Foolish Haints

An April May Snow

Paranormal Fiction Thriller

By

M. Scott Swanson

April May Snow Titles

Throw the Amulet

Throw the Bouquet

Throw the Cap

Throw the Dice

Throw the Elbow

Throw the Fastball

Throw the Gauntlet

Throw the Hissy

Foolish Aspirations

Foolish Beliefs

Foolish Cravings

Foolish Desires

Foolish Expectations

Foolish Fantasies

Foolish Games

Foolish Haints

Never miss an April May Snow release.

Join the reader's club!

www.mscottswanson.com

Evry frog praise e ownt pond.

(Everybody favors his own home.)

-Gullah proverb

Chapter 1

"Oh! For the love of..." I yell as I yank my foot out of the cool puddle of slime.

Travis, following so closely behind me we might as well be spooning, asks, "What happened?"

"I just murdered a new pair of Keds with some unidentified nastiness," I say as I stop to check the damage.

"In the itinerary, I told everyone to wear boots tonight," Miles's voice echoes from behind us.

I would love to tell Miles where he can save his itinerary, and it wouldn't be the cloud. Instead, I grind my teeth. I've promised myself to curb my smart mouth when my comments aren't helpful. The struggle is real.

"He does have a point," Travis says.

"Travis, I'm not in the mood."

He chuckles. "What? I'm just saying you could have bought two top-of-the-line pairs of hiking boots for the number of innocent tennis shoes you murdered this year. I have never seen a girl destroy a pair of shoes as quick as you."

I roll my eyes; Travis can't see that since I'm leading our paranormal group through the underground tunnel we discovered moments earlier. Jumping across the puddle, the heel of my other—still presentable—shoe strikes the edge of the liquid, splashing more goo onto me.

"You almost made it," Travis says as he turns on his camcorder light to size up the distance to cross.

The laugh of a child, specifically the eight-year-old, sandy-blond-haired boy we chased downstairs from the closed diner above, echoes against the ceramic tile walls. I pull my shoulders inward as the hair on my neck stands on end.

Travis lands behind me, the gear in his backpack rattling as the light from his camcorder temporarily blinds me. "That little booger is creepy." As I raise my hand to block the light from his camcorder, Travis angles it down and turns it off. "Sorry."

"It's probably best to keep the lighting to a minimum until we find him."

Travis pulls a flashlight from his utility belt and flicks it on low. The red LED glow coats the ceramic tile wall's pastel-blue pattern, giving it a macabre crimson glow.

"Personally, I don't think we need the light. The little dude's powder-blue glow will stick out from one hundred yards away as dark as it is down here."

Travis's comment gives me a jolt. During earlier paranormal excursions, I noticed he is keenly aware of ghostly presences in his vicinity. However, that "gift" has evolved into a much more potent skill set during the year I have collaborated with my brother's team.

In fact, while investigating the upstairs diner moments ago, Travis was the first to hear the giggles. And Travis flushed the diminutive's specter from his hiding place under the bar sink.

Except for Dusty, all of the members of the ghost-hunting enterprise that research and document paranormal experiences for my brother have become more gifted.

This evolution and growth of the team should put my mind at ease. Since, as quickly as I can get everything buttoned up in my current life, I'm due to move in with my "sort of, kind of" fiancé in Baltimore, Maryland. Knowing the entire team now has various skills should make my resignation from the projects less of a burden for my brother.

Instead, it leaves me overly concerned for the paranormal team that has grown into a second family for me.

The growth of their paranormal abilities confirms a suspicion I have held for years. When an individual is exposed to supernatural events, any latent skills in their genome will come forward and bask in the energy. That energy feeds the skills' growth. That sounds positive, except the paranormal skill set can eventually crowd out their *everyday* life.

Considering the team makes a living—or a profitable side hustle—by recording paranormal events, the skill growth would appear to be a boon … if it weren't for the *other* truth proven in my experience during the last year.

Supernatural entities are drawn to people with higher-level gifts. Often those entities are nefarious with dubious intentions.

I pause as we come to a tee in the tunnel. Travis sidles up to me as I shine my light in alternate directions.

"Well, this is a conundrum."

Laughing, I shoot him a sideways glance. "You can say that again." I raise my finger to stop him from repeating it. "Don't."

"You know me too well. We've obviously been working together for too long." He flashes a toothy smile that, due to the red light from my flashlight, creates a ghoulish, bloody appearance.

I wiggle my eyebrows and shake my finger at him for good measure. I'm thankful for the poor lighting, since I'm sure my feigned playful mood would not be convincing under normal circumstances. When Travis mentions we've worked together too long, I'm beset by a case of melancholy. This is our last ghost hunt as a team.

"Come catch me." While seeming playful as he punctuates his words with a laugh, the little boy's voice has an evil ring that makes me hold my breath.

Travis pushes me to the right as he takes the lead. "Did you hear that?"

"Yes."

Travis crosses before me, taking several steps down the left corridor. "Which way did it come from?"

"What's the holdup?" Chet Early asks as he enters my periphery. "I suppose it was too much to hope this was a quick excursion underground. Did you see which way he went?"

"No," Travis grouses as he passes in front of us again. "But the little brat is taunting us."

I try to ignore Travis's frustration and center myself. With any luck, I should be able to pull in enough ambient energy around us and use it to search for our diminutive, deceased juvenile delinquent.

"It feels like he is on the right," Chet says. "Have you used your app?"

"Have you used your app?" Travis mocks as he pulls out his cell phone.

It's challenging, but I stifle a giggle. I close my eyes to focus on my task using my natural abilities.

Chet rarely sees apparitions. Although he heard the little boy's ghost, he did not see him. Where Travis has developed the ability to see supernatural events, Chet's growing skill allows him to sense disruptions in the veil. While not perfect, his power is undoubtedly as accurate as the spook meter app Miles designed for the team.

"Is that a dead end?"

Liza's question distracts me, and I lose the tail of the energy I am harnessing. I exhale a puff of air rudely across my lips and open my eyes.

Liza grimaces. "Sorry."

"No worries." I look over her shoulder. "Where are Dusty and Miles?"

"Have you seen your brother jump?"

True that. "If Dusty wore the prescribed footwear, he could just walk through it."

"Assuming it's not six feet deep."

"Fair."

"Why would you have a tunnel under a diner, and the more

suspenseful question is, where is it leading?" Liza asks.

"I'm not sure. Given it's Murfreesboro, it could be from the Civil War. Then again, it could be a prohibition bootlegger tunnel. Either way, it doesn't lead to only one place. That's why we are stopped."

"I guess it's a good thing there are six of us, then," Liza says curtly as she turns back toward the direction we came. "Hey, Dusty. How about you and Miles set up there in case the ghost doubles back and gets by us."

"Oh … Okay. That's a good idea."

The apparent relief in Dusty's tone brings a smile to my face. I can visualize him standing on the puddle's far edge, deciphering the exact speed and height required to launch his three-hundred-pound-plus body safely across the obstacle.

Liza offers me a smug smile. "There. Planning session complete. You and Travis will take the left side of the tunnel, and Chet and I will peel off to the right."

"Why are you going to the right?" It is a meaningless question since it shouldn't matter, and a decision needs to be made.

"Because my boy Chet thinks the little ghost went to the right. If I have to walk around underground, I prefer it to be for a good reason."

Travis appears conflicted. Like the rest of the team, I know he wants to be where the action is. As Liza says, "Why go on a ghost hunt if you are not going to see anything?"

I hold a different value system than the rest of the team. While I find the adrenaline rush of a good ghost hunt exhilarating, more often than not, our adventures go cattywampus quickly. I will consider it a blessing if I can draw a sizable paycheck from my brother and be bored tonight.

"Nah. You're wrong, Chet," Travis says as he stalks off to the left.

I shrug my shoulders. "Well, happy hunting."

"Be safe," Liza says as she turns to follow Chet.

Travis has managed to get several strides in front of me, and his silhouette continues to gain separation.

"Hey, hold up."

"Pick up the pace, April."

"What's the hurry?"

"In the time it took for you and Liza to flap your gums, that pint-sized cretin could've already exited the tunnel."

He continues to gain distance from me, forcing me into a jog. "Well, that's no excuse for running pell-mell into a trap. Who would be the cretin then?"

"Trap, *please*. The little dude was cowering under the bar sink ten minutes ago. It's not like we're dealing with an archdemon. Besides, we could use footage of the tiny creep for this episode."

Despite a rocky start with the network, Dusty's paranormal team has had excellent luck capturing ghostly images for their cable show. This has fed the appetite of a particular niche market desiring to be scared by the unexplained. The show has built a ravenous fan base that seemingly reads, too, as Dusty's novels have seen a significant rise in sales.

The business is all Dusty's. Still, I have a healthy level of pride in the exponential growth of the team's revenue over the last year.

Would the team have been as successful without me? They are talented, so I'm positive they would have been. However, there is no denying my unique skill set of multiple supernatural talents has made the job easier for the team.

The weekend paranormal excursions were never more than a detour in my career path of becoming the most sought-after defense attorney in the Southeast. It is simply a profitable side job my brother reminds me regularly that he had to bribe me to participate in.

As my powers grow and, more importantly, my two grandmothers teach me how to harness and use my abilities, I appreciate these weekend adventures. When I leave Guntersville, Alabama, behind, the paranormal research trips are one of the things I will miss the most.

This is an incredibly odd thought considering how much I loathed my natural gifts only last year.

Despite my jogging, Travis's silhouette gets further away from me. "Travis, don't be stupid," I yell at him. My voice echoes across the tiled walls and ceiling as I continue down the dirt path.

Nausea punches me in the gut, and a vinegar taste permeates my mouth. I stop running and yell at Travis again, but his silhouette disappears into the dark.

Something has changed dramatically. My senses stand on edge as I peer down the corridor of gray-and-black shadows.

Someone, not Travis, is nearby. I feel a disturbance in the energy field inside the tunnel. Particles of chaos stream past and away from me in a blur as if a giant supernatural vacuum lies ahead. Over the trickle of water dripping from the ceiling, I hear the slow crunch of gritty soil before me. Above the dank, earthen smell of the path, a sudden infusion of sulfur wafts to my nose, and a gust of frigid air forces me to cross my arms across my chest.

"Hello? Is anyone there?"

I hold my breath while continuing to peer into the darkness. As if I concentrate and stare long enough, I'll be able to see what I sense. "Travis?"

I'm not scared. Or at least that is what I tell myself. But I do know that there is cause for concern. I look behind me and consider if I should return to Dusty and Miles to get their assistance. Then again, it is best to move forward and warn Travis about what I'm sensing.

I have the lousiest of luck. My final excursion would be when I become trapped in an underground tunnel with a hostile entity.

Deciding that I need to team back up with Travis as quickly as possible because, quite frankly, I don't want to be alone, I pick up my pace to a jog again. The deeper I go into the tunnel, the more tiles I find falling from the walls and ceiling. In scores of spots, tree roots have pushed through. Their rough, black tentacles come into my vision at the last moment, forcing me to duck, weave, and bob.

It's been half a year since I had a supernatural showdown with a lower-class demon in an alternate reality of his construct. To say I was scared out of my wits during the battle and that I had zero clue of how I was using my skills would be an understatement. Somehow, I managed to snatch victory from the jaws of defeat.

Winning a fight like that, where I felt I had no business being in the battle because I was in way over my head, has done wonders for my confidence. Still, I can't protect anybody that I can't see. Because of that simple fact, I'm increasingly anxious to find Travis quickly.

I slam into an earthen wall and fall back onto my butt. I groan as I put both hands to my nose to check if I broke it.

I had to have broken it. The pain is so excruciating, there is no way I didn't.

What the heck? Did I miss a turn?

Still cradling my nose with my right hand, I look side to side for the doorway I must have missed. I only see broken tiles on either side of me—no opening.

This must be wrong.

Pushing up to my feet, I press my hands against the wall. I can make out that it's solid, but I want to feel it to confirm. I turn my LED flashlight to full beam and reach as high as possible, finding nothing. Squatting to the dirt floor, I run my hands all along the cool, damp earth, knocking several jagged, marble-sized stones loose as I search.

"I must have missed the turn further back," I whisper.

Slowly and intentionally, I run my hand along the tile to the right as I study the tile to my left. No openings up here as I backtrack.

Where could Travis go if this is a dead end?

Reluctantly I decide my only plan of attack is to return to get Dusty and Miles's help to search for Travis. The extra sets of eyes will help.

An uneasy feeling claws at the back of my mind. I don't want to think about it, but I can't help it. It's as if Travis disappeared into thin air. And that's just not a thing.

The tunnel turns slightly as I continue to run my hand along the blue-glazed tile. I stop and stare in front of me at the dirt wall blocking the tunnel. Swiveling quickly, I flash my light down the way I just traveled and note the dirt wall blocking the opposite path.

"Oh, fudge! I'm trapped."

Chapter 2

Now, this royally chaps my butt. Here I am concerned Travis will run headfirst into a magical trap, and instead, I find myself doing the exact same thing.

To further confirm my disastrous change of fortune is not an illusion, I place my hand against the earthen wall blocking my path back to Dusty and Miles. Like the wall blocking me from Travis, this dirt wall is solid, too. So much for my hope of an optical illusion spell left to confuse anyone wandering into the tunnel.

I study the earthen obstruction looking for imperfections. If it is magic, it is a puzzle I'll need to figure out to free myself. Unfortunately, I haven't a clue what I am looking for in this perfect illusion. Perhaps some magical key latch to swing the dirt wall back and allow me to go on my merry way. That would be extraordinarily helpful.

An advantage of having forty paranormal-research trips under my belt is the mental catalog of experience built from similar situations. As I pace toward the other mass of dirt plugging the tunnel, I recall our team's trip to Sloss Furnaces in Birmingham.

As Liza and I walked through the old industrial building, brick walls shifted and blocked our path. Later, we discovered a powerful warlock was trying to scare us away from the site.

I ponder that experience while studying the dirt blocking me from Travis and squint my eyes severely. As if applying enough pressure on my brain will force a brilliant solution to pop out like a golden egg.

Again, no nifty keyholes or latch do I find.

In Birmingham, at the furnaces, Liza and I found the rest of our team because though the brick walls appeared solid, even to the touch, our voices carried through them efficiently. Once we could communicate with our team members, we shattered the warlock spell's power.

"Travis!" My voice echoes. I find this highly disconcerting. I don't have to be the daughter of a physicist, which I am, to know that there should be no echo in a twenty-five-foot chamber plugged in by dirt at either end.

Squashing down the uneasiness bubbling up from inside my gut, I whisper, "Just be thankful you've confirmed your hypothesis, April."

No. I don't usually talk to myself. But currently, I'm struggling to hold my nerves together.

Tentatively, I put my ear close to the dirt and listen. Travis's reply that I am so desperate to hear never comes.

Taking in a full breath, I shake my head in wonderment. If this blockage was formed by a spell, whoever spun the magic has profound skill. The illusion comes complete with a dank, earthen odor and a plethora of incredibly sharp, jagged sandstone edges jutting from the earth.

As I wait for Travis's reply, all I hear is the blood pumping in my eardrums. I swallow nervously, and it sounds exceedingly loud.

"Travis, can you hear me?"

Holding my breath, I wait and pray that I will hear my friend's voice. *Drip, drip, drip.* In addition to my blood, I now hear water dripping somewhere unseen. Its rhythmic beat is a loud cacophony in my otherwise silent, dark tomb.

My anxiety level continues to rise as I wait for Travis's voice. Apprehension twists my stomach. I close my eyes and pull in a deep breath through my nose.

You've got this, April. Use your head; use your powers.

I take inventory of my skill sets. What would best breach these dirt blockades? It's a more complicated question than what I would first believe.

Fire won't be effective. While a kinetic push might be successful, I don't like the idea of what will happen with any blowback in such tight quarters. I could, in effect, frag myself.

No, this calls for something slow and deliberate. Not exactly my usual mode of operation, but it's time to give it a try.

I attach my flashlight back to my utility belt to free my hands. Rubbing my palms together vigorously, I contemplate how best to try what I want to do—given I don't even know if I can do it.

A more compact approach would be safer. I put my thumbs together, placing both hands on the dirt wall and leaning forward. Shards of sandstone dig into my palms as the coolness of the dirt warms to my touch.

A grin stretches across my face as I feel my power building against the wall. A force that makes me feel unique and accomplished as I bring my skill set to bear against the magic of someone else's construct.

This is why I have studied relentlessly with my grandmothers to hone my skills. There has never been any question about the potency of my powers, only my ability to master them and use them in an organized and helpful manner.

I visualize the wall deteriorating granule by granule in a ten-inch diameter area around my fingers. All the chaotic energy present in my current tomb of solitary confinement swirls about me. Gold-and-blue microscopic, kinetic-potential flecks enter my sternum and pass through my hands. My magically created pressure builds against what I now know to be a façade of chert and soil.

If this doesn't work, I'm a failure.

My random thought is the equivalent of throwing ice water

on a flame. The chaotic energy I'm collecting to blow through the wall and secure my freedom loses focus and swirls away.

With all my being, I try to purge the unhelpful thought from my mind. I must fight it. I must not go down that rabbit hole right now. Still, I feel myself spinning out of control as the thought echoes through my mind.

April, you're a fraud—a fake—a failure. You're the queen of the three Fs!

It's a secret fear I have buried so well, so effectively, for so many years that not even I realized it until a few months ago. Some folks are claustrophobic. Others hate snakes or even have a weird aversion to things like clowns... Well, I suppose I understand the clown one.

I am terrified of being a failure. Despite a few scattered wins in the courtroom and my freaky paranormal world that I'm stuck with, the Atlanta debacle overshadows my recent successes. Until I accomplish my life goals, the ones that dogged me like the hounds of hell through seven years of study at the university, everyone will consider me the girl who settled.

Knowing I am a failure makes me sad. The currently more pressing crux of the issue is how sadness affects my ability to tap into my magical skill set at the intersection of normal and paranormal.

"No, April, not now," I whisper.

My grandmothers and I have determined that my emotions directly impact my unnatural power intensity. If I am excited or angry, I can exponentially level up the energy I am able to harness. Unfortunately, profound sadness stops my paranormal powers altogether. Talk about a beggar's bargain. I wish I had been present for those negotiations.

Then again, if I had been present, I would have walked away from the paranormal skill set deal altogether and never have found myself in my current predicament.

I attempt to regain control of my emotions to halt my tailspin into the pit of despair. I alter my focus from the inequities and failures that create my sadness.

Something else that doesn't make sense to me draws my attention.

The chaotic specks of blue-and-gold power I have been collecting do not fall away from me in the typical tumbling, swirling pattern that happened the other times I have failed. Instead, they form an inverted funnel and flow through the earthen wall in front of me in an orderly fashion.

That can't be right. This is the first time I've seen chaotic energy form an orderly mass in such a manner. Even when I siphon the fuel for my own magical use, the funnel to me will have random particles break free.

I drop my hands from the dirt façade before me. I might as well since I've managed to sabotage my magic.

But there is something more. Something with me in this dark tomb that I have found myself in. Or at least on the other side of the wall.

"Hello?"

Drip, drip, drip. Only the phantom driblet and the pulse drumming in my inner ear answer me.

Think, April.

A chill shoots up my spine as the logical conclusion comes to me, no matter how hard I want to find another explanation. Something magical is in the tunnel with me.

Pulling my flashlight off my toolbelt, I shine it in the direction from which we came. The façade of magical dirt continues to plug the opposite side of the tunnel, too.

No, I didn't expect to get that lucky. Still, a girl can hope, can't she? Turning the light back toward the obstacle directly before me, my light strobes wildly. I give it a good slap with my other hand and a vigorous shake—a Southern mechanic's magical fix-all—to no avail.

Strobe lights don't affect me in an adverse physical manner as they do some people. But they aggravate the tarnation out of me, and I don't need the distraction now, so I turn my flashlight off.

"Peaches." I can't help but go back to lamenting my terrible luck. What is the probability that I would be buried alive on my last paranormal excursion with my brother's team?

That is a stupid question. Given how most of my life goes, odds are even better that things would end up going sideways on this outing.

I grind my teeth in thought. My eyes inexplicably grow accustomed to the dark, and I can see the bits of white chert jutting from the wall.

That shouldn't be possible in the dark, except the magic used to construct the wall has formed a slightly luminescent sheen on the wall's surface. I also have a gut feeling, from the earlier odd flow of chaotic power, that whatever or whoever made this amazing illusion is gleefully waiting for me on the other side.

I would prefer to try my abilities on the opposite wall—the one leading back to my brother and the exit. Especially given my preference not to be ambushed by some amped-up, super-juiced supernatural being on the other side of this wall. However, I'm keenly aware that Travis, my friend and often research partner, is trapped on the same side as the entity.

No, I'm not a marine. Still, no man left behind at this high-stress moment makes all the sense in the world.

Squashing down my fear, I realize the only reasonable path is forward. I must help Travis while I still can.

I place my hands back on the wall. With the brief break from magical exertion, I notice the negativity I flogged myself with earlier has passed. Once again, the particles glittering around and behind me flow in my direction. The sparkling light forms a mantle on my shoulder as they track to my sternum, continuing down my hands in a consistent, pumping sensation.

The power surges on my palms as they grow incredibly hot against the dirt surface. The first part of the grand illusion begins to disintegrate as the energy I control flows with increasing force through my hands.

A massive bolt of energy rips from my chest and through my hands, disappearing into the wall without effect on the surface. It's an odd feeling, like someone tearing a shirt off of me. It leaves me feeling exposed and weak as my collected energy has been forcibly sapped.

Whatever is on the other side of the wall is substantially more powerful, or at least more skilled with their magic, than I am.

It's as if they can steal my magical energy. Of course, that's not even possible. At least I don't think it's possible.

I cover my chest with my arms as the temperature drops precipitously. Biting my lip, I wonder how long I can last in this hole and ruminate on how horrible a death it will be to waste away in this earthen tomb.

My chest and toes bump into the magical dirt wall.

Odd. I was at least an arm's length away from the dirt wall seconds earlier. I must have accidentally leaned forward and not noticed it as I considered the sobering reality that I might starve to death. There are hundreds of awful ways to kick the bucket, but shriveling away from want of food is at the top of my list.

I turn around. Perhaps I should go back for Miles and Dusty. If I can get to them, they can help me save Travis quicker than I can on my own.

A wave of anxiety rolls over me. I bet if I try the other side of the tunnel, Dusty and Miles won't be able to hear me any better than Travis at this end. If I can't yell loudly enough through the magic to get their attention and the wall pulls my magical energy from me when I try to use it, it can mean only one thing.

I'm going to die in here.

I lurch forward as the wall bumps into my backside.

No. I'm not imagining things.

I make a small, orbital flame in my right palm and pull out my strobing flashlight. I shine the strobing light at the far wall. The chamber has noticeably shortened from twenty-five feet to twenty feet long. These walls are moving in on me.

As fear constricts my chest, the walls creep in on me. Like a trapped animal, I run to the center of my short tunnel like it will buy me more time.

Instead, the walls continue sliding toward me at an increasing pace.

The glittering specks of blue and gold increase and flow off of my skin toward the earthen walls. It is as if my fear is creating the chaotic energy feeding this unexplained illusion.

Then don't feed it. It's not real, anyway.

As the thought of the illusion not actually existing registers with my mind, the movement of the walls, now making the chamber only ten feet long, ceases.

I can't contain my grin as I am relieved and proud of myself for having unlocked the secret.

"I'm not afraid," I yell at the wall in Travis's direction. It's true, too. I'm not scared of the magical dirt plug coming in any closer. Whether or not I fear the witch or warlock on the other side of the illusion, we'll cross that bridge when we get to it.

"Do you hear me? Your magic does not scare me. In fact, I find it to be a cheap parlor trick at best," I shout as I lean into the wall.

"Seriously? Is this the best you've got?"

I laugh. Admittedly, it sounds quite hysterical to me—not my regular laugh. As the wall in front of me turns to mush, my hands push through it. Without my quick reflexes, I would have fallen through it.

Standing back, I watch the illusion melt like a huge three-wick, chocolate-colored candle blasted with a welder's torch.

With great satisfaction, I observe the last of the magic wall seep into the dirt floor as the scent of sulfur and musk surrounds me.

I draw a deep breath as I steel my nerves to find Travis and bring him to safety. Odd magical walls are one thing. A friend lost in a warlock's version of an underground funhouse is an entirely different subject.

Exhaling, I set my shoulders and take a determined step into the darkness. A match lights in front of me. The silhouette of a man's face sucking on a cigarette appears before me.

I nearly pee myself.

Chapter 3

"You're sharp as a tack, ain't you, missy?"

The red ember from the lit end of a cigarette glows directly in front of me. "I'm not afraid of you. You're not real," I lie.

"Oh, I'm real, missy. And this ain't no place for a girl like you. You shouldn't have come down here."

My mind reels as I try to process all of the information at once. I realize that I am dealing with a specter of some sort, and I also have a suspicion that it is perturbed I am in its space.

"I'm only here to get my friend, and then we will leave."

The man chuckles, and his form illuminates. I take in the wiry, masculine vision. Standing six feet tall and one hundred and eighty pounds, he is mostly bald with a greasy comb-over. I guess his age to be a rode-hard-and-put-up-wet late forties. His uniform of choice is heavily scarred work boots, Dickie jeans, and a filthy wife beater. He is not from this decade. Of that much, I am sure. On a cursory glance, I would take him to be alive. However, the light blue glow that encases his form is a clue that I am speaking with someone who no longer counts birthdays.

He shakes his head from side to side. "You ain't gonna be able to help him much."

"Why?" I shoot back. "Who?"

He draws in a breath burning half his cigarette. He forms an

"O" with his purple lips and blows four perfect smoke rings. "I'd say they got him shriveled up like a dried-out prune by now."

His laugh jars me. It is annoying, like fingernails on a chalkboard. Rather than scare me—well, I am petrified deep down—this greasy ghost in front of me has done unchained my redneck.

"Mister, you got no idea what you're messing with."

"I know you're special. And Mama said that one day somebody might be able to get through her magic. She said, 'Delbert, and if'n they do, you got to put an end to them.'"

"Is that so?"

He grins, exposing decayed teeth. "It's important to keep the moonshine tunnels a secret. Even if it means killing a tasty-looking girl."

"Well, Delbert, it is Delbert, right?" I don't wait for him to respond. "All I got to say is that you better pack a lunch. Because it's going to take you all day to take me down."

Is that a factual statement? No. Still, one of my secret abilities—non-supernatural, that is—is bluffing. The hope of escaping this without a fight still has not abandoned me.

Delbert removes the cigarette butt from his lips and flicks it against the wall. "I suppose if that boy hadn't gone up top like I warned him not to, you might not be down here. Kirby don't listen proper to his elders."

"Is Kirby your son?"

Delbert wrinkles his face. "Heck no. I ain't got no children."

Well, I'm so surprised.

"Kirby stole down here a ways back. And you know I had to —" Delbert makes a slashing gesture across his neck. "You can't be too careful. Live lips are loose lips."

"Delbert, you need to step aside. I'm going to go search for my friend."

Delbert spits on the floor, looks up at me, and squints his eyes. "You do what you think you gotta do, missy. But you be sure and clear out once your business is done."

"I'm not looking for trouble. I just want to get my friend."

"Oh, you done found trouble. But I'm feeling gratuities today, and I'll let you by this time."

I'm within a frog's hair of correcting Delbert on his use of "gratuities" rather than "gracious," and somehow manage to hold my tongue. "Thank you."

Delbert walks through the blue tile wall to our left. "Oh, I wouldn't be thanking me yet," he says. "Because even though you hold the key, you'll never be free."

Chapter 4

I consider the oddness of Delbert's last words to me. Travis's scream startles me, jolting me into action. Carelessly, I rush down the dark hallway with my hands outstretched in either direction so I don't slam into the tile wall.

"Get away from me!"

Travis's shout has me wondering what exactly is after him. Travis is a sizable man, and for him to be distressed is alarming. Still, it does not slow me from going toward him.

The irony does not escape me that I was cautioning Travis from barreling down the tunnel only moments earlier without knowing what was in store. The notable difference being I *know* something terrible is on the other end, and I am still running blindly to his aid.

"I'm coming, Travis!"

"April, hurry!"

I hit the edge of the tile wall hard, and it knocks me sideways. *Magic-sucking ghost, be darned.* With a snap of my fingers, a small flame appears at the tip of my right index finger.

The flame lies on its side, as if blown by a gust of wind. As it flames out, I see my spent energy's blue-and-gold specks float to the tile wall. Delbert better be thankful he is dead. Otherwise, I would kill him the next time he shows his face.

"Argh... No!" Travis screams.

I wrench the flashlight from my toolbelt and sprint toward Travis's shriek of terror. The strobing effect of the light causes equilibrium issues for me. It feels like I am running three times as fast as I am from the intermittent flashes of reality tucked in between pitch-darkness.

I slow as I approach a left-handed dog-leg turn in front of me. Careful not to slam into the broken tiles at the turn, I pivot, and the vision revealed by the first strobe of my flashlight steals my breath.

Dreadful awe fills me as my flashlight's ten successive bursts of dim light confirm what I'm observing.

Travis is spread eagle on a massive spiderweb that spans the entire tunnel. The webbing is as thick as a climber's rope.

He continues to scream wildly while thrashing back and forth. He does not see me standing at the entrance to this leg of the tunnel.

It's not real, April. It's Travis's fear.

I know this terrifying vision is a construct of the fears within Travis. All the same, the illusion is so spectacular it seems undeniable.

"Travis! Travis, open your eyes!" I scream as I force myself forward.

He does not respond as he continues to buck and convulse, causing the wide webbing to shake. As it does, small pepper-like bits bounce from the long, white runners.

Despite his desperate need for aid, my feet stop ten paces away from him. The rope that forms the web shimmers and moves in an undulating fashion.

The magical illusion is breaking apart as the surface of the web takes on an unstable mirage quality. Yet only the webbing at the farthest edges is deteriorating in this manner, and the shimmer is moving closer toward Travis.

What the friggin'! That's not an optical imperfection of the illusion. Those are baby spiders in the thousands working their way down the web toward Travis.

I close the gap between us, place both hands on Travis's shoulders, and yell into his face, "Travis, I need you to open your eyes!"

I expect he won't, but his eyes fly open at my command as he screams again. I smell the burritos we had for dinner, as well as his fear.

"Look at me." Travis closes his eyes, and I slap his cheek. His eyes open wide. "I need you to stay with me. Focus on me, Travis."

It's enough to stop his screaming and struggle until he looks to his left and spots the swarm of baby spiders scurrying toward his bound hand. He renews his struggle, pulling against the webbing with additional vigor.

Thoroughly mesmerized, I watch the dusty-gold energy cloud emanate from Travis. It forms a matrix of tiny threads connecting directly to the thousands of microscopic, pin-sized spiders.

The tiny spiders double in size. It's as if each minuscule illusion is attached to an air compressor that fills them with a rush of air. Travis is the energy force that fuels the spiders' growth.

This is getting real in double time.

If those spiders continue to grow, before too long, they will be able to suck Travis dry, as Delbert alluded to. I must get Travis's attention and make him understand the key to this magic. He is the one feeding this illusion with his fear.

I press into Travis's chest as I grab the sides of his face, giving him no choice but to focus on me. "Travis!"

His wild eyes fixate on me. Silently, they implore me for my help.

"Travis, this is only in your mind."

"Spiders—everywhere!"

"No. You're causing this. It's not real."

He shakes his head as he licks his lips. "I can't..."

"Yes. You have to."

"They're gonna kill me."

"Travis, do you trust me?"

He continues to struggle and buck despite my weight pressing into him. He grunts and snorts as he tries with a renewed effort to free his left arm from the snare.

"You've got to calm yourself. Stop fighting and relax."

Travis emits a pathetic scoff as his jaw drops open. "Relax while they eat me?"

"No. It's not real. It's like a nightmare you created and brought to life."

"A nightmare?"

Oh, thank the Lord. I'm finally getting through to him. I hope he doesn't look to the side, where the spiders have increased to the circumference of blueberries with long legs.

"Yes. It's a spell that works off your fear. The more you fear it, the more dangerous it becomes."

He licks his lips again. "But they're..."

"Your fantasy."

The left side of his face ticks up with the beginnings of a grin. "Well, they wouldn't be my fantasy."

The sudden reemergence of the Travis I love fills my heart with joy, and I kiss him on the forehead.

"Then wake from your nightmare for me."

He keeps his eyes trained on mine, as if he has realized looking away is not a promising idea, and asks, "How exactly do I do that."

"Think about..."

Yep. I think I peed myself. Yeah, I'm positive I did.

But if the four-hundred-pound spider takes a bite from Travis's neck before he can banish his fear, I won't have to be embarrassed about creating a wet spot on my jeans.

Travis understands that something has gone terribly wrong. It could have been my eyes, but if I had to guess, it is most likely the gasp I make as I watch the colossal spider clack her manacles the size of my legs together.

"What is it?"

"Nothing."

"April…"

"Take care of your business. Think of anything that makes you happy or breaks the current thought."

The gargantuan, swollen-belly spider scurries closer to us, crawls up the wall of blue tiles, and proceeds to weave a rope-like thread that she splats against the ceiling. The babies, now golf ball sized, have paused inches from Travis's limbs. I watch as they commence weaving. They each pull a silk thread from their abdomen and roll it up in the folds of their black legs, as if making a ball of yarn.

I press closer to Travis and wrap my arms around him tightly. I can't blame him for his fears that we will die in this horrible manner. Still, dying with a friend seems thousands of times better than dying in a tomb alone.

Click-clack. Click-clack. With my eyes closed, I hear every rustle of all the thousands of legs in action around us. I can't look. Call me chicken, but I don't want to watch my death if this is it. I'm going to wait for it to happen.

Travis's heartbeat increases. I squeeze tighter and listen to the rhythmic sound as it gives me one sliver of peace before our imminent deaths.

Travis's heart is all I hear.

The awful clicking noise has stopped.

If we're dead, dying was much quicker and less painful than I anticipated. I'm not looking a gift horse in the mouth. I'm just saying it wasn't what I expected.

Cautiously, I open my eyes and find that the web that held Travis is gone. I tilt my head up and see Travis grinning down at me.

"If I had known you felt like this about me, April— I wish you had told me before you hooked up with Lee."

Embarrassed by my reaction while I thought we would die, I can't bear to face his cocky grin. I look down to hide my face.

I don't need to ask Travis what fantasy he used to banish the fear of spiders from his thoughts. The sizable lump in his jeans should be clue enough for an intelligent girl.

Chapter 5

I take a bite of my steamy, hot, crispy hashbrowns, and the stress of our near-death experience evaporates.

Even if Dusty were not my brother, I would love him as a boss. Not because he always listens to his team's advice or has an encouraging word ready for any team member who needs it, although that often is the case. I love my brother's management style because he understands the importance of breaking bread with the team.

Unfortunately, at this early-morning hour, our options are Waffle House on the north side of Murfreesboro or Waffle House on the south side of Murfreesboro.

Unlike my sorority sisters at the University of Alabama, I enjoy Waffle House.

It's hot and fast, and the price is right. Sure, with all the extra grease, it's best to avoid eating it daily. But right now, the excess fat is soothing my frayed nerves that were all standing on end only minutes ago.

"Dude, let me see that again." Travis reaches across the table for Chet's video recorder.

Chet raises the camera up. "Bro, be careful. Don't drag the strap through my syrup."

Travis snatches the camera out of Chet's hand. "Don't drag it through my syrup," he mocks. "I can't believe you got *my* video."

"I told you the ghost went to the right." Chet smirks.

"I could've sworn he zigged left."

"I'm so glad you had us separate, Liza. If you hadn't, we would have missed the video," I say.

"Well, yes. But the idea of you and Travis being alone to deal with that magical trap really upsets me."

The concern on Liza's face touches me. It was once quite different. At the start of our relationship, I'm positive Liza would have been rooting for the four-hundred-pound spider to suck me dry.

With time, we have bonded in a manner unlike I have connected with any female outside my family. Even though, despite the commonality of the supernatural, we are near polar opposites. I love her and think of her as a soul sister found.

"It was nothing. Travis made it sound worse than it was."

She purses her lips as she stares at me. A telltale sign that, once again, my inability to lie is still intact.

Miles takes the camcorder from Travis. "This is going to clean up nicely. Luis can get five to seven minutes of good video from this alone when he returns from El Salvador."

This being the last hurrah, it saddens me that Luis and Jason could not make it. However, the research trips because of the demanding twenty-two TV show episodes per year and Dusty's continued two books a year have predicated we travel every weekend.

But folks have lives they have to take care of. So recently, except for Dusty, Miles, and me, it's common for at least one of the team members to be absent from an excursion.

Miles looks up from Chet's incredible footage of the boy Travis flushed from the restaurant. "I only wish we had footage of that bootlegger you talked to, April. And I can only imagine what a video of a magical spiderweb would have done for our ratings."

It would be awesome to have a record of the impressive

spider—which I don't, since Travis dropped the camera on his sling before I found him spread eagle, screaming like a little girl—and my body camera was crushed against his chest.

It is fortunate that I don't have a video of the traumatic event. It would put me in a pickle if I did.

While I understand the value of having a recording of such a horrifying vision. I did promise Travis I would leave out the part about him being trapped like a bug on the spiderweb screaming his head off. Without the footage, my allegiances do not have to be torn.

Plus, if we don't discuss the fact Travis was trapped on the spiderweb, we won't have to explain how he managed to banish his arachnophobia long enough to dispel the magical trap.

I find it best not to unpackage embarrassing moments in a crowd. Friends should be allowed to keep a few secrets.

"I've been telling you, Dusty. It wouldn't be that expensive to get more body cams."

"Luis says it is rare the point of view is ever usable," Dusty counters.

"But that one time it *does* capture something. Hello, prime time," Liza grumbles as she looks away from Dusty.

Dusty's lips part, and his jaw remains open as he looks at Liza. She busies herself, putting picante sauce on her recently arrived omelet.

I struggle to contain my giggle.

Liza rarely argues with Dusty. Partly because she is a stickler for obeying the chain of command and believes in his leadership. The other reason she has hidden well from everyone, including my brother, is that she has a terrible crush on Dusty.

Unfortunately, my brother is too dense to catch on. That is a shame for both.

The conversation halts as we begin the assault on our meals. I will miss this. The eating with the team and companionable silence.

If anyone claimed eighteen months ago that when my tour of duty ends with my brother's team, I would be sad. I would have laughed in their face. Now I'm not only leaving my two brothers, parents, grandmothers, and uncle when I get on the last flight to Baltimore, I'm also leaving this eclectic and delightful group of unique people.

I have no reason to be melancholy. I have my law degree and significant litigation experience, I'm flush with cash, and I have an incredibly sexy professional ballplayer waiting for me in Maryland. That is, a sexy man who is also a talented cook and inexplicably loves me despite all my idiosyncrasies.

That sort of guy is worth dumping everything for. Right?

Yet, here I sit with people I was not sure I liked a year ago, and I feel tears welling in my eyes. It's, like, so stupid of me.

Liza stands as we near the end of our meal. "Hey, guys, I'll be right back."

I'm surprised as she walks out of the restaurant rather than to the restroom.

"Now, we know you're going to be busy, April. But if we get nominated for an Emmy, you must promise to attend the ceremony with us."

My smile stretches my face so hard it hurts. "I wouldn't miss that for the world."

"We will hold you to it," Miles adds.

That is the team's new goal. At one time, it was to cobble together enough facts from real ghost stories to put together a book and pitch a publisher. Then the goal became to make the series of books a bestselling hit.

When I was younger, it aggravated me that people would call me Dusty's or Chase's little sister. But now, I'm right proud to be called their sister.

I'm cataloging Dusty's face like I'll never see him again. His ice-blue eyes; full, red eyelashes; the round shape of his light-complexioned face; the monstrous black gauges in his ear lobes; and bushy, red beard which seems to go in every direction at once. The tears gather at the edges of my eyelids as I wonder how soon I will manage to only see him on the holidays.

"For she's a jolly good fellow!" The team breaking into the chorus bursts the tears on my eyelids, and they stream down my cheeks as I turn.

Liza smiles broadly. Her teeth-revealing smiles are rarer than solar eclipses and make her stunningly beautiful. She nods and tilts her head down, directing my eyesight to the box of cupcakes she holds.

The dozen softball-sized cupcakes have seven pink candles sparkling on them.

"... Which nobody can deny!"

"Blow them out," Miles says.

Liza's smile calms to her more customary smirk. "Seven for good luck. Not that you should need them. You're the luckiest girl I know."

I'm luckiest to have friends like this. I blow out the candles and wish this wasn't the end of our friendship's season.

Chapter 6

The crackle of the fire brings a grim smile to my assassin's face. It's still pitch-dark, but I know I am coming upon my prey.

The putrid fumes of plastic and treated lumber burning float in the air, wafting to my nostrils. A healthy dose of sulfur tangs the scent.

He wasn't expecting me tonight.

The fact my prey is dangerously close exhilarates me, and I lean into the senses that have already bloomed. The taste of vinegar fills my mouth as copper coats my palate, like I sucked in the mist of blood.

The left side of my face warms dramatically—so hot it feels as if my eyebrows and bangs may singe.

Come out, come out wherever you are.

I can't see him yet, but I know he is near. Tonight, I hope to capture him. Tonight, I want to end him.

Slowly, like the first hint of the morning sun rising out of the lake, the world turns from pitch-black to an apocalyptic scene of flames and smoke tumbling from a landscape of ruined structures.

I'm where I always begin. To my left is the collapsed east wall of the gutted-out Snow and Associates office building. There is no longer a fire in it, just a smoldering tail of smoke lifting into the purple-and-black sky above.

Austin, the demon I battled six months earlier, initially pulled me into this parallel reality to finish me. He and his horde of witches are naturally more potent in this realm than in my plane of existence.

Everything was working to Austin's plan. Until I realized that whatever I'm made of—a maddeningly long and circular conversation with the people who have the best chance of explaining it to me—is also more powerful in Austin's realm. More potent than I can understand.

Despite the flood of adrenaline causing me to feel impervious, I am mindful of my grandmothers' words. We spent considerable time searching for answers to why my powers are exponentially stronger in Austin's realm than in the normal realm. More importantly, why, when I use my energy in his domain, it brings an evil tilt to my personality.

Understand, there is no book of rules explaining my powers. I would gladly study it front to back and memorize every word if such a text existed.

The best we can figure out is that it's a yin-yang relationship. Nana points out that when I use my powers with a defensive motive specifically to protect others, I brighten the good in my personality.

On the contrary, aggressive attacks such as flame creation and hurling items—most notably the concussion grenade that I used to dispel Austin's witches—taint my soul.

I was incredibly agitated for a month after surviving the showdown in this world. I tended to strike out and be ugly to folks. More disturbing, I was drawn to using my powers for selfish entertainment rather than for good.

That is why my amulet and looking stone now reside in the special place I store them. Frozen in a block of ice inside of my freezer. I must stow them away, so I am not tempted to abuse their powers. It's easier that way.

The simple thought of the two powerful, magical items I own makes my palms itch. Yeah, Sméagol and I, we have that in common.

Even though I'm bursting with confidence as I walk across the shattered glass on the rippled asphalt that once was Gunter Avenue, I long for my items.

But they are not necessary. Now I know that on this side, in this reality, I'm ten times stronger than Austin ever dreamed of being. Granny eloquently said that "he screwed the pooch" when he brought me into his domain.

Flames lick out of the county courthouse's roof. It's been on fire for six months now if the time in this parallel reality is the same as where I live. The whole vision is Austin's construct, and he has either become too distracted by his change of fortune or too scared to show his face and do the work to alter the illusion.

"Austin," I sing melodically. "Austin, come out and play."

I make my way toward the dike that still holds back the deep-blue waters of Guntersville Lake. Flames dance across the top of the smooth, glassy surface. Large oil globules pulsate forward, carrying the fire like a homecoming boat float.

I stand where Austin stood when I uncorked the mother of all psychic blasts. To Austin's credit, he is one tough cookie. He survived the blast. Of course, now his pretty face is not as attractive as it once was.

His horde of witches fared even worse than his face.

Walking along the lip of the dike, I notice a dark black, greasy splotch on the dried ragweed crabgrass. Bending over, I slip the iron link necklace over the crook of my index finger and lift it to my side. It's the Talisman of the Hell Kite.

I press my finger against the top point of the pentagram—sharp enough to draw blood if I press any harder. In the center is a miniature likeness of Austin in his complete hell kite transformation.

Walking the now deserted streets of this apocalyptic version of my hometown, I have found a hundred identical pieces of jewelry if I have found one. I ball the chain in my hand, lean back, and toss it into the flaming lake.

For the past few months, I have wondered if Austin will

be able to rebuild his army of witches. His current speed of creation tells me no. Or, at the very least, it is a task that takes centuries to complete.

Movement in my periphery catches my eye. I watch intently as the shadow emerges from the woods on the far side of the lake.

I can't see his destroyed face, but I imagine it all the same as I watch him move to the bank of the lake. I raise my hand and wave. I don't bother to holler his name. My voice would not carry over the fires crackling across the lake's expanse even in this realm.

Austin raises his hand as if to wave and then gives me a single-finger salute. I rotate my wrist and return the favored gesture.

It is a joy to know that he wants no part of me. Still, one of these days, I'll catch him unaware, and regardless of what the use of attacking magic might do to my psyche, it'll be worth taking Austin out.

The flames' color dims, and I am cast back into pitch-dark. The heat of the fire dissipates, and the smell, save for the slightest taint of sulfur, disappears.

Traveling between the two realms—something my grandmothers warn me is too dangerous—has become as easy as getting up and walking to my parents' home for a cup of coffee.

I float through the darkness, absent of all sensory stimuli other than a slight chill on my skin to be credited to the sheen of sweat I develop while in Austin's world.

My floating motion halts. Something heavy has fallen across my legs, trapping me in the Void. I try to kick and push against the pressure. The weight holds me firmly in the icy darkness.

I scold myself for my arrogance. My grandmothers warned me this could happen. That I could be trapped in the expanse of the in-between. Now the worst has happened.

Twisting sideways, I hope to buy enough space to pull my legs free of whatever has trapped me so I can continue floating home. A sharp firebrand sears through my cartilage. The sudden pain jolts me into action. I sit up and grab my injured knee.

Instead, I capture two handfuls of thick, soft hair.

What looks like a pig in a fur coat is stretched across my legs. I have my hands deep into his silver-and-black mane. Puppy opens his eyes and frowns as if to ask, "What's up?"

"For the love of Pete..." I say as I try to push him off my legs with no effect.

"Get off, Puppy."

He grunts and shuts his eyes.

"Come on, man, I told you not on me. You can lay next to me but not on me."

He opens one eye at me but makes no effort to move.

I really do think I sprained my knee. This calls for drastic measures. "Cookie? Can we go get a cookie?"

He begins to make Puppy snores. I know he is faking because he does it all the time.

Fine. Time for the nuclear option. "Bacon?"

Miraculously, he jumps from his side onto all fours with no motion in between and locks eyes with me as if to check if I am trustworthy. I am if Mama went to the store recently. I know the only breakfast food in my refrigerator is strawberry Greek yogurt. I strongly suspect Puppy will not fall for that trick again.

I didn't realize what time it was when I woke up. Since it is only 4:30, I beat Mr. Chipper Early Bird, aka Chase, into the kitchen.

With a glint of pride, I hustle to the coffee maker, as it's cool to be the one to make the coffee for once. Besides, it is the one "cooking" skill I am one hundred percent confident I can do without poisoning anybody.

The aroma of coffee fills the kitchen, and I go to work foraging in my parents' refrigerator. "Oh, bless you, Mama," I say as I pull out a pack of bacon and hold it to my chest. This will save me from having to sleep with one eye open because Puppy never forgets.

Maybe it is a function of my power when walking in Austin's world, but I feel competent today. In fact, I'm feeling so froggy that as the bacon warms in the cast-iron skillet, I pull down the Bisquick and decide today is the day I will make biscuits.

How tough can it be? The directions seem straightforward.

Puppy bumps my legs, knocking me off the one-foot-tall plastic stool. He likes biscuits but wants all my attention focused on the bacon in the skillet.

"Mind your manners, young man."

At my rebuke, he drops his butt onto the tile and stares at me condescendingly.

"And you can wipe that look off your face, too," I say as I dump the milk into the white powder and mix it with a fork.

I remove the first few slices of crispy bacon from the skillet, drop in five raw pieces, pivot to cut out the last biscuit and place it on the round, stoneware baking dish. Quickly, and feeling extremely capable, I slap generously sized butter chips on each biscuit top.

Chase will be so surprised. I hate that I waited until the end of my stay to finally get the nerve to learn how to cook and contribute to the rest of the family. But hey, better late than never. Right?

A flock of butterflies tickles my stomach as I slide the biscuits onto the rack and set the timer. I leave the light on in the oven so I can watch my masterpieces come to fruition.

Grabbing one of the slices of bacon, I blow on it to ensure it's cool enough for Puppy. I take a bite of it to be extra sure.

Puppy whines and stomps his front paws as he scoots closer to me. "You've been a good boy. Yes, you have."

I hold the bacon toward him. This isn't my first rodeo. I'm

thankful for my cat-like reflexes that leave the bacon hanging in mid-air as Puppy's multitude of teeth take up the space where my hand was seconds earlier. He snaps loudly as saliva flies to the floor.

"You like that bacon, don't you."

Puppy shuffles his front paws and whines. I take another test bite of a piece of bacon and repeat the levitating bacon trick.

I don't think he even chews, so I'm not sure why he likes bacon so much. There is no way he could taste it. Still, to each their own. He can eat his breakfast in any manner he pleases.

He whines, but I ignore him. Two slices are enough for now. I bend over and watch the biscuits bake.

I am so excited. These are going to be delicious. I know this because the biscuits smell perfect.

The timer for the biscuits goes off, and Puppy gets up and starts to do three-sixties in the kitchen. My dog is an even more serious food junkie than I am. He has significant food issues.

I grab hold of the stoneware pan with oven mitts. Slowly and carefully, I pull my beautiful biscuits from the oven.

"Did you cook biscuits?"

I jolt. The pan nearly flies out of my hands as biscuits jump four inches off the surface before landing neatly back inside the circular stoneware. "Bless it, Chase! You nearly gave me a heart attack and caused me to burn myself."

Chase frowns as he cocks his head to the side. "I'm not sure those two medical issues are in the same category of bad."

He is right, so I ignore his comment. "I made breakfast. I hope you're hungry."

Chase ambles over to the coffee and pulls down a mug as he suspiciously eyes the bacon and biscuits. "I see that."

"I wonder why I haven't tried biscuits before. It really wasn't that difficult. And I need to learn because I want to be able to cook for Lee."

"Yeah," Chase says haltingly as he walks closer to the biscuits and inspects them. He blows on the coffee he holds in his left hand as he presses one of the biscuits with his right pointer finger.

They are beautiful. Golden brown, just like Mama's. "Do you want some jelly for yours?" I ask as I open the refrigerator.

"Hmm… I think I'm just gonna do butter and steal a couple pieces of bacon."

"Suit yourself."

"Have you already fed Bear?"

Everyone in my family has created a different name for my dog. Mama called him Fabio, Chase used to call him Fang, and Daddy called him Bear. Bear now carries the day as his preferred family name. He is still Puppy to me, and always will be, but I can concede that his middle name is now Bear.

"I haven't given him any biscuits yet."

Chase squints his eyes as if he is about to ask a question and then decides not to. Instead, Chase cuts the top off one of the biscuits and quarters it. He bends over and holds the biscuit out to Puppy. "Hey, buddy, you hungry?"

Ever so gently, Puppy accepts the quartered biscuit from Chase. If I were smart, I would have the dog whisperer teach me that trick before we leave for Maryland.

Puppy snaps his head back, and the biscuit sitting on the edge of his lip disappears down his esophagus. Then Puppy drops his muzzle and opens his mouth. His tongue seems to go back into his throat, and the biscuit rolls out onto the floor.

"What the heck, Puppy?"

Chase's eyebrows narrow. "I guess he is not a biscuit fan."

I know that is not true. Puppy loves biscuits. Biscuits plain, biscuits with gravy, biscuits with sausage, biscuits with… Well, you get the picture. Puppy has never met a biscuit he didn't like.

Chase lathers the other half of the biscuit with butter and takes a bite. He chews, and chews, and chews.

My first foray into baking something besides Rice Krispies Treats may not have been the raving success I first thought. "Well?"

"They are different."

"What's the matter with them?"

"I didn't say anything was." Bits of crumbs drop out of Chase's mouth. He takes a big swig of coffee and looks like a pelican trying to swallow too big of a fish as his eyes bug out.

"You don't like them."

"No, they're great. They'll really stick with you all day."

Puppy whines and leaves the room. I assume he is afraid I'll make him eat the quarter of a biscuit he spat out.

Chicken.

A foul odor assaults my nose. It's a pungent stench reminiscent of a decaying body on a hot summer day with a tinge of bile-filled vomit.

Chase covers his face. "Oh, Jiminy Cricket, what is that?"

"Is that you or Puppy?"

"Wait, did you give Bear bacon?"

"Just a little."

"Darn it, April. You know that dog can't eat bacon." Chase tosses out his coffee in the sink and doesn't bother to rinse the basin. He marches toward the sliding glass door and yanks it open.

Fighting back my gag reflex, I ask, "Where are you going?"

"To find a skunk to squeeze so I can get this smell out of my nose."

Chapter 7

Surreal. That is the best way to sum up how this morning feels.

I spent eighteen years escaping the familial gravitational pull of Guntersville the first time, and I was ecstatic when I did. So much so that I didn't let the door hit me in the butt when I left for college.

Life changes have always made me feel alive. Beginning with a clean slate somewhere different always appeals to me.

So why am I swamped with melancholy and sadness mere hours away from my next big adventure? I've only been back in my hometown for eighteen months. It's not like I have set down new, deep roots in this Podunk town.

Still, I have pangs of anxiety as I walk through the quiet law office and pack the last smattering of personal items. It's like I'm a potted plant, and somebody is yanking me by the stem. Except it is my blood vessels—rather than a white web of roots —being torn from the earth that I cling to in vain, leaving half of my body buried unseen below the dirt.

If I had accepted Uncle Howard's generous offer and continued the law practice, I would have needed to hire an assistant and another lawyer. The business has been booming over the last few months. It required a Herculean effort to clear the last of my cases and direct any new business to other lawyers. Unfortunately, most of the opportunities had to be directed to Huntsville since the legal bench in Guntersville is exceedingly thin these days.

Not my problem.

I try to console myself with the refrain I have used for over a decade anytime something is inconvenient to my plans. Still, it now rings hollow to me. Somewhere during my journey, I have inadvertently made it my problem. For the first time, I care about how my choices affect the people around me.

Life was easier before this recent phenomenon.

Because they are kind, any of my clients would say I was professional in finding their new representation, given I'm leaving town tomorrow. That doesn't prevent me from feeling like I'm abandoning them in their hour of need.

But what am I supposed to do? The man I love is waiting for me in another state. It's impossible to be in two places at one time.

If we were to try a long-distance relationship, it would end in disaster. In fact, that is what we've been doing since February. Even though Lee hasn't mentioned anything about it, I feel less connected to him. I don't want that. I love him, and I want to be as close of a couple as we can be.

I see how my parents interact in their loving, successful relationship. That is what I crave. Why shouldn't I have that, too?

I'm debating if I want to pick out the pens that still work in my top desk drawer or dump them all in the garbage bag. My cell phone rings. Checking my phone's display, it reads Andy Ricketts.

Andy and his partner, Thelma Banks, run the local party supply and rental store called Party Perfect. I got Andy out of a legal jam last month when one of his tents collapsed during a freakishly strong rainstorm. The storm would have been enough to sour the wedding of the bellicose bride whose family hired his services. The tent collapsing and trapping dozens of guests underneath? Well, that simply turned her perfect day into purgatory.

The negotiation for a settlement took way more meetings than would have typically been required to allow the emotional aspect of the wedding ending in such a manner to cool off. Against her daughter's continued demands for blood, the bride's mother convinced her husband, one of the most extraordinary enablers of the princess syndrome I have ever met, to agree the catastrophe was nothing more than an unfortunate accident brought on by the whims of mother nature.

At first, Andy did not want to settle. I understood his position since, technically, the equipment was installed correctly and met all the wind code requirements.

I explained to Andy the settlement was half of what his legal fees for fighting the case in court would cost. Also, the compromise would protect him from a jury awarding the plaintiff a substantial judgment that could bankrupt him. He agreed, and we settled things discreetly.

The phone continues to ring in my hand as I wonder why he is calling. I referred him to White and Lowe for future needs, a good firm for small businesses out of Huntsville.

The intelligent thing for me to do is allow his call to go to voicemail and hope Andy can take the hint. Unfortunately, my curiosity will not allow me to make a clean break from my clients.

"Hi, Andy."

"Oh, April. Thank you so much for answering."

I blush since I didn't plan on being considerate enough to answer the phone. "No problem. Is everything all right with Jenny and the kids?"

I'm playing it like this is a social call.

"Oh… Yeah. Hey, April, I know you said I needed to go to White and Lowe in the future."

"Yes. I did."

"I need your help with something only you can manage."

"Andy, they are a capable firm."

"Well, they can't help me with this situation."

I fight the urge to bang my head on top of my desk. "I assure you they can, Andy. I selected that firm specifically because of their past history with small businesses like yours."

"I'm sure that is the case, and I appreciate the recommendation. But I have a particularly sensitive situation to take care of."

As a matter of reflex, I check the time on my phone. I'm not leaving today. It's only my overriding sense of lack of time. "Andy, I'm leaving the state tomorrow. I urge you to contact White and Lowe. I'm sure they can handle anything that is pressing."

"No. You are the only one that can take care of this."

I snort a laugh. "Andy, all Alabama attorneys have to take the same bar exam. There is nothing I can do for you that they can't."

"You don't understand. It's Thelma."

Andy's tone gives me pause. And, of course, my ever-present curiosity kicks in. "What is the matter with Thelma?"

"She's not right, and she won't get any help."

"What do you mean?"

"The past few weeks, she has been going in and out... It's hard to explain. It's like one minute it's good old reliable Thelma, and the next minute she is confused and doesn't know where she is at."

Thelma is no spring chick. If I were to guess, she could have taken full Social Security benefits five years ago. Consequently, I wouldn't be overly surprised if she starts to have an occasional senior moment. "Andy, I'm sorry to hear that. But I need to understand what that has to do with me."

"Isn't it obvious?"

If I had a dollar for every time, somebody said that... "Andy, if I have to ask, it's not obvious."

"Well, I can't leave my family's future at risk. I've offered to buy her out, and she refuses."

That's the thing about it with clients. One minute you're on a lazy Sunday drive, and the next minute, we take a hard left and hit the accelerator. "You want to dissolve the partnership?"

"I don't want to. But I have to."

"But you two built that business together."

"Yes. But that is no reason for me to stand idly by while she destroys it."

If I didn't know Andy to be such a serious man, I would think he was adding drama to the situation. "How is she destroying the company?"

"She refuses to let anybody other than her do the books. Which is fine. I prefer to take care of the sales and set-ups. But last week, I was embarrassed to find out that our largest paper goods supplier cut us off because they hadn't been paid in three months."

"Okay."

"No, not okay. If you lose your credit line in this business, you're out of business."

"Andy, I'm sure it was just an honest mistake. There is no way Thelma would purposely hurt your company."

"Not on purpose. But it doesn't matter whether it's intentional or not. She is doing it with increasing regularity. I'm telling you I can't work with her anymore."

"And when you talk to her about it?"

"She becomes angry. She thinks I'm trying to drive her out of the business."

I'm glad Andy and I aren't meeting face to face, so he doesn't see my expression. "Andy, if you're trying to dissolve the partnership, you are driving her out of the business."

He huffs. "I want to give Thelma her fair due. But I can't work with her anymore."

"So why can't White and Lowe take care of this for you?"

"Because she will listen to you. You're my only opportunity to offer her a fair deal, and be positive she will accept it."

Andy must be desperate or delusional. Although Thelma became an occasional businesswoman mentor of mine since the bridezilla settlement, it's not like the excellent advice flows both ways between us.

"Look, I can't draw this out. At the rate she is messing up, I've got to do something now. I can get you all the financials from last year so you can confirm the generosity of my offer. But, April, I don't think anybody will be able to get her to listen but you."

It sounds like the proverbial "trying to get a horse to drink water when it needs to pee." Still, if Thelma has medical issues, a solid buyout from Andy might be the best solution for everyone and save their long-term relationship. At the very least, I owe it to them to have that conversation with Thelma.

"Andy, send me the documents. I'll have my CPA look at the financials and do a quick valuation. When I return to town at the end of ball season, I'll talk with Thelma."

"Ugh... As much as I want to have a World Series winner from our town, I'll have to hope they get swept in the division playoffs."

"Hey, now!"

"Sorry. I didn't mean to be selfish. Thank you, April, and please tell Lee good luck tomorrow in the game. I'll be hoping he pitches a shutout ... and that Thelma goes on a vacation ... which she never does."

"Don't thank me yet. I will present your offer to Thelma once I have confirmed the deal's value, but only after talking to her and getting a feel for her condition. If she is as you say, I will try to convince her to accept the offer since it sounds like the best solution for both of you.

"Still, if she decides she doesn't want to sell her part of the company, you'll need to deal with White and Lowe. I will not be a part of forcing either of you to do something against your will."

Chapter 8

Puppy has not mastered the whole "riding in a canoe" thing. Still, he refuses to let me go on my own, and if I leave him behind, he will sulk over the perceived slight for days. If I put him in the canoe first, he hops out. If I get in first, he dives into the canoe, and his weight threatens to turn us over for an unplanned swim.

I canoe several evenings a week now. It's excellent exercise for my upper body and even better for the mind.

Once my furry copilot is finally situated. I push off from the dock and stroke past the boathouse. The brisk wind forms small wave caps on the lake's surface.

The sun sits on the tips of the pine trees to the west. I'll have to do this quickly. I don't want to be caught on the water without a signal light in the dark.

For years, the idea of canoeing or swimming alone in the lake petrified me, and for good reason. Being pulled under and nearly drowned by a spirit at the age of eight can cause a phobia.

The ghost pulled me under, leaving an indelible stinging sensation on my left ankle. I have always called the spirit the Old Man in the Lake.

Imagine my surprise after my battle with Austin earlier in the year when my parents shared details about a man named

Randolph, who disappeared decades earlier. I have no way of confirming if Randolph and the Old Man in the Lake are one and the same, but I have my suspicions.

Randolph was in his early thirties at the time of his disappearance. My Aunt Dionis, who was pregnant with his child, insisted that she could see him at the bottom of the lake.

I realize most people would write this off as a delusional nightmare from a woman grieving that her love abandoned her during her moment of greatest need. However, Dionis has visited me, and I know she was afflicted with the same "gifts" I am.

Dionis had consistent dreams and visions of Randolph drowning. She was positive he had died even though her family disparaged him for ducking out on his responsibilities.

She was convinced he would not have abandoned her.

Dionis's belief that Randolph had drowned was her undoing. After giving birth to their child, she walked into Guntersville Lake six months later and was never seen again.

Until she showed up in my room two years ago.

I pass by the yacht club on my right and admire the enormous, gas-guzzling flotilla of the rich—sometimes cash-strapped—not-so-famous.

Dionis is right about Randolph. I know this because Austin parted the lake's water during my battle with the witches. At the bottom of the lake, I could make out a pathetic being struggling along the muddy bottom of the lake, his feet encased in concrete blocks. Although he was doing Austin's bidding and was a spectral being, he did not strike fear in my heart. In fact, in retrospect, he was a sympathetic sight.

Still, he tormented me for twenty years. In many ways, my going out on the lake alone is my tiny way of taunting him back.

If I were to stay in Guntersville, I would like to bring closure to how Randolph met his end. From the sounds of it, he made plenty of enemies in Guntersville. Still, there is a vast difference between enemies and someone willing to kill you.

I circle Duck Island, slowly alternating the sides I paddle, when I unexpectantly grind to a halt on a mudbank I did not notice. Three ducks land on the shallow water twenty feet away, paddle, then walk up onto the island's edge. Puppy launches himself out of the canoe.

Catching a bird has been on his bucket list for a long time.

"Bless it! Puppy, get back here!"

Does my dog, who loves me, mind me? Of course not.

I hop out of the boat onto the mudbank, thankful I was mindful enough to wear my water shoes and pull my canoe up to the island's shore. Puppy has already disappeared into the thicket.

I consider following my dog, but after taking inventory of the thorned bushes, I think twice. "Not today."

His barking sounds like it's on the back side of the island, which is only forty yards across. I circle around the island, careful not to slip on the large, slimy, flat rocks at the shoreline.

Arriving on the backside, I find my dog standing at the edge of the brush. Puppy has a large, brown, angry-looking thorny branch running along his furry belly.

"How did you expect this to end, silly dog?"

He whimpers. I set my jaw and squat to see how best to free him.

"Well, you've done this up right, mister," I say as I pull ineffectively on the branch buried in his coat.

I set to work pulling his cotton-like undercoat free of the razor-sharp thorns. It's a tedious project. I have six inches of cane left to remove when I drive a thorn halfway through my thumb.

"Mother of pearl, that smarts!"

I jerk my thumb back and shove it in my mouth. "Bless it, Puppy. You're the thorn in my butt some days," I mumble.

He snorts at me. Displeased that I have failed to free him yet, I'm sure.

The taste of blood confirms the thorn did a number on my thumb. That will be aggravating for the better part of the week.

Well, in for a penny, in for a pound. I bend over, hoping to make quick work of the last of the thorny cane. Gritting my teeth, I ignore the blood I smear on Puppy's light gray belly and toss the remaining stick to the side.

"You're welcome."

He huffs and sits on his haunches.

"No, sir. We don't have time to rest."

Reluctantly, he obeys, and we are off like a herd of turtles. Walking back to the other side of the island, where I grounded our canoe. I'm forced to coax and bribe him every few steps as we cross the stones at the water's edge.

At the side of the canoe, Puppy decides he doesn't like the angle and refuses to jump into the boat. A wrestling match ensues as I struggle to lift my furry pig over the side as he freaks out, twisting and turning in my arms like one colossal muscle.

We didn't have time for the extracurricular duck hunt. The last slice of the sun disappears below the tallest pines as I labor to find a rhythm with my paddling.

The temperature drops precipitously as we pass the yacht club, and my thumb throbs nonstop.

"I can't believe you ran off like that," I scold Puppy. Actually, I can. I'd be more surprised if he hadn't. Life goals are essential. Even if it is something as idiotic as catching a bird.

He rotates his ears, laying them flat against the back of his head, but refuses to turn around and acknowledge me. I'll accept Puppy's contriteness as his apology. Devoted friends don't require apologies to always be verbalized.

Shifting my grip, I rotate the paddle to the right side of the canoe. My hand stings from the damage to my thumb. Bummer.

I shake my hand to stop the tingling sensation, and droplets of blood fly into the air, landing on the lake's surface. An eerie, azure mist rises from the indigo surface.

Well, that's new. I've never noticed that before, but I can't remember ever bleeding in the lake in this manner.

Either way, the odd, bright blue smoke can't be anything good.

The solution to this mystery is simple. If I bleed into the lake, it causes a magical mist to rise, but since I will soon be in Baltimore... See, no mystery to be resolved. Now I just need to get to our dock as quickly as possible.

A glimmer of light in my right periphery cuts through the night.

Despite the increasingly bizarre, magical fog thickening on the lake that knots my stomach in dread, I pause, focusing on where the flash originated. It does not return.

I surmise it was headlights, while at the same time I slap down the logic that there is no road or path in that direction, and I dip my paddle through the thick fog to paddle us to the boat house.

As I stroke the water, a single shimmer strobe again appears on the shore.

All right now, I'm not imagining that.

Despite the throbbing injury to my thumb, I paddle in a sprint toward the flash on the shoreline. It appears to have come from between two humongous cedar trees. Each cedar towers forty feet into the air, and is easily twenty feet wide at its base.

Funny, I don't recall ever noticing that vacant lot. The Mercers' two-story colonial to the right has been there for as long as I can remember. The brand-new McMansion to the left was completed while I was at school.

The lot between them, the one with the cedar forest, appears out of nowhere.

The glimmer reappears between the two trees. The shock of light is five feet tall and four feet wide. Like a search beam, it throws a ray out across the increasingly dark surface of the water while adding a luminescent glow to the azure mist.

My curiosity is thoroughly piqued, and I paddle like a scalded haint toward the light. Closing the distance quickly, I am within fifty yards of the shore. The light vanishes.

Chapter 9

Puppy whimpers and launches onto the decking as our canoe pulls level with my parents' boat dock. He makes tracks up the weathered boards as his nails scratch the surface.

"Hey, don't mind me. I'll get the gear put up by myself."

I love that dog, but for the life of me, he is a riddle to me. One moment I can't get him to give me room in the bed, and the next minute he abandons me.

Never mind. I forget that Puppy is male. He can't help it; it's in his DNA.

I pull the canoe into the boathouse, placing the lifejackets and paddle into the center. I latch the drawstring to the hooks Daddy mounted on the stern and bow. Since I will be gone, I need to tidy it up and hang the canoe in its proper place.

All this putting everything in its proper place before I leave is beginning to have a theme. I hope the excitement of moving on to the next chapter of my life will hurry up and improve my attitude. I'm ready for these daily steps not to carry the "last time" message that fills me with a melancholy reflection on my decision.

And what exactly is my decision?

I've wondered recently if my decision to move with Lee is actually a decision or the next blind move in my tailspin since the destruction of my master plan. Seriously, do I find Lee exceedingly attractive? Yes, I do, but at the same time, there has been no mention of marriage. Only recently did he finally quit avoiding the question of what I will do with Puppy when we move.

It was as I suspected. Lee would be undisturbed to allow my family to care for Puppy while we are in Baltimore. The discussion about where Puppy will reside while April lives with Lee is the closest we've come to an all-out argument.

He made some excellent points—only because they were low-hanging fruit. Such as Puppy is used to my family, and Puppy enjoys the lake.

Only my persistent reiteration that Puppy is my friend, and I will need him for the company as Lee travels to away games convinced him. Begrudgingly, he agreed Puppy would be allowed to come with me.

It is not something he gave into willingly. He was saying yes, but I could see on his face that it was not his desire to give in on that point, and he might revisit it with regret later.

I often wonder if Lee would react similarly if I broached what has yet to be discussed—the question that he has never asked.

To be fair, I've never spoken of marriage, either. Currently, the relationship is convenient for us in its present state. The real question may not be so much something for Lee to ask me as it is for me to ask my heart. Am I ready to commit my life to Lee and raise a family later?

I don't have a suitable answer to that inquiry presently. I know that if I do marry, it will be as the vows prescribe, "For better or for worse." Let's face the facts; forever is a long time. And at this point, the best answer I can come up with to that inquiry about marriage is a resounding maybe.

It's best to heed one of Chase's favorite stanzas: "Be careful what you ask for. It might be more than you asked for."

The scent of flaming hamburger grease reaches my nostrils, and the mystery of Puppy's abandonment of me is quickly solved. The dog loves me with all his heart, but his stomach still trumps his emotional attachment to me.

My tall, athletically built brother, Chase, works a spatula with deft proficiency. His attractive profile is illuminated in a burst of yellow-orange flame from the grill.

My traitorous dog sits at Chase's left boot, staring dreamily at the man and hoping his master spatula skills will fail and drop a patty from heaven.

"Howard always said that is your best trait," Chase says without turning toward me.

His comment surprises me. I thought I was in stealth mode, and he did not indicate seeing me. "What trait is that?"

"Perfect timing."

I snort an unladylike laugh. "Well, you're sadly mistaken. I can fill a notebook full of instances to the contrary without any effort—college ruled."

Chase angles his face toward me. "Uh-huh." He redirects his attention to the grill.

"Can I buy a plate, or is this a private party?"

"Your money will never be any good here, Tink. But Dusty is inside getting the rest of the meal together if you want to help."

It's a straightforward, thoughtful statement from my brother that drops an acidic ball of angst into my stomach. The sting of this morning's biscuit failure is fresh on my mind.

I am trying to get better at carrying my load on the culinary-contribution front. Unfortunately, it's a long and slow process.

My feet stay frozen to the deck three steps from the glass door to my parents' kitchen. Chase turns his head, and his eyebrows draw together.

Think, April, think.

The epiphany blissfully blooms in my mind. I remember Mama had a bag of zucchini in the fridge when I searched for bacon this morning. "How about I throw together a zucchini bake?"

The flash of the quick-moving spatula ceases over the flame. Chase grimaces, his expression reminiscent of someone required to tell their friend they accidentally backed over their cat.

"Nah. That's okay. Dusty and I already have enough fixings. I meant help him bring it outside."

Now I feel even more pressure to contribute to the basket of fish and bread. "It won't take me but a few seconds."

"Really, April. This is almost done. Some other time."

"But I want to."

Chase opens his mouth to say something, closes it, and presses his lips together. The sliding door opens. Dusty appears, holding a lighter.

"Just in time, April." His broad smile moves his red beard, tilting the tip toward me.

"Does Mama still have the zucchini in the fridge?"

"I suppose she might..." Dusty trails off as he looks over my left shoulder toward the grill. I turn to look at Chase, and he snaps his head so his attention is redirected to the burgers on the grill.

"She d-does," Dusty stammers. "But this morning, she told me those are earmarked for a batch of pickled squash."

Even in the failing light, Dusty's white skin turns a shade darker. "Doesn't Mama use squash for pickled squash rather than zucchini?"

"A new recipe?"

"When did she start back to pickling items? I thought she said it took too much time."

Dusty shrugs as he hurries by me. "Don't expect me to explain the ways of our mom, April."

Fair enough, even though I feel like I am being subverted. I turn my attention to Chase, and he appears disappointed that our eyes meet.

"You could grab the outdoor dishes and fill some glasses with tea. That would be awfully helpful," he says with a winning smile.

Fine. Considering I nearly choked him with this morning's biscuits, Chase may be the voice of reason. The silver lining is I can use the thirty minutes required to make something edible to instead put the finishing touches on the items I will take with me on my trip to Baltimore.

It's a shame the initial plan of moving up this week has been delayed since Lee's team has made the playoffs. Now I'm to go up with minimal items, and as soon as the season is complete, we will drive down and rent a U-Haul to move me up.

My goal is to have everything organized and boxed. Then, when we come down after a World Series win, it won't take more than a day to load up Puppy and make my final exit from Guntersville.

I light the citronella candles around the outdoor seating area, even though the mosquitoes have subsided since we recently had some very cool mornings. Autumn, my favorite part of the year, has finally arrived in the South.

It hurts my feelings that I will miss Halloween in Guntersville.

I'll also miss cheering for the Crimson Tide as they put together another championship season. Especially since their state rivals choke leads and fire their coach on Twitter every Saturday. It's the best time to be a Bama girl. The worst time to be leaving for Maryland.

You cannot buy dinners like my brothers cook. After an hour of gorging myself with hamburger steak, mashed potatoes slathered in brown gravy, and honey-glazed carrots, I sit back and undo the button on my jeans. I admonish myself for pigging out when I have been doing so well not to overeat lately.

My eyes glaze over, and my mind fogs. I could use a long nap or an early bed call, and it's not just the caloric coma I have put myself into. I have been going ninety to nothing trying to take care of everything that must be set right before I leave, and it's taken every hour of every day. More so, it has emotionally bankrupted me.

I'm too tired to feel much of anything.

Dusty and Chase's conversation shifts to the annual men's retreat they began when they graduated from high school. Once a year, twenty-five to thirty of their friends get together and go on an extended weekend. This will often revolve around outdoor activities ranging from fishing to bird hunting to golfing. A few times, the focal point was more touristy to a famous city such as New Orleans or Nashville because many of the men had yet to travel out of Alabama.

While the group and location constantly change, the event remains intact because of my brothers—the core that the other men choose to orbit. Some friends have fallen to the wayside due to family or work obligations. Still, the men that can make it always rave about the trips.

Since increasingly more of the group has become married and/or fathers, the locations have moved closer to Guntersville. While not married, my brothers are mindful that the group stays closer to Guntersville these days in case anyone is needed at home for an emergency; they can make it back within a few hours' drive.

This year's excursion is a fishing trip to Joe Wheeler State Park. The boys have it planned out for a five-day, four-night trip. They will stay at the lodge and already have the menu, hiking, and fishing itinerary set.

"I want to go."

The words blurt out of my mouth before I think about it. My brothers quit talking and raise their eyebrows at me.

"What? I know most of the guys who are coming." Not a totally accurate statement, but I do know more than I don't.

"Uh...no," Chase scoffs.

"Definitely not happening," Dusty adds.

"Why not?"

"Well, for starters, many of these men are married," Dusty says.

"And?"

"And the only way they got kitchen passes is because their wives know there are no women on this trip. Moreover, their wives know we have no intentions of going to seedy establishments where women are..." Chase motions with his hands. "You know."

"Geez, Chase. It's not like I'm gonna be hitting on your friends. I have a fiancé, after all."

"Yeah, but that won't matter to their wives and girlfriends. You should know these things."

I do, inherently. Still, coming home in a few months and going on the trip with my brothers has captured my interest. "They don't have to know."

Dusty starts to say something, but Chase lays his hand on Dusty's shoulder. "No. End of conversation."

I snort and shake my head. "I don't see why y'all are this way about it."

"Because guys need guy time just like girls need girl time. April, you need to plan a trip with your girlfriends if you want to get away for a weekend. You can't be included in a guy trip. It's just not done."

Typically, my brothers will give in to me if I'm persistent enough. Of the two, Chase is the easiest to convince. However, his jaw is set, and the hardness in his eyes tells me I have ventured several steps over the line with my request.

"You know, April. It brings up a topic we have wanted to talk to you about, but the opportunity never seems right."

I glare at Dusty. Not getting my way with them is a little much to bear, and it will take a minute to get over it. "What's that?"

"You spend too much time at work, hanging out with the family, or holed up in your apartment. It's not healthy," Dusty says.

"What are you talking about?"

"Why do you never hang out with your chick friends?" Chase interjects.

"Chick friends?"

He makes a waving motion with his hand. "Girls, women, females, whatever we're allowed to call y'all nowadays."

"Like girlfriends?"

"Sure, okay, girlfriends," Chase says.

"Because I don't have any."

My snippy statement hangs in the air as the three of us stare at each other. *Odd, I wouldn't have thought about it without this conversation.*

Liza and I have become close over the last year, but when she left for Michigan for four months, I didn't keep in touch with her. Likewise, while Jackie Rains and I are no longer enemies, I've made no real effort to restart our friendship. And since Susan's wedding, I have yet to reach out to any of the girls from my sorority.

"I've never told you what to do," Dusty says. "But I feel it's healthy for everyone to have someone from the same sex to confide in. It can be a smaller group than we put together. But you might want to develop at least one strong friendship," Dusty says in a voice barely above a whisper.

Even as gently as he put it, his statement feels like a rebuke. Still, he might be right. Nana, Granny, and Mama have been my female interaction partners recently. But they are one and two generations removed from the things I am experiencing.

Once I arrive in Baltimore, I must prioritize developing friendships with a few women. I'll have the ins and outs to learn about being a ball player's wife—well, fiancée—and need to become comfortable in my new city. The sooner I put together a group to help me navigate that, the sooner I'll acclimate to my new surroundings.

Chapter 10

It's 7:30 AM, and I am walking inside Snow and Associates. I took the phone off the hook yesterday when I left. Consequently, it's so quiet I swear I can hear the hum of the HVAC unit in my eardrums.

Everything is packed away. All the folders are in order and ready to review if Uncle Howard needs them for some deposition in the future. Assuming he can break away from his marinara empire long enough to help his former clients if they are subpoenaed for some old documents.

Standing at my desk, I look around the office for one more bittersweet moment. I remember all the highs and lows of the last year and all the lessons I learned from Uncle Howard. They will serve me well in the future.

My return to Guntersville was for a reason. I had yet to learn that the degree I earned from the university was all book knowledge. It took the mentorship of a thoughtful, practicing lawyer to round out my abilities.

I am better prepared for my future now than when I arrived in Atlanta a year and a half ago. When I get to Baltimore, I will have exceptional talents and skills to offer my clients.

The front door opens, drawing my attention to it. My private investigator for the last six months, Baker Diaz, enters with a gift in his right hand.

"I was worried I missed you. I kept calling and getting a busy signal." His eyes shift toward the desk phone. "Mystery solved. You took the phone off the hook."

"I see no reason to disappoint clients by answering the phone and telling them I can't help them."

Baker shoves his free hand in his right pocket. "I suppose there is some wisdom in that."

"To what do I owe the honor of your visit?"

He approaches and holds out a box—eighteen inches square —wrapped in bright green wrapping paper. "A little something you can't open until your first day as a lawyer in your new career." As I take it, he produces a sizeable brown folder with a ribbon tie clasp from below the gift. "And then the infamous Dottie folder. You can open it today."

I roll my eyes. "I am not taking that cold case with me."

"No. But you should have it filed away if anybody local ever needs the information."

I accept the folder from him. Reluctantly. Dottie is the one bit of business I won't be able to tidy up before leaving Guntersville. When her house burned down and a body was found in the basement, we assumed Dottie died tragically in the fire.

In retrospect, I would have been satisfied with that news. Nothing ever seems to be that clean-cut in my professional career, though. One of my good friends, an excellent medical examiner, Shane, believes the remains were not Dottie's. Unfortunately, since there is no salvageable DNA on the body, we have not been able to identify the female in the basement.

Diaz has been searching for Dottie in case Shane's theory is correct. He has had the same results as Shane. Nada.

"I'm sorry I didn't locate her for you."

"Baker, I know that woman is slipperier than owl poop. You did your best, and I appreciate you staying on it and working as diligently as you did."

"It wasn't without compensation, and I wish I had been able to provide better results."

I appreciate his honesty and have to laugh. "Well, that would make two of us."

"When are you leaving, April?"

"My butt must be in its seat on flight eleven thirty-four to Baltimore at three o'clock."

He nods his head slightly. "I hope it's everything you wish it to be. I know I'm rooting for you."

"I appreciate that, Baker."

The door shuts behind him. My thoughts go to the contents of the package I hold. I can't help it. My curiosity is perpetually stuck in overdrive. Still, I promised Baker I would wait until I began my next job. Since he was such a friendly and dependable business partner, I'll have to live with it and save it for a surprise.

Dottie's folder on the other hand? I drop the large envelope inside a cardboard filing box at the top of a stack I have made in the corner. I apply a liberal amount of packing tape for no good reason and step back to admire the files that hold "April's cases in Alabama."

It is a healthy amount of production, if I do say so myself.

The unassuming boxes contain more than paper and forms. They hold people's lives and real-world events that required my expertise and moxie to solve. For once, I allow myself a little pride as I review the stack in the corner.

The self-congratulatory moment is over quickly. I grab my purse from the bottom drawer of my desk for the last time and walk toward the front door. I scan the tiny office that has become a pivotal part of my life and whisper, "Goodbye."

The front door opens, bumping me rudely on the butt.

"Oh, excuse me," Lane says, his face flushing red. "I've been trying to call you, but your lines have been busy."

I consider explaining that I took the phone off the hook but think better of it. "I was heading out."

"You can't." Lane raises his hands and inclines his head. "I mean to say I need your help desperately."

"I'm sorry, Lane. I have a plane to catch at three o'clock."

"Perfect. That is sufficient time to help Kat Krasinski. She needs a lawyer. I can replace you next week when Lynn comes back from vacation."

I must be staring at Lane as if he has grown a second head because his facial expression changes from hope to complete confusion. "What?"

"Lane, the shop is closed. Snow and Associates is no more."

"Right, I understand that. Still, you have a few hours, and I need you to do this last thing for me."

"No. I wish I could, but I'm done here."

His brow furrows as the left side of his lip twitches into a grin. "A young lady is being charged with attempted murder, and you are not willing to help?"

"I didn't say I didn't want to. I'm saying I can't because I'm leaving."

"I heard you—at three o'clock—but it's nine now. You have plenty of time to help her through the interview process."

Lane has always been pushy, but this is beyond the pale even for him. "Lane, I don't think you understand. I'm leaving, and because Howard has decided to put his full-time effort into the pizza parlor, this place is no longer an option for your department's overflow cases."

"And you need to understand that this case requires your assistance. You are still a part of this community, and this is specifically up your alley."

"Up my alley?" I scoff. "What would that be?"

"Kat Krasinski shot her boyfriend Liam's ear off today." Lane continues to look at me with an expression of anticipation.

"And that is a case I am particularly suited for because…?"

"Because she is a female, and she is charged with attempted murder."

I'm not gonna lie. Ever since Charlotte King's case, a mother of four wrongly accused of murdering her husband, I have had a soft spot for women charged with a crime against their spouse or lover. Still, that doesn't change the reality that I, April, must be on a plane at 3:00 PM, or I'll have a physically imposing athlete in a particularly sour mood.

"Lane, truly, I would love to help. But there is no way I can and still make my flight."

"I can provide a police escort if necessary."

"All the way to Huntsville? I'm so sure."

Lane smiles. "It sounded good. Who knows. If I ask Pete Lau nicely and his team ran the interrogation too long, he might do it."

The name Pete Lau sends a chill through me—the equivalent of a creepy dude touching my cheek. Pete Lau is the new police captain. I can't even begin to explain how much the police department in Guntersville has changed since Jacob left and Pete Lau became the new captain of the force when Captain Ricks retired.

"I'll pass on the escort. Tell me again what she did."

Lane takes a step closer. "Kat and Liam have had issues for a while now. They have been living together for two years. During that time, there have been three domestic dispute calls. Finally, better sense prevailed, and Liam moved out two months ago. This culminated with Kat getting a restraining order."

I make a circling motion with my finger to speed Lane up with the explanation. Although I'm intrigued by the details, I still have a travel schedule.

"To put it bluntly, Liam beat the living tar out of her a month ago and was sentenced to eight months in jail for domestic abuse."

"If he is in jail, how does he manage to get his ear shot off."

Lane shuffles his feet as a distressed expression comes over him. "The new state's attorney has sent a mandate requiring us to release first-time offenders early if no weapon is involved."

My ire jumps up a notch. "State Attorney Giles has never heard of anybody being killed by somebody else's hands?"

Lane frowns as he shoves his fists into the front pockets of his trousers. "Come on, April. Don't make me explain how politics work in this state."

"I was just wondering if we are still grounded in reality. Guns and knives are not the only things used to kill people."

"I'm only following orders here, April."

"You let the scum bag out early."

"I let this piece of trash out because I was told to."

"Same result. The ending is predictable, yet I want to hear it from you anyway."

"Liam made a beeline to his ex's home, who was instrumental in his arrest. You can get the rest of the story from Kat, but from what I understand, when he broke down the door to her trailer, she was waiting on the other side with a twenty-two rifle."

"Not my choice, but good for her."

Lane narrows his eyes.

"What? I'm just saying. If we're back to protecting ourselves because nobody else will—"

"April..."

I pull in a deep breath and favor Lane with my sweetest smile. "She pointed the rifle at his face and blew an ear off?"

I'm seething on the inside. Plus, there is no way I would have missed that shot. If somebody ever used me as their personal punching bag and then kicked in my door, I'll be shooting two rounds—one for his left eye and one for the right—and my aim is perfect.

"No, she missed with the first two shots. Then, as Liam ran to his car to escape, she split his right ear with a round."

"Sounds like he should count himself lucky and stay away from her."

"I'm not here to argue that with you, April. Still, he has asked us to press charges for attempted murder, and attempted murder is a crime of focus for the state attorney. So, given the evidence, we will be prosecuting."

"And your solution is to sic Pete Lau on her to get a confession?"

"I don't have any choice as to who the police captain is." He sighs as he looks away from me. "Besides, she has already confessed, but I don't think it fair that she did not have a lawyer, and she finally requested one."

It figures. Like being trapped during the last ghost hunt before leaving Guntersville, a case would present itself where an innocent woman is accused of something stupid before I leave town. The correct course of action is to continue to beg off Lane and tell him to do something different. But my conscience won't let me.

"What interrogation room does Lau have her in?"

Chapter 11

I had hoped my impromptu trip to the jail would allow me to visit my friend Jade. Unfortunately, she is off today, and I'm led back by a new guard I'm unfamiliar with. The young man directs me to interrogation room number two. As I approach, I see Captain Lau outside, watching the interrogation through the one-way glass.

"Hi, Pete. Care to let me in to discuss things with my client?" I know that calling Pete by his first name aggravates him immensely. Something I'm particularly proud of, given the man thinks the sun comes up just to hear him crow.

"Not necessary, Snow. We'll be done in a few minutes."

"You'll be done in three seconds if you don't let me speak to my client."

I give him my best death stare. He returns his version, and we hold it for several seconds before he finally acquiesces. We continue to glare at one another like two fighters at the weigh-in.

We're in the same weight classification. I'm confident I can take him.

"Understand, this won't change anything. Kat will be prosecuted for attempted murder."

"Thank you kindly, Pete. You have a blessed day now," I say as I enter the interrogation room where Dorsett and Colby hold court. "Detectives, if you please, I have some things to discuss with my client."

Dorsett opens his mouth to protest, but Colby grabs him by the arm. I've become good acquaintances with both. One I respect immensely; the other I wouldn't spit on if he were on fire.

The door clicks shut behind them, and I smile at Kat. From what I can tell, she is a tall woman—slightly taller than me—with a strong jawline, pug nose, and wide-set brown eyes. Her thin, brown hair hangs loosely around her eyes and needs a trim. I sit in the seat, still warm from Dorsett. "Hi, Kat. I am your temporary public defender, April Snow."

"It's about time. Can you get me out of here? These turkeys are driving me crazy."

"I hope to. But for now, how about you bring me up to speed with what happened between you and Liam? After that, we'll try to answer the detectives' questions to get you released."

Kat slouches in her chair as she squints her eyes. "So, you're as useless as tits on a boar, too."

"Aren't you just precious?" I say as I open my backpack and pull out my laptop. "How about you describe Liam's and your relationship."

Kat gathers a handful of her hair in her right hand and breaks off the split ends one strand at a time. "We've been dating for the better part of two years and living together the last year and a half. "Well, minus the last month when he has been in jail for beating the stew out of me."

"Was there an incident that brought on the violence?"

Kat wrinkles her face as if she has bitten into a lemon. "What? Are you into victim shaming?"

"Not at all. Still, I'm not ignorant that when men lose their Jesus, half the time it's because something triggered them. The other half of the time, it's alcohol or drugs."

She looks away from me and clicks her tongue. "I suppose Liam got his underwear in a bunch because Leslie and I went to Choppers. But we were only going to have a drink."

Choppers is a less-than-desirable bar on the outskirts of Boaz. The mayor has been trying to close it down for a decade. I believe nobody should patronize that bar unless they are looking for trouble.

"And what happened that night?"

"I came home, and he asked where I had been. And I told him none of his beeswax. Then he used my head like a battering ram against every wall in the living room."

"That's when you took out the restraining order?"

She raises her eyebrows. "And you wouldn't have?"

I continue writing notes on my pad. "There wouldn't have been any need to." I look up and meet her gaze. "A restraining order would be pointless since I would have killed him."

Kat laughs hysterically. "Okay. I feel you, girl. And don't think that I didn't consider it. All the same, I'd rather not spend the rest of my days in jail for killing him."

"See there. You've already proven that you're smarter than your representation."

She smiles. "That's all right. I trust her fully."

Chapter 12

I call Daddy at noon to ask if he has time to go online and try to reschedule me for a later flight out of Huntsville. A few minutes later, the confirmation comes in that I am now on the 5:10 flight.

My stomach turns as I realize how insanely tight my schedule to make it to Baltimore in time for Lee's game has become. The best I can calculate is that Lee will already be on the mound when I arrive at the stadium.

But seriously, what am I supposed to do? Lane didn't have a public defender to help Kat, and I couldn't leave her alone with Dorsett and Colby.

I reenter the interrogation room and signal Dorsett and Colby that they can follow me. I take inventory of my temporary client. Despite Kat's blustering and posturing, I can see she is exhausted.

I won't allow her to make a mistake. Still, with Dorsett's continued hostility at Lau's request, I question what goodwill Kat's cooperation with the investigation is buying her. I'm near the point of pulling the plug on this circus.

Dorsett reenters and puffs his chest out. He slams his fist on the table, causing Kat and me to jump. "Are you done playing games?"

"What the heck, Dorsett?" Colby turns to me and says, "I

apologize for that, April."

"You're not the one who owes us an apology." I glare at Dorsett.

Dorsett snarls, revealing his upper teeth. "Sue me. I am getting impatient with her runaround."

"You have yet to see runaround, Dorsett. And thank you for the suggestion. I'll take the time to consider if it's worth our effort to sue you."

Dorsett crosses his arms over his massive chest as he grunts a growl.

Colby adjusts his attention from his admonished partner to Kat. "Understand that all we're trying to do is develop the timeline. There are a few aspects of it that I need help understanding. I would appreciate it if you could elaborate."

Kat shakes her head. "Colby, just ask a question, and I'll answer it."

"From the look of it, Kat, you were lying in wait to ambush Liam. I want to know if that is the truth."

"Colby, before we answer that, I have a question for you."

"Come on, April. This is our interrogation."

I smirk and wait. Colby releases an exasperated breath through his teeth. "Oh, all right. What is it?"

"How do you lie in wait and ambush an intruder in *your* home?"

"I don't understand."

"Precisely. Me either. My client was at her house. Her, H-E-R, home. She has a restraining order against Liam, and when he breaks into *her* home, *her* castle, it is considered an ambush when she protects herself?"

"She tried to murder him," Dorsett hollers.

Colby raises his hand toward Dorsett. "April, this is different."

"Different how? If *you* protect your family from an intruder, will you be charged with attempted murder?"

"They had history." Colby's tone is patient and pleading. He is trying to defuse the April bomb that he knows is pending.

"And by my estimation, that only makes it worse. Kat had a restraining order against Liam. For sending her to the emergency room. And that is for the only time she reported it."

"So what? We're supposed to tell Liam to count his blessings that she is a bad shot?"

"I am not a bad shot," Kat snaps.

"Kat, let me handle this."

She promptly ignores my command. "It took two warning shots to get it through that man's thick head that he better leave my trailer. That third shot was a reminder in case he forgot."

So not helpful.

I hang my head in defeat. I can help my client if she can learn to follow instructions.

"A reminder?" Colby asks.

"You darn near shot his ear plum off," Dorsett shouts as he walks toward her.

"I only planned to zing one by his ear. His truck was to the left. How was I supposed to know the dingbat was going to zig right. He always has been unpredictable like that."

It's not funny. Honestly, it's not. But I struggle mightily to push the giggle down inside me so I don't erupt into a belly laugh.

"That's just it, Miss Krasinski. You purposely attempted to murder him."

I rest my hand on her shoulder as I answer Colby. "You fellas aren't listening. She had every right to drop him like a sack of potatoes when he broke into the trailer. Instead, she fired warning shots which he finally heeded and left the premises. By my account—except that he should be charged for disregarding a restraining order—no harm, no foul, and you should release Kat now."

The interrogation room door opens, and Pete Lau enters. "Can't you two complete an interrogation successfully?" he scolds the detectives. "Enough of this happy horse puck, Counselor Snow. How about you do your job and explain to your client that she is looking at some serious time. You should convince her to work with us now so we can ask DA Lane for leniency."

I squint and cock my head as I stare at Pete. "Tell me again where you got your law degree, Pete."

Pete loops his thumbs into his utility belt as he squares his shoulders. "I'm a police captain. It doesn't require a law degree."

I open my eyes wider. "Oh, *that's right*. Well, how about you let me do my job, and I won't tell you how to do yours."

"I know you think you're something special, Ms. Snow. But you're just another two-bit shyster lawyer getting in the way of the law."

There are many things about Guntersville that I will miss. But if I were to take inventory of those items, Pete Lau would not be found on that list. Fortunately for me, he is a recent addition to my town. The town I am leaving today.

I move closer to Pete until my Keds tap the toe of his smartly shined, black jump boots that he tucks his pants into before lacing. I tilt my nose down since I am two inches taller.

He takes a step back and rests his hand on top of his strapped Glock.

"Pete, you're left with two options as I, too, am tired of this horse puck. You either charge my client with attempted murder, which I know you're not prepared to do because your case is weaker than a straw bridge, or she walks out of here with me."

Pete's expression changes dramatically. He glances at his two detectives.

I tap him on the chest. "They can't help you, Pete. It's time to make a decision."

He narrows his eyes as he inhales sharply. He points his finger at Kat. "Ms. Krasinski, don't you leave town." He turns smartly in his jumper boots and marches out of the room, reminiscent of a paratrooper from a banana republic dictatorship.

Chapter 13

I really need to be at the airport. I now risk missing the later flight that Daddy was kind enough to arrange for me. Still, because her car is at her trailer, Kat needs a ride home.

At speeds that would make a moonshine runner proud, I navigate my IROC through the curves of State Route 227, praying none of the mysterious sinkholes have reappeared in our path. Kat never flinches, grabs the armrest, or stomps on the invisible brake on the passenger side floorboard. I slide on gravel as I brake to a stop in front of her double-wide at the trailer park tucked away on a heavily wooded, ten-acre plot.

"That was one ballsy move," she says as she opens the door.

I assume she is talking about my driving. "I'm sorry. I'm in a rush to get to the airport."

She doubles over to look into my Camaro. "I'm talking about how you put Captain Lau in his place." She clutches the roofline of my car and shakes her head. "You're one tough broad. Thank you for doing that for me."

It's one of the rare moments where I'm speechless. I have an uneasy, forced grin on my face.

Kat taps the top of my car. "Well, I know you have a plane to catch. I won't keep you. Thank you, and thank you for the ride."

She makes an awkward waving motion before shutting the door. Awkward because she seems like a tough broad herself, and the wave is out of character.

I try not to throw gravel as I back up, but I hear a few pieces click under my car. I shift into drive, and my tires spin on damp pine needles before biting into the gravel. The Moonshine Xpress has left the depot and is scorching a trail toward Huntsville's airport.

I need to get to the airport as soon as possible. The problem is the airport is in Madison, even though it's named Huntsville International Airport. This means I must drive through Huntsville and all the way through Madison, no easy task on any day, but now I have put myself in the heaviest rush-hour traffic of the day.

If I make the flight, it will only be by the grace of God. The GPS has me arriving five minutes after the flight takes off, and I still must check a bag, get through security, and board.

I'm uncomfortable with it, but I'm going entirely too fast on Highway 431, attempting to eke out every minute of extra travel time I can. I'm playing a demented version of Beat the Clock, where the deck is stacked against me. Everyone in the hypothetical audience from the front row to the back wall shakes their head and says, "Not a chance she makes that flight."

Oh, April, what have you done? Once foolish, always foolish.

But what were my options? I couldn't leave Kat with no defense attorney. With her attitude, she was sure to dig even deeper into the legal hole she was already in.

And if I hadn't stayed the weekend for the paranormal trip to Murfreesboro, Dusty wouldn't have gotten the footage we did of the ghost hiding in the diner. The film they got of the wild goose chase through the bootlegger tunnels is absolutely riveting.

Those are things that I could affect. I understand it's a big deal that Lee is pitching tonight. I also know many of his peers only dream of throwing in the playoffs.

But I can't help him pitch. Whether I'm at the game or not doesn't impact his performance.

I *want* to be in the stands supporting him. It's just that things I can do—things that are important to my career and family—sort of got in the way. Is that my fault?

I burst into Huntsville on 431, and it's reminiscent of the parting of the Red Sea as every stoplight miraculously turns green as I approach. Few, if any, vehicles are taking the left-hand lane for some bizarre reason. With a thankful heart, I watch as, minute by minute, I shave time from my estimated arrival time at the airport.

While driving, I'm trying to devise a reasonable explanation that Lee will appreciate. The thing is, Lee lives an incredibly regimented life. As a professional ballplayer, the team tells him where to be 168 times a year for games, where to spend spring practice, team meetings, and other preparations. Still, even if he weren't a professional ball player, he would live every minute of his life by his calendar. It's just how Lee is wired.

We couldn't be any more different in that regard. I typically make a rough outline each Sunday of what I want my week to look like. That holds until about nine o'clock on Monday morning. It's not that I don't want to keep to a schedule. It's that critical stuff invariably comes up that only I can handle.

Lee doesn't and never will understand.

I swerve into the long-term parking at the airport and am amazed as my unnervingly lucky hot streak continues. As I turn down the lane, an SUV pulls out of a front-row space. I gratefully accept the gift.

The thought hits me as I yank my suitcase out of the back of the car. There is a ninety-nine percent probability that I have left behind two or three essential items. I must take comfort in the fact that I am not as broke as I used to be, and if I must, I'll buy what I need.

The check-in counter for my airline is vacant of customers, and I rush to the desk. "Hi. I am checking in for flight seven thirty-six to Baltimore," I say as I hand her my driver's license and show her my ticket information.

"Alright," she says as her fingers tap along the keyboard. The keystrokes stop, and she raises her eyes. "Oh my. Your flight is boarding now."

I close my eyes and sigh. "My fiancé is going to murder me."

"I doubt that. Listen, hang a left when you get through security, and you'll be fifty feet from your gate." She hands me my ticket and offers me an encouraging smile.

"Thanks for your help."

"No worries. I'm rooting for you," she says as I jog to the security check-in and pull off my tennis shoes.

Now I do believe in miracles. And obviously, given the affliction of my paranormal gifts, I believe in divine intervention.

I also know there are doubters. However, they would change their tune if they were with me today. Once again, there is no crowd. I walk directly up to the security guard, show my ID, and grab a big bucket to throw my shoes, purse, and backpack in without hardly stopping from a fast walk. Everybody knows that must be a miracle.

Maybe the whole Lee thing is supposed to happen, which is why everything is working in my favor.

Struggling to slip my laptop into my backpack, I don't bother to put on my tennis shoes as I sprint for the gate. Rounding the corner to the left, as the attendant instructed me, Gate B2 appears in front of me like a glorious finish line—sans the ribbon to run through. Unfortunately, the attendant who scans the boarding passes is stepping away from his station. I increase my speed to a level that risks a hamstring strain.

"One more," I yell in an overly loud but hopefully pleasant voice.

His eyebrows knit. "For Baltimore?"

I stop at his podium and fight the urge to double over to catch my breath. "Yes, sir."

"Well, you're certainly teasing the bell. Still, you're lucky. There is one seat left on the flight, which is weird nowadays."

"One seat is all I need."

He squints as his brow wrinkles.

I realize my brain is oxygen-deprived and not working. Still, my mouth continues to release nonsensical statements on its own.

He scans my phone and waves me through. "Have a pleasant flight."

"Thank you," I holler as I rush down the ramp and gleefully hop across the threshold onto the plane.

I must look like a domestic terrorist with a backpack of explosives. The three flight attendants' eyes open wider. To be helpful, I put their minds at ease. "I hear y'all have one seat left."

Everyone sighs a breath of relief. Their practiced smiles return.

"Yes, all the way back on the left." The male flight attendant directs me with a flourishing wave of his hand.

Trepidation sets in as I walk back to the airliner's tail. Seated in the very back aisle are two men my height, one in the aisle seat and the other in the window seat. Both men look to be one Twinkie short of weighing in at three hundred and fifty pounds.

Still, I'm exceedingly grateful that the flight isn't completely booked and, equally important, the door to the plane was yet to be closed. I offer the two nearly round gentlemen my sweetest smile. "Hi. Do y'all mind if I sit here?"

I know, it's another stupid, oxygen-deprived statement. Especially given they don't have the authority to tell me yes or no, and there is nowhere else for me to sit.

"Not at all." The older businessman on the aisle seat says as he struggles up from his chair. I slip past him and smack my knee on the armrest. Holding in my whimper because, as Kat says, I'm a tough broad, I manage to pirouette and sit down.

Newsflash, as I take my seat, I sit on a healthy portion of the window dude's left thigh and slide into place. The legroom on this aisle is inexplicably a third less than the skimpy legroom for all the other seats on the flight.

Aisle seat businessman sits back down, his thighs squashing

my legs together, and both men's shoulders are pinning me to the back of my seat. I could not be more effectively stapled in place than if I were in a five-point-harness seat.

Remaining grateful for making the flight, I look on the bright side. Lord forbid, but I'm perfectly safe if we crash or are forced to make an emergency landing. I'm buckled up, fully restrained, and have an overabundance of shock-absorbing cushiony packaging surrounding me.

Besides, this will only be a couple of hours of discomfort. Then I'll be in Baltimore, and my new life will begin. Like any hardship, if I know how long it will take, I can increase my mental fortitude and deal with it.

The attendant who helped me find the last seat lifts the microphone. "Folks, we have a bit of bad news. The plane has a slight mechanical adjustment that must be made before taking off. Please make yourselves comfortable, and we'll update you on our progress. I'm sure the captain will be able to get us in the air and on our way to beautiful Baltimore, Maryland, in a few minutes."

Lee and I aren't supposed to be together. I mean, how many times have I flown, and this is the first time I have been delayed on the tarmac.

Time crawls. The heat generated between me and the human packing material surrounding me increases, and my glistening arms feel sticky.

I'm not in a full-blown sweat yet. Still, if the plane doesn't get in the air soon, I'll be surprised if there is a dry bit of clothing on me by the time we land.

So, I do the one thing that works best for me whenever life makes me uncomfortable. I distract myself with things that make me happy.

Inexplicably, my chunky, furry friend comes to mind. I shouldn't feel any anxiety about traveling to Baltimore. Still, I won't have my support group with me for this trip, which makes me sad and apprehensive.

On the one hand, if I had brought Puppy with me, there

would have been no way I would have gotten on the flight in time and checked him into the live cargo area. Still, a little kernel of doubt continues to root and grow in my gut. I have an odd feeling I will need his understanding ear this week. It makes no sense. Right?

I don't kid myself. Puppy doesn't need me like I need him. And in some ways, I wonder if I'm doing him a disservice by moving him away from the lake home when I leave.

"Hi, folks. The captain informed me that the mechanics will have us ready in an hour. That should put us getting into Baltimore at nine o'clock instead of seven. But hey, it's about getting there safely, right?"

Fudge. I'm in big trouble.

Touching down at nine o'clock, collecting my luggage, assuming it made it on the flight, and driving out to the stadium... The only way the game will still be going on is if it goes into extra innings. Even that is not helpful since Lee is the starting pitcher and will be off the mound when I arrive.

The best way to control this is head-on. "Excuse me."

I break free of my two friends who have grafted to me and lean forward to fish my phone out of my backpack. Taking a deep breath, I think of the best way to break the news to Lee.

Grinning, I type. *Hi, baby. I'm stuck on the tarmac in Huntsville. By how long it is taking, I think they're putting a new wing on the plane. Let me know when your game starts. I'll see you soon. Love you.*

I cradle the phone in my lap, staring at it as if peering into my looking stone. I hope for a *No worries, babe. Be safe. I love you,* message. A heart emoji right about now would feel like a win. Heck, a thumbs-up would be better than nothing.

I'm being an idiot since he is probably already warming up his arm. He hasn't even thought about his phone or his less-than-reliable girlfriend.

Three dots appear on my screen. The anticipation of receiving Lee's written absolution increases my heart rate.

I pull the phone closer, cradling it just below my face. The three dots disappear.

Chapter 14

"Camden Yards, please," I say as I enter the Uber.

The round-faced man in his late fifties turns and gawks at me. "Are you sure?"

I need some clarification. "Did they change the name of the stadium the Orioles play at?"

"Not hardly."

Not sure what the trouble is, I add, "I'm going to the game."

"The only way you'll see that game is on SportsCenter tonight. It finished fifteen minutes ago. The Orioles…"

I raise my hands. "Ah-ah-ah! Don't tell me anything."

He chuckles. "Wouldn't dream of it, lady."

I look out both windows and then make a rolling motion with my right hand. "Can we go now?"

"To the stadium?"

"Yes."

He shrugs as he turns and pulls the car onto the road. "Whatever you say, lady."

If I weren't already fully consumed with the terrible turn of events facing me, I might be perturbed by my driver's tone. But right now, I need him to get me to the stadium as soon as possible.

There is a chance, or at least it's my hope, that if I can arrive at the stadium before Lee and the team leave, my groveling for his forgiveness will be much more effective at the stadium. I can't bear for him to be upset with me. I'll need to patch this up immediately if I have any designs on this being a pleasant visit.

I take in the brightly lit city as we approach downtown. Reminiscent of my first foray into the large market, Baltimore is huge. Tall buildings are lit up, signaling an incredible opportunity for a young, aggressive attorney.

There is more opportunity for an attorney in one block of Baltimore than in the entire city of Guntersville. From a career standpoint, I'm making the right decision.

The Uber driver pauses in a huge, vacant parking lot. It is incredibly dark. He throws his right arm over the seat and points. "That is the stadium. You said you wanted to come here, but I can't sleep tonight if I drop you off alone."

"Do you think the teams have already left?"

He licks his lips as he considers his words. "Well, I don't want to be a spoiler, so if I were to guess, one of the teams is a few beers into a celebration while the other has hit the showers and is in bed trying to forget the game."

Geez, things keep deteriorating. I had best go directly to Lee's apartment and wait for him.

I give my driver Lee's address. He pulls the car out of the parking lot. I sit back and watch the lights as we drive out of the urban setting and into the suburbs.

Even though I barely visited, Lee thoughtfully ensured I had a key to the apartment. Even so, I have been there enough that my back stiffens as we pass familiar landmarks and draw closer. I contemplate our impending conversation.

I see Lee's tricked-out Denali pickup truck in the parking lot, and my stomach turns over. That means he is already home.

That should be good since I won't have to wait in his apartment alone.

Instead, I realize I need more time to be ready for this conversation. Despite wanting to be responsible and meet my shortcomings of the day head-on, I need to figure out how to explain what caused me to be late tonight and not sound like I put Lee last.

My suspicions tell me that the next thirty minutes will decide whom I will spend my life with for the next thirty years.

Chapter 15

The elevator opens on the fourth floor. The long hallway to Lee's suite could not be any more daunting even if it were the Overlook Hotel and Jack Torrance was running up and down the hall with an ax.

I don't anticipate Lee channeling an angry axman with cabin fever. And even if I did, I'm way past the stage of my life of avoiding uncomfortable conversations. If I haven't learned anything else during my recent stay in Guntersville, I've learned Mama is right about disappointing news. Ripping the proverbial Band-Aid off sooner works better than slowly and later.

As I approach the door to his apartment, I steady my breathing and manufacture a welcoming smile. I'm prepared to knock on the door, and the ever-present saying of my brothers pops into my head.

"It is what it is."

Yes, it is.

I raise my fist to knock, and a woman's peel of laughter emanates from behind the door. Her laughter is followed by the familiar baritone voice of a ball player I am most intimate with. He also sounds like he is having a swell old time.

My ire spikes, and it's all I can do to grab hold of my redneck before she kicks in the door.

Still, why am I knocking on the door when I have a key? I am supposed to be in there. The laughing girl is not.

I search through my purse, my ballistic emotions causing me to overlook my key on the first pass. Clutching it too tightly in my now sweaty hand, I jam my house key home into the lock, syncing perfectly with another peel of her insidious laughter.

I open the door and step through as if I'm charging the gates of hell. A petite, too-cute-to-be-in-my-fiancé's-apartment-alone-with-him brunette swivels quickly. Her expression tells me everything I need to know about her intentions.

My glare settles on my two-timing—sort of—fiancé. He smiles as his chin juts up in greeting. "Hey, babe. I'm glad you got here safely."

I plan to ask Lee who the little brunette is and what she is doing in his apartment. Still, my mouth skips a beat as a vision of me grabbing her by her long, chestnut hair and swinging her about the living room flashes across my mind, stealing my train of thought.

"Gidget here is from the marketing department. We're discussing a couple of merchandising ideas after tonight's win."

I open and close my mouth rapidly as I do my best imitation of a goldfish.

Gidget's expression changes to a smirk. With my female-relationship superpowers, I deduce Gidget believes she has captured the high ground. She moves to Lee's side, placing her hand on his forearm. "After tonight's game, everybody wants a piece of Lee," she says with a too-sweet lilt, making me want to punch her lights out.

I don't know about *everybody*, but I am sure of a little brunette who wants a piece. But the odds are she won't see tomorrow if she doesn't quit touching him.

"Tell me again why you're here?" I manage to say evenly.

Lee frowns. "April, I just told you Gidget is with the marketing department."

"She must be awfully dedicated. I don't know any respectable businesswoman making house calls so close to midnight. Folks might think she has ulterior motives."

"I hear you keep some crazy hours for your clientele yourself."

"Yeah, but I'm not trying to get laid by any of my clients."

"Whoa!" Lee scolds as he holds his hands up to keep us apart.

"Somebody has got to take care of your man. You sure don't."

And just like that, decades of training myself to keep my redneck roots concealed go out the window. Gidget doesn't know what hit her as I'm on her like a duck on a June bug. She doesn't even offer to block my attack. Even Lee takes a step back.

I have her by the hair but accidentally grab her barrette, which messes with my grip. I'm so angry my left hand isn't doing anything other than holding onto her puffy-shouldered dress jacket.

Who is this woman? Doesn't she know that shoulder pads went out in the eighties?

Strong arms go around my waist, and my feet lift off the floor. I'm kicking wildly with my Keds but not connecting with anything as I continue to hold on to Gidget.

"Stop it!"

Lee's uncharacteristically stern voice reverberates in my mind. Despite my desire to pound the flyweight into a pulp, I open my hands and release Gidget.

Gidget scrambles backward until her butt slams into the wall. Which proves she is not totally stupid.

"April, what has gotten into you?" Lee grumbles in my ear.

Little Gidget might be wise, but she overestimates her ability. She doesn't know what she is messing with as she shakes her finger at me. "She's crazy, Lee!"

"You haven't seen crazy yet!" I scream.

Lee makes a shushing noise close to my ear. "Gidget, I'll see you tomorrow at the office."

She frowns but acquiesces to his request. Her eyes look

toward the door, and I spy her purse. She will have to go dangerously close to me to retrieve it.

Enough of this.

What do I care if Lee wants to date junior high schoolers instead of me? Better to learn that now than later in our relationship.

"No. Don't let me break up y'all's little spin-the-bottle party. I'm leaving." I try to shake off Lee's arms. He drops them to my waist.

"And where would you be going at this time of night?"

AHHH! I want to scream so loudly that every window in Baltimore explodes. I frigging hate the fact that his logic is so sound. At this hour, with the playoff crowd in town, the probability of me finding a room—at least one that doesn't charge by the hour—is next to nil.

I slump my shoulders in defeat. Gidget, the junior high brainiac, sees her opening and walks quickly by me, clicking her heels as she retrieves her clutch.

At the door, she flashes what I assume she considers her sexy, "I'm always available" expression. "Call me if you need me, Lee."

"Thank you for your help, Gidget."

I snarl in her direction. "Don't let the door hit your scrawny butt on the way out."

Chapter 16

"I'm hungry. I'm going to fix omelets. Do you want one?" Lee asks.

"No, because then I'll want to stay."

"I won't let you," Lee says.

His comment does not have even a hint of nastiness to it. Still, he might as well have punched me in the gut. I'm left gasping for air.

I'm thankful that he is digging for ingredients in the fridge so he doesn't see the devastated expression on my face.

What did you expect, April? Isn't this just a self-fulfilling prophecy?

"I don't understand."

Lee comes out of the fridge. He holds a pack of eggs in one hand and a carton of half and half in the other. "April, we need to talk. We both know this isn't working."

Despite agreeing with his evaluation of our relationship, for some stupid reason, I choose to argue. "What do you mean? What's not working?"

He blows a gust of air through his lips. "Really?"

"You're ending us because I missed your game?"

"No. I'm ending it because we are good people that deserve to be with someone we want and who wants us back."

"You can't be serious. Is missing your game enough for you

to throw our whole relationship away?"

Lee stops with an egg over the edge of a stainless-steel mixing bowl. He grinds his teeth and takes a deep breath. "No. April, if you had said you weren't coming to tonight's game, I would have understood."

"So, it's because I said I was going to come, and I wasn't able to?"

Lee shakes his head from side to side and cracks four eggs into the steel bowl. He pours some half and half into the bowl and begins to whisk it. Slowly.

"Well?"

"You know, I'd like to have a civil discussion about this. Preferably without drama."

"Well, I'm sorry. But the only drama I see is coming from you."

Lee lifts an onion from a hanging basket. He sets to task deftly dicing the onion. I sit on a barstool across from him and watch his work.

My intention is to wait him out. Patience is not my best virtue. Well, that's an understatement. He has something important to say, and rather than guess, it behooves me to shut my mouth and wait for him to explain. A lot is riding on this conversation. I want to make sure I understand and get it right.

I expect him to clarify his position when he dumps the onions in his Teflon-coated skillet to sauté them in butter. Instead, he continues to ignore me and opens the refrigerator.

He retrieves a small bell pepper, a Roma tomato, and five mushrooms this time.

Dag burn! Whoever does Lee's grocery shopping for him rocks. If I ever find out that it is Gidget, the "call me if you need me" junior high girl, I guarantee an aisle cleanup will be needed in the produce area.

My stomach rumbles as the scent of bell pepper and onion sautéing fills the room. I wasn't hungry, but Lee isn't exactly playing fair. When he said omelet, I wasn't anticipating him going all out as usual. I expected a couple of scrambled eggs with cheese slices, and I hadn't even earned a hardboiled egg.

"I can't have this be ugly."

His words break the silence. They are by no means what I expected. "Okay."

He whisks the eggs aggressively and pours half of the mixture into a smaller skillet. "I let it ride during the summer, partly to give you room to make your decision even though I figured it was made all along. It didn't bother me much. It's just been another year playing ball. Honestly, the distraction of women off the table gave me plenty of time to focus on honing my craft."

I think to make a smart-aleck comment like, "You're welcome," since, from what I understand, he pitched a terrific game in a playoff series. But he begins anew, his words pouring out faster. I realize it's not and never was intended to be a conversation.

"Before I met you, the second time around, I was a jerk with women. I would sleep with women I had no intention of ever having a relationship with. I'm sure I have partners whose names I can't even remember if you required it of me.

"I'm not saying this to brag or say I'm proud. In fact, now, I'm mostly ashamed of it."

I shift my butt on the barstool because the topic makes me uncomfortable. I know about Lee's past, but it's not my business because it happened when we weren't dating.

He flips the first omelet over.

"The truth is that I had never considered the possibility of settling down. When you and I met the second time, that became a powerful desire. Now I know I want to marry soon and start a family."

He looks up for the first time since he started the omelets, and our eyes meet. "You will never understand how desperately I wanted it to be you."

I want to tell him how much I've longed to hear that from him, and suddenly I am convicted. As I stare into his eyes, I realize he has been professing his love all along. It has always

been me. I was the one who was the last to say, "I love you"—
the last to commit to our future life together.

Because I feel I need to, I open my mouth to say something
—anything. But what can my response be when I've had the
epiphany that points the accusing finger at me? I'm the issue
with this relationship. I am the reason it's not working.

Lee favors me with a rueful smile. His eyes glisten. He
diverts his attention back to the task of finishing the first
omelet.

The silence between us hangs heavily. Only the slight sizzle
of sautéing vegetables breaks the intense noise vacuum.

Lee pulls a red Fiestaware plate from the shelf above his
head to the right. He deftly slides the completed omelet onto
the plate. Then he lifts a fork and places it on the cheerfully
colored plate he sets before me.

"I'm sorry, I don't have any bacon to go with it," he says as he
pours the egg for the second omelet into his skillet.

I want to say thank you for the omelet. I need to say I'm
sorry for being such a lousy girlfriend. Yet it feels like I poured
a pound of cornstarch down my throat, making it impossible
to speak.

"The funny thing is, if I thought that there was even the
slightest chance that one day you would come around, that I
could be enough for you, I would wait. For *you*, I would wait for
as long as it takes.

"But the writing has been on the wall almost from the start
of our relationship. And Lord knows I have turned it over in my
head at every angle, trying to figure out how to make it work
for both of us."

Sighing, I slide my arms onto the bar top and lean forward. "I
genuinely wish it were different. I want it to be," I whisper.

"I know." He turns his head to the side while swiping his left
eye with his wrist. Quickly, he returns to his task of the second
omelet.

"What now?" I ask.

Lee turns his face toward the ceiling and blows an

exasperated breath. "Give me a minute, April. Okay?"

Giving him the privacy I can manage, given our close quarters, I look down at my plate. Bless it. That must be the fluffiest, most beautiful omelet I've ever seen.

What is wrong with you, April Snow?

I must be the most messed-up person in the world. Forget that Lee could double as a male model and earns a healthy seven-figure salary playing ball. The man's saintly disposition alone at a painful moment like this should be enough to move any woman in her right mind to lock him up with a long-term contract.

That's it. I'm plumb out of my mind. As Dusty would joke from time to time, "You just ain't right, April." As I stare awkwardly at my plate, I realize no truer words have ever been spoken.

Lee slides a stool over and sits at the kitchen counter side of the bar. Placing his plate in front of him, he draws a deep breath and favors me with a wan smile.

"Do you think you'll take over your uncle's practice?"

I'm thankful for the change of topic, although it is as uncomfortable as the breakup conversation. "I don't know. I still have my dreams, but I'd be fooling myself if I tried to say there aren't days I enjoy working in Guntersville. Some of my favorite people are there. Of course, some of my least favorites, too."

Lee laughs. "That would be because you're cantankerous."

"I am not."

"You do know denial is a dangerous weakness."

"Whatever." I narrow my eyes at Lee and take a bite of my omelet. This is odd, considering that ten minutes earlier, I thought there was no way I could eat. I am at once glad I did, as it is scrumptious. "Dang, Lee. You should consider opening a restaurant when you finally hang up your cleats."

"Thanks, but my cooking is only good when I'm doing it for someone I care about."

My stomach rolls over, and I stop chewing. Lee notices my

expression and raises his hand. "I'm sorry. And I was the one who said 'no drama.'"

"It's okay." I form a smile, which is no easy task given how his comment cuts my heart. "So, do you think you're gonna stay with Baltimore?"

He shrugs. "Baseball teams are fickle. After tonight's game, I think I'm an Oriole at least for next year. But you never know. If we have a slow start next season, it may mean I'll be one of the first ones traded."

"For what it's worth, I'm fiercely proud of you. You stayed with your dream for so long, and now it is coming to fruition for you."

"Thanks. I have yet to think about it much"—he makes a to-and-fro motion with his hand—"because I knew this conversation was coming."

"I'm sorry to spoil your moment with my, as usual, bad timing."

"Don't," he says. "I don't think either one of us needs to be sorry. We did our best, and things just didn't work out. Only fools expect to win every game. Besides, this will allow each of us to find the right person."

I point toward his front door. "I know. You had a willing partner leave a hot minute ago."

"Stop it."

I snort. "What? She was ready to jump your bones."

"She isn't exactly subtle. Still, I'm not interested in Gidget like that. I'm interested in her getting me my next advertising opportunity, so I can capitalize on this win. But that is as far as my interest goes with her."

I shrug my shoulders. "I'm just saying, if you get lonely."

"How about you worry about you, and I'll worry about me."

"Well, since I'm now relegated to the friend zone, it is my sworn duty to warn you."

Lee narrows his eyes as he cocks his head to the side. "No. We're not in the friend zone."

My eyebrows creep together as I try to process his statement.

"What do you mean?"

He arches his eyebrows. "You and me? Tonight ... is it. I can't handle being friends with you, April. That would be too much."

Lee might as well have thrown a fastball and hit me in the chest. It feels like my heart stops, and I find I cannot breathe.

Struggling to recover, I scoff, "We're bound to run into each other when you come home to Guntersville during the off-season."

"That is a favor I need you to do for me. Your mom has been so sweet to me and worked incredibly hard to decorate that place for me. I trust her and want her to get the commission off of the sale, but there is no way I can tell her that I'm selling the place."

"You're selling your lake house?"

"It was always sort of a silly purchase. I suppose it was a thumb in everyone's eye in Guntersville who assumed I had the talent but not the discipline to be a success. Come to find out, there are lakes up here in Maryland." He exaggerates a smile. "Who knew? Plus, once I found Annapolis, there was never a doubt where I want to live now."

I realize, the longer we talk, I never really wanted to marry Lee. I'm sexually attracted to him, and he is easy company.

But forever? Yeah, that seems like such a long time.

Still, as it dawns on me that the only time I will ever see Lee in the future will be on TV, it makes me sad. The suddenness and completeness of this breakup are shocking.

"I will tell her for you."

"Thanks. That is a relief." He lifts my plate off of the bar top and washes it. "The guest room is made up, including clean sheets."

"Thank you."

"You're welcome. I've got to be at the training complex early in the morning. You can leave the apartment key on the bar when you go."

My mind is so jumbled, I may as well have a concussion.

Thoughts of what could have been and the history of this being our second near miss in a long-term relationship make it difficult to deal with the new reality. This is the end of my Lee era.

Even though something is crumbling inside, and I wonder if I'm making the biggest mistake of my life, I muster up the sweetest smile I can. "Thank you again for the room, Lee."

Chapter 17

The sheets are so tangled around my legs that I must roll over to free myself. It's not the bed. Lord knows whoever furnished Lee's apartment understands the value of an excellent mattress and luxurious sheets.

My sleeping difficulties arose because I must be the most foolish person I know. At any point last night, I could have stopped the conversation from going in the direction it did.

Lee was practically begging me to tell him he was wrong. That I wanted to stay in Baltimore.

It would have been easy to say, "I'm sorry I made you feel that way, Lee. I never meant to make you feel like less than the man of my dreams. I want to spend my life with you and our future children."

Instead, I sat back and let him come to his own conclusion. Which, if I'm being truthful, is the only conclusion he could arrive at. What sort of girlfriend ducks out at every opportunity to go on ghost-hunting excursions with her brother?

I had six months to get my butt up to Baltimore, and last night I made a halfhearted attempt to do what I promised Lee. My gosh, long-distance relationships are impossible, and I created a self-imposed one.

The poor guy. He truly was holding out hope that I would

come around.

Still, why is it my fault our lives didn't dovetail as he assumed they would? We are two separate people. Relationships are always messy.

I'm not being fair.

The truth is, there is not one logical reason for me not to move forward with Lee. There certainly isn't anyone else. And if it's some career aspiration that has yet to be scratched, I sure haven't been actively pursuing it for the last few months.

Man, I'm not fit to be in a relationship with anybody. I can't even understand myself. How can I expect someone else to understand me?

My self-loathing is not as enjoyable in Lee's apartment as it typically is in my place. It is best to take my shower and leave...

Peaches. What am I gonna do?

I could go home. But I'm not in a mental state where I can share this latest train wreck with the rest of my family or ask Howard for the law office back. Assuming he hasn't already leased the office out.

There is nothing wrong with me taking the week off. I can text Howard the basics and then take a week's vacation to get my mind around the rest of my life.

In theory, that sounds great, except I'm alone and have nothing planned. Plus, I need transportation.

Groaning, I flop back onto the bed. Oh, for Pete's sake.

I allow myself a mini pity party. It makes my disposition worse.

Attempting to do something constructive, I resolve to wash the grime of last night's travel off of me. I cringe as I remember still having the sweat from my pair of human airline seat restraints on my skin. I pad to the en suite bathroom and turn the shower on.

Steam flows across the large bathroom ceiling, and I enter the shower. As the water blasts in a massaging motion on my tense shoulders, I give over my anxiety and breathe.

Even if I did make a mistake, l know I'll be okay. To Lee's

point, he deserves somebody dying to be with him.

Not Gidget. But somebody who will love him completely.

The water sluices over my face. My skin becomes tender from the heat and high-water pressure. At first, I had thought I could stay in the shower all day—spend my entire week off here—but I need to figure out what I'm doing and get gone.

As I towel dry my hair, it comes to me that Baltimore is less than an hour from DC. My good friend Martin lives in DC.

Well now. Isn't that fortunate? April won't have to convalesce alone with her broken heart. Martin was always a good listener.

I wrap a towel around my waist and turban wrap my hair in a second towel. Stepping back into the bedroom, I hunt for my phone.

As I reach to lift it from the nightstand, it rings. Reading the word *Trisha* brings a smile to my face.

"Good morning, sunshine," I say.

"April, where are you right now?"

The urgency in her tone piques my curiosity. Once again, the Snow grapevine has worked beyond the speed of light. How could Trisha, who lives in Nashville with my uncle Norman, already know that Lee and I have broken up?

Especially since, until midnight last night, I didn't know that I was broken up with Lee.

"I'm still at Lee's place in Baltimore. But I am getting over myself, and now that I have a shower, I'll do the mature thing, fly home, and lick my wounds privately at my apartment."

"What are you talking about?"

Okay, so the Snow grapevine has yet to develop its own psychic ability, and Trisha doesn't know about last night. And April hasn't gotten over herself.

"I'm sorry, Trisha. I suppose I'm still processing last night."

"Oh my gosh, April. Did something happen between you and Lee?"

I snort. "You can say that again, sister."

"He wasn't cheating on you, was he?"

A rueful smile stretches my face. "No. Exactly the opposite."

"Stop with the suspense building. Hurry up and tell me before I burst."

Talking about the demise of Lee's and my relationship is the last thing I want to do. But now that I hear Trisha's voice, I know I need to, and she is the one person in the world I'm comfortable being honest with, including how I was the one who sabotaged the relationship.

"Well, what started it was I missed his game last night."

She emits a gasp. "Lee's first playoff start?"

Rubbing salt in my wound isn't exactly the response I was hoping for from her. I snap back, "When did you become such a baseball aficionado?"

"Hello, Pensacola."

I giggle as I remember Trisha's weeklong romance with a young farm boy from Iowa who was an exceptional pitcher in the minors. "Fair."

"How could you miss such an important event?"

"It wasn't on purpose. Dusty had this excursion to Murfreesboro that ended up being a bust until the last few hours. Then we found something great for his TV show, and it ran me late back to Guntersville. Then while I was packing up to get the office ready to turn over to Howard, the DA dropped a case on me. It was a young lady who is wrongfully accused of attempting to murder her boyfriend."

"And your point is?"

If we were Facetiming, she would see my death stare. Instead, realizing that my stare is wasted, I huff loudly. "That I was busy with important things."

"No. That's not acceptable."

"What—"

"April, before you have children, the relationship with a man you intend to marry and spend the rest of your life with takes precedence over everything else."

I sit heavily on the edge of the bed and lean forward until my head is between my knees. My towel turban falls to the floor, and I make a weak attempt to catch it.

That is the thing about my family. Everyone is so blasted logical. I react according to my emotions and varying levels of drama. While everyone in my extended family operates on a constant logic-oriented risk-to-reward and priority-based matrix.

Consequently, it's all too often that I explain one of my drama episodes only to have one of my family members drop an unwanted truth bomb on me. One that rattles my world and makes me stop and consider if my approach is entirely wrong.

In this case, there is no denying that Trisha is one hundred percent correct.

"I suppose that was the root cause of the situation," I whisper.

"How so?"

"It didn't work out because I never moved him to the top of my priority list. I knew in my heart all along that it wasn't right. Yet I can tell you right now that as much as I enjoyed being around him, and Lord knows I love how he loved me, I never could make him my first priority. Bless it, Trisha. I could barely squeeze him into the top five."

Trisha gasps for the second time during the conversation, and I roll my eyes. "I know. I'm just broken." I clutch my curly, damp hair, waiting for her answer that never comes. "So, I think this girl will be forced to take a long break from the opposite sex. I plan to focus on my career as soon as I figure out what that is and keep all of the relationships I have with men strictly on a friendly basis."

"That's a smart idea coming out of a serious relationship. I know we're different, but it would take a long time for me to process what went wrong before I'm ready to enter a new one."

"Exactly. It's like, tried this, done that. Move on to something I can be successful at and forget about the whole happily ever after. It's not in the cards for me."

"Uh, no. I am not talking about you taking an oath of chastity and becoming a warrior nun. It's healthy to give yourself an opportunity to reflect on what happened between you and Lee so that the next time it will work out better for you."

"Darn it. Being a warrior nun sounds a lot more enjoyable."

Trisha laughs. "Lord knows you would be a formidable one."

I straighten my back and push out my chest. "Thank you for the compliment."

"I didn't know I gave you one."

"Sure, you did. April, the warrior nun."

"You're a loon."

"Something I've been told thousands of times."

We break into a bout of giggling as if nothing has changed since we were little girls at sleepover parties. My laughter stops as the pain hits my heart.

"I miss you."

"I miss you, too."

"I sure do wish we lived closer together."

She scoffs, "Says my cousin who constantly threatens to move to some faraway city."

"Well, it seems the universe is stacked against that, so you can continue to find me in north Alabama if you need me."

"Sure, I can. Until the next grand adventure."

I groan.

Trisha sucks in a breath. "Oh, you almost made me forget. Are you heading straight back home, or could you take some time off?"

"Why? What's up?"

"Dad has an Army buddy down on Turtle Key who needs help with a case. He asked me to go with him to Savannah and says I can bring a friend."

Since retiring from the Nashville Police Department, my uncle Norman has created a thriving private detective practice. Still, I am interested in why he would take a job so far from Nashville.

"Why doesn't his friend hire somebody local?"

"It's a sensitive topic, from what I understand. Plus, Turtle

Key has its own culture. The locals are selective on who they let in."

In passing, Nana Hirsch, in her interest in making sure that I am aware of as many different subsets of magic as possible, has spoken of the Gullah culture. Given their unique blend of Islamic beliefs with hints of Christianity and black magic, which would seem incompatible, like the origin disparities of my gifts, I can understand why they are reticent to bring someone into their world.

When people hold rigid truths, they can bend reality neatly into their values. It's difficult to bring someone into your world who does not understand or respect your different belief system.

"Well?"

"Well, what?

"Are you going to be my plus one to Savannah?"

"Absolutely!"

Chapter 18

It takes me longer than expected to secure a rental for the drive to Savannah. I considered flying since it's a nine-hour drive, but the check-in and flight would have taken six hours. Plus, with the rental, Trisha and I will have a vehicle and be free to go wherever we want.

I could use some alone time, too. Minus the 350-pound dual male restraining system I had on my last flight.

It is ten o'clock as I take the onramp to I-95, and the GPS shows I'll arrive in Savannah by seven. I set the cruise control five miles over the speed limit and start the task of getting my life back on track.

Using my time as effectively as possible, I dictate an entirely too-long text to Howard explaining that I've had a change of plans and to please not lease out the law office. I also remind him that I am still working on the pending partnership dissolution of Andy Ricketts and Thelma Banks in case one of them reaches out to him.

I send the text and obsess that I don't hear the pleasant ding of a reply coming back. I'm hoping for something like "That's great news, April," and worry that I might instead get "I'm sorry, I've already leased the office out to a nice antique business."

Oh well. Either way, I'll have to deal with the consequences of my earlier indecision.

Now comes the second most crucial point of contact in Guntersville. There is no way a text will suffice for him. I draw a deep breath, trying to steady my nerves.

Don't be a chicken, April. Just call the man.

A phrase Chase uses when faced with asking somebody for something that might perturb them comes to mind, and I smile. He always says, "It's not like they're going to kill you and eat you."

While I'm still tickled by remembering Chase's phrase, I call Lane. On the fourth ring, I'm grateful I'll be able to leave a voicemail since my adrenaline rush is wearing off.

"April?"

"Yes, sir."

"I wasn't expecting a call from you. Is everything all right?"

If ever there were a loaded question I'm not prepared to answer, Lane just asked it. I'm wise enough not to give him the laundry list of issues I gave Trisha earlier this morning. "I've had a change of plans, and I want to get you in the loop, Lane."

"Oh?"

"Yes, sir. I've decided I'll be staying in Guntersville."

"Wow. That's an about-face."

"Yes."

"Not to get into your business, but is this a long-term decision or one of temporary convenience?"

"Long term." I think, but given my history, who really knows.

"That is some welcome news. I appreciate you sharing this with me."

"Do you know if Howard has leased my building yet? I haven't been able to reach him this morning."

"If he has, he did not bother to mention it to his number-one friend."

"Good."

Lane laughs. "I suppose he figured that either he would get tired of the pizza empire, or you might decide to move back home."

"I believe he plans to continue his quest to become the king of pizza."

"I believe you are correct."

I muster up my courage to complete the true purpose of this call directly. "Lane, can I continue to work your overflow cases for the defense department."

"Somebody has to work them, and until I can get a full roster back, I can certainly use the help."

"Thank you!"

"Starting with Kat Krasinski since you have a history with her."

I wouldn't call one interview history, but that will be a first client. "Y'all charged her?"

"I haven't done anything. But I can tell you that Captain Lau continues to collect information on her. Assuming he finds something, she will need someone who knows how to clear folks of murder charges. I seem to remember a sharp lawyer who can put together an excellent defense."

"What's his problem?"

"The man's doing his job, April. Sometimes police work is gut feelings and intuition. I will not fault the man for following his intuition. So, if he does find something, there is one case for you."

"Do you think it will hold for a few days? I plan to take a week off while I am up here. I thought I might do some exploring."

"The wheels of justice turn slowly, Miss Snow."

And they can be exceptionally dysfunctional at times. "Did Lau at least bring Liam in for violating the restraining order?"

"That was humorous. You should have seen Liam's face when Lau brought him in. I believe because Kat clipped his ear, Liam assumed everyone would forget about him violating the order."

"Good. I don't like the dynamics of their relationship. If Liam doesn't abide by the restraining order, there is no telling how that situation could snowball."

"Between missing a chunk of his ear and spending time in jail, I pray he will realize Kat is too expensive for his taste."

"Let's hope he is smart enough to put that together."

"Yes." Lane grunts. "Goodness. Where has the time gone? I've got a meeting to get to, Counselor. I appreciate the call and want you to know I am pleased to have you back in Guntersville."

"Thank you, Lane."

It's hard not to draw the marked difference between the ending of Kat and Liam's relationship and what I experienced with Lee last night. The lack of drama in our adult conversation helped me understand that it is the correct decision for us. The tone of the discussion was all Lee.

Kat and I are more similar than I would like to admit. Unfortunately for her, Liam is no Lee.

Even though the relationship between Lee and I did not work out, I learned something valuable from it. It is from a source most unexpected, considering how wild he was in high school. Still, Lee showed me what being fully committed to a relationship looks like and how to be an adult if things end. I should take notes to ensure that the next time I'm involved with somebody, I manage the relationship as he did.

Of course, that's not going to happen. Because I will only be concerned about my career and my family from here on out. Since I am the human version of a Venus fly trap—drawing men in only to hurt them—I'll do the male half of the species a favor and take myself out of the game.

There. That is April proving how adult she is.

My phone dings and displays a text from Howard. I shouldn't since I'm driving, but I still glance.

"I knew you'd be back."

Chapter 19

I can't recall a margarita ever tasting so sweet and refreshing. I sit with Trisha in the old tavern. It's as if God smiled on me today and made her call with this invitation.

Star Chase Tavern is three blocks from the main squares of Savannah. The tavern has a fascinating history. Having a speakeasy set up in the back of the warehouse during the '30s, it continued as a legitimate bar after prohibition ended.

Of more interest, at least to me, is the rumor that it was the meeting place for a coven of witches during the late 1800s. Given the incredible residual energy throughout the tavern, I have no trouble believing the validity of what others would consider an outlandish claim.

After a brief wait, we are escorted to a small table in the back. The dimly lit location is more suitable for a romantic couple's dinner.

Realizing I have made today more about me, I ask Trisha, "How are your law school classes?"

"Good." She rocks her head from side to side. "Actually, it's tough some nights. I'm super interested, but it's a bit much some days after work."

Trisha didn't have the advantages I grew up with. She earned her way through school at Western Kentucky before starting law school at night. She has always worked a full-time job while getting her education.

"I'm proud of you for continuing to work so hard. I know it must be difficult."

She laughs as she trails her finger along the condensation on her glass. "I have you to thank for that."

"How's that."

"Since you completed your law degree, it motivates me to finish mine."

"It's not the same."

"It doesn't matter. We don't all start in the same place. That doesn't excuse me from finishing the race."

Her optimism and determination always bring a smile to my face. It's one of the many things I love about my cousin.

"So, have you quit pining for your married boss?" I tease.

"Stop it. Just because I find my boss attractive doesn't mean I'm pining for him."

"I'm only teasing you."

"It's a good reminder not to share everything with you."

"Touché." I laugh.

Trisha shudders. "Yuck, did you feel that?"

So much energy tingles in the air that asking me what I *don't* feel would be easier to answer. Still, I scan the room out of an abundance of caution.

"It's like somebody walked over my grave," she adds.

"No. I didn't notice anything unusual."

The tavern is still near total capacity. The mirrored bar, forty feet long with a complement of five bartenders, is packed. Every seat has a patron, and at least one person waits for a drink behind each of them.

The sizeable, antique-decorated dining room is walled in dark-wood planks that form a reverse ship hull for the ceiling. Throughout the large room, there are scores of round tables. The three walls not occupied by the bar are lined with pew-style booths made of pine turned black with age. They are upholstered with hunter-green leather cushions and easily seat six.

In the center of the room is a large, rectangular table with high-backed chairs. A party of seven women occupies the table. The diverse palette of physical appearances—all attractive and of varying ages—and the visible joy of their camaraderie draws my attention.

Normally, a group of women enjoying a meal together in companionship—something I should do more often, per my brothers' recent observation—is nothing particularly remarkable.

My interest would not be so keen without the slight illumination surrounding the seven women from their shoulders up. Their smoky, glowing power mingles and cojoins over the table's center. The merged energy floating over the middle of the table glows brighter at moments, dims, then grows more brilliant again during their conversations.

I'm quite familiar with this magical creation.

Nana calls the odd glow a "coven coalescence." A fancy phrase for the mixing of the coven's powers. The meeting of their energy makes the addition of their abilities more significant than the sum of the individual forces.

"April?"

I return my attention to my cousin. "Hmm?"

"Did you talk to Howard?"

"I texted him. He texted me back that everything is good."

"That's nice of him not to make you explain everything."

I roll my eyes. "I think he is tired of my drama. Heck, I know *I'm* tired of my drama."

"Don't be so hard on yourself. It takes work to figure out who and what you want to be. Gosh, then add the idea of finding somebody who wants to be with you for the rest of your life... That is a huge decision with a multitude of long-term implications. I can't even begin to comprehend it. I don't understand how people can ever decide someone is the right person for them."

"Not made any easier by our parents who set the bar so high for what a successful marriage should look like."

Trisha squints her eyes. "I'm glad I've seen what a loving marriage looks like. Call me a hopeless romantic, but it'll help me identify a good partner. With a little luck, I can emulate my parents enough to give our relationship a fighting chance."

Trisha has dated less than I have. This goes back to the fact that while I was trying on different guys like they were blouses at a seventy-five-percent-off sale, she was working to send herself through school. She is a hard-core romanticist and, at the minimum, a bit Pollyannaish about how life works.

The last of my naivety evaporated with the end of my relationship with Lee. I do not expect a happily ever after ending any longer. However, I may settle for a "good enough for now" relationship once I am successful in my career.

The sensation of a granddaddy longlegs spider crawling across my neck adds to the energy tingle inside the bar. My eyes naturally go back to the seven women in the middle of the dining hall. The coven coalescence hanging over the center of their table continues to grow, both in magnitude and brightness.

In my periphery, a quick glimmer, like sunlight striking a mirror, draws my attention to the doorway. Standing in the arched entrance is a man just under six feet tall. He glares at the women.

Trisha continues to describe how her parents met— a story I've heard many times before to the point I can recount it to her —and I watch the man.

He pushes off the wall he's propped up against and momentarily looks across the room. Following his glance, I find an equally formidable man with dark skin and a head shaved bald. The second man's complete focus is on the center table, too.

Something besides the weirdness that they are watching the women troubles me. I try to figure out what it is while listening to Trisha.

"Hey."

A wooden chair slams beside me, and I nearly jump out of

my skin. "What the devil?" I exclaim.

A humongous man grins at me as he sits on the chair. Despite the crowd's clamor, I hear the chair groan as if it will give out under the man's massive size.

"Yeah, I've been mistaken for him occasionally, but he won't make an appearance tonight."

The man is easily six feet seven inches and 330 pounds. If Jesus Christ decided to beef up and play offensive tackle for the Green Bay Packers during his second coming, I would be looking at him. His long, sandy-blonde hair touches his shoulders, and his strawberry-blonde beard juts forward eighteen inches from his chin. He has a moderately large, aquiline nose and prominent, golden-green eyes—bright and full of life.

Immediately, I am concerned this man is part of the other two men's group. It's possible, given that all three, in their own manner, look like they could be downright lethal.

"I'm Trisha. What's your name?"

Since a monster-sized man sat beside me, I momentarily forgot about my naïve cousin, who has never met a stranger. I fight the urge to put my hand over her mouth.

"Hi, Trisha, my name is Scott."

I see my opportunity to hop into the fray and quickly end this civility. "Nice to meet you, Scott, but we are having a conversation."

He leans forward. I smell coconut oil on him.

"Really? What are we talking about?" he asks as his eyes widen.

I make a flailing motion with my hand. "Nunya."

"Onions?"

I need help deciphering if Scott is joking with me or if he misheard me.

Trisha, laughing, cuts in. "Nunya. Like none of your business. But never mind April. She is in a foul mood."

Now I want to slap Trisha, since she conveniently gave Scott my name.

"What troubles you, April?"

"Presently?" I arch my eyebrows. "You."

"My, my. You're as cuddly as a porcupine."

"Seriously, don't pay her any mind."

I realize that Trisha and I have two vastly different expectations for tonight. I thought it would be a girls' night, which I desperately need. Trisha, as usual, is ready to start a conversation with anybody who will talk to her.

Also, I find Scott aggravating. Who does he think he is, dropping in on two girls he doesn't know. Not even a decent pickup line. He merely says, "Hey, here I am. What are y'all talking about? Let me put my two cents in." *Really, who asked you, Scott?*

Fine. I can use it to my advantage to keep an eye on the two scoundrels I noticed earlier. Assuming Scott is not collaborating with them.

The coven energy field has changed its color from green to blue to now a swirling silver. Rather than the small orb the women initially created, a mass like a miniature hurricane now rotates over their table.

It's interesting. The group is simply sharing a friendly meal. I don't notice anything of a supernatural nature that the women are doing to create the anomaly above them.

Is it possible they don't know they are creating the energy force?

I ponder the thought. Mainly because until Nana and Granny instructed me on my abilities, I didn't realize that I was marshaling the kinetic energy stored in the atmosphere my entire life.

Nana and I often create a similar energy mass when working together. I would take the precautions not to expose it to the public, only because I know we produce it. Even though it may be one in one hundred million people who could see it, I would never knowingly take the risk in anyone else's view.

Watching the women from the farthest wall, the large, bald Black man glances momentarily to his right. Following the quick tick of his eyes, I identify a third team member. A tall, wispy woman with straight, purple hair bobbed at her ears. She wears no makeup on her porcelain-white skin except lipstick in the same shade of purple as her hair.

She is a strikingly tall woman, at least six feet. Her knee-high boots with spiked heels add another three inches to her height.

Our eyes meet across the room. I should look away. Whatever they're doing, assuming that they are up to no good and it's not just my imagination fabricating a bit of fantasy, is of no concern to me.

Although her two male partners look deadly, if they plan on robbing or otherwise attacking the seven women, they are as stupid as they are lethal looking. I'll take the odds of seven on three any day.

The women at the table don't look like a group of Karens. At least three of them appear as if they might know a thing or two about defending themselves.

All that be as it may, I have this overriding feeling that I'm witnessing the start of something larger. It doesn't involve me directly, but it wouldn't hurt me to intervene. If for no reason other than to aggravate the tall, witchy woman still staring at me.

First, I need to ensure that Trisha is safe with Sasquatch Scott. I stand and purposefully catch my foot on the back of my chair. I grab Scott's shoulder with my left hand as I pretend to recover my balance and open my mind to glean any information from him.

I must conceal a laugh. I feel sunshine, hear the ocean's roar, and taste fresh oranges on my tongue. Scott may be aggravating as a goat in your pumpkin patch, but he is harmless.

His hand lays on top of mine, and I get another jolt.

"Whoopsie daisy," he says.

"Sorry, I caught my foot on my chair."

"That's okay, Grace."

I cut Trisha's giggle off with a death stare. "I'll be back in a second."

"Do you need me to go with you?"

"No, you stay here and entertain your company." I favor her with an exaggerated fake smile before turning away.

The thin, purple-haired witch—I don't know if she is, only that she looks like one—stands straighter as I move toward the table and the seven women. I make a waving motion at her.

It's false bravado as I check either side of my periphery to ensure neither of the men is approaching. That is when I realize what has been aggravating me about the three lookouts' positioning. They are strategically blocking the exits. To leave, the women will have to walk by one of them.

I take my cue from Scott. I grab a chair from the table next to them and slide it to the corner of their table. The coven coalescence brewing above them makes a snapping noise as it dissipates.

"Hi, ladies. I don't mean to startle you, and please don't look, but you are being watched."

The youngest woman at the table turns her head to the left.

"Lauren, she said don't look."

The younger woman, Lauren, jerks her head back toward me. "Sorry."

"I wish I could tell you more, but it's just something I noticed."

"How long have they been there?" an attractive woman in her mid-forties asks.

"Less than a half hour. I believe they were here when I came in, but y'all were here before we were seated."

She nods her head. "Thank you for telling us."

"Don't mention it. I know if it were me they were watching, I would appreciate someone alerting me. You can't be too careful these days."

"That is the truth of it." She turns to her coven. "Ladies, it's time we head back to the B and B. No dilly-dallying, and if you must use the restroom, you'll have to wait until we are back in our rooms."

"Do you need a distraction?"

"How do you mean?"

"What is your plan to get by them?"

I watch her scan the room's layout without moving her head. "They have blocked the exits, but not the hallway to the other dining area. From there, we can access the gift shop and exit the tavern." She raises her eyebrows. "Is everybody clear?"

They all nod their heads in agreement.

As a lawyer, I've learned how to make tangential inquiries to provide me with the answers I want without asking direct questions. "Too bad y'all don't have the skills that the witch coven who used to meet here had. You could turn yourselves invisible or give the three folks spying on you food poisoning."

Their expressions are varied but priceless. The woman who appears in charge of the group says, "I didn't get your name."

I touch my breastbone with my fingertip. "I am April."

"I'm Rita, April. Thank you for your help tonight."

Rita scans her group, and they all nod their heads. When she rises, they simultaneously push back their chairs, grab their purses, and follow her out in an orderly manner.

I watch the purple witch's confusion as she decides whether to follow them or stay at her post. When she turns her ire on me and glares, I simply smile and turn my back as I walk toward Trisha and Scott.

They are rolling with laughter as if enjoying an event at the comedy club. I take my seat, this time without falling onto Scott.

He looks at me and sobers. "Tell me. Did everything come out all right?"

Trisha peels into another bout of laughter, and Scott joins her.

I really don't like Scott.

Chapter 20

I'm barely awake as we drive toward Tybee Island the next day. After speaking with Rita and her "we don't know we're a coven" group, the nine-hour drive to Savannah from Baltimore suddenly caught up with me. I was so tired I couldn't even take much note of our hotel room other than it had a bed, and I fell perfectly into the middle of it and never moved.

Trisha, as usual, read my mind and offered to drive this morning. It allows me to take in the sawgrass swamps and wetlands as we travel toward the popular tourist attraction.

As we take a right onto the main road down the island, I am quite surprised at the age of most of the buildings. It has a circa-1960 feel to it. I've become used to Pensacola, where you can count on a hurricane every twenty to thirty years to wipe everything clean and make the citizens build it all new again.

We find a space in the public parking area, grab our cooler, umbrella, and beach chairs, and wrestle them across the asphalt and the wooden boardwalk leading down to the sand.

It is the beach—the salt spray is in the air and the sand is present—but it is darker than the white coastline of the Gulf Coast I'm used to.

"Where do you want to set up?"

Trisha is already struggling and would be content to set up here. But it's about four umbrellas deep to the water. Which is way too crowded for my liking. I look to the far right and see something much more pleasing. "It's a lot less crowded down there."

As the sunbather population decreases, the smell of dank, fetid water fills the air. I notice a vast sandbar formed twenty yards past the ocean's waterline.

"Gawd. What is that stench? It's enough to knock a dog off a gut wagon."

Trisha giggles. "I thought you had eaten something that disagreed with you last night."

"The only thing I'm disagreeable about is your choice of company," I grouse. I drop the cooler and my umbrella. "Let's set up here."

"Why do you always do that?"

"I always do what, Trisha?" I grumble as I drop to my knees and screw the umbrella anchor into the sand.

"Be so mean to people you don't even know."

"I'm sorry, Trisha. If you're into him, that's cool. I don't care what you do. He seems like a good enough guy. It was aggravating because we haven't caught up in a while."

"He wasn't into me. He was into you, dum-dum."

"Well, he hung around and talked to you."

She plops into her chair and straightens her sunglasses. "Because he is a nice guy and didn't want me to sit there alone."

I sit next to her. "All right, it's all my fault, and I'll own it. I'm rude and shouldn't have left you alone."

"See, it doesn't kill you to admit you're wrong."

"I was being facetious."

"Yeah, me too."

The smell, as if somebody has dumped a hundred porta potties into the ocean, does not dissipate. Still, I become used to it. I assume this because I find myself dozing off.

With the day's warmth and a gentle breeze blowing, the troubles that have been mine the last week melt away. Good company and vacation time can change your perspective on life.

The closer I come to sleep, the further my mental partitions lower. The paranormal activity in the area is nothing in magnitude to what I experience in Guntersville. It's also not the collective kaleidoscope of energy I sensed at the Star Chase Tavern last night.

Yet it is present. It's like a low thrum in my head.

I am glad that it is such a low energy level. Unlike last night where the energy signatures were mostly good, there are some quite evil ones here.

"This is a pleasant surprise. It's like finding a four-leaf clover."

I nearly fall out of my chair at the familiar voice in my ear.

"Scott, you've got to quit doing that. You're too friggin' big to be sneaking up on people."

He grins. "That is why my friends call me the phantom."

"I bet you don't want to be a real phantom. But somebody might accidentally make you one if you keep sneaking up on people."

I notice his peculiar attire as he drops his butt on the sand. Granted, it's late fall, but it's still eighty-two degrees today, and easily ninety percent humidity. Scott wears a ridiculously large broadband hardhat, a bandana, a fully buttoned up long-sleeved shirt, baggy work jeans, and thickly scarred work boots.

"Aren't you a little overdressed for the beach?"

"Oh, I always wear protection."

I fight it, I really do, but I smirk nonetheless. "Well, that's good to know."

He makes a funny face at me. It's obvious his double entendre was inadvertent.

"So, what are you doing out here anyway? Stalker much?"

He frowns and points over his shoulder. "No, I'm remodeling the Seahorse, and I happened to see you walking out here."

I rotate in my chair to see where he is pointing. A four-story motel behind us looks to have been built in the '50s. "Tear it down."

"Yeah. My partner had planned on doing that, but the locals didn't want the high rise he was planning, and they were able to label it as a local historical site."

"They can do that?"

He grins. "Of course, they can. It's their island and their zoning laws."

True that. Just because you buy a property doesn't mean you get to do what you want with it.

"Wait a minute." I check my phone and see we've already been set up for two hours. "You watched us come out, and you waited this long to come to say hello?"

"I had to wait for a break. I've got twenty-five guys in there."

"Break? *You* had to wait for the break."

"That and it was a debate if you were worth braving this section of the beach. I don't like the smell of the runoff here. There is no telling what is coming out of those marshlands. You know it's best not to swim in that."

Bless it. That explains the God-forsaken smell. It also explains why Trisha and I have this large section of the beach all to ourselves.

"Well, that's good to know. I appreciate the information."

"See, I can be a handy guy to have around."

"Uh-huh."

"I was wondering, are you seeing anyone?"

I hold my hand up. "Let me stop you right there, Scott. I just got out of a relationship and plan to take a decade or two off from dating."

He barks a laugh. "A decade or two?"

"Absolutely."

He grimaces. "It was a nasty breakup?"

"No... Truthfully, it was a rather pleasant evening."

Scott's expression is quizzical. I understand. I'm still confused about how calm the separation was, too. Inexplicably, the ease of the breakup is as disconcerting as not having Lee in my life anymore.

He recovers. "Anyway, I thought it fair to warn you. You

don't realize it yet, but you're going to fall in love with me. What do you say to that?"

"You'll be highly disappointed at all your time wasted on that endeavor. Before you start building a house on a property, you better check who controls the zoning."

He points his finger at me. "I like what you did there." Scott rises to his feet and swipes sand from his butt. "Challenge accepted, April."

He walks away before I can say anything else to him. I'm dumbfounded that he can be so confident yet woefully unprepared to accept my quip as a challenge. Other than my first name, he doesn't know anything about me. How would he even find me?

Idiot.

That tickles me, and I settle back into my chair and grin.

Despite the brackish water stench, I have no plans to move. But I look to the side and confirm Scott's information. A nasty, green gully runs to the sea thirty yards to our right.

"Oh, my. I must have dozed off," Trisha says. "Did I miss anything?"

"Only a Sasquatch sighting."

Chapter 21

Trisha insists we move away from the green watershed. I welcome the absence of the funky smell flowing from the marsh. However, I do not appreciate the multitude of people's backs that now block our view of the Atlantic Ocean.

Understand, typically, I would enjoy people-watching. The beach is always a spectacular location for that activity.

The trouble is, I am about peopled out. After a year and a half of serving the community of Guntersville, my brother's paranormal team, nearly fifty property owners of suspected haunted hotspots, and most recently, negotiating the choppy waters of a relationship that I wasn't fully committed to, I feel the need to have less human interaction, not more.

I am afflicted with a twinge of aggravation, as opposed to interest, as I watch a group of young men playing frisbee. The frown forming on my face as I watch a couple holding hands walking in front of me confirms I made the correct decision about Lee.

Ending our relationship before we did something stupid like getting married and having children, after the initial sadness, has a freeing quality. Maybe I'm selfish, but there is a lot to be said for only having to worry about myself.

Even going back to Guntersville seems right, at least for now. Nothing will prevent me from sliding to Huntsville or Nashville in a few years. But currently my hometown is oddly appealing to me. I'm learning much about my chosen profession and my natural flair for litigation.

Those are the benefits before I throw in that it will allow me to remain close to my family. Most importantly my grandmothers, while I continue to master my paranormal skills.

Yes. Fully developing my "gifts" is another decision I've taken this week. Simply burying my head and hoping my "gifts" will atrophy again is not an option. Especially considering a hell kite is waiting to settle a score with me.

"Are you hungry?" Trisha asks.

"Yes, but I would prefer to stay out here longer."

"How about we get a sandwich and bring it back to eat?"

I consider the probability of said hypothetical sandwich having a high degree of sand before I finish eating it and frown. "Maybe in a bit."

"What time is it anyway?"

"Don't know, don't care."

Trisha leans over the arm of her chair and commences digging in our beach bag. I glance to the right and watch the healthy amount of sand she tracks into the bag.

She finds her phone in the last place it could be, grabs it, and rolls back into her seat. "It's four o'clock."

"Hmm."

"Oh no!"

The alarm in Trisha's voice shakes me from my warm cocoon of leisurely bliss. I wait for her to announce the emergency. Instead, she is busy pecking at the screen of her phone.

She puts her phone to her ear, and I ask, "What is it?"

"My dad's been trying to..." She looks away from me. "Sorry, Dad. We were on the beach, and I just got your message."

"Oh." Trisha turns her attention to me. Her eyes open wide with urgency. "Dad needs to talk to you. He has left you several voicemails."

Instinctively, I roll to the side and begin digging in our beach bag. Norman and I have a great relationship since I am his niece. Still, his trying to call me, especially while I'm with Trisha, is highly unusual.

"Peaches. Where is my phone." I'm as lousy of a phone hunter as Trisha.

"Here, just use mine."

Well, that would make entirely too much sense. I stop digging in the bag and accept Trisha's phone. "What's the matter, Norman?"

"April, I know you and Trisha are on vacation, but something has come up where your help would benefit me."

"Uh … I can give you some basic legal information, Norman. But I don't have a license in Georgia."

"Oh, no, honey. It's not legal."

I get a funny tightness in my gut. "Illegal?"

Norman releases a bark of laughter that startles me. I giggle as he continues to laugh, albeit more from relief than amusement.

His laugh winds down. "No, honey. Your uncle Norman would never ask you to do anything illegal."

While I am relieved that the foundation I've built my relationship on with Norman remains rock-bed solid, I am at a total loss on how to help him. "Then how can I help?"

"First, promise to tell me if you can't or don't want to do this. But, if you can, you would be helping me repay a personal debt."

The manner of his request reminds me of the other skill I have, and I pray that is not where we're going. Not because I wouldn't gladly do anything possible to help Norman or a friend he owes a debt to. It is because I assumed Norman didn't know of my paranormal skills.

I've never had conversations with Norman about them. I have talked to Trisha about them. I shoot an accusatory glance in her direction.

"What?" she mouths.

I roll my eyes. "Yes, sir. What do you need me to do."

"Your granny says that you have both the touch and visions."

That is a surprise I didn't expect. Although I should have since Granny is Norman's much-older sister-in-law, who practically raised him after the sudden death of his parents while growing up. "Yes."

"I'm working on a case for a good friend, and those skills would be beneficial."

Because I'm a defense attorney who does a little side investigating on my own when I don't farm it out, my paranormal skills are occasionally helpful. Still, I find them suspect at best.

"April?"

"I'm here. Tell me what's happening and why you think I can help. It's not that I don't want to do this. It's only that I want to make sure that what you need is something I can deliver so I don't disappoint you and your friend."

"Honestly, you couldn't be a disappointment at this point. We've run into nothing but dead ends with all conventional methods."

I'm sure he would prefer I take his statement at face value. Still, there is a slight hitch in my uncle's otherwise usually confident and deliberate delivery. "And?"

He sighs heavily. "Given the environment, I have an itching suspicion that we might be dealing with something of a paranormal nature."

"Do you care to share why you feel that way? Or will I be forced to pump you for information?"

"I'd rather not pollute your paradigm before you get down here and see for yourself."

I snort a rude laugh. "I bet you do. Just tell me. I'd rather know what I'm walking into."

"The investigation site is Turtle Key. It's one of the barrier islands off the Georgia coast."

"Your friend is Gullah?"

"He is. But first, he is a friend who served with me in Iraq. I've covered the case detail with Aduwa several times, and we haven't a clue that gives us a single thread to follow."

"But that doesn't answer why you feel a paranormal may be involved."

"Granny said that Pauline has been teaching you all manner of witchcraft that she is familiar with. Is that correct?"

"Well, one person's witchcraft is another person's religion based on the physical world. But yes, Nana has been teaching me what she knows."

"Are you familiar with haints?"

"Are you serious?"

"Come on, don't make me defend what I don't even necessarily believe in." He pauses. "Some older folks have reported seeing a Gumby and think it has carried the three people off."

"Duppy." I correct him.

He pauses and releases another bark of laughter. "I thought that sounded weird."

"Yes, sir. I am not interested if they have a tall green playdough character snatching people off the streets."

Nana instructed me on the Gullah Geechee population because she believes they are a storied and essential part of the Southern tapestry. Their history is quite different than other Southern populations.

According to her, their religion is an eclectic blend of Islam colored with hints of Christianity. From a barbaric practice called seasoning, where plantation owners first shipped Africans to labor on Caribbean islands before bringing them to America, some supernatural beliefs from other African cultures bled into the Gullah belief system—faiths of a dark-magic flavor.

After the Civil War, General Sherman released the Gullah. The community, under constant threat from mainlanders not keen on freed slaves, banded together. By combining resources, they bought land on their barrier island to build a better life for themselves.

Over time, young people moved away for jobs and love. This has left the community fighting for its survival.

Nana can be quite salty about populations with divergent religions being displaced. Given our distant Cherokee ancestry, the mother of all triggers in her kitchen is to mention the Trail of Tears.

"Do you think it's a good idea? I mean, are they okay with this?"

"Aduwa trusts me. If he called for my help, I know he is at his wit's end and is willing to do anything to solve this case."

"It sounds like he is an excellent detective, like his friend from the army."

"He is a concerned citizen. There is no police force on the island, April."

"Oh."

"The sheriff's department has been notified of Jumare's disappearance. But the mainland police forces routinely put the island's needs at the bottom of their list."

"Then it's a missing person case?" This grabs my interest as I have had marginal success with such investigations.

"Yes. Jumare is Aduwa's nephew."

Chapter 22

Because time could be essential to whether or not we find Jumare alive, Trisha and I load my rental car and opt for a drive-through meal. As we merge onto the interstate, a true toad strangler hits, and I must slow to give the windshield wipers an opportunity to work, even set on high.

I explain the basics of the case to Trisha. Looking at her serious expression in my periphery, I sense she is highly concerned.

I am too.

If I had known a boy's life would hinge on my supernatural talents, I would have thawed out my amulet and looking stone. Hindsight being twenty-twenty and all.

Instead, the only spiritual item I have with me is the crucifix that Liza gave me. Great against demons. I have no clue if it will affect haints.

"Your dad said the ferry leaves at four thirty?"

"Yeah. Do you think we're gonna make it?"

"If it rains this hard, we'll do better by stopping and renting a boat." I flash her a grin. She is not amused.

"Will this rain make it more difficult for you to use your skills?"

I squint my eyes. "Yeah, no. Rain doesn't tamp down spiritual energies. It's not like I'm a bloodhound using my nose."

"Good."

I divert my view to my phone and watch as the expected time of arrival changes from 4:10 to 4:11. The next ferry out to the barrier island is tomorrow morning at eight. My shoulders pull up toward my earlobes from the tension of being rushed and knowing we will not make it at our current speed.

Screw it. Go big or go home.

I push the accelerator down.

"April! I felt the car hydroplane!"

"Don't break my concentration, Chicken Little."

It sure is a good thing the ferry goes super slow. It gives Trisha plenty of time to get over being angry at me.

Being an only child, she can't understand, so I might as well not try to explain. I am confident in my driving skills for a reason. Having grown up racing Chase and Dusty with every manner of motorized and pedal-powered vehicle available, I don't believe we were ever in danger driving at top speed to make the ferry. Much.

Besides, given that Jumare is in real danger, the ends justify the means in this instance.

As the ferry plows through the murky, green water, I look across Trisha and out the window. Her coloring is coming back nicely.

"I bet this isn't what you had in mind when you invited me to the beach."

She favors me with a death glare and returns her attention outside the window. I want to give Trisha her space, but I can't since the captain insisted we stay inside during the ride. Obviously, somebody before has gotten rowdy and fallen off the boat. I am bored out of my gourd.

"Do you know Aduwa? I've never heard your dad mention him before."

She huffs dramatically before answering me without facing me. "They served together. I don't know the full story, except Dad says Aduwa saved his life one day."

That is a sobering thought. There would have been no Trisha if Norman hadn't returned home from the first Gulf War. And with no Trisha, my life would be a lot less enjoyable.

I owe Aduwa a debt of gratitude as well. I'm learning all sorts of stuff about myself on this trip.

The sun peaks through the cloud cover at our back, illuminating the rain before us. A million drops of gold and silver form a curtain for us to pass through.

"The devil is beating his wife," Trisha mumbles.

The old saying chills my bones. I am holding out hope that this is just a case of a young man going on his version of a walkabout.

As the rain comes to an abrupt stop, I see the shadow of a dock ahead. On the other side are yards and yards of marsh grass.

The setting sun lights each blade on fire in a luminescent green and gold. I'm thankful that the weather has been colder in the evening. Hopefully, that will limit the mosquito, snake, and alligator populations.

The captain reverses the propellers. The ferry glides within a foot of the dock, and the crew hops to the deck and temporarily ties off the vessel.

"We thank you for riding the Turtle Key ferry today. As you disembark, please make sure to take all your belongings. Watch your step while on the island, please enjoy your stay, and don't feed the alligators."

I see Uncle Norman on the dock and wave at him through our window. He waves back.

Next to him stands a formidable dark-skinned man and a tall girl.

"Who is the girl?" I ask Trisha.

"I haven't a clue."

Chapter 23

Norman introduces us to Aduwa and his niece Laila. Aduwa ushers us into his Chevy Suburban and drives us down a hard-packed red dirt road.

I take in the eclectic collection of humungous vacation beach houses built next to older, modest clapboard homes. Nana said some of these communities are dissolving piece by piece as the land is sold to wealthy vacationers.

Despite the initial warm introductions and close proximity, with each pothole, I bump into either Trisha or Laila as we ride in the backseat, and it is awkwardly quiet.

"Have you always lived here?"

Aduwa finds me in the rearview mirror. "I grew up here and have a place on the island, but I work as a mechanical engineer during the week in Jacksonville."

"Oh, wow. That must be difficult keeping up two houses. I have a hard time keeping up with my one-room apartment."

"It's important." Aduwa meets my stare in the reflection of the rearview mirror.

So much for trying to liven things up and make small talk. It's never been my talent, anyway.

"My uncle is trying to say that having one foot in the new world is difficult while trying to honor your past."

"Laila, I don't need you to speak for me."

She grins at me and mimics her uncle as she mouths "I don't need you to speak for me."

I stifle a giggle by placing my fist against my lip. Laila looks almost fourteen but is obviously brave. I never would have considered giving Norman that kind of lip at her age.

"How long has Jumare been gone?" Trisha asks.

"Six days," Aduwa says.

"I picked him up, and we rode the ferry together last Friday when he got out of school. We went to our Gramma's, but he left before dinner."

That is the first red flag for me. I've been around enough teenage boys to know you don't want to get between them and the table once the dinner bell rings.

"Gramma was concerned, but we also figured he might have gone on a hunt and forgot to tell us. He can be forgetful sometimes."

"Laila."

"It's the truth. Saying it ain't isn't gonna make it any different. Some days, I think that boy would forget his butt if it weren't screwed on tight. Don't get me wrong, I love Jumare, but he can be vexing, too."

"You go to school on the mainland?"

"College," she says with an air of dignity. "I stay there during the week. Jumare has to ride the ferry each day since there is no school on Turtle Key."

I let that sink in for a minute. Mostly, I have always enjoyed school. But having to ride a ferry both ways each day might significantly decrease my affection for scholastic endeavors.

"What are you studying?"

"I want to be a lawyer."

I light up like a Christmas tree. "Really? That's what I am. What made you decide to pursue that?"

"Laila and I have seen that the only way we get anything for the island is through the court system. She wants to be the next champion for her island," Aduwa says.

I cock my head to the right as I stare at her. She beams a

smile. Yes, I see where she has the charisma and confidence of a successful litigator.

I pray that she doesn't ask me why I became a lawyer. The fact that my uncle is one, and it seemed like a way to make a good living, doesn't exactly compare with her altruistic reasoning.

That may not be fair to me. Although that might be why I initially got into law school, the ability to sometimes set a severe wrong correct has kept me intrigued for the last year and a half.

Still, I change the conversation before she asks. "Norman tells me there is suspicion that something unnatural has happened to your brother?"

"Just a bunch of grannies talking is what it is."

Laila purses her lips as she shakes her head. "Uncle Aduwa is a strict Muslim. He doesn't believe in a lot of the old ways."

"It has more to do with science than with my religion. There is no such thing as dead people walking about grabbing people. That is what people make up to scare their kids from going into the forest."

"And yet they still do."

"That would be called 'selective evolution.'"

Laila leans toward me, cups her hands, and whispers, "People are always afraid of what they don't understand."

Once again, I'm forced to stifle my laugh. Laila is going to get me in trouble yet.

A conspiratorial grin graces her face. She points at my hand and crooks her finger. Intrigued, I open my left hand and hold it out to her. She runs two fingers of her right hand across my palm.

A spark flashes on my palm, and the tingle travels to my shoulder. Laila leans back and chuckles. "I thought so."

Chapter 24

Aduwa turns left off the dirt road that runs parallel to the beach. We cross over several short, steel bridges that span marsh areas. The heavy rust on the bridge spans makes me glad that Aduwa is not driving a bus. The old bridges would not hold out.

The marsh ends, and we are engulfed by heavy vegetation that forms a tunnel of varying shades of green. The leafy walls the foliage creates grow narrower the further we go into the living pathway. Bush branches swipe at the sides of our SUV as Spanish moss sways in the canopy above.

The vegetation would be dense just from this area's multitude of live oaks. But the undergrowth completely fills out all the earth below the trees.

This is country ... coastal style.

As quickly as the vegetation cave began, we emerge into an open area. We pass a trailer on our left that looks like it's been battling the barrier island winds and salt for a decade too long. Three wooden structures are next to it, spaced out comfortably on two-acre plots.

They are squat, single-story buildings of approximately 1,200 square feet, and a perfect rectangle save for the porches. By their design, I venture that whoever built one built all three.

Each is painted a distinct color: one yellow, one white, and another a loud salmon color. Each has one thing in common. Haint-blue trim is prominent around every doorway and windowpane.

I'm eager to explore and investigate the porches' ceiling. I'm curious if Nana's story about the Geechee's beliefs about the spirits being confused by the ocean-blue paint is genuine or a myth.

Laila taps me with her elbow and points out the window. "If you get bored, the Pick 'em Up store is the only place for entertainment."

I take in the utilitarian, concrete-block building with a nearly flat tin roof. The fifteen-thousand-square-foot store appears to be an oversized five-and-dime.

I look back to Laila, and she grins. "It's a happening town."

"A young lady like yourself should be focused on her studies, not her social life," Aduwa says.

"It can't be much of a social life when I know everybody on the island. Half of them are twice my age, and the other half are related to me."

"I hear you there, Laila. I have the same problem in my hometown."

She flashes me a wicked smile. "You do? How many people do you have in your town?"

"Guntersville has almost eight thousand people."

"I see." She leans forward. "Uncle Aduwa, how many folks do we have in town?"

"Since Jimmy White and Mary Johnson left the island, seventy-nine."

"They didn't leave the island, Aduwa. Nobody takes the ferry off the island with no record of a ticket or abandons all their possessions in their home."

"When people get the itch to leave, sometimes they want to start over without any reminders of their past."

Laila shakes her head as she looks at me.

"There are two other missing people?"

"Yes. But Aduwa is content to disregard their

disappearance."

"Laila, don't be getting things stirred up," Aduwa grumbles, then blows an exasperated breath between his teeth. "Norman, don't pay her any mind. I swear that girl lives to stir things up."

Laila ignores him as she explains to me with animated expressions. "Some people prefer to ignore things happening right before their face."

"And what would it be that I'm ignoring, Laila?"

"I've been telling you for a month. We've got a serial killer on the island. And he is picking us off one by one."

"That is complete bull, and you know it."

"Granny Ruby thinks it's one of those white developers."

"Granny Ruby needs to stay out of the whiskey."

"You know that woman has never drunk a drop of liquor in her life. And what really irks you is a white developer would have a motive and opportunity by being on the island."

"This is what happens, Norman. You send them off to college to study criminal justice. The next thing you know, everything becomes a conspiracy theory."

"Until it's not a conspiracy theory," Trisha interjects.

"When trying to solve a crime, it does help to look at all possible contingencies," I add.

"My father always told me there is nothing more dangerous than educated women, and now I'm learning that for a fact."

"And all three aspiring lawyers, too." Norman gets too much joy by reminding Aduwa that we are or aspire to be lawyers.

"We're here," Laila announces.

"Delivered finally from my trial," Aduwa grouses.

"I love you, too." Laila gives Aduwa a love punch on his shoulder and motions for me to open the door.

I step onto hard-packed dirt with barely a hint of vegetation gracing its surface. In front of the SUV is another single-level rectangular home built by the same contractor. However, this one is immaculately painted with a fresh coat of bright white. The porch has been enclosed in heavy, clear 8 mil plastic, with the bottom portion covered with tin siding.

I see someone harbors a similar aversion to being eaten alive by mosquitoes.

Haint-blue paint borders the screen door to the porch and the two windows to the side.

"Come on, don't be shy. Come meet Gramma."

Trisha walks in front of the vehicle and sidles up next to me. "Do you feel out of place?"

"Well, we are. But we're also guests. You should take it all in and relax."

She nods. "Yes. It's just…"

"Y'all coming?" Norman asks as he follows Aduwa through the open porch door.

Trisha and I step forward as I ask, "Just what?"

"I can't explain it. It's like something is watching me and wanting me to leave."

I open the door for her. "Nonsense. You're only nervous because you're out of your element."

She sets an expression of determination on her face, and I'm glad that my comment has temporarily allowed her to put her awkward feelings aside.

But I don't totally disregard her discomfort. Because I know something about Trisha that she doesn't understand about herself.

Like my brother Dusty, Trisha has a rudimentary sixth sense of paranormal events. They've never been more than the sense of heebie-jeebies or something freaking her out, but they have always been accurate when she does get a feeling.

This is important to me since from the moment I stepped off the ferry, the paranormal energy in the air has been so thick I could cut it with a knife. I assume the heavy blanket of power is from the emotional hardship experienced at a place formerly dominated by a working plantation, followed by a community trying to scratch out an existence. In other words, I discount the overwhelming sensation I initially felt in the energy signature of Turtle Key.

I expect the island to have a high touch of emotion

remaining from the decades of slavery. I reason the preponderance of the feelings potent enough to linger as residual energy must be from the generations of souls long since passed to the other side of the veil. Souls that cannot be helpful to our current endeavor.

Trisha is correct. When I filter out the cacophony of noise and focus on a single negative kernel, I feel something unseemly watching us. It is not happy we are on the island.

We step from the porch into the house, and it reminds me of visiting Nana. Something is cooking, and the small foyer is filled with the delicious scent of a meal I cannot identify. A silky-smooth energy hums lightly in the air, signifying someone with a touch of magic toiling industriously at something they enjoy.

The room's walls are filled with pictures of what I assume to be family. Some photos are shiny new, but many are yellowed with age.

A worn recliner sits to the right of an equally shabby sofa. Each one is draped with a colorful quilt.

I enter the kitchen through the doorway that Norman stands just inside of. The light, not all from the light fixture, is bright enough to force me to squint my eyes.

Gramma has Aduwa's round face but is willowy in stature like Laila. From the heavy creases at the edges of her eyes and lips, I wouldn't put her a day under eighty.

She moves toward Trisha and me with grace and speed belying her age. "I'm so glad to meet you. I'm Beulah, but everybody calls me Gramma, and I expect the same from you," she says as she takes Trisha's hands and favors her with a smile.

"Such a beautiful young woman. Looks are the only thing I miss about being young," she says as she moves closer.

She touches my hand, and I get a snap of electricity that feels like being struck on the hand with one of those one-inch-wide rubber bands. We can see the energy burst between us, and we both smirk. "Thank you for coming to help find my Jumare."

"Yes, ma'am. Thank you for opening your home to me." I look over her shoulder at the stove. "But you shouldn't have gone through the trouble of cooking for us."

"We're not family until we break bread together."

It's a common theme I've heard throughout the South my entire life. Breaking bread with another is paramount to building a tight, trusting relationship.

For varied reasons, Gramma's use of that phrase brings tears to my eyes. It could be I feel Gramma's anxiety over Jumare's disappearance. It could be our commonality of having powers that we keep secret from the rest of the world. Or it may be because I'm touched she cooked for us, given the incredible burden she is bearing.

I am in the presence of a woman of unimaginable emotional strength.

"Yes, ma'am. Thank you."

"Plus, we don't have any restaurants on the island. I couldn't let you starve your first night."

I laugh and nearly spill the tears that have gathered in my eyes.

∞∞∞

It is like being in the middle of a tennis match during dinner. Trisha and I answer one question by Laila, only for Gramma to follow it up with another. I don't mind, but underneath their kindness and interest, it feels as if they want to avoid discussing our task.

"Gramma, I understand you are concerned that Jumare's disappearance might be tied to a supernatural element?"

She stares pointedly at Aduwa.

He sighs and pushes back his chair. "And that would be my cue to look at the timing belt on my truck." He moves to the head of the table and kisses Gramma's forehead. "Thank you for dinner."

"Thank you for understanding."

She waits until Aduwa has exited onto the porch. "I don't know your experience, only that I've been told you have the sight. What's your religion, child."

Gramma looks at me as if Trisha and Norman are not even in the room.

"I suppose Christian while doing a forty-year walk in the wilderness."

Gramma smiles. "It was the Jews who spent forty years in the wilderness."

"What can I say. I'm confused."

"Do you know what a haint is?"

"A ghost."

She favors me with a hint of a smile. "Christians believe that there is a corporal body and a soul. When you die, having been saved by the grace of Christ, your soul ascends into heaven. The Geechee believe there is a corporal body, a soul, and a spirit. The spirit remains on earth forever."

Nana missed that subtle but significant difference during our discussion about the Geechee. If their belief is reality, that would mean that the paranormal world is quite crowded with past generations. This has a hint of authenticity to me. I've often wondered how in tarnation so many "spirits" are stuck in purgatory to fill my head with their constant noise.

"The spirits maintain the person's personality traits of when they were alive. Good people try to help their descendants; bad people continue to try to afflict their enemies."

"And that is what you believe?"

Her shoulders slump, and she suddenly looks her age. "I have tried to leave the old ways behind. I know that it does not fit within the teachings of Allah. Still, to turn a blind eye to things when they show themselves is foolish."

"I'm not sure I follow you."

Laila lays her hand on Gramma's. "Do you mind?"

"Please. My breath isn't what it used to be."

Laila turns her attention to me. A determination blazes in her eyes. "Four years ago, there were easily thirty feral cats running around the neighborhood. They were good for keeping the rodents down, so we all would set food out and didn't pay them any mind. You won't find a single cat in the community anymore." She waves her hand in front of her face. "All gone."

"Coyotes?" Norman asks.

"Or a python," Trisha ads.

Laila ignores them and continues. "Next thing you know, dogs disappear after the cats are gone. Six different families' dogs all disappeared within three months."

"I'm with Trisha. That sounds more like a boa."

"Two were pit bulls, and one was a Great Dane."

"That's one big snake," Trisha says.

"Then, before Jumare, two other people disappeared without a trace. The entire community searched, but nobody knew what happened to them. Aduwa and the others in charge have tried to make us believe they simply picked up and left. After working hard to get what they had, nobody leaves without taking their belongings and selling or deeding the property to somebody else."

"And the sheriff?"

Gramma laughs and waves her hand. I look back to Laila, who has a rueful expression. "It's island life as a Black community, April. We had to sue the county for a water tank big enough for the island's needs and an electric incinerator for the garbage."

"Lily lost her son two years ago because he had an accident, and by the time the helicopter came, he bled out."

"That was bad." Laila nods her head. "No healthcare, no school, no trash pickup, and the sheriff will come out here and take down a report, but that is all that ever happens."

Two things come to mind. First, I consider Guntersville country. Everything is a matter of perspective. Turtle Key is *country*, for sure.

Country living, distilled down to its essence, is "if it's going to get done, you better get at it." Turtle Key lives by the same creed.

A second more troubling thing comes to mind. Gramma and Laila's scenario sounds eerily familiar to the situation Trisha and I dealt with in Pensacola two years ago. A sibling warlock and witch team had found an altar previously used for sacrifices. Their belief, and they were correct, was that the altar could imbue them with powers. They had started out stealing the life force from dogs and were looking for a human with spiritual abilities when they set their sights on me.

Stealing life force energies from other beings is as old as the dark craft is.

Gramma's façade of happiness unexpectantly crumbles, and she puts her face into her hands. "I asked that boy to burn his hair, or at least flush it. But he wouldn't listen to me. He'd be, "Oh, Gramma. There you go again with that old island nonsense." Just like his uncle Aduwa. Too smart to be fooled by witchcraft. But I know that's what happened to him. Someone got hold of his hair and put a root on him, and now I lost my baby."

"Root?" I ask.

"It's like a spell or a curse," Laila says.

"Gramma, I'm sure you're distraught because Jumare's missing, but why would you assume someone has put a root on him?"

"I'm not assuming…" Gramma drops her hands into her lap. "Ade told me as much."

I have too much new information coming at me to process. My mouth is opening and closing as if I'm chewing gum.

"She is the neighbor down the street. Ade and Gramma used to quilt together."

"We do quilt together. Ade told me her rheumatism in her hands has been feeling better, and she can quilt now like she did in her forties."

Norman clears his throat. "April, we've already talked to

Miss Ade."

Gramma overlooks Norman. "Ade said she couldn't sleep the Friday before last, and she saw Jumare at one in the morning, walking past her porch and toward Bucky's place. She called out to him and said, 'Jumare Washington, where are you going at this hour? Does your Gramma know?' She says he kept walking, and we haven't seen him since."

"Ade comes across as the type of woman who likes to keep the pot stirred. There are too many inconsistencies with her story, and they shift like sand," Norman says.

"She doesn't have any cause to lie."

"I thought you said Jumare didn't come to dinner that night, Laila."

"He didn't. That was the first thing that told me something was bad wrong."

"What happened between him getting off the ferry and Miss Ade seeing him at one in the morning?"

My question is greeted with silence. As we exchange stupid glances because none of us have the answer, I know what my first step in the investigation is.

"Ladies, we need to have a discussion with Miss Ade," I say as I push my chair back.

"You're wasting your time, April. Shouldn't we start by showing you Jumare's room and letting you get some readings off some items?"

I smirk at my uncle. "Who's running this paranormal investigation anyway?"

"I'm just saying that that old woman is a waste of time. I've talked to her at length, which got me nothing."

"Yeah, but maybe it's time for a heart-to-heart between girls." I motion for Trisha and Laila to follow me.

Norman claims Miss Ade likes to keep the pot stirred. She ain't seen a swizzle stick like me yet.

Chapter 25

Laila takes the lead as we exit Gramma's house. We cross the rutted, muddy road and walk toward a shambled-looking house. It's twilight now. The best I can see, the home is a well-weathered shade of purple.

Three small sheds sit to the right of the house. An old truck with all four tires flat is to the left, with saw grass growing up through the fender and bumper.

I steal a peek at Trisha. She appears as nervous as a long-tailed cat around a rocking chair.

Her facial expression confirms my feeling. There is something not quite right about this place.

"Laila, has there been any trouble between your family and Miss Ade?"

She screws up her face. "Oh, no. Ade can be a bit strange at times—she is certainly old school—but she has been Gramma's friend since before I was born."

We walk up the path of broken shells that lead to her front porch. Laila takes the stairs two at a time and knocks on the screen door. The front door is open. "Miss Ade? It's Laila. I have some company from the mainland."

Trisha and I stand at the bottom stair.

Laila cups her hands around her eyes and peers through the screen. "Miss Ade?"

"I'm right here, girl."

We all jump to the left. Laila stumbles and nearly goes tea kettle over the spout as she bumps the porch railing. She puts her hand on her chest. "You scared the ghost out of me, Miss Ade."

"Been sitting here the whole time. Saw you coming down the lane."

"Why didn't you say something?"

"I reckon I didn't want to. I don't feel like talking right now."

"It sure would be helpful if you change your mind. These two ladies came from Nashville to help find my brother."

Ade fishes something out of her apron pocket and puts it in her mouth. We watch as she chews on it like cud.

"Miss Ade."

"You try my patience." She motions for Laila to enter. Laila opens the screen door, holding it open for Trisha and me. "I told y'all a week ago that the obeah man got him. If the police had listened to me, Jumare would already be home. But I'm sure he's done something bad to him by now." She accentuates this by pursing her lips while shaking her head.

"Miss Ade, Bucky ain't no more an obeah man than you are a witch. Can't you at least tell these girls one more time what happened that night you saw my brother?"

Ade leans forward in the rocking chair until her butt comes out of the seat. She braces on her hands and squints her eyes in my direction.

"Looks like some of those vacationers to me."

If I'm to get her to warm up to me, it's now or never. "We were on vacation up in Savannah, Miss Ade. But then we heard about Jumare and hurried on down here to see if we could do anything to help."

"My white folk's name is Adeline. Friends and family call me Ade. You're neither."

I grit my teeth as I gather myself. "My apologies."

"And unless you're a voodoo priestess, which you'd be the whitest one I've ever seen, there is nothing you can do to help a dead man."

I narrow my eyes and take one step closer. "I understand. Still, I'll hold out hope that we will find Jumare alive until we don't."

"Miss Ade, you know Gramma's heart is broken because of Jumare's disappearance. I can't believe you won't do whatever is necessary to help."

"Beulah had no business trying to raise you two. Ain't right for old folks to be raising kids."

The hurt expression that flashes across Laila's face tears at my heart. Adeline's proclamation has a vicious sting.

"Gramma did a fine job," Laila whispers.

Adeline fishes in her pocket again. I take a step closer, and in the failing light, I swear it looks like she shoves a white carrot in her mouth.

"Adeline, I don't want to disturb your peace any more than I have to. But you should also know I'm not leaving until you tell me what happened."

"You think you're special, so I have to tell you whatever you want me to say?"

"No, ma'am. I'm asking you to because you are friends with Beulah, and she is in a terrible sort right now. I'm gonna be honest with you. I have no idea if I can help. What you tell me may or may not be significant.

"What I can tell you is I'm not leaving until you describe to me what happened the night that you saw Jumare, and as soon as you do, I'll get out of your hair and you won't have to see me again."

She chews the sticks in her mouth, then shoves another piece against the inside of her cheek, causing a bulge. "For Beulah, I'll tell you, but I don't understand why folks keep asking me about this. It's the last time I'll tell the story."

"Yes, ma'am." I move to Laila's side. I hear Trisha's steps behind me.

"My rheumatism is so bad some nights I can't sleep. Last Friday, and I know it was Friday because the moon was full, my hip was hurting, and sometimes when I rock in the rocking chair, it'll loosen it up.

"So, I'm out here rockin', listening to the toads while watching the moon, and then what happens? Here comes Jumare Washington walking down the road.

"Jumare isn't old enough to walk around like that alone at night, and I know Beulah wouldn't let him. I thought it best I call out to him and tell him to get home rather than let him skulk about like an alley cat. When I did, he told me he was going to Bucky's."

Laila gasps. "You said he didn't talk to you. That when you called out his name, he didn't respond."

Miss Ade knits her eyebrows together on her heavily weathered face. "Did I?"

"You did."

"I didn't want to get Bucky in trouble. Just because he is an obeah doesn't mean I have the right to out him." Adeline looks pointedly at Laila. "People have a right to hide their abilities if people wouldn't understand them."

Norman warned me that her story was constantly shifting. Since it's been a while since she gave her last account, it's best to play along and see where the trajectory of this recounting goes.

"What happened then?"

Adeline gives me a disgusted look as if I am daft. "How do you mean?"

"He told you he was going to Bucky's, and that was it?"

She shoves another stick in her mouth and can barely close her lips as she chews. "I told Jumare to go home. He said no. Something about Bucky was going to give him something. But he never said exactly what. Now he's gone."

"What do you think Bucky had for him?"

"Nothing. That's why he is dead. It was the bait to snare him with."

It's fair that Adeline may have just concluded that Jumare is dead. Still, her insistence that he is no longer with the living aggravates the stew out of me.

"If Bucky did kill Jumare, what do you think he would've done with him?" Trisha asks.

Adeline smirks as she shakes her head. "After he drained his essence? I'd say he dropped him in the salt marsh. By now, you'll be lucky to find a thigh bone between the gators and the crabs."

Laila makes a sobbing noise and pushes between Trisha and me. Before I can say anything, she is jogging toward Gramma's house.

I return my attention to Adeline. "How can you be so cruel to the granddaughter of your friend?"

"Great-granddaughter." She makes a twirling motion with her finger. "We had a deal. You need to make yourself scarce now."

I've never been fond of being dismissed, but we did have a deal. There is also the fact that I can talk to Adeline for the next three days, and like Norman told me, I'll get fifty different stories, and all of them will lead to a dead end.

"Come on, Trisha."

As I reach the broken-shell walkway, Adeline cackles. "I was just kidding about the saltwater marsh. I wanted to see if I could get a rise out of that girl. She has always been way too high-strung."

Turning, I focus on Adeline through the screen of her porch walking toward her as she speaks.

"I'm not saying I know where he is at, and these ears may be old, but I still hear pretty good. If I were you and had a mind to find Jumare, I would be looking at the barn storage behind Bucky's house. The other day, I was walking and kept hearing something in his barn."

I want to scream. "And you're just now telling us?" But I also realize it won't be helpful. Heck, I wonder if what she tells me will be beneficial or even trustworthy. Still, given that I have zero leads, it'll give me something to focus on.

"I got something else to tell you."

"Yes, ma'am."

"You have to come here 'cause I got to whisper in your ear."

A cold chill runs up my spine. That's illogical. Adeline is just an elderly woman, even though her house feels like it has known evil before. With what I have faced during the last two years, a woman who can barely get out of a rocking chair will not spike my fear meter.

Out of trying to prove to myself that I'm not afraid of her, I make a show of stomping up her stairs. My only hesitation is when I'm standing in front of her.

"I have to whisper in your ear. Closer."

I bend over to put my ear next to her mouth. She pets the top of my head, and I pull back.

"Sorry. I've always wanted to touch a white person's hair to know how it feels."

Feeling violated and highly aggravated, I'm undecided if I want to learn what she has to tell me or if I'm ready to leave.

"I'm sorry I couldn't help myself. Please lean in closer, and let me tell you."

"How about you tell me where I am."

She crooks a gnarled finger at me. "Come here. Let me tell you."

If I listen to the limited common sense God gave me, I will hear, "No! Just leave." Still, my abnormally high curiosity is doing me in again. Despite her creepy petting of my head, I come close to her mouth again.

The rush of her moist breath warms my earlobe. "I know what you are."

Chapter 26

I don't believe Adeline's story about Bucky being an obeah. The idea that a predominantly Muslim community with a touch of Christianity would have a full-fledged obeah within their midst does not ring true.

Still, I'm not in a position to write anything off yet.

If we need to talk to Bucky to get some answers, it's the only conceivable way forward. As the sky blesses us with drizzling rain, we step onto the red dirt lane.

"Do you want to get some umbrellas?"

"No. If you haven't noticed, I'm not made of sugar. I won't melt." I motion with my thumb toward Trisha. "Trisha—it's tough to say."

"I am fine, thank you very much." Trisha turns her attention to Laila. "Obeahs are like witch doctors?"

"Loosely translated, that is a decent way to describe them."

"So, does he like make potions and do spells?" Trisha asks.

Laila laughs uncontrollably.

I shrug and continue to lead our group. I don't know about Bucky's abilities, but thinking about people using their magical talent for making potions reminds me of Nana. Given several of her failures over the years, some quite comical, I hope Bucky is a better potion maker than Nana.

Laila catches control of her laughter and explains, "He

makes potions, but none are magical."

Trisha becomes exasperated with the riddle and frowns. "I don't understand."

"Bucky grows… Let us say a lot of unconventional products."

"Like marijuana?" Trisha asks in such a conspiratorial tone, I nearly laugh too.

"That, poppies, hallucinogenic mushrooms, and he even raises hallucinogenic toads."

Trisha squints her eyes. "Now I know you're pulling my leg."

"I got no reason to lie."

Trisha runs her hands through her hair, flicking it back. "Toads. Honestly?"

We continue down the lane, and as we approach a clump of wilderness at the elbow of the path, Laila points ahead. "See that red house out in the field with the sheds to the side?"

"Yes."

"That is Bucky's place."

"Oh."

A quarter of a mile in front of us is a square red building with a minimal-slant tin roof in desperate need of care. It looks like it has been built in eight stages, and none of the additions match perfectly. In particular, the addition to the left sits several inches below the rest of the structure. I can only know for sure by going in, but I would be surprised if it has seven-foot ceilings inside.

"That's the house?" Trisha asks.

"Yes. It has been in Bucky's family for nearly a hundred and fifty years."

"Yeah, that front door is circa 1800."

"He doesn't care much about materialistic things."

"Do you believe what Gramma said—Miss Ade's claim he is an obeah?"

"Do I believe there are obeahs? Absolutely. But I also know empirically that Bucky is not one. Is he the best place to get some superb recreational drugs if that is what you're into? Yes. For a love potion? I wouldn't advise it unless you're willing to go to jail for slipping somebody some Molly."

"Can you think of any reason Jumare would have been around that?"

"Jumare is not into drugs." Laila shrugs. "If I'm using my imagination, there might be an outside chance Bucky offered Jumare cash to help him move something around. But there are at least ten other people Bucky would have asked before Jumare."

We turn down the dirt drive toward the house. The home looked better from a distance. I count at least four clapboards that have worked their way loose, and the three wooden storage units to the right are not in much better condition as the doors look swollen shut.

"Honestly, Miss Ade's claim doesn't square with me. I've always thought of Bucky as a harmless, entertaining guy. I can't imagine him hurting an animal, much less murdering or kidnapping anyone."

I take Laila's evaluation into thoughtful consideration. Still, through my legal career experience, I am confident in something my uncle told me early on.

People will surprise you.

I understand people's motives and match them with their personality styles. Except when selecting a life partner, my social skills and determination are as much of a superpower as my paranormal gifts. Who knows, perhaps my magical abilities assist me in that.

Yet despite my excellent abilities, I have been surprised, good and bad, on several occasions during the last few years.

I know to expect the most probable scenario but be prepared to pivot if the facts change. It's all about adaptability.

"Here, let me," Laila says as she slides past me and pulls the stuck screen door that whines as if its hinges have never been oiled. She steps in front of the splintering, green front door and taps beside the neck-high single window smeared with red clay.

No answer.

Laila knocks on the front door again. As we wait, she turns briefly, offering me an unsure smile.

"Bucky. Bucky, it's Laila from up the street." She says as she raps harder with her knuckles.

"He won't be out in his fields with it raining," Laila says under her breath.

I watch her back as she shifts her weight from side to side. She has developed a severe case of fidgets.

"Should we try the back door?" Trisha offers.

Laila cups her hands and looks in through the smeared window. "His house doesn't have a back door."

"That could be a problem during a fire." I watch Trisha scan the multitude of bags of fertilizer and newspapers in the corners of the porch. "Not that there is anything that could possibly catch fire."

Laila knocks on the door with greater vigor. "Bucky. Bucky, it's Laila. Open up."

Still, no answer from Bucky. Besides the rain falling on the tin roof and the wind cutting through the screen, there is no noise. Nobody is rustling inside the house or saying they are on their way.

"This isn't like him. He is always home."

"Maybe he walked down to the Pick 'em Up store."

Laila sighs. "I suppose since it's raining."

"You seem concerned about him," Trisha says.

"I've just got the beehives under my skin suddenly. It's nothing."

"Do you think maybe we should check inside for him?" Trisha asks. "Maybe he was evaluating the potency of his crops and passed out. He could need our help."

"I'd like to check on him, but Bucky is likely to think we're trying to steal from him or hurt him. He has been swearing for ten years that he knows a secret, and the president is sending somebody to kill him."

Trisha laughs. "Which president?"

Laila rolls her eyes. "Whoever is in the office at the time, if he can recall."

She steps past us and off the porch into the rain. "I want to check out back in case Bucky is working in the rain."

Walking around Bucky's house, my tennis shoes squish with each step. We're funneled toward the backfield through dozens of fifty-five-gallon drums and abandoned tractor implements. None of the tools look like they have been operational this decade.

From the front of the house, I had spied a twenty-acre field of corn in the back. As we exit the maze of discarded drums, we are close enough to the crop that I see it's not corn.

"Sugarcane?"

Laila looks over her shoulder at me. "Mostly. He grows the field for local use and sells some to a small boutique candy shop in Savannah that buys from him. Plus, it conceals his other crops."

"Huh. If I didn't know any better, I'd think Bucky is a long-lost cousin from the folks I know around Sand Mountain back home. If you're dealing with things the government has an issue with, it's best to be clever."

Laila wraps her arms across her chest. The rain, which has picked up, slides down her face. Still, it's so muggy I know she is not crossing her arms to keep herself warm.

She is concerned for her neighbor. I get it. Many folks in my hometown have similar issues when making healthy life choices. Still, I would worry if they were missing and doing something out of character. I like predictability. It's comforting.

"I guess we could check for him at the store," she says with a defeated tone.

A feeble, faint noise rises on the wind.

Due to the extraordinarily loud paranormal signature of the island, I have been keeping my protective partitions up at full strength the entire time we've been here.

Bless it. I have been defeating the whole purpose of having come on this trip.

Cautiously, I lower the partitions, and a high degree of white noise enters my mind. Concentrating, I work to eliminate the superfluous commotion and chase down the single channel of what sounds like a male voice.

"What is it?" Trisha asks.

I hold up my hand, gesturing for her to be quiet.

It's so faint I cannot even discern whether it's on this side of the veil. It is suddenly interrupted by a croaking noise.

"Do you hear that?" Laila asks.

"Toads?" Trisha squinches her face.

As they discuss the source of the croaking, I lose the male voice I believe I heard on the wind.

A single toad, the improbable size of a football, jumps out from the sugarcane. Its sudden appearance startling me, I take two steps back.

"What the devil?"

"Don't say that," Laila scolds.

Trisha grimaces. "Sorry."

As I become used to the football-sized toad before us, I convince myself that it must simply be a freakishly huge species of toad native to Turtle Key. A pinkish-red cable shoots out of the sugarcane, wraps around the toad, and disappears him.

"Aargh!" Trisha yells.

"What the devil!" Laila screams.

I nearly jump out of my skin. I retreat ten feet as I watch where the toad had once been and knock over a fifty-five-gallon drum with my butt.

"How big does another frog have to be to do that?" Trisha yells.

"Oh, no. I ain't doing this," Laila says.

"Laila, do y'all typically have toads that big?"

She twists up her face in disbelief. "What? The size of an alligator."

"I'm just asking."

"Maybe we should get back to the front," Trisha says.

I hope the frog has nothing to do with our inability to find Bucky. I need to know if it is. Still, the invisible toad with the rubbery red truck winch accessory is certainly large enough to maul Bucky, if not disappear him. I'm not eager to be his next meal.

As I hear the faint male voice again, I become increasingly concerned that Bucky is toad food. While still unintelligible, the voice could very well be Bucky trying to communicate with me from the other side of the veil.

I draw in toward my sternum as much of the plentiful chaotic energy as I dare. I hope to identify if the voice is on the other side of the veil—as in Bucky is dead—or if he lives, and I can get a sense of where he is located.

Honestly, as weirdly cattywampus as everything has become, I'm hoping it is Bucky I am reaching out to, not something more nefarious. Such as a hell kite who believes I owe him a pound of flesh. Literally.

A clamorous sound fills my mind. As if a hundred people are simultaneously beating the dust out of area rugs. I watch Laila and Trisha stare into the sugarcane. They backpedal, and I know they hear it too.

"Birds?"

Perfectly timed with Laila's question, giant gray-and-black moths flood out of the cane by the thousands.

We are engulfed in the storm of insects. I swipe at my face and drop to the muddy ground as they track around us in some bizarre migratory path.

As the sound of beating wings diminishes and the tiny, pelting collisions against my body cease, I cautiously unwrap my arms from across my face to survey the damage.

Laila looks as if she is nearing the end of her sanity.

I try to make light of the situation. "I take it y'all don't normally see flocks of butterflies either."

"No." She points at one of the insects killed in the crush of their mass exodus. "They're not butterflies. They are black witch moths."

"Sorry, biology wasn't my strongest subject."

"No. Black witch moths signify someone will die soon."

Fudge. I remember now. Nana has been pushing so much historical knowledge at me that I never know what will be essential to remember.

"Bucky?" Trisha asks.

Between the odd, masculine voice, the pitched level of paranormal energy at the sugarcane's edge, and Bucky's disappearance, it seems like a safe bet that something has happened to Bucky. Whether he is alive or dead, I know everything emanates from the sugarcane field.

What must be done is clear, even if it makes my skin crawl.

"Y'all stay here. Get help if I don't come back."

Trisha grabs my arm. "What are you doing?"

"I am going into the sugarcane to see what is causing this." I slide her hand off my arm.

"Let's go get Gramma."

"I've got this."

Neither of my partners appear convinced. Heck, *I'm* not convinced. Still, I will myself to the sugarcane field's edge, my ruined Keds making sucking noises in the marshy area.

The rain slows to a mist as the sun breaks through, changing the color of the cane leaves from evergreen to fluorescent green. The breeze switches directions, and balmy air flows from the field, the scent of decay and death lingering on the field's warm breath.

I swallow hard as I work up the nerve to move between the tall stalks.

My first step into the field is more of a hop, and an incredible crunching noise generates a few yards in front of me. Stalks are laid to the side, and a groan emanates from the crops. I move to retreat, but before I can turn, something crashes into me.

Chapter 27

I cringe as I struggle to wrestle the dead weight off of me. The back of my shirt is soaked, and rocks cut into my side as I roll over.

I come to my knees, expecting the person who slammed into me to attack me with a weapon or, at the very least, to grab my legs.

The ashen man does not move. His coal-colored eyes are deeply sunken into his orbital sockets, blinking slowly as droplets of rain strike his face.

"Jumare!" Laila yells. She bumps against me as she drops to her knees next to us.

"My gosh, what's happened to him?" Trisha asks.

The distress on what should be a young man's face is extraordinary.

His clothes are shredded, exposing his rib cage so I can easily count every bone. His cheekbones stick out prominently, and his skin has an odd, gray tone.

If he were walking, I would mistake him for a zombie.

The thought brings a level of concern to me. While Laila holds his face talking to him, I lean down and press my ear to his chest. The heartbeat, although faint, is present, and I lean back in relief.

"Is he going to live?" Trisha whispers.

Laila and I share a glance. She answers Trisha. "Yes. But call my uncle and your dad quick."

"We need to get him out of the rain," Laila says.

"You get his head, and I'll get his legs. We will commandeer Bucky's sofa whether he likes it or not. "

Laila frowns. "Bucky may have done this to him."

"All I've got to say to that is he better hope that's not true." I slide my arms around Jumare's legs and nod, gesturing for Laila to not be concerned about Bucky's response.

Even though he is taller than Laila and me, Jumare is sickeningly light. It's as if someone has hollowed him out, replacing his skeletal system with bird bones.

As we walk sideways, carrying him to Bucky's front door, Laila and I share a knowing glance again. This is not normal. People do not drop fifty pounds after disappearing for a week. This is some sort of magic that has caused Jumare to waste away.

We step inside the porch and come to the front door. Laila tries to adjust her hold on Jumare to knock on the door. I lay Jumare's feet on the floor and grab him under his shoulders, lifting his weight from Laila. "Screw that. He had an opportunity to answer the door earlier. Kick it in, Laila."

Her startled expression tells me she is not comfortable with that. Then she sets her face with grim determination and turns toward the door. Striking with the bottom of her right foot, a crunching noise fills the porch as the wood breaks before the latch. Laila kicks at it again, and the door flies open.

"Let's get him inside and get him warm."

We resume our original hold and quickstep him into the living area of Bucky's house.

The place reeks of marijuana, mildew, and some odd, metallic scent. Still, there is no garbage, and for a single man living as a hermit, that surprises me.

I rub one of Jumare's hands in mine. Momentarily, I consider using my healing powers. Still, given that I don't know precisely what happened to him, I must wait.

As I try to warm him with the friction from my hands, Laila says, "I've got to get him some blankets."

"Yes. Do you know where they're at?"

"No. I've never been inside Bucky's before."

Her initial bravery is wearing off. I don't want to stress her any more than necessary. "Here. Lay down next to Jumare and hold him while I find blankets."

Laila nods and quickly slides in next to Jumare, pulling him tight to her. "Hang in there, Jumare. You're okay now."

I take a second to watch the siblings lying together. I know how my brothers can make me feel safe if I ever get in a bad spot. At the same time, I can't even bear to imagine if I found one of them looking like Jumare does right now. He is knocking on death's door.

I hustle through an inner doorway, finding myself in a small kitchen. To the left is a dark hallway, and I quickly take it.

I see three doors: one on the left, one on the right, and one straight forward. The one straight ahead must be the bathroom, which should lead to a linen closet.

I open the door and get a start. There is a tall, lanky man sprawled out over a bed. This must be Bucky.

My task is urgent. Still, it's difficult to tell if Bucky is sleeping or another casualty. That seems incredibly important to me now, if for no other reason than I don't want Bucky to wake up and ambush our triage of Jumare in the living room.

Cautiously, I approach the bed to get close enough to Bucky to check if he is breathing.

"April?"

Uncle Norman's booming voice makes me snap to attention. Bucky groans and rolls to his side. Alarm flashes across his face as he rubs his eyes and opens them.

"Who are you?"

I should stand my ground, but I backtrack as I say, "I'm a friend of Jumare's family."

The incredibly tall man rises into a sitting position. "But why are you in my house?"

"April, are you back there?"

Bucky's eyes open wider. He grabs something silver off of the nightstand and yells, "You came here to rob me?"

I am speechless. This is quickly turning into a complete crap show. I fully understand Bucky's alarm, even discounting that Laila indicated the man has psychotic tendencies.

"You need to tell me why you're here."

"Blankets?"

Bucky furrows his brow. "You broke into my house for blankets?"

The door behind me slams open wider, and Norman stands in the doorway. Bucky raises a hunting knife and jabs at the air.

Norman reaches for his right hip. I grab his right hand and hold it at his side. "No!"

Norman's startled expression tells me he thinks I've lost my mind. He may be right.

"Why are you stealing my blankets?"

Norman and I cut our stare off short, and I turn to Bucky. "We found Jumare Washington in your sugarcane field. We're trying to get him warm."

Bucky lowers the blade to his thigh as his mouth drops open. "Jumare was in my cane field?"

"Yes."

Bucky sits heavily on the edge of his bed. "It stormed last night."

"Bucky, blankets."

"Oh man, yeah." He stands and looks down at the knife in his hand as if to wonder how it got there. He sets it on the nightstand and moves toward Norman and me.

"I keep them in the storage room bedroom."

"Where is he!" Aduwa's voice reverberates through the house.

"You should catch Aduwa before he does something we'll all regret."

∞ ∞ ∞

Bucky's concern for Jumare, genuine and complete, confirms to me he had nothing to do with what took place with the teenager. Sure, a real mastermind criminal might have been able to fake his concern. But Bucky, addled by the copious amounts of drugs he has taken, is no mastermind. If that man had a brilliant thought, it would die of loneliness.

It all makes him an effortless read for my improving "gifts."

Unfortunately, my impressions of the man's character brook no favor with Aduwa. He and Norman restrain Bucky to turn him over when the authorities arrive.

It is understandable. In the world of science and logic, all details point toward Bucky. Still, much science was once a mystery. That is why an open mind is of the utmost importance. Aduwa does not currently have an open mind.

Aduwa also insists on calling the life flight helicopter to take Jumare to the emergency room. Given that his nephew looks like he recently completed a three-year stint in a POW camp, I can understand why.

But the injuries were inflicted by magic. For that reason, the emergency room is not the best course of action.

Thankfully, before I am forced to object to the driven man's decision, Gramma informs him he will not call for the helicopter. She understands what Laila and I already know. What happened to Jumare, conventional medicine will not help. To take him to the emergency room would only give cause to alarm folks about some dreadful, unknown virus.

Now that we saved him, or Jumare saved himself from the magical spell, lots of rest is what he needs to improve his condition. Fortunately, he has Gramma, who specializes in caring for her family.

∞ ∞ ∞

Gramma sets about the task of healing her entire family after the traumatic events of the day. According to her rules, we are family now that we've broken bread together. She lavishes her tremendous gratitude on us through her cooking.

Who would have ever thought that chicken and beans could be so delicious? Of course, besides the fact that Gramma cooks everything with love, I am so hungry after the events of today that I'm not surprised I'm making a pig of myself.

Laila makes it a point to henpeck Jumare about eating the soup Gramma prepared for him. If there were any doubt about the magic versus "real" injuries to him, the fact he is already filling back in speaks volumes.

Still, what needs to be speaking is Jumare. He looks less bewildered but is yet to be able to communicate with us.

The magic used on him has put him through a trauma that may remain long after he has physically healed.

It isn't as much that his physical being wasted away. His spiritual essence was being sucked out from inside of him.

Fortunately, because he is young and essence recovers quickest in loving environments, I am sure he will return to his familiar ways in a few days—hopefully with a new respect for things of a paranormal nature and Gramma's warnings.

As happy as Gramma, Laila, Trisha, and I are that our mission of bringing Jumare safely home is done, Aduwa is livid.

He is not satisfied with the knowledge that Jumare has returned and will make a full recovery. Aduwa is out for retribution. He is consumed with when Bucky will be prosecuted for his crime. His negativity lowers the spirit of Gramma's home, and she sends Aduwa to his house to be angry alone.

I am concerned for Trisha's well-being. Since we found Jumare and were worried that he would die, she has been quieter than usual, and her coloring has never improved.

It gives me an idea. "Laila, do y'all have beaches people go to here?"

"Do we have beaches?" She laughs. "We're on an island. Besides, why do you think you can't throw a rock without hitting a beachside mansion here?"

I shrug.

"I'm told we have some of the most beautiful beaches in the world," Gramma says. "Of course, they're the only ones I've ever seen. But that is what folks say."

"I know it's too soon because we just found Jumare today, but could you give us directions? I would love for Trisha and me to see your beach."

"I'll take you if you want."

"Oh, I can do it. I know you want to stay here with Jumare."

"That is a wonderful idea. You should take your friends, Laila. You don't ever have any fun."

Laila shoots Gramma a sideways glance. "I have plenty of fun." She smiles at me. "But I want to take you to the beach to show my appreciation."

"Are you sure? I really don't want to put you out."

"No, I insist."

"Thank you."

I sit back and smile like the Cheshire cat. What a glorious day. I helped return a missing boy to his family. I am full as a tick, and I will be able to see the purported most beautiful beaches in the world tomorrow.

I am the luckiest girl in the world.

Chapter 28

Once you've been to the sugar-white beaches of the Gulf Coast, few will ever match their beauty. Still, whoever told Gramma that the beaches of Turtle Key are the most beautiful in the world could be forgiven. Turtle Key is likely the most beautiful beach they've ever seen if they haven't visited the Gulf Coast. However, they hold a solid second place with the unblemished shoreline and the intriguing jungle behind us. It gives our little adventure a Robinson Crusoe vibe to it.

Gramma has been sweet enough to pack us a picnic lunch. If Trisha's sunscreen holds out, we will make a day of it.

Laila shows us her skill with a boogie board. I watch Trisha temporarily master it before collecting a scraped elbow and a partially sprained wrist. That convinces me to make beach towel surfing on the sand my sport today.

After lunch, we lie out under the sail tent. Before I realize I'm sleepy, I conk out.

Waking up from my cat nap, I find Laila on her back with her mouth parted open and Trisha lying on her tummy, her head tilted toward me. Laila's heavy mouth breathing combines with Trisha's whistling snores in a most disconcerting racket causing me to giggle. Bless it.

The thought of returning to my slumber is impossible, not solely due to the racket of my companions. Something nibbles under my skin, alerting me to a change in the paranormal currents.

I scan the beach, finding it not as deserted as I thought. A woman—her head and body concealed by a silky, green-and-black flowing material, walks away from us. Other than the solitary woman, we are alone on the beach.

How cool is it to have your own secluded beach?

The sun slides toward the horizon; I know it is late afternoon.

Taking a stroll alone along the beach seems like a beautiful idea. I glance over at my cousin and our new best friend. As much as I'd like to, I don't want to be rude and wake them.

I sigh and wiggle my butt to make a deeper hole in the sand while grabbing another towel to roll up and put under my neck. It allows me to better view the white-capped waves breaking against the shore as I watch them between my feet.

Don't get me wrong, lying here with the kiss of salt in the air is absolutely delectable. Still, there is an antsiness to my condition that a long stroll exploring the shoreline would help immensely.

I am so thankful Trisha called me when I was stranded with no plan in Baltimore. Of course, I wish the awful thing that happened to Jumare wasn't what precipitated our invite to this paradise. Still, the missing family member condition of the Washington family disengaged me from my life drama. It has helped me change my perspective and examine my circumstances more effectively—with less emotion.

Now I realize I was attracted to Lee, but I never did, nor would I, genuinely love the man. As much as men hate to hear a woman say—*it's not you, it's me*—in this case, it is the undeniable truth.

There is nothing not to like about Lee. How many people would love to have a spouse who could set them up for financial independence, dote on them, and make them feel special? Let's not forget to mention providing unbelievable sexual pleasures in bed.

Yes. I am obviously spoiled beyond any salvation. If Lee Darby isn't marriage material, I need to quit searching.

The curious thing is that initially, I had that thought as a temper tantrum. Sort of like, *fine, I'll take my ball and go home*, only to feign leaving. Or if I do leave, just show up the next day to play as if nothing ever happened the day before. I've never been convinced I could stop looking for "my man," at least not for more than the prerequisite few weeks to sulk about the last breakup.

But the more I think about it, why do I need a guy? Why have I been so eager to find someone? I no longer care for the perpetual state of serial monogamy while constantly measuring if the man I am with that week is marriage material.

It's simply exhausting.

I often ask myself, "Why do I look at every man as if he is a potential lifelong mate." I now realize that my mind was twisted into conformity somewhere along the line.

Understandably, this happened to me, given that my parents —my first role models—met as children, married in their early twenties, and are still to this day inseparable. Talk about setting the bar extremely high for their children.

Then there is the fact I am getting older. At twenty-seven, I'm getting to that age where people ask passive-aggressively, "You're not engaged?" Many of my friends are already married, and several have children.

Why shouldn't I be behind them on the relationship measuring stick? They graduated with the highest degree they wanted five years ago. Meanwhile, I went back for a second helping of knowledge dump and have spent the last two years working with my uncle.

I know this now. Mama met Lee again by chance. She thought he would be a great match and introduced us.

Mama's belief about Lee would only make her intelligent. He would have made an excellent match for any "normal" girl. This proves Mama is becoming forgetful as she obviously failed to remember she has anything but a normal daughter.

Still, the point is that Mama believes it is time for me to marry and went through the trouble of hunting down a suitable life partner for her daughter. Being the pleaser I am, I spent a year with Lee because I believed it was what I was supposed to do.

Wow. And I thought arranged marriages disappeared in the Western Hemisphere.

Rising to a sitting position, I stretch and grab my toes. I hold the leg stretch for several seconds and enjoy the slow burn.

I shouldn't abandon my friends for a walk, but I am now drawn to the ocean.

It's unusual. Mainly because of my vivid imagination. The one where I have a leg torn off by a shark or a Portuguese man o' war sticks on my face, scarring my complexion for the rest of my life as it pumps its chemicals into my skin. Still, besides all the mortal danger of the activity, I have the urge to go swimming.

I crawl off of my towel, careful not to make any noise that might wake my companions. Once clear of the tent, I high-step it down to the water, reveling in the knowledge that I am young and free.

"Fudge!" Just stepping my feet into the tide, I darn near freeze. It's so blasted cold.

I look over my shoulder, and the girls have not stirred. The heavy sound of the surf and the wind must have carried my curse word away.

Something catches my eye past the breakers. A yellow float bobs up and down, disappearing behind each swelling wave. It must mark either a crab or a spiny lobster trap.

My competitive streak bubbles up, and I set a goal. I'm going to swim out and touch the bobber. I size up the distance and put it at forty yards. Not too far. I could make that distance easily in the lake.

Still, with the tide working against me and the absolute need for a wetsuit to prevent hypothermia, it should be challenging enough.

And what does it prove if I swim to the marker? It's a game I've played all my life. Set a physical goal, like making a shot from half-court or throwing a rock at a bottle. If I complete the task successfully, I take it as a good omen that I will accomplish the life goal I wish for.

It's not the most truthful game since I choose the task. I have the freedom to set it as a challenge yet something I'm confident I can accomplish.

I set the prize. April May will no longer give a flying flip what other people think. I'll live as I see fit, regardless of the social norms. It is my life.

I smile, quite pleased with myself. If I live by my new creed of not giving a flip about what anyone else thinks I should be doing, I will live my best life and be the greatest success.

Pumped with the adrenaline of living my new, better version of life, I push deeper into the surf. A wave crashes against my midsection, exploding salt water and grit upward into my face.

"Mother of pearl, that's cold!"

Too late to wimp out now. My new life attitude is at stake. I dive under the next wave and open my eyes. The saltwater burns but quickly normalizes with the saline of my eyes.

I come up and pause with my teeth chattering from the cold. *Freestyle or breaststroke?* Something I should have planned out before hitting the water...

For no reason other than to loosen my spine, which went into paralysis when I dove into the frigid water, I choose breaststroke. I frog kick in synchronization with the pull of my arms and make some progress toward the yellow float.

Halfway to my goal, my energy leeches away. I better make quick work of it. I switch to free stroke and go into a sprint burn.

The idea is that I will get to the marker and then simply float back on the current afterward. That will require minimal energy for my return.

I'm so focused on the efficiency of my stroke that I am a yard past when I see the yellow float in my periphery of the splashing water. I stretch and pound the marker with my right fist, then raise my hands and scream in exaltation.

April May is officially a free woman. As Kat said, "I'm a tough broad." So, you better not mess with me.

The celebration ends quickly as my lungs are on fire, and I can't seem to suck in enough air. I roll onto my back, using the salt in the water and my curves to float.

The ocean's surface ebbs and flows as I listen to the breakers crashing against the shore increase in volume.

I'm exhausted, and every ounce of physical energy is spent. Still, I have miraculously normalized to the water's frigid temperature, enjoying the sun's warmth on my face and chest.

So peaceful.

The slow rock of the ocean—just me and the energy of this universe.

My stomach cramps violently, forcing me to curl into a fetal position. I know that's not wise, but this is as if somebody has run me through with a sword.

I lose buoyancy as I allow all the air to rush out of me and close into an oversized bowling ball. I somehow tilt to the side and sink toward the ocean floor.

Knowing I must overcome the intense shooting pain and somehow get to the shore, I try to straighten my body so I might swim. My back ignores my brain's commands, and I remain bent like a closed jackknife.

I continue to sink. The undercurrent swings me forward and back as I drop down, down until my hip rests on the sand.

Desperate, I attempt to unfold myself again. It brings another bout of pain, like a firebrand burning in my gut. The last oxygen-depleted bubbles escape my mouth as I scream from the agony coursing through me.

Hands grab both of my arms, and I am yanked to the surface that, seconds earlier, I believed I would never see again. I greedily suck in the air mixed with salt water that drips from my face.

"April, that's not funny!" Trisha yells too close to my face.

"Are you okay? Did you swallow any?"

Laila is asking me too many questions all at once. I can't process any of this as I finally have oxygen, but now I have a splitting headache.

"Oh my! She was really drowning."

"Come on. Let's get you to the shore," Laila says.

Between the girls tugging on me, the waves crashing into my back, and the cramps in my stomach causing my legs not to work correctly, I wonder if I've been saved from drowning, only to be mauled to death.

Laila and Trisha half carry, half drag me onto the shore, where they unceremoniously drop me as they collapse next to me. We sound like three faulty respirators as we try to catch our breath.

"Bless it, April!" Trisha sucks in another deep breath. "You know better than to go swimming by yourself."

I'd like to remind her that I am three times the swimmer she'll ever be since I was raised on the water and constantly competed with two older brothers. Still, it's all I can do to breathe right now and deal with the dull pain of the stabbing in my abdomen that is slowly lessening.

"The tide is not that strong today. Did you get a cramp?" Laila asks.

I want to give a long explanation. Instead, I must opt for pointing at my stomach. "Stabbing cramp." I choke out.

Laila purses her lips. "That's odd. We all ate the same thing."

She says what has already occurred to me. As much as I'd like to write this off as an unfortunate case of food poisoning, I've never felt anything like this pain before, and how it was so sudden gives me pause.

Trisha stands and extends her hand. I shake my head no.

"Give her a second," Laila says.

Trisha narrows her eyes as she places her hands on her hips.

I know she is aggravated with me. Partly because I scared

her. The other is I have managed to ruin a perfectly wonderful day. I might even feel bad about it if I thought I had brought this on. But this pain is unnatural.

Trisha looks back at the ocean, as if sizing up how far the buoy is. She places both hands over her forehead as a visor. "That's far enough out for a tiger shark to have taken a bite of you," she scolds.

I can't help it. A giggle bubbles up from inside me. Trisha is going to make the best helicopter mom ever.

"Oh no," she says as she trots into the knee-high surf and bends over. She stands back up, races over four more feet, and reaches out again. This time she comes up with whatever she is chasing.

I watch her in amusement as her focus shifts quickly from my near-death experience to something floating on the water that she feels the need to rescue from the surf. She grimaces as if picking up something incredibly nasty.

"Seaweed?"

She looks up from what is in her hand and wrinkles her nose in her all-too-familiar expression. "No. I thought it was a little girl's doll."

Trisha wades back toward us, her arms swinging left to right to keep her balance in the surf. She holds the object out with her thumb and forefinger as if touching it is too disgusting.

"Put it down!"

Laila's alarmed command causes me to jerk.

Trisha obeys and drops the item on the sand. She stands on her toes as her hands go into the air. "Oh Lord, what is it? What did I touch?"

Laila runs to her and grabs a piece of driftwood as she closes in. She stands over the object and flicks it onto the shore with the stick.

"I've never seen one in person."

"What is it?" I ask despite believing the information will give me the heebie-jeebies for a month.

"Dark magic."

Two words that by themselves are innocuous. Yet, in combination, they send an icicle straight up my spine.

"Oh, no way."

Laila tilts her head. "Yes way."

I want to move over to the group and join the inspection and the conversation. As I do, the pain renews in my ribs, and I clamp my arm and hand around it tightly.

"That looks like a pin," Trisha says.

As I take faltering steps toward her, Laila reaches down. Her hand pulls away from the doll in the sand. The pressure at my side releases, and I fall to my knees in gratitude. Laila notices my reaction, and her eyes open wide. She stands and scans the beach.

I do the same and see the woman I noticed earlier, three hundred yards off, walking into the forest. Laila is off like a flash. Her long legs turn up the sand as she closes the distance quickly.

"Laila, don't!" This is not the time to go blindly after someone who may be responsible. Whoever created the magic that had control of me is not only talented with their skill, but they also have a high degree of power.

"Should I go get her?" Trisha asks, looking as if she is a runner at the starting block.

"No. You call your dad and watch over the doll. I'll go get Laila."

Trisha looks at me as if I have lost my mind. I understand because there is no way I could run and catch up with Laila, given that my rib cage still aches.

I turn to walk toward the jungle and spot Laila coming in our direction. She waves her hand at me, signaling me to stay where I am. I'm not going to argue with that.

"Can this really work? I mean, how can a doll control someone?"

It's a fair question. One that rattles another factoid loose in my mind. For a likeness to affect its victim, it must be made with something personal from the target. Since I don't know anybody here other than people I trust, how in the world could this happen to me?

I check if my earrings are still on my earlobes. The zirconium studs I wear all the time unless I'm going on a date are still in place. I stare at the doll, wondering what could make it operational, how someone got it from me, and, most importantly, who.

"Whoever it was, they stepped into the woods and somehow left not a bit of a trail."

"Do you have any ideas who could have made this?"

Laila shakes her head. "Folks still secretly believe in dark magic. But it's been frowned upon for generations."

"What about Miss Ade calling Bucky an obeah."

Laila rolls her eyes. "That's only Ade stirring up stuff. You'd learn to take anything she says with a grain of salt."

"I think somebody is still practicing."

"Practicing? I'd say they're a master at it. They darn near drowned you."

We lock our eyes. I can't believe how insensitive Laila is being. She hints at a smile, and we burst into laughter. It feels good. I needed a laugh desperately.

"Seriously. We'll take this back in one of the leftover grocery bags and let Gramma take a look at it. She can tell us something about it. If not her, Ade can."

"It seems like so few people have access to me that it should be easy to limit who could have done this." The idea of someone collecting something from me without my knowledge is creepy and leaves me feeling violated.

"That is why I want Gramma to inspect the doll. She might find the personal item that we're not seeing."

It's a sound plan, and since I know Gramma has more abilities than she lets onto, I hope she can identify what was used to tie me to the doll since it is my best chance of identifying who tried to drown me.

I am certain of one thing: since Bucky is in jail today, Aduwa is barking up the wrong tree. Jumare's kidnapper is still on the loose, and Bucky has been wrongfully accused.

Chapter 29

"Humph," Gramma grunts as she moves her nose closer to the voodoo doll on the kitchen table. She works the tweezers at the neck of the likeness, then picks the straw figure up while making a circling motion around its neck.

Gramma holds the tweezers above her head toward the hooded light above us. "Look familiar?" she asks.

A long strand of dirty-blonde hair floats on the light cross breeze through the home. "You young folk need to be careful where you put your hair."

I raise my hand in exasperation. "But who? When?"

Gramma removes her glasses and sighs. "I have no clue. Granny Hattie was the last person to use the old magic on the island. She has been dead for nearly fifty years."

"But you must agree that somebody is practicing the dark arts again with what happened to Jumare this week and me today."

Gramma grimaces as she pushes up from her chair. She walks over to the twenty-four-quart stock pot of gumbo simmering on the stove. "What I know is you and your family need to leave in the morning. I've enjoyed the visit, and I'll be eternally grateful that you returned Jumare to me. But it's too dangerous here for you now."

"Gramma, I can't leave when this is going on. Who is to say

that tomorrow it's not Laila or you that this person hurts."

"That will be our responsibility to take care of. I see now that involving mainlanders in our business was a mistake. I'm sorry I put you at risk."

"You can't mean that. I'm not going."

"April…" Norman warns.

"No." I glare at Norman, then return my focus to Gramma as she sets the wooden spoon on a plate. "Listen, I understand that you may have some reservations. And I don't want to step on anyone's toes. But I also can't live with myself if I might help in some small way now that I've met you."

"Young people. You're always trying to save stuff—keep everything as it is—not realizing everything changes."

"… I don't understand."

"Exactly. You're all out there fighting to preserve. Preserve what? Young folks wanna save the island, to keep the culture, but then they move away."

"Gramma, let's not get into that again," Aduwa says.

She holds her hand up to Aduwa. "Young man, don't you dare interrupt me. My bones are aching, and I've been walking on this earth way too long for you to be trying to stop me from speaking my mind. Now I know you think your heart is in the right place when you talk to the county mayor about getting us police officers or trash pickup. But what does it matter if the only people left on the island are old folks who will be gone in thirty years anyway? What do you think you're saving?"

"Our heritage," Laila says.

"Heritage is lived. It's not in a museum. Do you plan to live here, Laila?"

"On the weekends."

"Like your uncle." Gramma shakes her head vehemently. "We are the culture. Not just the land. Yes, the taxes are increasing quickly because of the property value rising with the white people building their beach houses; that's a problem. And I'm not saying that it won't make me eventually sell my property to them because I can't afford those taxes. But if y'all aren't going to live here, who cares."

"Gramma…" Aduwa says with a tone of aggravation.

She picks up the wooden spoon and steps toward him, waving it in the air. "Boy, I gave you good warning that you would not interrupt me."

Aduwa leans back in his chair. "Sorry, ma'am."

She moves over to her chair and sits heavily on it. She slaps the wooden spoon in front of her as she leans forward. "Y'all done got my blood pressure up."

"I'm sorry. I just want to help."

"I know, sweetie. I know you do."

My nose tingles as my eyes turn liquid. I would like to know if my grandmothers feel the same way about how I wanted to move away from Guntersville for a better opportunity.

You can't blame a young person for moving to put themselves in the best possible situation for success. Like my grandmothers, Gramma wouldn't begrudge Laila and Aduwa for wanting to improve their lot.

Still, as I watch her and how it works her up. I realize it must be a bitter pill to swallow. I'm sure when she was raising her children, she hoped, and even assumed, they would all stay one big, happy family on the island for all time.

"There's nothing left to be solved. We have our man."

I favor Aduwa a droll smile. "Then explain the goofy doll that almost drowned me today."

"If it is magical, I'm sure Bucky placed it there earlier, and when you got close, it took effect." Aduwa sits back, appearing pleased with his explanation.

I look at Gramma and raise my eyebrows.

"That's not how this works," she grumbles.

Aduwa shrugs. "Maybe he has an accomplice. If he does, I'm sure the sheriffs will get it out of him."

"The sheriffs aren't even going to understand the situation since it's dealing with something they don't want to believe," Laila interjects.

Aduwa stands and pushes his chair under the table. "I've

got some paperwork to tend to. I'll see you tomorrow. We have the perpetrator in custody. Everyone can rest easy, and Norman and his family can return to Savannah and enjoy the rest of their vacation." Aduwa kisses Gramma on the forehead. "Thank you for the gumbo." He straightens and waits for her reply. She doesn't. He nods his head and turns to the door.

Chapter 30

We settle into Laila's room. I take the cot while Trisha and Laila sleep on the two twin beds in the room.

It's impossible for me to sleep. My mind is spinning with all the different possibilities.

I can't explain why I am convinced Bucky wasn't involved in Jumare's abduction. Jumare was found on Bucky's property. Bucky also has convenient access to any number of drugs that might have aided in the kidnapping of Jumare. And there is Miss Ade's testimony that she saw Jumare, and when asking him where he was going at such a late hour, he said Bucky had something for him.

Of course, Ade's version of events would be easier to confirm if Jumare could speak about his kidnapping. Instead, it is as if his mind was wiped clean by amnesia from when he said goodbye to Laila at the ferry's dock the day he disappeared.

Aduwa is confident it is Bucky. While not nearly as vocal in his accusation, Norman appears ready to accept that same truth.

My gut tells me Bucky is an unwitting participant. And I've come to know not to discount my gut feelings.

True, they can be capricious and ambiguous. Still, they are an excellent indicator of odd or supernatural things.

And then there were today's events at the beach. It's

becoming apparent that Laila was right to chase after the shrouded figure. That could be one thing that Aduwa is correct about. Bucky would have to have an accomplice to have enacted the voodoo ambush on me today. Especially since he is cooling his heels in the Jacksonville jail.

If we catch that person, we may be closer to putting an end to the danger. "Laila, does Bucky have a sibling or a girlfriend?"

I wait in the shadowed moonglow room. Rolling to my side, I squint to see if Laila's eyes are open. I only see the silhouette of her face.

"Laila? Are you awake?"

Still nothing. I was in Bucky's home, so I try to recall walking through the hallways and living area to remember any family pictures I viewed on the walls.

Bless it. All I recall is the dark, faux-wood paneling as I hurried through the home, searching for a blanket to help warm Jumare. I wasn't committing the surroundings to my memory as if I was investigating a potential crime scene.

Not that it matters in the greater scope of things, but Gramma is wrong. Of course, I would never tell her to her face. This is of a supernatural nature, and given my high skill set, I could be helpful even though I'm learning as I go regarding this specific magic technique.

It's their issue, and you're no longer invited, April.

That's the truth. Even though I don't like it, I understand the Washington family's feelings. I can only imagine how I would react if someone came into Guntersville and told me how best to prepare for Austin's expected counterattack. I can't say that I would be as charitable as Gramma has been toward me.

Our saving grace at this point is that Aduwa requested Norman's assistance in the first place. From Gramma's point of view, we have served our purpose. But she should let me finish the job now that I'm on the trail.

Get over yourself, April.

Yes, I'm overthinking this, but it's just a function of my overactive curiosity. Anyone in their right mind would gladly accept the permission to leave and return to their sorely needed vacation with the excellent company of their cousin.

Me? No, I've got to continue picking at the scab until I figure out what is wrong on the island and bring it to a satisfactory conclusion. All the while, I'm simply irritating the family who has been kind enough to open up their home and allow me a glimpse of their fascinating culture.

Granny always says the worst guest is the one who overstays their welcome. I mean not to be that guest.

Frustrated, I pull a pillow over my head and clamp it tight. Of course, covering my ears won't do anything for all the noises. Those are inside my head.

∞∞∞

My skin tingles, and the scent of ozone fills the night air. I bury my nose deeper into my pillow, replacing the smell with that of fresh lilac fabric softener.

The haze in my mind begins to disintegrate. Ozone? Why would there be ozone in the air?

Possibly a lightning strike.

I slide the pillow covering my face to the side. There is no rain falling outside. That kills my original hypothesis unless it's an incoming thunderstorm preceded by thunderclouds and lightning strikes.

But the scent is dense with a high tang that I can taste on my tongue.

I smack my tongue on the roof of my mouth. Then run the tip across my teeth.

Gramma's gumbo was delicious, but she must use a lot of spices I'm not used to. There's a funky taste setting up in my mouth.

It would be best to ignore the need to brush my teeth and fall back to sleep. Instead, I swallow harder and more often, making me wake up even more.

Fudge. I'll have to brush my teeth now, or I'll never fall back asleep. I'll need to gargle with hydrogen peroxide, too.

Rolling over, I'm startled by the bright blue glow illuminating the room. It's rare to see a moon glow blue, and even rarer for it to be so incredibly bright.

That is odd. I swivel and peer out the window, then return my attention to Laila. It's not from the moon outside, whose illumination is clearly silvery white.

While it's mildly disconcerting, I'm not alarmed because I know Laila has paranormal powers. She may be experiencing a dream where she is marshaling her forces. If her dream requires her to use her magic, it might make sense that she is creating the glowing blue, transparent shield around her.

Huh. I'd like to know if I ever do that when I sleep. Lee never mentioned it when we were together. Of course, Lee always slept the sleep of the dead. The rest of the time, I was in my apartment by myself.

Intrigued, I set my bare feet on the wooden-slat floor while contemplating how disrespectful it would be for me to investigate further. On a scale of one to ten, ten being the rudest, I would venture it to be a nine and a half. I would be livid if I woke to a friend staring at me while I slept.

As if there is nothing creepy about that. How would I attempt to explain that one away if I were caught?

I'll get the opportunity to figure it out if she wakes. I can't resist, and I walk across the rough floor.

Yes, It's Laila creating the magical field cocooning her. The closer I get, the more intense the thrum of energy emanating from her becomes. A stream of chaotic, colorful energy flecks fly by my face toward her at an incredible pace.

How I pray that I don't do the same thing when I sleep. If I'm ever with a guy again, and they are unaware of my supernatural powers, I might give him a heart attack.

I can't begin to imagine being normal and waking up to a partner who glows blue while shooting off little bits of energy that sting like static shocks. Growing up in a paranormal family it's only interesting. But if a person had no clue that such a thing could happen, it would have to scare the bejesus out of them.

It would be an unfortunate way for a promising relationship to end.

I'm grinning broadly as I watch her. It reminds me of how Mama complains about Daddy snoring while he sleeps. I've heard him before. It's like little bitty baby snores. I don't know how that could possibly be a big deal.

But Laila's snores sound like she is sucking on a soda through a straw. Slurp, slurp, slurp.

Bless it. How does Laila make that noise while she is asleep? It's all too funny.

I reach out to touch her blue energy field. Just because I can't seem to help myself.

My finger pierces the blue glow at her collarbone.

The magical blue field rises from her body. A monstrous face comprised of a pug nose, pointed ears that stand up from his scalp, and long fangs protruding over his swollen lips, turns toward me and snaps.

I step back, trip, and try to scream. Nothing comes out.

The blue specter leaps from Laila's bed toward me. Landing inches from my face, it opens its mouth wide enough to shove a human head inside as talons elongate from his hands as he holds them out wide. The specter is only three feet tall, but its bare feet are four times larger than the usual proportion for a human, reminiscent of a baby gerbil. Its stomach hangs, round and heavy, and gravity tugs at it as if at full gestation.

Frozen in fear, I can only take in every aspect of the grotesque vision. As if sensing I do not have the wherewithal to defend myself, the blue shadow beast leaps onto my cot and hurdles through the open window.

Knocked out of my catatonic state by the incredible sight, I move to the window and watch the beast run across the street toward Miss Ade's home.

Chapter 31

My scream is only delayed. A mewing, bloodcurdling cry emits from me like an alarm, waking Trisha and Laila as I hunt for my shoes.

Without question, they jump out of bed, gathering their robes and shoes too.

Pulling on our shoes, we run through the living room, hitting the back door at a full-out run. We reach the porch and slap open the screen door.

We must warn Miss Ade. She might be a cantankerous old cuss, but that grotesque monster... I would feel awful if anything happened to the old woman in her sleep.

I cringe, wondering what would have happened if we hadn't been spending the night with Laila. Or if I had been calm and fallen asleep like I needed to.

I take Miss Ade's stairs two at a time and throw the screen door open. "Miss Ade!" I scream through the glass pane as I beat on the door. "Adeline, wake up!"

"April, I'm going around back." Trisha's announcement makes me uneasy, and I think of asking Laila to go with her. At least somebody with paranormal abilities should be with Trisha. As I steal a glance, I see that even though Laila has followed us, she is about to collapse from exhaustion.

I can't worry about that right now and beat on the door.

"Ade, you're in danger!"

Laila walks over to the two windows next to the rocking chair and leans against the wall between them.

"Ade!"

Laila leans over and tugs on the window. It slides up easily. The open entrance to Ade's home gives me pause. I want to save her if the blue specter ran into her house. Similarly, I don't need the old woman getting any more upset with me than she already is, even though I'm not long for this island.

Laila seems to understand and crawls over the sill and tumbles through the window. Her energy reserves are obviously depleted to a dangerous level.

"Ade?" Laila's voice is barely above her talking volume.

I feel the need to help her and scream through the window. "Miss Ade, wake up!"

Laila flips the lights on in the living room. I yell again for Ade as Laila walks toward the kitchen.

"Is my house on fire?" Ade says as she appears in the doorway, pulling on a housecoat. A plastic bonnet covers her head.

"No, ma'am." Laila doubles over as she attempts to catch her breath.

"Laila, are you okay?"

I take that as an opportunity to enter the house and swing my legs over the windowsill. "Hi, Miss... Adeline. You didn't see anything odd in your house."

She scowls at me pointedly with her yellowed, bloodshot eyes. "You mean besides you?"

Chagrin flushes over me as my ears heat up. "Yes, ma'am."

Ade shifts the bonnet on her head. "No. I was busy getting my beauty sleep."

Well, if this isn't uniquely awkward. I favor Ade with a nervous smile as I give thanks to the Lord that she isn't armed with a shotgun. "We're terribly sorry for bothering you."

A violent knock reverberates through the kitchen from the back door. Laila tenses into a guarded posture.

"Hello!"

I let out an exasperated breath. "It's Trisha."

"What sort of Tomfoolery are y'all up to?"

I move toward the kitchen and realize it's not my place to be invading this woman's home anymore as Laila holds up her hand. "I'll give Trisha the all's clear."

Laila disappears into the kitchen, Ade watching her back with a frown before she turns her attention to me. "Ain't been nothing but trouble since you've been on the island. I didn't think there was anything worse than those white vacationers. But you proved me wrong."

My face heats even more inexplicably as I didn't realize I could be any more embarrassed than I already am. "Yes, ma'am. I truly am sorry."

"I don't need you to be sorry. I need you to get gone. We have been fine on this island for decades. We don't need help from you."

"I understand."

Chapter 32

Gramma's mind about an extended stay of company changed when we explained to her what took place with Laila. After eating the breakfast of sausage gravy and biscuits Gramma prepared, Laila appears to be recouping some of her vitality.

We sit on the front porch watching the hive of activity this morning. The sheriff's department from the mainland sent deputies to assist a handful of islanders as they check for the two missing people.

The sheriff, like Aduwa, is convinced that Bucky is in the wholesale business of killing folks. Using my legal training—even though Bucky had the opportunity—for the life of me, I can't think of a motive. Even less so after talking to Jumare and realizing there is nothing for Bucky to have gained unless he is some sort of sick sadist, which is always possible.

Trisha and I continue to sip our coffee. The salty breeze from the ocean blends with the pungent scent of the nearby marsh. The sun lights the vegetation surrounding the porch into a brilliant green.

I watch Miss Ade taking a morning stroll. Her silky yellow dress lifts serenely on the breeze. She turns toward the commotion where the searchers are and disappears down the side of Bucky's cane field.

After we scared the tar out of her last night with the false alarm, I'm surprised she is out so early. Either way, I hope I don't cross her path today. It is all so embarrassing.

"Do you want to go for a swim in a bit?" Trisha asks.

I pause the coffee mug halfway to my lips. I shoot Trisha a sideways glance. "You're not serious."

She straightens her posture as her eyes widen. "Oh, I forgot."

The screen door opens, drawing our attention. Laila steps out in a full-length, brilliant-red dress.

"Nice dress."

"Thank you," she whispers as she sits in the last rocking chair.

"Seems a little warm for a dress with that long of a hem, though."

She favors me with a droll stare. "It keeps the ghosts away."

"A long hem?"

She rolls her eyes and takes a sip of her coffee.

"I just never heard that before."

"Not the hem, silly. The color red."

Huh. Just goes to show you learn something new every day. I've never heard that from either one of my grandmothers. Still, I may significantly change my wardrobe if we don't encounter ghosts today.

"Are you feeling better this morning?" Trisha asks.

"Yeah, like a car hit me instead of an eighteen-wheeler."

I smirk at Trisha. She mouths "what?"

We sit in companionable silence, enjoying our coffee and watching the activity at Bucky's.

"Do you think they'll find them?" Trisha asks.

"Not where they're looking. I can't believe those fools still think Bucky is involved."

"Your uncle is an influential man on the island."

"Yes. I've just never known Aduwa to disconnect from logic. After what happened last night, how can they think Bucky had anything to do with those disappearances?"

We watch as people walk in and out of Bucky's house. For the life of me, I pray they don't find anybody. The crime scene is so messed up now everybody on the island would be a suspect.

"I want to thank you again for saving me last night."

I scoff, "Well, if I saved you, it was only because you rescued me at the beach. I suppose we can call it even now."

"Sounds good."

The deputies open Bucky's barn, and the islanders helping with the search move items from inside.

Something has been annoying me ever since we found Jumare. Only this morning during breakfast, it occurred to me what has been sticking in my craw all this time.

While the girls and I stood at the edge of the sugarcane field the other day, it was as if a tidal wave of magic rushed toward us. That was followed by the small freaky frog, which had to have been of some sort of magical origins, followed by the Shetland pony-sized frog that ate the first frog.

Then, unexpectedly, we were in a random migratory flight of black witch moths again flying at us at the specific moment they decided to flee the field. Lastly, a walking, unconscious Jumare comes stumbling out of the sugarcane field and falls directly into my arms.

Coincidence? I think not.

It had to be magic. There is no way all of those things appeared spontaneously, including Jumare, who was walking dead, to come toward us.

Initially, I thought the magical entity I felt did that—pushed the whacky cacophony of living organisms toward our group. But I can't understand what they would have gained from the unsettling events.

It is possible the first two items, the toads and then the flock of moths, were meant to scare us away. But to give us Jumare? How does that benefit a witch or a warlock who has gone through the trouble of kidnapping him to sap his life force?

After last night's attack, I have no doubt that whoever is behind this is bent on taking the life force from others for their own benefit to power up. Especially those from magical bloodlines.

The supernatural criminal person did not cause those things at the sugarcane. It was me. My wishful thoughts to find Jumare extracted him and every other magic item from the sugarcane field.

That is a sobering thought. Mark it down as one more magical skill I'll have to learn to manage in the future. *Wonderful.*

"Does anybody want a refill?"

I favor Trisha with a smile for her characteristic of always thinking of others first. "Thank you, but I believe if I have any more caffeine, I'll end up scratching my skin off."

The screen door slaps shut behind her as she goes for her refill.

"She isn't touched, is she?" Laila asks.

"I think she has a little niggle of something in her. But no, nothing like yours."

Laila has the thousand-yard stare. "Lucky girl."

"Very lucky indeed."

It's like looking at one of those visual puzzles where suddenly someone points out that the word fly is in it, and you can't unsee it. Something suddenly jumps out to me in the sugarcane field behind Bucky's property, where we found Jumare, and I point.

"Laila, why does the sugarcane do that there?"

"Do what?"

I stand and walk toward the plastic covering of the porch, placing my face near it as I study the field's topography. "Look in about three hundred yards from the edge of the field. Does it look like a portion is significantly taller than the rest?"

Laila grunts as she stands. She moves next to me. "That is odd."

"Is there like a hill or a mound out there?"

"If there is, I've never noticed it before. And I've been looking out from this screened porch my entire life."

The wind buffets through the corners of the plastic

covering, blowing my hair back. I stare at the round, six-foot wide, flag-like growth toward the back center of the sugarcane field. Its presence makes my tummy bubble. I wish I had not noticed it.

Laila says, "You're gonna make us go check it out, aren't you?"

"I'm sorry."

Chapter 33

Worst idea ever.

Between the mosquitoes biting and the uneven ground at the sugarcane bases poking up through the rich earth, conspiring to twist my ankle with every step, I sense my interest wavering. Uncovering the secret of the extra-tall sugarcane seems less important with every passing second. But now that we're one hundred yards into the sugarcane, we should investigate, as it's as far to get back as it is to carry on forward.

I have countless abrasions on my thighs and an annoying narrow cut on my hand. Those only add to my aggravation when I feel the first hint of energy being organized by a magical spell.

Still in her full-length red dress, Laila grabs my arm, and I stop. I watch as she turns her head so her left ear points forward.

"What are we doing?" Trisha whispers.

I tried to convince Trisha to stay behind precisely because of her propensity to ask questions at the most inopportune time, like right now, when I'm thinking and do not have a satisfactory answer to her reasonable question. But she insisted, and it seemed too mean of me to tell her that she couldn't come.

"Do you hear it?"

I lowered my defenses entirely before we entered the field so I might feel or hear anything that wanted to make itself known. Still, I don't sense anything.

"No."

Laila shakes her head. "Maybe it wasn't anything."

I doubt that's the case. Given what already tumbled out of this cane field the other day, I would be surprised if she didn't hear voices.

I walk forward and hesitate. Peaches. I have no clue which way is the correct direction. I had lined up with the sun when we began, but a heavy cloud cover has rolled in since.

A faint murmur echoes in my mind. Similar to a small creek in the distance. The sound is intermittently broken up into one-second segments, ten seconds apart. I turn to my left at a thirty-five-degree angle and pick up my pace.

Swatting cane stalks to the left and right, I make my way quickly through the dense growth. I'm confident I will end up with many more cuts than would be the case if I took my time. Still, I am driven by a burning desire to finish this task and figure out what we are dealing with.

I hear Laila's grunt of exertion behind me, and while I feel bad because I know she is physically drained, I can't stop. Trisha is mumbling "Mom approved" cuss words as we go.

The voices grow louder, forming a continuous hum of imperceptible speech as a strange, pungent odor invades the air around us.

"Wait! I hear them now," Laila says.

Hear … but hear what is the question. Have we found the two people that are missing? Or are we running blindly into something dangerous?

I am beyond caring since I am on the hunt now. My blood pressure pumps in my ears as my adrenaline spikes. Locking my jaw, I set my expression with the intense determination that consumes my focus. Yet on the inside, I feel an inappropriate giggle of anticipation may gurgle out of me.

As I sprint through the cane, I've thrown all caution to the wind. Each step throws me side to side as my feet find flat purchase against the cane stalk bases.

The dismaying stench of the marsh continues to build with every breath I suck in. I can taste the decay on my tongue. My left foot sinks unexpectedly into the soil. As I try to regain my balance with my right foot, I trip on a stone and fall pell-mell into a sugarcane stalk, catching it rudely against my shoulder and chin.

Dag nab it! That hurts!

Rolling to my butt, I check my collarbone to confirm I didn't break it. With my bones intact despite feeling like I have been struck by a tree, I check my chin for blood and curse at the splotch of hot, crimson fluid on my palm. I must have sliced the tarnation out of the bottom of my chin to bleed this much.

I scramble to all fours to ask Laila and Trisha to look at the damage I have done. They are busy projectile vomiting their breakfast of biscuits and gravy.

Chapter 34

It's hard to shake the heebie-jeebies when I know my left foot went through a dead man's chest and my right foot kicked a woman's head off. This is my new reality.

I took a hot shower—twice—but I still feel filthy. Trisha lost everything she had eaten on this trip and has since gone to bed. Laila, perfectly understandable given the turn of events since we showed up, appears as if she has developed a debilitating case of PTSD.

I could be there and probably should be in that situation, except my butt is chapped. Somebody—with magical abilities —is wreaking havoc on this already fragile community. I haven't a clue who. They could be a wealthy, white developer like Miss Ade claims. Or a crazy supernatural person who took a ride on the ferry one day, intending to murder people in the most gruesome manner possible.

What I know is that a supernatural is harvesting people's energy, which makes me assume they are stealing the life force to level up. I might have powerful skills, but messing with somebody actively trying to power up does not seem wise.

If not me, who? Laila's power is basic animism knowledge and the ability to hear through the veil. Gramma, I suspect her powers are more significant, but let's be honest about it, a good old fashioned family argument can tucker her out.

Which leaves me. I must figure this out and find a way to end it.

Awesome. I'm all pumped to charge a hill and protect this unique community against evil magic. The only trouble with that is I still need to figure out who is responsible for these grotesque acts.

And that aggravates the stew out of me. How is it that I am stumped after the hundreds of legal and paranormal mysteries I have helped solve?

I could make the excuse that I'm not in my element, except for the fact that every one of my paranormal events has been away from my comfort zone and home.

I am frustrated that I thought I would be relaxing on the beach. Instead, I am being measured and found unworthy of this mystery. It's aggravating that Norman has put me in this position.

After all the free dinners, free trips, and sage advice he has given me, the one time he asks me for help, I can't deliver. It wounds my pride that I can't manage a single reciprocating favor.

For once, I thought I could be a giver instead of a taker. I loathe feeling like some pubescent child with my hand out asking for the next treat. I want to contribute and move our relationship into a new dawn. I need it to become a peer-to-peer—adult to adult—connection. I respect him so much, and I am hungry for him to know I appreciate him and that I'm not a charity case that has leeched to him because of familial ties.

Norman has always been gracious and never hinted at any resentment toward my eager acceptance of his gifts. That's because Trisha and I love each other's company, and he loves his daughter unconditionally. If something delights Trisha, Norman will make it happen.

But that is the dynamic of their relationship. It is separate from how I want to improve my belief of how Norman views me.

I stand and walk outside. The dank air assaults my nostrils

and only adds to my deteriorating disposition. I crumple onto one of the metal seats on the porch.

This should be easy to solve. Eh, if it's a wealthy land developer outside the circle of people I have been visiting with, it would be more challenging to solve than I think.

But the idea of a white developer running rampant and murdering people feels as improbable as Bucky killing folks he knows.

What would a developer have to gain? If they want Bucky's property, wouldn't it be easier to kill Bucky than frame him for murder?

Don't even get me started on Bucky. There is no chance in Hades that man could pull off three kidnappings. Then to hide two bodies in his field? He has killed a lot of brain cells, but that's stupid on too many levels.

Sure, I'm sometimes wrong, but some things don't even begin to be difficult to read, and Bucky would be one of them.

Through the quavering plastic covering the screen, I stare toward Bucky's field and grind my teeth. Yes. All the answers lie out there somewhere. But so far, all I'm getting are dead bodies and more questions.

Miss Ade appears from behind her home. She has a small sack that she swings back and forth. The breeze increases and ripples her ankle-length dress's royal-blue silk fabric. The brilliant blue of her hijab shines brightly in the sun.

Her screen door snaps shut behind her, and she disappears from my sight.

Son of a monkey's uncle. I lunge from the metal chair, making a beeline for the front door.

"Laila!"

Chapter 35

I watch the silhouette of her face through the screen of her porch as we approach. She smiles, and that throws me off my game.

"Miss Ade, do you have a moment for us to speak with you?"

"If'n you're coming to apologize for the other night, you don't have to. After I thought about it, I appreciate that y'all were looking out for me."

"I appreciate you being open-minded about that." I open the screen door, and her smile fades.

"What are you girls up to?"

"We still have some questions about the day we found Jumare."

She shifts in her chair. "Don't know how much more I can tell you about your brother. You and your girl found him."

"In Bucky's cane field."

She looks at me pointedly. "That's what I heard."

"But why were you so certain my brother was out there."

"It made sense to me." She shrugs her shoulder. "If anybody is gonna be sapping their energy, he's got to hide them somewhere. There's no better place than a cane field."

"Ade, you never told us we should check the sugarcane field. In fact, you said that we should check Bucky's barn."

"Hmm... Did I now? I don't quite remember the discussion

going that way, Laila."

"I do, and it did," I say.

"Why are you still here?"

"I suppose I'm just one of those girls who doesn't leave until the job is done."

"Ade, you need to tell me what you know about Jumare's disappearance."

"You're staring at me like I had something to do with Jumare being in that field."

"Did you?"

Ade looks at me with such hatred that the insides of my chest flutter. "You need to watch what you say about folks." Ade lifts a glass of lemonade, taking a sip as if she hasn't a concern in the world.

"Ade..."

"Child, you best be getting home before I have words with your gramma."

Laila moves closer to her. "My gramma would want the truth."

"The truth? I gave you the truth, and he is in jail now. But you can't be satisfied with that." Ade lifts the glass of lemonade toward her lip.

Laila reaches for the glass in Ade's hand. Cat quick, Ade slaps Laila's hand, inadvertently knocking the glass out of her hand. It falls to the porch floor and shatters.

"You won't be trying any of that old world magic on me, missy. You just remember that. I promise I'll chew you up and spit you out like cane fiber." She narrows her eyes. "Try to read my thoughts from my drinking glass. What's gotten into you?"

Laila stares at Ade with such intense hostility that I place my hand on her shoulder. In case she fails to control herself. "Let's go back to Gramma's and regroup."

"Why don't you listen to your friend?"

"I know you had something to do with it, Ade. Mark my words. I will tell Gramma. It will rain down fire on your head when she finds out what you have done."

"Don't be promising things you can't deliver, girl. Now you get on with yourself."

"Laila, come on, let's go."

"I'll be back, old woman."

Ade cackles, raising the hair on the back of my neck. Laila lurches forward, as if to attack her, but stops. Her feint fools me, and I step toward Laila to pull her off Ade.

Ade reaches into her apron and shoves a cane stick into her mouth. "You heard your friend. Get out."

Laila growls and spins on her feet. She bumps shoulders with me and slaps the screen door open.

I stare at Ade, and she laughs, revealing yellow teeth and the white stick protruding on the side of her gums.

"Laila!" I run to catch her. "Hey, wait up. What was that all about?"

"Nothing."

"Stop, won't you? Tell me what that was about."

She stops and faces me. Fire burns behind her dark eyes as she snarls. Her upper lip lifts, revealing her teeth.

"Seriously, calm down. Tell me what happened."

"She's lying!"

I snort. "Yeah, I figured that out."

"She knew all along." Laila jabs her finger in the direction of Ade's house.

I check to ensure we're far enough from Ade that she can't hear our conversation. She has disappeared from her front porch altogether.

"Yes, I am getting the same feeling. So, what do we do now?"

Laila balls up her fists and shakes them. She doesn't say anything. Instead, she holds her breath and turns a shade darker.

"Laila?"

"What, April? What do you want me to say? She's got everybody thinking it was Bucky. Heck, Bucky might be involved, too. Who can be sure?"

"We both know he didn't do anything," I whisper.

"Yeah, well, tell that to my uncle."

"I'll tell him if you think it would be better coming from me."

"It doesn't matter who it comes from. Aduwa's mind is made up, and he won't change it," she grumbles.

"We'll have to make him change his mind."

She blows a blast of air rudely between her lips. "You've got a better chance of seeing pigs fly."

"I'd say around here, I've got a higher chance of seeing that happen than anywhere else."

She glares at me until the hardness melts away, and she laughs. "Girl, you are so not right."

I favor her with a toothy grin. "That's funny. I get that a lot."

She walks toward Gramma's house. "I bet."

We cross the lane and enter Gramma's yard. While we're still alone, I ask, "Do you have something against lemonade?"

She shoots me a squinting glare and shakes her head. "Stop it."

"Are you allergic to it or have some agenda against citrus farmers?"

"Stop it, April."

"I will when you tell me what that was about."

She stops at the screen door and faces me. "There are things about my world you'll never understand. So please quit asking."

"I think you would be surprised."

She drops her chin to her chest and closes her eyes. "You're not gonna quit asking, are you?"

"I've only got so many cards to play, and persistency is my best."

She presses her fingertips to her forehead. "The old-world magic teaches that if you touch a cup someone drinks from, you can read their spirit. The earth-bound part can reveal their intentions. I never believed in the myth until it happened to me one day when I picked up Jumare's glass while clearing the breakfast dishes and learned he planned on skipping school."

My eyes open wider. "That is way cooler than how I have to

touch someone to get a reading."

"I don't have control of it and don't even know if it's reliable. Still, given the situation, getting an unreliable read would be better than nothing."

I appreciate Laila's moxie. It crossed my mind to see if I could get close enough to get a reading from Ade, but now that she knows I'm on to her, I doubt she would let me get within an arm's length.

"Fudge!"

Laila turns, her hand on the screen door. An alarmed expression flashes across her face. "What now?"

"She got my hair."

"Ade? When?"

I stomp my foot and look back toward Ade's house. "When she told me to come closer to tell me a secret. That egg-suckin' dawg. I can't believe I didn't realize what she was up to."

The jigsaw puzzles continue to fall into place. "And the lady on the beach... Ade wears dresses and head scarves like that all the time."

Laila gasps. "Oh my gosh, you're right. Come on, we've got to tell Gramma."

Chapter 36

I expect to find them in the kitchen and pull up short when I see Gramma, Aduwa, and Norman sitting in the living room. My gut turns as if we are sneaking home after curfew, and the entire family awaits us.

"My ladies. Is the devil chasing you?"

I would find Aduwa's comment humorous if I were sure we weren't in immediate danger.

"I'm glad you're all here," Laila says.

Me? I wanted to catch Gramma by herself. But I now understand that Laila has much more intestinal fortitude than I do.

"What's up, dear?" Gramma asks.

Laila steps closer to her but gives a hesitant glance toward her uncle. "Where is Jumare?"

"He is resting, dear."

"What's the matter with you, Laila? You're acting sketchy."

She ignores her uncle and pulls up a chair across from Gramma. "Good. I don't want him to hear this."

I'm the only person left standing in the room. Since no chairs are available, that will only change if I want to split Norman and Aduwa on the sofa. No, thank you. I'll just pop my hip and cross my arms.

"Laila, you're flushed. Tell me what the trouble is."

She laces her hands in front of her. "Gramma, it wasn't Bucky who kidnapped those people."

"Oh, I'm not listening to any more of this fabrication." Aduwa stands, and Gramma points at him.

"Sit down, young man. The very least you can do is hear your niece out."

Slowly, and with a condescending stare, Aduwa sits on the edge of the sofa covering his knees with his hands as he leans forward.

"Gramma, I know you and Ade have been friends for a long time. So, I need you to withhold judgment until I tell you everything."

"I'm withholding judgment now, dear. Didn't I tell your uncle to hear you out?"

"Yes, ma'am." She nods. "When we were on the beach, the day that April nearly drowned, the only person on the beach with us was a woman wearing a silk dress and a hijab."

Gramma shrugs and turns her hands palms up.

"I know, not a totally foreign costume on the island. But still, the only person that would've had an opportunity to place the voodoo doll in the water had to be that woman."

"Unless it was someone else while y'all took a nap."

I shift my weight from one leg to the other. Aduwa makes an excellent point that I'm not going to confirm. I recall that the three of us dozed off at least once.

"Except, the likeness was activated by April's hair. And we could never determine who had the opportunity to collect the strands or how."

"So now you're telling me that it was Ade."

"The first day that we went to talk to her. When everybody said that it would be pointless. For some reason, Ade asked April to get closer to her. She claimed to want to tell her a secret. And when she did, Ade did the oddest thing ever."

"Yes?"

"She petted her on the head."

Gramma makes an amused expression. "Ade petted April?"

"Yes, ma'am."

Gramma lifts her fist to her chin, focusing on the floor. Laila waits for her.

"You think that's when she stole a few strands of April's hair?"

"It makes sense to me. Do you feel that could have happened?"

Gramma closes her eyes. "Laila, you've known Ade your whole life. You know that's not like her. She can be peculiar, but she has always been the first to help our family."

"Yes, ma'am. I understand that. But April's hair."

She pinches the bridge of her nose. "I don't know. I can't believe that she would do anything to Jumare. She even babysat him. Watched him for me."

"You said that her arthritis was acting up. Would this allow her to heal herself?"

Gramma raises her hand. "Give me a second, child."

I shift my weight as the silence continues. Before this event, I was not privy to the family's relationship with Ade.

From where I'm standing, Ade is a vindictive, mean old woman I wouldn't even think had a friend. A thought has occurred to me more than once. How can Gramma keep her as a friend? The two are complete opposites.

"It's not that I disagree with you. It troubles me that April was only on the island for two days when the attack occurred. Our family should've been the only ones with access to anything of hers."

"You cannot suggest that you believe your lifelong friend tried to kill your grandchild. Have you lost your mind, Gramma?"

Gramma shakes her finger at Aduwa. "You will not talk to me like that in my home."

"I'm sorry." Aduwa waves his hands in the air. "I am always quiet about this magical nonsense you're constantly discussing. It's okay. It doesn't hurt if you believe it. I would expect it to be like children having imaginary friends that eventually pass. Still, most of the time, it's no harm, no foul, Gramma. But you're talking about your closest friend. You really believe that she is capable of this?"

Gramma swallows as her eyes narrow. "No. I don't believe it, or at least I don't want to believe it. But can you explain the coincidences? She had access to April. She's constantly in the cane field, yet three girls, who never go into the field, find two bodies in minutes. She's been there every day since our neighbors have gone."

Aduwa leans back on the sofa. He rubs his forehead as he bites his lip.

"Could you just talk to her and see what you feel, Gramma?"

"I could, Laila, but we've known each other so long, I would know if she's lying. I may be old, but if I sense she is lying, I'll knock her into next week, leaving her looking both ways for Sunday. Then I'd have a stroke 'cause I can't catch my air. Rules for old lady catfights are that there never is a winner. Just a bunch of hurt pride and fractured bones."

Gramma's comment brings a smirk to my face. I would love to see that bout and put my money on her, but I must admit, physically, the two women are a draw, and I already know Ade is a murderer. She wouldn't be pulling her punches.

"What do you feel we should do?"

Aduwa shakes his head and leans forward, placing his elbows on his knees. "Nothing."

We stare at Aduwa.

"Nothing has been said that convinces me that it's not Bucky. We have our man. Read the evidence. One, it's Bucky's field, and two, trying to put the murders on Ade is the equivalent of putting it on you three because you were walking in the field."

"I wouldn't exactly call it the same, Aduwa," Norman offers.

"What about her chewing on the sugarcane?" Trisha blurts.

"What about it, dear?"

"I don't know. It seems odd that Ade is chewing cane all the time."

Aduwa scoffs as he stands. "Please."

"It's something fieldworkers have been doing for centuries. Just a little bit of sweetness to curb your appetite is all."

Trisha listens politely to Gramma's explanation, but I know she's not accepting it as the gospel by the expression on her face.

Now that she's mentioned it, it seems odd to me, too. I initially wrote it off as a cultural peculiarity, but the woman doesn't chew a piece or two daily. She consumes it like her life depends on it.

"Ladies. I do appreciate your continued interest in making sure that justice is served. Still, I implore you to spend the remainder of your time on the island swimming or relaxing on the beach. We have our suspect, and he will pay for his crimes." Aduwa turns his attention to Gramma. "Norman is going to help me with the tires on my truck."

Gramma braces her arms to push out of her chair, and Norman raises his hand. "Beulah, please don't. You don't have to stand when family leaves the room, and you needn't see me out."

She favors Norman with a smile.

As I watch the men leave, I contemplate Aduwa's doggedness about it being Bucky who committed the crime. If I'm being honest about the facts, it makes much more sense that a man his size kidnaps three people than Ade committing the crime. Except for my hair, which Bucky may have somehow broken into the house and pinched from my brush, everything makes more sense that it was him and not Ade.

Still, I believe I am merely trying to convince myself of that. Either way, we will soon know whether we're right. Because I have learned one thing in the last two years. A killer's gonna kill.

Chapter 37

I have sufficiently worked myself into a tizzy. Consequently, despite the breeze through the open windows, my body is on fire because my mind is in overdrive.

The refrain from a classic Beatles song that Uncle Howard loves keeps playing in my mind. *Let it be, let it be, hear the wisdom let it be.* That's a lot easier said than done. Granted, the entire reason for being on the island was to recover Jumare. Fantastic job. Well done!

And yet it's not enough. It's that tiny niggle that teases my brain. The one that says, *You left something undone, April. Quit being a lazy nincompoop. Figure it out.*

And I have been trying nonstop ever since the conversation with Aduwa. I know that to move forward with anybody other than Bucky being responsible for the murders, I'll need buy-in from Aduwa. His opinion carries tremendous weight in this community.

He is the de facto judge of all things on the island. That being the circumstance, why am I having such difficulty putting together a case against Ade?

Then again, it has a lot to do with that aforementioned niggle in the back of my brain. If this were a court of law and I were the district attorney, I wouldn't have played any cards yet. I wouldn't have taken Bucky into custody. Instead, I would continue discussing things with Ade. My hope would be that, at some point, the woman slips up and tells me something more conclusive than what I am deriving from circumstantial evidence.

Bless it. This is worrying me smooth.

I flop onto my back for at least the twentieth time. I turn onto my side and look at Trisha and Laila across the room. Both girls appear to be in a deep sleep. Laila is thankfully sans the blue glow tonight.

The thought latches in my brain like the barb of a fishhook. It wasn't a blue glow she created. The light was an entity lying on top of her.

Things happened quickly, and I had not calmed enough earlier to consider the events. The immediate need was to warn Ade that something had run into her house. It left me with little time to consider the nature of the ghost on Laila, attempting to steal her essence.

But still—now that I recollect what I witnessed—it was the most peculiar-looking ghost. Almost as if it was a caricature rather than a person.

But of whom?

Obviously, there are no three-foot-tall people on the island with hollow fangs that they use for power-sucking straws.

And, although it's hard to be sure because the only color was silver, in a blue hue, if I had to take a gander, the entity was of a deceased white man.

I roll onto my back and stare at the ceiling while trying to recreate my mind's vision. It's tricky. The abnormally long feet, fangs, and shiny blue bubble push all other details of the specter out of my mind. Slowly, I flesh out the rest of the ghostly attacker.

Grotesquely fat, so much so that it appeared as if it were pregnant. Yes, I remember that now.

Also, a cleft chin with curly, lamb chop sideburns. This is even more peculiar since there was nary a hair on its otherwise bald head save for large tufts just above his ears. Its full lips were swollen, but I cannot be sure if that is their normal state or if it is a function of it feeding on Laila as she slept.

Overall, not helpful.

Besides, it's not like anybody will ask me to pick a ghost out of a lineup. That would be too convenient.

Regardless of its natural beauty and the kindness of its population, this island is whacked. Guntersville is bad? Well, this place has so many unrelated entities running around for such a small population base that it's unfathomable.

If nothing else, it helps me change my perspective. Anytime I want to complain about living in Guntersville, I can always think back to my time on Turtle Key and feel better about my predicament.

I groan and sit up. One thing I am not fond of is acts of futility. Which I now realize my sleeping tonight is.

I stand and look out the window. Ade's house is to the right of the center through the opening. To the right of that is Bucky's dilapidated monstrosity.

As the heavy cloud cover clears from the full silver moon, I crane my neck and identify the shadows of the tall cane field swaying in the late-night breeze.

It's beyond me why I can't take the win and enjoy myself. It may be the injustice of Bucky being accused of a crime I don't believe he committed. But now that I've learned more about Ade, I don't think she is any more inclined to be a murderer than Bucky. Which only makes sense. Whether at the Pick 'em Up store or the ferry boat, everyone I have met in this small community is welcoming and gracious. I must've said something initially that offended Ade.

That does make sense. It would not be the first time someone has reacted negatively to me.

Despite the murders, magical virility, and complicated relationships, the island is a slice of paradise. I've always been partial to property next to water. This little island, Turtle Key, must have been the best-kept secret for the last century. It really does surprise me that it's only now being encroached on by wealthy vacationers.

It's not exactly your own private island, a common fantasy for many people. Still, it's as close as you possibly could get.

The heavy cloud cover rolls over the full moon again, blocking all but the silver outline at the edges of the fast-moving cloud cover. I wonder if it's the same on the Atlantic coast, but it looks and smells like we're about to get a toad strangler.

I sigh deeply as the last of the angst dissipates from me. Aduwa was not being mean or dismissive. If anything, he was speaking the truth. My job, which Aduwa—through Norman —summoned me here for, is complete. Jumare is resting peacefully in his bedroom, regaining his strength. I've got a lot to keep me busy when I return to Guntersville, so now is the time to relax and put things I can't explain out of my mind.

Lifting my knee, I balance my weight against the mattress, reaching for my pillow to fluff it. As I do, an odd, red glow illuminates the back of Ade's house.

Curious, I pause and squint. Fire?

It's only possible if a fire can sway and move. The odd glow slides from the left side of the back of the house toward the right.

Ade making a trip to the cane field with a lantern?

No. That couldn't be. That odd glow is too bright for a lantern, and most burn yellow to orange. This is a fiery red.

I climb onto my bed. To better look through the window, I brace my hands at the bottom of the sill and lean out.

A flaming wild boar appears from the back of Ade's house and tears up the earth as it runs toward Bucky's barn. The boar, its shoulders easily taller than me, cannot be of this world even if it weren't for the flames reaching high into the night sky from its back.

I recoil in shock, nearly losing my balance. My nails bite into the wood of the sill, catching myself.

What in tarnation am I looking at?

This place gets weirder by the minute. I believe it would be more relaxing to return home to Guntersville and deal with a few unreasonable clients.

The boar crosses behind Bucky's incredibly quickly and disappears into the sugarcane field. Only a slight halo glow and the occasional lick of a flame now show.

I watch as the boar continues a beeline through the field. It disappears as it enters the abnormally tall area in the center, where I inadvertently disturbed the resting place of two Turtle Key citizens.

Weirdest thing ever. What manner of magic deals with a flaming boar?

I'm so intent on the oddity that I've witnessed that I'm slow on the come about the real issue at hand. The boar appeared to exit Ade's house before running to the sugarcane field.

Oh my gosh. It wasn't Ade or Bucky. It's this spirit that is the boar. It must be some sort of demon or, at the very least, a consort of one like the hounds of hell.

It came out of Ade's house. Did it somehow carry Ade off into the field? Is that how everyone ended up in the center of the sugarcane?

I look back over my shoulder at my cousin and my new friend. Neither has stirred from their slumber. It's not surprising, given the dreadfully stressful few days we've experienced. Backup would be good. It would be beneficial. But given the false alarm I created when we went looking for the blue ghost feeding on Laila, I'm not ready yet to wake the whole crew and barge in on Miss Ade again.

Aduwa's sage advice rings in my head. I could let it go and mind my own business. Obviously, things are happening here that I have yet to gain experience with.

If I hadn't heard that Ade has been a wonderful friend to the family, I would be less inclined to check on her well-being.

It's not like I was about to fall asleep. There is no possibility of me sleeping without the knowledge that she is safe. If I were to wake in the morning and learn something harmed her, I'd never forgive myself if I could have helped.

There must be a better plan than sneaking out the front door since the floor squeaked so loudly last time that I woke everybody up. I look over the windowsill and measure the drop to be four feet. I can do it.

I swing one long leg, followed by the other, through the window and balance my butt on the ledge to gather my thoughts.

April May Snow, you are plumb out of your mind.

The cloud cover clears momentarily, and the rutted dirt lane is lit in silver. I look to the far right and wonder if the boar will remain in the field or if it will return to Ade's home. All things I can't know. I do know Ade may need my help.

Shoving off the ledge, I drop onto the dirt below. I land awkwardly as my bare foot strikes the point of a rock, and I fall forward. I catch myself before tumbling into the vegetation in front of me.

You really planned this one out, April.

I walk on the dew-covered zoysia in Gramma's yard rather than risk cutting my feet on the crushed-shell driveway. Damp grass blades slide between my toes while the brisk breeze chills the dew on my feet with each step.

A plan takes root in my mind as I reach the lane. My heartbeat slows, as plans, regardless of how idiotic, are more soothing to my nerves than reacting blindly.

I can't know the probability of the boar returning to Ade's home tonight. Finding someone besides its victim could be a bonus midnight snack for the beast. Or something to eliminate quickly by running its flaming tusks through me. Either way, I must determine my best defense for that contingency.

Lucky for me, I'm a witch with just enough training to be scary, and Turtle Key is chock-full of chaotic ambient energy.

As I slink my way over to Ade's home, I marshal an abundance of the free-flowing energy into my core. I don't plan on doing anything with it at the moment. However, if I could somehow miraculously form moccasins, I would certainly do that and save the soles of my feet from their current torture.

I need to hold the reserves for quick access. If I must protect Ade with a shield or, heaven forbid, use a more aggressive method of magic to ward off the beast, I intend to have the prerequisite power at the ready.

Blue-and-silver reflective dust swirls toward me in an organized pattern. As it does, my confidence grows with each step, and I feel fuller and heavier. It's a heady experience, like the largest adrenaline dump I've ever experienced, times twenty. As I arrive at Ade's screen door and scan the inside of her porch, I have doubts about my approach.

Since the flaming boar came from the backyard, it would make more sense for Ade to be at the rear of her house. The most probable location is her kitchen. Still, I can check the living room windows while I'm here.

An overriding sense of dread crashes into me as I open the screen door to her porch. I sense a distinctly different residual magic and know it to be powerful and old. Unfortunately, it is a construct of something I can't identify. Whatever I feel, I have not previously experienced.

"Just beautiful," I grumble as I cup my hands to look inside the windows. I take my time because I have a full charge of energy if I need it to protect myself. I see no sign of Ade in her living room.

With my hypothesis proven, I exit the porch and walk toward the back of her house. My knees falter as I step on particularly sharp rocks. The light mist forms a sheen on my face.

Arriving at Ade's back door, I look over my shoulder to ensure I'm not being stalked by a boar.

Satisfied I am safe, I again cup my hands against the window and peer inside. Breathing in deeply, I scan the room. I hope Ade is tucked in bed, and I will be soon, too, once I confirm this is yet another false alarm.

My breath catches as I see something I can't readily identify on the floor.

"Fudge!"

Chapter 38

The sight of Ade crumpled on her kitchen floor jolts me into action. I lift a potted plant on the table to my side and throw the fern through one of the door's glass panes.

Without clearing the jagged remnants of the glass, I reach through the opening, praying she has a turn lock rather than a deadbolt. I slap the far side of the door several times and realize there is no key to turn.

"Bless it," I grumble. "Ade! Can you hear me!"

She appears dead, or at the very least, completely incapacitated. But I must do something while trying to figure out how to get myself inside to help her.

How difficult would it have been for her to have a regular lock? I grab the doorknob and yank on it in frustration. The doorknob moves freely, and I pull. The door swings open. Thankfully, due to the current emergency, I don't have adequate time to admonish my stupidity, and I move forward to check on Ade.

The glass splitting the sole of my right foot hurts like a banshee. "Give me a break!" I rise onto my tiptoes and navigate through the maze of large shards of glass scattered across the floor.

I drop to my knees at Ade's side and look behind at my injured foot. Yes, I know Ade is in trouble, but the shard of glass

I see protruding from my foot makes me queasy and messes with my nervous system.

With the adrenaline rush from the emergency, I don't hesitate as I pinch the glass and pull it free. The relief is immediate as blood streams freely from the puckered wound at the ball of my foot.

I redirect my attention to Ade on the floor. Leaning forward, I reach for her shoulders. I stiffen, and I contort my face in confusion. "What in the world?"

I pat Ade on the back, causing a dull thud to echo in the silent room. As if continuing with the madness will change the results, I rise on my knees and pat the middle of Ade's back, buttocks, and thighs. The results are the same, thud-thud-thud, as my hand strikes through to the floor. I pinch her calves and lift.

My stomach's gorge rises, and I might lose it. Ade has more severe issues than being unconscious. Her clothed skin is all the remains of the woman. It's as if everything inside her skin has been vacuumed out of her.

As the new reality sets in, my incessant curiosity takes over, and I move to her face. Gently I lift her right eyelid and grimace. I am greeted by her dull, brown, yellowed eyes looking lifelessly back at me.

Sitting back on my haunches, I rack my brain for anything that Nana or Granny have told me about something like what I'm experiencing now. Surely, there is no way that I have stumbled across something new in the paranormal world. Yet as I sit here, it sure does look to be the case.

Perfect. Just what I need ... something out of the ordinary for my freaky April skill set.

Convinced that unless I have a sudden epiphany, there's not much I can do for Ade, I pull my right leg under me to examine the damage to my foot.

"Hey, April. Let's go and spend some relaxing time on the beach. Oh wow, I would love that..." I mock as I stare at the substantial gash on my foot.

"Oh, you know that super cool heal-people-with-your-touch thing. Yeah, that doesn't work on you either."

As I stand to find something in the kitchen to stop the bleeding from my foot, I mull over how I have begun talking to myself regularly. It probably indicates some psychotic episode for which I need help. But what are they gonna say? I'm cracked? Heck, I already know that.

I hop on my left leg toward the sink. I'd prefer not to have a cut on my foot, but I'm grateful for a task so that I'm not simply staring at Ade's deflated body with no idea how to help her.

I lift myself onto the counter and swing my feet into the sink. The icy water makes me grit my teeth as I watch the thick, red blood dilute with the water and run into the white, porcelain sink before the pink stream flows to the drain.

Isn't this the nature of life? Whenever I've leveled up and found a modicum of success, along comes a case that knocks me sideways.

In the paranormal world, it's even worse. To date, I have not met a single weirdo like me who has even a third of the potential I do. I have two wonderful mentors, yet I've still managed to unearth something they have yet to mention.

If I were smart, I would claim mental disability and stay in my parents' boathouse for the rest of my life. I'm a magnet for all things evil and odd which could harm the rest of the world.

Stop making everything about you, April.

I tie a terry cloth hand towel across the top of my foot. It's not likely to stay in place, but I won't be going anywhere fast.

Triage task over, I have no choice but to look at what horrifies me. Ade on the floor, deflated like a three-week-old balloon souvenir from a kids' party.

Not a good look for her.

I get another jolt of recognition and frown. Ade's dress and head scarf are identical to what the lady on the beach wore the day the voodoo doll tried to drown me.

Again, circumstantial evidence, as I never saw her with the

doll. Still, it is a strong indicator of her guilt.

I can't even be angry with her. How dreadful to have something suck the insides out of you.

I wonder if this has something to do with the blue sucking ghost I chased off of Laila the other night. Did I save Laila from this same end?

Poor Ade. Nobody deserves this.

Even if she did try to kill me, she must've had her reasons. If I had to guess, it's the hurt of watching her world be sold off parcel by parcel to people who want to dramatically change it.

It does give me pause, as I do understand. When I come home to Guntersville and see that someone has cleared off a dilapidated building, even though it was an eyesore, it gives me a sense of loss, even if it is replaced by something newer and more functional.

I can only imagine if the loss was something incredibly significant, like my high school being torn down for a shopping mall or, in the case of Ade, the forest that she explored as a child becoming a strip of vacation homes for people that only visit the island on their vacation time.

The epiphany has yet to happen. And, like a knucklehead, I dove out the bedroom window without my cell phone.

Walking back to Gramma's with the cut foot will be challenging. But not as difficult as explaining the situation over at Ade's house. There's no use delaying the inevitable, and I check the condition of my foot one more time and swing my feet out of the sink.

A strange red glow catches my eye.

Chapter 39

"Fudge nuts!" My eyes open so wide they feel like they will pop out of my head as my chest constricts.

The flaming red boar sends clouds of dirt up behind it as it gallops toward Ade's house. Through the kitchen window, I have all the information I need. It says one thing: April, make yourself scarce.

Still, I must take one more look at the fiery beast who has closed half the distance between Bucky's and Ade's homes.

Another choice to be made, besides freezing in terror and watching the unusual oddity or fleeing Ade's home... *Would I be better served to go out the back or the front door if I choose to run?*

Easy—front door. I saw the boar coming from the back of Ade's home earlier. It only makes sense that if it returns to the crime scene, it'll be at the back door.

I drop my feet to the floor, and the shooting pain in my right foot returns, buckling my knee.

Toughen up, buttercup.

I grit my teeth and hobble toward the living room. Tears leak out the sides of my eyes, and I'm unsure if it's from pain or fear.

That's silly. It's both.

I clear the doorway into the living room, making good speed, half hopping and half limping toward the door, when an eerie red glow appears on the porch.

So much for sound logic, April. I pivot, forgetting that my right foot is damaged, and scream in pain.

The boar roars, vibrating the walls.

I may have peed a little.

Back door... Back door... Run!

I'm faced with enduring the pain in my foot or being eaten alive by the world's largest walking BBQ. "Please, Lord, I'll never eat barbecue again," I say, as if this is all a karmic issue.

In a weird, hobbling sprint, I pass by Ade's deflated body, and the doorway fills with flames. The boar snorts as it paws at the ground.

I don't see any manner of escape. I'm cooked.

Backpedaling, I keep my eyes on the fiery image before me. The boar snorts, and napalm globules and smoke puffs shoot out its nostrils. I dodge to the left to avoid the flames shooting out and falling to the floor in front of me.

A calmness comes over me as I realize I'm trapped, and this is where I will meet my end if I do not come up with a solution quickly.

The boar moves forward and approaches Ade.

My sense is she is dead. Still, my protective side pops into action. I try to collect energy to form a protective barrier between us and the entity.

I concentrate on coalescing enough magic energy to utilize one of my favorite skill sets: creating an impenetrable defensive bubble. I am alarmed as only a few specks of chaos flow toward me. My heart flutters as I wrestle to squash down the thought that pops into my head.

Now that I struggle to find the slightest bit of ambient energy in an area that I know has been extremely high, it becomes clear that the energy is unavailable for a reason. The boar in front of me is sucking all the available power out of the air.

Without the juice to initiate my paranormal skill set, I can do nothing for Ade. I backpedal, and a fresh idea comes into my mind, although the probability of success is minuscule. If I run out the front door, the boar will come around the house before I escape.

But what if I can drive further into the house? Make it difficult for it to get to me.

Despite the low odds of success, it is my only chance. The final decision is when it blows another plume of sticky flame across the kitchen, catching the pantry to my right on fire.

My confidence wavers. All that is left is to backtrack until I see an opportunity to break out the door. Possibly right before the boar comes across the threshold leading to the living room.

I take another step back and yelp. The scent of singed hair fills my nostrils. My shoulders ache as if I have just received a sunburn.

Pivoting to look behind me, I make a squeaking noise as my breath catches in my throat.

The threshold leading to the living room is a curtain of flames. It's as if the entire entryway is ringed with Bunsen burners, positioned six inches apart on full-flame gas. The heat is so intense I bring my hand up to shield my face as it begins to warm.

There's no way I can run through that. The flames would cook me even if I passed through and found the living room free of fire. And I can't be assured that it won't be in flames, too.

Still, desperation changes my logic, and I peer through the raging plume of blue flame. I must confirm if the living room is clear of fire. It's crazy. Even if not, I will have second- and third-degree burns across my face and body. But burns must be better than having my innards sucked out.

I jump as something pierces my tender shoulders, holding me in place.

"Medium, rare, or well done, I can never decide." The female voice has the same effect as fingernails across the chalkboard, and I squirm to try and free myself.

"Oh, the governor will enjoy you. He likes them feisty and juicy."

Despite the sharp pain in my shoulders, I turn my head to see who has a hold of me. I glimpse Ade's face. My stomach flips as I am jerked into the air, and my face is pile driven onto the wooden floor.

"Eh-eh-eh, you shouldn't have come here, blondie."

I struggle to catch my breath as she mounts my back and digs her nails deeper into my shoulders. I fight the pain of my bruised ribs and jaw, which I swear is dislocated. The copper taste of blood blooms in my mouth.

The flaming boar has disappeared. Half of the kitchen cabinetry is covered in flames, and the smoke forms a thick blanket covering the ceiling.

Ade is reanimated, and the boar is gone. What manner of strange devilry is this?

"The governor told me to bring you to him straight away." I feel Ade's cold lips against my ear. "But he might not mind me having a little taste. That's not too much to ask. Changing form requires a lot of energy. The governor should understand."

The phrase "a little taste of me" clues me in to the idea I am the object of a feast and encourages me to find an energy reserve I did not realize I owned.

I wriggle and spin my hips. Ade's balance falters, and she pushes her weight onto my shoulders, flattening me again to the floor.

I let out a grunt and mew in defeat.

"On second thought, the governor is very thirsty. He mustn't know I stole a taste of your magic, or he might cook Atlas." Ade positions her lips next to my ear. "Atlas promises to be gentle, blondie." Ade sits back and chuckles gleefully. "But, boy, what the governor will do to you when he devours you! The governor is not gentle. No, not gentle in the least."

Inexplicably, she increases her weight and pins me down. My clavicle bone crushes against the wooden slats of the flooring.

"Now hold still and accept the inevitable." A gust of wind at the back of my neck separates my hair. A putrid stench overpowers the smoke fumes in the room, causing me to gag. Something flicks, cold and wet, like the tip of a water snake, at the base of my neck. My toes and fingers curl in repulsion as she licks my neck. A soft, sucking noise ensues, I notice a disturbance in my body's energy, and I whimper.

The pain of my injuries intensifies, and it becomes a battle to take my next breath. Suddenly, I feel as if I am so exhausted that I've been up for the last six nights straight and so hungry and thirsty that I have not had any nourishment in the same amount of time.

The soft, sucking noise stops, and Ade smacks her lips. "Oh, so powerful. The governor will be well pleased."

Her weight lifts from my shoulders, yet I am so tired I remain with my arms flat on the floor and my face turned to the side. I don't have the energy, nor the will, to escape.

I am filled with deep sorrow. Given the nature of my paranormal abilities, this is a double whammy for me since sadness prevents me from recharging my battery.

Of all the times before that I have thought I would perish, the only occasion that equals now is when Austin's witches bound me and carried me into the parted lake.

This time, I know no Antoine will come to my rescue. This time I will not have the benefit of my potent paranormal amulet.

How foolish I've been not to bring the magical gifts my family gave me on this excursion. How childish that I never acquired the discipline to use them only for altruistic purposes, forcing me to store them out of reach.

Ade pulls my arms back behind me. My wrists burn fiercely as something cinches them together and pricks my skin with thousands of electrical charges.

"That will hold you until I get you to the governor."

Ade laces her hands under my wrists and yanks me up onto my feet with unimaginable strength. I fear my shoulders will dislocate, and I cry out in pain.

"Hey, duppy!"

Laila's voice I recognize, but I must be close to passing out because I do not understand what she said.

Ade emits a terrible scream and releases me. Despite my befuddled state, it jolts me awake. I watch her charge the back door.

"Count this, demon!"

Ade screams and pulls at her hair. A tuft of black-and-silver strands comes free in both hands, and she drops to her knees.

I locate Laila standing in the doorway. I'm overwhelmed with relief, and my knees buckle, causing me to fall rudely on my butt.

Ade is bent over on all fours a few feet away from me, her long fingers sliding across the floor at lightning speed. "Thirty-eight, thirty-nine, forty." She counts with her entire focus on the handful of spilled white grain.

Laila's eyes widen as she sees me and starts toward me. "April!"

I move my mouth to say her name, but nothing comes out. I choke on the word.

"I can't hold her long. Can you help?"

"Help?"

Ade's counting begins to sound jubilant. Laila turns and tosses a second handful of rice toward the pile Ade's already collected and counted.

"No! You miserable girl." Ade screams and resumes counting again. "One, two, three."

This time her pace of counting is even faster. As she draws her long, pointed finger across the wooden floor, she leaves a trace of blood on the honey-and-gray boards.

"April, I need your help. I can't keep her at bay until sunrise."

But my hands are tied... No, my hands are free. When did that happen?

"Can you bind her?"

I don't know anything as complicated as a binding spell. Even if I did, that would be an offensive move rather than a defensive, potentially throwing me into a dark magic imbalance.

In a stupor, I watch Ade count her rice piece by piece, leaving a bloody trail. The smoke billows to the ceiling, the cabinetry blazes, and Laila hollers at me inches from my face. All the sound has left the world, as has feeling, taste, and smell. My reality has distilled down to this hellish, chaotic scene before me.

I read Laila's lips. She says that she has nothing left to make Ade recount the rice. That seems mildly humorous to me now, which I understand to be nonsensical, given it is all that keeps Ade from focusing on my destruction. Her concentration on the rice has distracted her enough to break the binding spell on me.

The binding spell felt like how the witches bound me to carry me over the lake. The chains did not have the same appearance, yet they had the same feel. As if recalling a memorized recipe I have never baked, I know exactly how to cast the binding spell. The words are not mine and are foreign, but they are the way of the magic.

The chaotic energy in the room swirls a thick fog of blue and gold. A multitude of tiny flecks floats freely in the kitchen. With minimal effort, the chaotic mass flows in an orderly fashion toward my chest, clearing my mind and filling me with purpose.

I stand, my legs steady, and walk toward Ade. She's down to the last few pieces of rice to count, the floor in front of her streaked profusely with blood.

"Hey, demon!"

She turns her head. The snout of the flaming boar is thinly overlaid against her dark, weathered skin and yellowed eyes. The combined facial images of the two faces competing for the same real estate are disconcerting.

She has no time for me and returns to her counting. I swipe my bare foot through the pile she has counted, flinging rice across the room.

"No! You treacherous woman. Why did you do that?" She

doesn't bother to look at me. Instead, she resumes counting the rice. The tip of her right pointer finger leaves bits of shredded skin on the wooden planks.

For her safety and ours, I enact the bind by taking my crucifix off and removing it from its sterling silver chain. I chant the secret phrases that have remained residual in my mind from Austin's witches and Ade. I scream it in a declaration as I hold the limp, silver chain at arm's length.

"Corpus animam et mentem cum catena ego ligaveris. Corpus animam et mentem cum catena ego ligaveris. Corpus animam et mentem cum catena ego ligaveris"

The fog energy in the kitchen shakes as if jolted by a seismic wave, aligning and flowing toward me in a blindingly fast, bright rope of light. The power swells my insides, and I may explode like a balloon filled past its capacity.

I'm relieved as the energy flows quickly down my arm and to the chain dangling from my hand. The crucifix's chain sparkles golden as it snaps to attention, the clasp reaching out toward Ade.

I straddle Ade and loop her free hand with the slipknot the chain magically forms. Shifting my weight, I wrestle her other hand away from counting the rice. My anger and fear have boiled my emotions so high I must check myself so as not to use too much force. I pull back firmly on the golden chain. As Ade's hands come behind her, I shift my stance to support her shoulder with my left hand to prevent her from face-planting onto the floor from her kneeling position.

Laila rushes in front of Ade and pushes her shoulders down as Ade attempts to stand. I am thankful for the help, as I was losing my balance. Not wasting any more time, I loop the extra length of the magical chain around Ade's ankles and tie it off snugly.

"What have you done?!"

With Ade, or the demon, now detained, I feel for the first time like I have a fighter's chance of getting out of this alive. Thanks to Laila's bravery. "It's just temporary, Ade. Until we can figure out how to help you."

"You don't know what you've done. The governor will make you wish you had died a thousand deaths already."

"Some days, I feel like I already have."

Laila drapes her arm across my shoulders, and we shock each other with a transference of magical energy.

She laughs nervously. "Are you okay?"

"Thanks to you, I am."

"But thanks to you, we might make it to the morning."

I exhale a breath I had not realized I was holding. "Yes. Is that what we need to do?"

"The best I know, but I have never done this before."

"Fair."

"Laila? April?"

"Oh, shoot. I forgot about Trisha," Laila says as she approaches the door. "It's all clear, Trisha."

"Why is Trisha here?" I blurt before checking the harshness of my tone.

Laila screws up her face as she gestures with her thumb over her shoulder. "Trisha is why I knew to come here and look for you."

"What do you mean?"

"Untie me!" Ade screams.

"Shut your mouth, demon scum."

Laila grimaces. "Are you talking to Ade or the demon?"

"Point taken."

Trisha sucks her breath in hard, and it draws my attention. She points at Ade.

I shrug. "She needs a time out."

"Untie me!"

Ade's wailing is becoming rather annoying. "If you don't want me to shove a magical sock in it, you'll want to shut your mouth."

"You can do that?"

I favor Laila with a droll stare.

"Oh. We're stuck listening to her until the sun rises."

"She's like a vampire?" Trisha asks.

"No!"

Laila says it as if Trisha is silly to have asked. It was a valid question. I, too, wonder why a ghost would care whether it's daylight or night.

The idea that I had a fighter's chance of making it off of this island alive deteriorates with every passing moment. The three of us exchange expressions of solemn determination. I do not doubt that the two women with me would do anything possible to protect the island from whatever demon has taken over Ade.

The only issue is we have scant information available to proceed. Not to mention we don't have the training to deal with this.

"What about Gramma?" Trisha asks.

"I would," Laila stammers, "it's just her heart has not been the best these last few years, and I don't want to pull her into this if we can avoid it."

I fully understand that. My granny recently traveled with my paranormal team, and I worried about her the entire time. And she doesn't have a heart condition.

"I understand," Trisha says. "April, didn't you say your granny was teaching you paranormal skills."

My head snaps back, and I scowl as if I smell something offensive. "I said that?"

"You said your granny was passing her knowledge to you on some things. We're all aware that she can't cook, and she used to be an expeller of demons in her youth."

Why is this common knowledge to everyone in my extended family? I only recently learned that it is factual that Granny used to expel demons. Until she recently shared that revelation with me, I believed it to be a family joke. Her insistence that I had the "gift" too is the cherry on top of the butterscotch sundae.

"April. Wouldn't this be a relevant situation?"

"I suppose," I growl.

"Well?" Trisha holds out her hands and turns them palms up.

"For Pete's sake, Trisha. It's not like I've had the opportunity to practice or anything." I gesture toward the chain at Ade's back. "I didn't even know I could do that, and while doing it, I thought my guts would explode all over the wall."

"But they didn't," Trisha says pointedly.

"Could have."

"And didn't."

"You might be able to separate the demon from Ade?" Laila asks.

I have something snarky to say on the tip of my tongue. But Laila's expression is so hopeful and sweet that I swallow my mean words.

Granny has spent hours discussing with me the entire process of expelling demons. She shared scores of cases she worked on before her children were born.

Honestly, even if she is correct and I can expel demons, I had fully hoped to get through this life without ever needing to try it. While extremely interesting and riveting, Granny's stories are scarier than any slasher film I have seen. I prefer not to take part in my own real-life version of a horror flick.

Still, with Trisha standing with her fist on her hips while she squints her eyes at me and Laila's doleful expression, I feel my resolve slipping.

Dag nab it. I'm really gonna do this.

"Guys, listen. I can try, but I don't know what the end result will be." I gesture toward Ade. "Right now, we've got her tied up, and she is not going anywhere. I can't say the same if a flaming, red boar starts running around the house, shooting napalm out its nostrils."

"What?" Laila and Trisha ask in unison.

I see my opportunity to slip out of this chore, and my eyes widen as I grin. "Oh yeah. A few minutes ago, before y'all got here. Let me tell you, there is something far scarier than Miss Ade counting rice like a deranged lunatic. How would you like a shoulder-high, two-ton flaming boar chasing you?" I nod emphatically. "True story."

"That's unlike any duppy in the tales," Laila says.

"What is a duppy?" Trisha asks.

"The spirit of the dead. Some are good. Others are bad such as the rolling calf."

Trisha's nose flares. "Rolling what?"

"Calf..." Laila shakes her head. "It doesn't matter. It's a specific type of demon from the old religion."

I point toward Laila. "See. We don't want to turn that thing loose again. Atlas would kill the three of us in a blink of an eye, then disappear back into the cane field from where he came."

"So, what? We're gonna leave Ade as she is for the rest of her life?" Trisha asks.

I stare down at Ade and shrug my shoulders. "It seems safer to me."

"Safer is not always an option, April."

"It is until somebody has a better solution. Feel free to kick in at any time."

Ade makes a squealing pig noise. The decibels are so high they force me to cover my ears.

It dawns on me that she is calling for the governor. I dive forward to cover her mouth, and she clamps down on my hand with incredible force.

"Mother of pearls!" I scream as I pull my hand out of her mouth and examine the teeth marks left. I fight to remember that it's Atlas, not Ade, who bit me, so I don't knock her out.

"That looks safe."

I favor Trisha with a death stare.

"April, can you loosen the chain enough to allow Ade to walk?"

Laila raises her eyebrows, and I stare at her as if she has lost her everlasting mind. "Why would we do that?"

Laila scoffs, "I realized Ade took down her blue bottle tree six months ago. She had one in her front yard and one in her backyard, and then one day, they weren't there anymore."

"And?"

"Spirits become intrigued by the bottles, and because they're curious by nature, they go inside them and can't figure out how to escape. In the morning, the sun burns them up in the bottle," Trisha says.

I favor Trisha with a smirk.

"What? Gramma told us at dinner the other night when I asked her what they were about."

"It's true," Laila says.

I sigh derisively. "We *think* it's true."

"Most myths are based on some truth," Trisha counters.

"Or they're meant to explain something that spooked us."

"April, I have to agree with Trisha on this. I assumed duppies were a fanciful legend until you told me what you witnessed with Ade."

Who am I to disagree with them. I just turned a twenty-four-inch sterling necklace into a six-foot-long magical golden chain with a binding spell no one has ever taught me. If that's not stretching the bounds of belief in the paranormal, I'm not sure what is.

"What's the plan?" I ask Laila.

"You said the boar came from the sugarcane field. To decrease the damage if the bottles don't capture it, we should do it near the cane so the demon will seek to return to its lair rather than continue the fight."

Trisha gestures towards the window. "Bucky had several of the bottle trees in his backyard."

"Yes." Laila nods her head. "That's precisely where we should try to expel the demon."

While Laila and Trisha continue to build up confidence in their plan, mine slips a gear. A dangerous predicament, as I know if my faith falters, so does my paranormal ability.

"And what if it doesn't work? What if I'm not able to expel Atlas?"

Laila bites her lip and looks down at the floor.

"How will the binding affect Ade when the morning sun

comes up, Laila?" Trisha asks.

Laila shakes her head. "I'm not sure. I know the duppies are only supposed to be able to travel at night. And the possessed person's skin protects them during the day. But I am concerned if being bound will change the equation."

That is precisely why I hate dealing with paranormal situations. Everything is based on myth and conjecture. Even if you had a solid plan or hypothesis, you would want to be able to practice it over and over until you have it correct. Often, in the paranormal realm, you get one chance. More importantly, if you fail, somebody loses their life.

I don't believe anything will happen to Ade when the sun rises. Everything in my gut tells me that Atlas will recede further inside Ade like any other day. Then I'll be able to unbind her and deal with her as her usual cantankerous, old woman self.

"Perhaps before we do something as drastic as attempt an exorcism, we should wait until the morning and see if she becomes Ade again."

"And if she and the boar you call Atlas burn up and turn into a pile of ash?"

"Come on, Trisha."

"We don't know that it won't happen, April." Laila points at the chain. "Will you loosen this up so she can walk, please?"

Laila would have to say please. It's difficult to deny people when they're being pleasant.

Something in my gut tells me this is beyond my abilities. In fact, I have an overriding fear that we will rue the day we attempt this exorcism. If we survive it at all.

"April?"

I narrow my eyes at Trisha. From her point of view, it is a simple request. Still, it's not like I understand how I created the chain in the first place. The thought of loosening it gives me the heebie-jeebies.

I visualize releasing a link or two to allow Ade to walk to Bucky's house. My mind is filled with visions of the golden chain breaking apart link by link and then reconstituting itself into the silver, serpentine chain of my crucifix. Thereby releasing Atlas to eat us as he pleases.

"April," Trisha scolds.

"What? I'm thinking about how to do this."

"Give her time, Trisha."

I'm thankful for Laila's understanding. I favor her with an appreciative smile and return to the task.

I know there's no way out of this. Our plan is correct about expeditiously getting Ade, who is carrying Atlas inside of her, to the cane field.

I consider if Ade is light enough for the three of us to carry. Still, I am sure that the other two will not brook that suggestion.

Kneeling at Ade's back, I cup my hands around the knot that ties her wrist snuggly to her ankles. I feign to unhook the bow, then stop.

The idea of running from the flaming boar again is not appealing. Laila and Trisha do not understand the danger. As soon as I release this bow, if the chain fails, Atlas will emerge from Ade and feast on us.

But why hasn't he already? If he could, undoubtedly, Atlas would've emerged from Ade and run for the protection of this governor character he speaks of continually.

It doesn't take a rocket scientist to figure out if he were to leave Ade's body, and she deflates again into the skin-only form I found her in earlier, a chain cannot bind her.

And yet he remains inside her, even though it's still dark enough to exit and make his escape. Again, assuming the information Gramma gave Trisha is correct.

Bless it. If only paranormal events came with an instruction guide.

"April, if we don't move soon, it will be dawn. The demon might fight the expulsion more if it knows that exiting Ade will kill it."

I frown at Laila's astute observation. We're in a conundrum, and the only way forward is to have faith that we can improvise effectively and quickly enough if Atlas is released and goes on a rampage.

I hold the golden bow of the chain in my hand, and all the worry and angst flow from my mind. I completely understand the magic I have created that binds Ade's ankles. With the smallest effort, by visualizing the bow untying, the knot releases and the chain pools around Ade's feet.

I examine the new formation of the chain and judge it to have enough slack for Ade to stand. I place my arms and hands under her shoulders and bend my knees.

"Ade, can you stand for me?"

"Why certainly, child."

The overly helpful tone from her startles me and pushes my senses to high alert. Atlas, not Ade, obviously sees an advantage to do as I ask.

Not necessarily a good thing.

She comes to her feet, and the golden chain makes a light, tinkling noise against the scarred pine floor. She moves toward the back door.

Laila and I share an uneasy glance. By her expression, Trisha assumes that everything is hunky-dory. To her, we are making progress in our stated plan, and she opens the door.

The light mist from earlier has turned into sputtering rain. My bare feet squish into the mud, sending goo between my toes as I clutch the chain behind Ade's back. I do not have to instruct her where to go.

Atlas is obviously more than ready to return to his governor. It will not take coercion to get him to return home.

If we're lucky, and if the myths are accurate, we may be fortunate and Atlas will become entangled in the blue bottles and burn up at the first light of day. I have a better chance of winning Friday's Powerball, but a girl can dream.

An uneasiness rises in my gut. I'm not optimistic I can accomplish the trick I must perform. I have no choice but to separate Atlas from Ade through expulsion. I've already seen the result of Atlas leaving of his own volition. If he leaves Ade a deflated bag of skin, we will have accomplished nothing besides killing her.

I ponder the multitude of hours in training with Granny. Despite the many discussions about the hundreds of cases she worked on during her storied career, I am still waiting for her to give me basic instructions on how to proceed with an expulsion. That is, I don't know the mechanics of it, or at the very least, I have yet to glean it from what she has shared.

The four of us slog through an ever-increasing rain. Ade, in the lead, seems to be following a homing beacon to the back of Bucky's house. With each step, dread builds in me, and I become certain I cannot do my part.

"Is there anything I need to do to help?" Laila asks.

My spirit no longer falters as one of Nana's teachings comes to mind and reignites my hope. In essence, it's incredibly silly of me. Even though neither of them has the magical abilities I do, they still qualify. We still make the cut.

"Yes. When we arrive at the edge of the cane field, I need us to form a circle around Ade and join hands."

Laila favors me with a sideways grin that I don't understand. She says nothing and nods her agreement.

Nana insists that a coven's power is nothing to trifle with. Honestly, I'm not one hundred percent sure the three of us qualify as a coven. Still, the thought of it helps me stabilize my emotions and fortify the idea that I can force Atlas to leave Ade in a manner that allows her to live through this ordeal.

Ade weaves between the farm implements in Bucky's backyard as the silhouette of the sugarcane comes into view. I must pull the chain taut at Ade's back as she breaks suddenly to the left in a sprint. I fumble my flashlight as I wrap the chain around my hand to grip it tighter. The misdirected light illuminates the blue bottle tree to our right.

I smirk as Ade's wince inadvertently confirms one of the island myths. My satisfaction is short-lived as I realize he will not be stupid enough to be snared by the bottle's trance now that he knows their location.

"You don't want to go that way, girl," Ade says.

"I am the one in charge tonight."

"You would do well to understand that I'm in charge. Once I tell the governor how poorly you have treated me, he will plant you in the field, too."

"Why?" I tug Ade toward the blue bottle tree as I shine my light on them, causing them to sparkle with an unnatural glitter that surprises me.

"Come now. Here I thought you were intelligent."

"You wouldn't be the first person to make that mistake. Why don't you enlighten me?"

Ade emits a derisive snort. "Never mind then."

"Whatever. I didn't care to know anyway."

Ade bows up, moving a step closer. "How rude."

"Not really. I'm not that curious about you or your governor, is all. I find you to be a bore." I titter a laugh and feign amusement. "Look at what I have done—bore, boar—how funny."

Ade stands toe to toe with me, glowering. Her irises turn from her usual darkest brown to an inky black with a pinpoint of hell's fire in the center.

"You mock me."

I roll my eyes. "It's not that I mean to be inhospitable, Atlas. It's just that when folks have overstayed their welcome, it's necessary to give them a hint. Even if it isn't subtle."

Ade leans back. The edges of her lips hint at a smile. "You should pay the governor a call."

I motion toward the bottles with my flashlight. "Geez, my social card is all filled up, I'm afraid."

Ade's eyes flit between the bottles and me. "One last thing before I leave. You should try the cane from the center of the field."

She snickers, sending a shockwave of déjà vu through me and making me dizzy. An idea so diabolical pops into my head that it is my fervent wish to push it out as quickly as it arrives.

Ade lurches forward and runs toward the field, pulling me with her. I stumble along and must lean back at a severe angle to anchor my feet, preventing her from entering the cane field. I continue to slide as the woman pulls with unfathomable strength.

I am losing this tug of war.

Ade is a row deep into the field, and my feet push onto the first thick, sharp clump of cropped cane bases. Given that it is Atlas's domain, I want to avoid being pulled into the cane field. I consider releasing my hold on the chain, which means I will lose Ade, the demon who possesses her, and my crucifix's chain.

Arms wrap around my waist, anchoring me to the ground. Laila's right leg appears next to mine, and she pulls with so much force it crushes my stomach.

"Tie her back like she was, April!" Trisha yells.

Why didn't I think of that?

The magic returns to me easily enough, and I chant the binding spell again.

Ade screams in frustration as she is forced to her knees once again. Her displeasure forms a grin on my lips.

"Let's get her back to the bottles," Trisha says as she leans over to lift Ade.

Oh, now *everybody wants to carry her.*

We lift Ade and carry her the ten yards to the bottle tree. I'm ashamed I allowed this little woman to drag me into the cane field. She can't weigh more than 110 pounds.

"My governor will split you open."

I know it's only Atlas speaking, but it is disturbing and creepy to hear Ade speak the words he thinks.

"Shut your mouth," Trisha says.

I nearly burst into laughter. Trisha telling a demon to shut its mouth. If that's not the height of ballsy or stupidity, I don't know what is.

"Trisha, give me your hand," Laila says.

Trisha raises her eyebrows yet does as Laila asks. I take each of their unoccupied hands, forming a circle around Ade.

Ade throws her head back and lets out the loudest pig squeal I've ever heard. I resist the temptation to cover my ears. Trisha and Laila shrug their shoulders toward their ears as they battle against the horrendous noise.

What does Atlas think the governor will do? Does he believe the governor can break our impromptu coven of three and free him?

No. I'm now confident the obscene, three-foot-tall caricature I saw sucking on Laila is the governor. Anything given to stealthily ambushing its prey does not have the intestinal fortitude to endanger itself when a comrade is in need.

Atlas is on his own, and we're coming for his hide.

Despite the continued squealing noise reverberating over the deluge of rain, strange energy unlike anything I have ever experienced causes a rippling sensation in my hands and arms.

The left side of my lips twitches up in amazement. The power of the coven. The feeling is precisely as Nana described.

Yet expulsion has nothing to do with animism. If I should be concerned about the conflict between my two belief systems, I am not. In fact, I am merely even more amused by the fact that Laila's religion adds a third paradox to our newly constituted coven.

The power continues to surge from my two sisters as their best traits—confidence, oneness of purpose, and empathy—flow freely to me as if they are my skill set, too.

It's as if a magical box in my mind opens, and a file, most likely labeled "other superfluous garbage from Granny," comes into view. There, dangling like a magic key on a rack, is precisely what I need.

Post haste, I mentally clutch the key and pronounce the words I heard Granny speak but believed I had never committed to memory.

"Liberar, Liberar, Liberar."

Ade's spine stiffens as she snaps to attention. Yet the

moment of expected triumph doesn't come, as nothing happens. Huge, heavy drops of rain splat on the ground around us. Trisha and Laila stare at me expectantly.

Still, my resolve will not falter as I grip their hands tighter and repeat the chant again.

Ade screams, falling prone at our feet. I am sure I will see the flaming boar expelled from her body at any moment.

Ade convulses, and black bile projects from her mouth into the puddle she lies in. It trails between Laila's and Trisha's feet, growing, the leading part morphing into a giant python head slithering back into the cane field.

I squeeze their hands tighter in case they lose their nerve at the unsettling sight of Ade convulsing and choking while the black fluid runs freely from her mouth. There is a loud sucking noise as the last tail of the liquid comes free from her mouth, and she shudders.

I want to free Ade from the chain. I also want to hold her in my arms and tell her everything will be all right. I can't release her yet. I must wait until the last rivulet of the inky fluid— Atlas—disappears into the cane field.

Trisha attempts to yank free. Of course, my sister of empathy wants to check on Ade. I squeeze her hand tighter to hold her steady while I narrow my eyes toward her. Trisha's expression changes, alerting me she understands the need to remain strong. We watch the last flick of the python's formed tail as it disappears from our sight three rows into the field.

So much for the hope that we could trap Atlas in one of the bottles. Because of the rainstorm, it would be a while before we saw the sunlight anyway.

"Vinctus dimittere vincula eorum."

The chain slides loose around Ade's wrist as it unties and streams away from her, forming a golden coil of links in the weeds. Ade coughs again. I take one more anxious look toward the sugarcane to ensure we are free of Atlas.

We are safe. Atlas has left for the comfort of the governor.

I drop to my knees next to Ade. "Are you all right? Is it you?"

Ade's yellowed eyes open, and I'm taken aback by the smile she favors me with. "Yes. Where is Beulah?"

Chapter 40

"How could you do something so irresponsible, Ade?" Gramma says.

"But you don't understand, Beulah. The tapestry that Esther told us about. It's there, on the old plantation."

"No! It was just a story that an old woman told us as young girls to keep our interest. And the plantation is gone."

Ade sets her jaw and scowls. "It was not a fairy tale. Esther would not lie to us."

"Heavens to Betsy. Esther didn't lie to us. It was a story. There is no such thing as a tapestry that answers questions."

"She says there was, and I believe her."

Gramma huffs and crosses her arms.

"You say she told you. But I thought Esther has been dead for a long time," Trisha says.

"Nearly fifty years," Gramma grumbles. "She told us that story when we were little girls."

"That doesn't make it any less true."

"But if she's been dead for fifty years, I don't understand how she told you it's still there, Ade," Trisha says.

"She spoke to me in my dreams."

"Ade Anderson, are you telling me this all happened because you had a dream?"

Ade glares at Gramma. "My dreams have always been

powerful. You've just never believed in them."

"Oh, I believe in them. I believe they're a whole heap of trouble. They're less dependable than the almanac."

"Like I said, Beulah ... you've never properly respected my dreams."

I know a thing or two about dreams and their reliability. Once, mine were dubious at best. The more practice I have with them, or perhaps it's the wisdom I have acquired with age, they're spot on more often than not.

"Ade, how often do you believe your dreams are accurate?" I ask.

She appears to relax as she disengages from glaring at Gramma, and I believe she comprehends I have the same gift. She folds her hands in front of her and takes her time with thought.

"When I was younger, seldom were they true. Now it's rare that they don't show me the future."

"This dream with Esther. Can you describe it to me?"

"I was sneaking through a fine garden. One of those types rich people on TV pay an army of gardeners to keep up. The grass under my feet felt like a shag carpet with a touch of dew.

"There was a barn door up ahead. I had to cross a pea-gravel path to get to it. I'm surprised I saw it since a massive oak nearly blocked it from my view."

She favors me with a smile. "That's when I know it's a dream, you see. Oaks that large can't grow on the barrier island."

I nod and narrow my gaze the slightest to encourage her to continue.

"I leaned against the barn door and put my shoulder to it. To open it a bit and steal me a look." She waves her hand in front of her nose. "That's when it hit me. The scent of the devil. As far as my eyes could see, there were stacks of casks. Now, I haven't ever tried any."

Beulah clears her throat, and Ade favors her with a sour, tightlipped expression.

"Go on," I urge.

Ade huffs as she returns her attention to me. "Well, it was rum. Hundreds of barrels of rum. This was odd since I'd never been to a distillery before. Still, somehow I knew what was in those barrels."

"How did you know?" Laila asks.

Ade holds her finger up toward Laila. "That's when I realized it wasn't me in the dream. I was possessed by a dream floater."

The term gives me a sudden jolt as if having my cover blown. "Dream floater" is one of the many odd skills I possess. I rarely share the times I use the ability due to Nana's insistence that it is highly problematic and can even curse me to spend the rest of my life in a vacuum void of all sensory stimuli until I die of starvation. All the same I find the skill to be one of my most intriguing.

"Honestly, Ade."

"What is that?" Laila asks. "I've not heard that term before."

"Because it doesn't exist," Gramma says. "Nobody has that much power."

"It is rare," Ade concedes to Laila. "But there is no other explanation."

"You were Esther?" Trisha asks.

Ade's teeth show as she leans forward with excitement. "Don't you understand? I was seeing the world through Esther's eyes. A moment from her youth."

"Honestly, Ade. You're making way too many assumptions for a dream. It could've been anybody, or a random dream altogether."

"No. I know for a fact because I investigated the distillery and found a door to an office. And hanging behind the manager's desk was the tapestry of truth. It looked exactly how Esther described it to us."

"It still does not prove that it was Esther."

Ade licks her lips. "Except when I asked the tapestry a question, I had a strange stutter."

Gramma leans back and puts her hand on her chest.

I bounce my attention from Gramma to Ade, then back to

Gramma. "Did I miss something?"

Gramma sighs. "Esther had a terrible stuttering issue until she became comfortable with people."

Trisha leans forward. "Forget that. What did she ask?"

Ade's expression turns sorrowful as she tilts her head to the side. "She asked if she would ever find true love."

My phone rings, and I nearly jump out of my skin. I snatch it from my back pocket. "Darn it. I'm sorry."

I read the display, and my stomach turns. "Excuse me. I need to take this one."

I leave the room as I answer my phone. "Thelma, it's good to hear from you. What can I help you with?"

"Where are you?"

Thelma's demand causes the same physical reaction as when my mother asks where I've been. I shake that off as quickly as possible to sound professional.

"Currently enjoying a week's vacation. Why do you ask?"

"That would explain why no one is at your office."

"It would."

"Just so you know. This is strictly a courtesy call. I understand that you and Andy have been working behind my back to separate me from the company I built. You need to know that I'll be hiring a new lawyer tomorrow from Huntsville and will be filing a complaint."

"Thelma, it's not like that."

She snorts. "Really? You're conspiring with my partner to file a motion for me to be removed from my company? How is that not like that?"

"Who told you that there's a motion to be filed? I assure you there's no such thing."

"I have my sources."

My ire spikes. "Thelma, your sources are wrong. But we must sit and talk when I get back to town."

"Talk about what? The battle lines have been drawn. You've chosen your side."

"Thelma, you need to hear me out in person."

"Why should I?"

"Because I've always had your best interest at heart."

There's a long silence. I would say something to break it, but there's nothing else to add.

"When will you be back?"

That is an excellent question. In fact, I'm still determining whether the real question shouldn't be *if* I will be back, given the folly being hatched in the living room.

"Two, three days at the most."

Thelma sighs heavily. "I suppose I can wait. But I won't wait any longer than that, and I'm only doing this because it's you."

"I understand, and I appreciate it."

"All right, then. Safe travels."

"Thank you, Thelma. And I assure you it will all work out in the end."

"I hope you're right for all of our sakes."

I shake my head as I push my phone into my back pocket. I wonder who the bozo was that told Thelma. It doesn't matter in the big picture. After the initial shock that she was calling me, all it did was help me deal with a client issue I should have tended to the moment I decided I was reopening Snow and Associates.

"Absolutely not," Laila says vehemently as I reenter the living room.

"The more people, the safer," Gramma says.

I feel uneasy as it seems an excursion has already been planned, and the only thing left to decide is the team members. "Safer for what?"

Laila gestures with her thumb. "Gramma wants Ade to show her where she went."

"That's an awful idea," I blurt out before I can stop it.

"How are we supposed to make the island safe if we don't eliminate that black thing that came out of Ade?"

I laugh at Trisha, which makes her ball her fist. "The black python that went into the cane field is nothing compared to the boar. And I've got a feeling the governor is that three-foot-tall, soul-sucking duppy who attacked Laila."

"Which is precisely why we have to go," Trisha insists.

I shake my head as I look between Ade and Trisha. "You're wrong about more people being better. We should involve Norman and Aduwa in the search if you hold to that logic. Of course, it would only be more cannon fodder for the governor. So, in that case, it might be safer for some of us." I look at Ade pointedly. "Only magical people should be involved. It's not safe for anybody else. And they wouldn't be helpful anyway. That includes Trisha."

"I'm not letting you go without me."

"Yeah. You're not going, cuz."

"She has magical abilities," Laila says. "If it weren't for Trisha, I wouldn't have known you were at Ade's house."

"But she..."

"I don't know what Laila is talking about, but it seems I have a ticket for this party, April." Trisha smirks.

I scan our expedition crew. We have a woman who was recently possessed by a demon, another elderly woman with a heart condition, partnered with two younger women—one with enough spiritual acuity to get the heebie-jeebies around ghosts, and another with enough magic to be dangerous.

Yep. We're going to die a horrible death.

Chapter 41

The thunderstorm passes, but the drops of rain striking our faces have been replaced by a plethora of insects flooding the steamy air. The slow climb uphill is treacherous due to the slick ground and abundant vegetation. There is no trail to the ruins of the old plantation house.

Forget duppies and flaming boars. The mosquitoes and noseeums are so thick as we push through the damp foliage that they suck as much blood as a vampire.

Trisha slaps the back of her neck. "Shiitake, that hurts!"

Ade reaches into the leather saddlebags she collected from her house on the way to investigate the plantation. "You smell like honey. Put this spray on you." Ade hands her a plastic spray bottle with some homemade concoction in it.

"Thank you," Trisha says as she squirts the liquid liberally on her arms and legs.

Similarly, I have welts all over my body from bug bites. But when I'm in Trisha's company, my motto is never to let an opportunity to kid her be wasted. "I've been telling you to eat more garlic."

Trisha stops and holds out her right leg to spray the purple concoction more thoroughly. "Well, if you have any of it, I'll take that, too." She slaps at her right arm and growls. "I'd eat that garlic bulb like an apple right now."

Laila and I laugh at her. "You have to shuck the skin off the cloves first."

"I'll just consider it roughage. That will fix two problems at the same time."

"TMI, girl." Laila giggles.

Trisha tilts her head and grins at us. The wind shifts, and she blanches.

A musky urine smell causes me to sidestep Trisha.

She turns the half-empty spray bottle over and sniffs it. Trisha grimaces as she pulls back. "Oh, my word!"

"Is that you?" I ask.

"What is in this stuff?"

Laila covers her nose with the back of her hand. Ade and Gramma have gained separation from us, and she hollers at them. "Ade, what's in the spray?"

"Just milkweed berries and billy goat urine. It'll keep those bugs off of you."

Laila's lips curl back, exposing her teeth. "Yuck. It would've been helpful to know before you sprayed it all over you."

Trisha extends her arms out and drops the spray. "I've got goat pee-pee on me?"

It's not funny. But I'm still downwind from Trisha, and when the breeze picks up, the gosh-awful smell makes me squint my eyes and turn away. I break into an inappropriate belly laugh as soon as I escape the odor.

"April, it's not funny," Trisha whines.

I beg to disagree, but I'm already hurting her feelings with the inappropriate laughter. "At least the bugs won't bite you."

"Ade does know her stuff about natural fixes. I believe her if she says it'll keep the bugs away." Laila moves strategically upwind of Trisha.

Still struggling to turn off my tickle box, I add, "Skeeters, snakes, dogs, and people... Nothing is getting close to you other than a female goat."

"Every dog has its day, April."

I burst into another round of laughter as I join Laila upwind.

"When is this dog gonna want to get around you?"

We must double-time it to catch up with Ade and Gramma. For a woman who just underwent an exorcism and another who supposedly has a heart condition, they sure can truck it through the bush.

Me? I've been mud surfing for the last half-hour. It seems like with every other step, one or both of my feet slide out from under me, and I must hold my arms out so as not to fall on my bum.

I'm deflecting a kamikaze mosquito the size of a B-52 bomber, and I notice the inarticulate mumblings. This causes me to freeze.

"Did we just walk into a graveyard?"

The two older women stop and gape at me. "Why do you ask that?"

Ade's stare is so intense that it causes me to blush. Even in this company, where everyone is at least open to paranormal abilities, it is still challenging to explain things when the other person has a different skill set.

Still, I am figuring out Ade's and Gramma's abilities, which is an excellent time to probe for more details. "Do you hear voices?"

The two women purse their lips as they squint their eyes in concentration. Gramma shakes her head. Ade clicks her tongue. "I can't say that I do."

"I do," Laila says. She points to a grouping of date trees off to the right that appears too perfectly organized. "But the voices of the dead are coming from over there."

Well, I'll be a monkey's uncle. I'm already aware Laila has significant reservoirs of power. But I am figuring out to what degree and what manner of gifts she possesses. I believe, albeit from a different subset of magic, she has been gifted with a varied arsenal of abilities like mine.

Gramma breaks in the direction that Laila pointed.

"Beulah, where are you going?"

"To see if there is a burial site. Don't tell me you don't know what this could mean, Ade."

"We don't have time for that. I'm not certain where at in the old manor we must go, and we only have a few more hours of light."

"We'll need to mark it so we can clean it up and show our respect."

"Beulah!"

While I understand Gramma's desire to locate and mark gravesites while we are here, I look at the sun as it approaches the horizon and agree with Ade that perhaps we should stick with one task at a time. Nothing prevents Gramma from coming up here later and finding the gravesite then.

"She won't let it go," Laila says as she steps by me and follows Gramma.

Peaches. We're not moving forward until we locate the source of those voices babbling in my head.

Laila is correct. As we approach the odd grove of date trees, the voices increase in volume and clarity. Unfortunately, so many are talking at once that it's impossible to make anything out of the garbled mess.

Unless this collection of souls is any different than other burial plots I have visited, it's most likely a loop discussion. Often the words from the long dead are distilled down to a few regrets or grievances they have held onto for decades which they repeat into infinity.

Laila slides past Gramma and says, "It's further back here."

Gramma pushes back foliage as she walks with her highly polished walking stick. "Watch your step. You don't want to trip over any grave markers."

It comes to me in a rush of clarity. "Laila, stop."

She does and rotates at her hips, looking in my direction.

"There won't be stone grave markers."

"Okay," she drawls.

I walk forward slowly as I scan the topography between the five date trees that form a perfect rectangle, with one in the center. I drop to my knees and look at the surface of the jungle floor, crawling forward as I search for what I think I will find.

"We don't have time for this," Ade says. Still, I remain focused on my task.

The tail end of the refrain echoes in my mind once again as gently as a breeze. *"The night she is chosen. The bond never broken."*

My hand, following the topography under the large fern in front of me, dips, and I crawl between the foliage. Despite having the advantage of understanding what I would find, my stomach tightens as I recognize the six-foot-long indentation in the soil.

"I found one of them," I whisper.

"I can't make out what they are saying?" Laila complains.

"They're speaking?" Gramma asks Laila.

"I think there is an unmarked grave over here."

I sit up and take note of where Trisha is. She is two feet inside the rectangle formed by the four date trees. I look over my shoulder and confirm that I have a tree two feet to my back.

"I have a bad feeling about this," Ade says.

My mind is racing so quickly that I'm developing contingency plans as soon as I'm casting them off as not what needs to be done. It is not helpful for me to let my mind go to the point of who could do this. And it may not have been a who. It could've been the former population, as I don't know the age of these graves.

I sense that the five women buried here had connections with one another. Whoever killed them planned to feed on their bodies' residual essence via the date trees.

Given the recent murders in the cane field, I can't help but believe this has something to do with Atlas's governor.

"There's another witch's grave over here."

I look up and find Laila across the burial ground between the trees. I'm no longer shocked at her abilities as I latch onto the word "witch," meaning she, too, has been able to identify them.

I'm already positive that there are five witches from the

coven. Still, I must walk the perimeter of the trees and find the remaining two indentions on the jungle floor.

Gramma puts her hands to her chest and gasps. Her eyes open wide as they flit from grave to grave. "It's the Silent Coven's grave site," she mumbles.

"Gramma, are you okay?" Trisha asks.

Gramma continues to shake her head from side to side as Ade moves to the center of the perimeter of the tree line and scowls. The two women's eyes lock.

"Ade, the graves of the Silent Coven. Just like Esther described."

"It's only some old family graves, Beulah. We need to move along. We've got business to deal with."

Gramma drops to her knees beside me and swipes foliage side to side. With the tip of her fingers, she gingerly strokes an odd-shaped medallion that comes into view.

"The markers. The prophecy Esther told us about, Ade."

The rustling foliage clues me in that Trisha and Laila are approaching for their own view. I crouch closer to examine the crudely cast, star-shaped medallion with a crescent moon emblazoned on it. Highly oxidized, the iron has turned to a pocked, ruddy, brownish red. Still, given that the symbols closely approximate the Muslim witches' competing religions, I can easily discern the signs despite the years of decay from the harsh environment.

"Beulah, you're too old for those stories to still have roots in your mind."

"No, it must be."

"Who are they, Gramma?" Laila asks.

"Esther," Gramma gestures with her hand toward Ade. "Our childhood mentor..."

Laila nods.

"She always spoke of a powerful coven of five extraordinary elemental witches who also follow the Muslim belief of Allah."

"This is where they were buried?" Laila asks.

"Yes. More importantly, this is where the coven was tortured and murdered."

"Why?" Trisha cries.

Gramma's lips tighten as she falls silent.

Ade's voice interrupts the silence. "They dared to conspire to win their people's freedom from the governor."

The title of "governor" runs a chill up my spine. I twist about quickly to confirm it is Ade and make sure Atlas hasn't reemerged.

I can't read her expression. It is Ade, not Atlas, but the kind and dry-witted woman I have traveled with the last few hours has disappeared.

"Ade, they could help us."

Ade scoffs, "Beulah, it was an old woman's tale to entertain two little girls. It is only a myth. And even if it weren't, they're long gone, as would be their powers."

Gramma's attention flits from tree to tree, and her eyes narrow. "No. See the dates. That's the method."

"No, that's you believing in tall tales when you're too old for it, Beulah." Ade stomps her foot. "We are losing critical sunlight. I do not want to face the governor in the dark."

"I don't understand how you can believe in the tapestry and dismiss what you see with your eyes."

"I see it, but graves can't help me. The tapestry can."

Gramma tilts her head. Her mouth opens, and her eyes widen. "Ade! You knew. You knew where they were buried."

"I did not." She crosses her arms.

Gramma stands and moves toward Ade. Ade takes a step back.

"Don't you dare try to lie to me. How long have you known?"

"I didn't say I did."

Gramma points an accusing finger at Ade's nose. "I know you too well. Tell me, when did you find their graves."

The two women glare at one another, their noses nearly touching. It's like watching two mountain rams posturing for a clash of horns.

"Rather than Ade tell us when, can you explain the

significance, Gramma?" Trisha asks as she approaches the two women.

They discontinue their standoff and take a deep breath. Ade answers, "Esther believed the coven could be reconstituted one day."

Trisha emits a derisive laugh. "You might have to explain more than that. This morning, I didn't believe things like exorcisms existed outside of movies. Now you're saying it's possible to bring people buried for a century back to life?"

Gramma places her hand on Trisha's shoulder. "It's a lot to take in, even for those who can draw on our powers." She turns on Ade. "So why would you keep this a secret?"

Ade raises her hands plaintively. "It wasn't the plan. I wanted to make sense of it all first. Besides Beulah, we are the only two left on the island that can draw from the old power. Everyone else has lost their way."

"Three," Laila says.

"Yes. Three," Ade corrects herself.

Laila reaches up and grabs a date from the center tree. She raises it to her mouth, and Ade screams, "Don't!"

"You've tasted from the tree, too?"

"Yes."

Laila smirks. I have a clear understanding of what she is about to do. Because I would do it, too.

She pops a date in her mouth with a flourish of her hand, bites down, and convulses. Laila jams her finger in her mouth to extricate the fruit as she gags and coughs.

Trisha rushes to her aid, as does Gramma. I stand in shock and horror as my eyebrows leap into my hairline.

"What the heck is that?" Laila manages to sputter.

"The dark."

An icy chill runs up my spine for the second time, causing every hair on the back of my arms and neck to stand on end as I am covered in gooseflesh. Ade doesn't need to explain. From my own experience, I know what she means.

The dark. That wicked itch assaults me every time I

offensively use my powers. The siren calls to move one more grain of rice onto the golden pan on the evil side of the scale. I never know when the scale will finally tilt, driving me to the dark side for all eternity.

"I thought you said they were trying to free their people. That they were good," Trisha complains.

"The warriors' hearts turn black to keep the innocence pure and safe."

The two older women shift their attention to Laila. She shrugs her shoulders.

"It's not like those myths aren't recorded. I find them interesting."

"You know their names and elements?" Gramma asks, her voice full of awe.

"Talitha of fire, Mildred of water, Josephine of earth, Bella of wind, and the leader, the center of the coven, Adeline Anderson." Laila nods her head in Ade's direction, raising her eyebrows pointedly. "I believe she's your ancestor."

"Yes. But..." Ade points toward Laila. "Her magic must have been dark."

Gramma sighs. "Which means even if the coven could be reconstituted, they may be the end of us."

The silence goes on way too long for my liking. Ade made an excellent point before she was caught in her lie. We are losing light, and approaching a hostile entity seems more palatable during the day.

"SOOO," I say to add levity to the situation, "should we soldier on to the old plantation or call it a day, return to the house, and regroup?"

I suggest this, knowing that I must leave for Guntersville as soon as possible. Trisha and Norman are also ready to travel home to Nashville, meaning it would be Ade, Beulah, and Laila on their own.

Then again, that's the way it should be. It is, after all, their world that I've inserted myself into. In addition, Trisha tagging along is more of a liability than an asset on the excursion.

It's difficult for me to decide. If this were happening in Guntersville, while the extra help might be desirable, it might be outweighed by the fact that they don't know the people's ways or the magic.

"We should strike while the iron is hot," Laila says.

"Yes," Ade agrees.

"Are you sure we shouldn't try to bring back the coven? It seems like a sign that we found them."

Gramma favors Trisha with a kind smile. "But for good or evil? We can't be certain. It's too dangerous for us to call on them when we don't know. Still, it does give me strength as I now understand Esther's purpose in telling us the tale. She wanted Ade and me to believe that heroes never really die. If you try to do something great, even if it ends badly, it's better than living your life in silent desperation."

"Oh," Trisha whispers.

Ade gestures toward the slope we were climbing earlier. "It's still a long hike ahead of us. It's best we get started."

We fall into single file, with Ade in the lead. I trail the group and am left alone with my thoughts.

Mainly, how powerful is this governor, who has been feasting on the souls of a coven for a century, and how stupid are we for charging blindly into his lair. This has all the makings of a terrible mistake.

Chapter 42

It's dusk and ungodly hot as the first pile of rubble marking the old slave quarters comes into view. I knew we were close because of the faint whispers increasing in my mind.

It's a dichotomy of feelings stirring in the air. One of desperation and futility fused with hope and love for family.

It has a sobering effect on me as we move further up the field, long grown over with brush and bent saplings.

"The old manor is a hundred yards ahead," Ade says.

"Shouldn't we already see it?" Trisha asks.

"In the 1920s, it burnt down. Much of the stonework has been carried off to make foundations for our homes."

"It sounds like a fitting use for the stones to me," I say.

"A great-great-nephew of the governor, who committed the execution of the Silent Coven, died in that fire," Laila says.

"That's hogwash. The man had serious gambling debts and staged his death," Ade says.

"I'm only repeating what the archived newspapers reported."

"And those aren't island papers. Those city folks will stick together, especially where money is involved."

What may have at one time been a row of slave quarters on a plantation of pristine fields, has all but disappeared into the crevices of time past. Where order and structure once existed, chaos reigns supreme.

The slave quarters' only distinguishable remnants are moss- and fern-covered heaps rising from the unkempt ground. There are no discernible fields, only a wide swath of brush with the occasional crooked pine or palm, its seed transferred long ago on the brisk, coastal breeze.

I raise the partitions slightly in my mind, and the whispers are snuffed out. Only the sounds of the bugs hiding in the sea of tall grass surrounding us break the silence.

I know how being here, in this place of broken dreams, makes me feel. I wonder. I can only imagine how unsettling visiting this place must be for the descendants of the population that worked these fields and built the structures that now lie ruined and rotting.

Ade comes to a halt, stopping our party. She points at a spot in the brush and gestures with her finger. "That's the east-side wall of the manor—or where it was."

I follow the motion of her finger, revealing a twenty-inch-wide section where vegetation is finding it difficult to grow. The ground appears rockier than the rest of the soil, and I realize the remaining stone footers lie below the ground.

"The manor stairs are over there." Ade points.

"How often have you come here?"

Ade clicks her tongue. "I'm not sure. Maybe once a month."

"Ade!"

"What? There's no harm in it, Beulah."

"Besides being used as a meat suit for a demon," Laila grumbles.

"I doubt this is the lair for the governor and Atlas."

"I visit to look for the staff of Adeline. The one that allowed her to harvest and wield greater power to assist the Elementals in her coven."

"I thought you believed Esther's stories to be a myth."

Ade at least has the sound mind to act chagrined over being caught in her own web of lies. "After finding the coven's burial site and tasting the fruit, I was sure the staff was true, too."

"You've been playing a dangerous game, Ade."

She nods in somber agreement. Her eyelids hood her yellow-stained eyes. "Yes. But I am an old, tired woman. If I gain my ancestor's staff and power, I should be able to rejuvenate myself. And if it costs me my life, the price is not nearly as dear as it once was."

"Ade, you can't mean that," Beulah scolds.

"You wouldn't understand. You have your family. I have nobody."

"You have me. And my family is your family."

She favors Gramma with a sardonic smile. "The truth is, once I tasted the power, it became the only thing I wanted."

Beulah shakes her head. "Then you are truly lost. The Ade I know would always put her friends before something as meaningless as power."

"I guess things change."

"I suppose they have."

Listening in on the two women dissolving their friendship is too voyeuristic a feeling even for me, so I turn away. Laila and Trisha are searching across the remains of what would've been the crawlspace of the manor.

I walk quickly over to them, taking care not to step on anything that looks like it might puncture the bottom of my tennis shoes or cause me to fall.

"This can't be it," Laila mutters.

"The foundation perimeter is not very large. It won't take us that long to search it," Trisha says.

I agree with Laila. If this is where the governor resides, he could have done much better for himself.

Now that we're here, searching through the ruins of the manor appears to be an act of futility. There is little left of a mansion now. The plantation most resembles any other unkempt area of the island.

I kick at a section of a charred painting frame. It flops over, revealing the tiniest scrap of canvas under a staple. I wonder if it was a portrait showing the governor and his family surrounded by their ill-gotten fortune.

"Karma is a witch," I grumble.

It is apropos that a structure meant to be a symbol of prosperity constructed off of the labor of an enslaved population should be burned and stripped of its very foundation. If it still stood, the only means of redemption would be to convert it into a community service center and museum to honor the rich history of the population that built it.

It never should have reverted to a distant nephew who, for lack of appreciation, used the facility for illegal purposes and ended up destroying it.

"Do you think Jumare would have passed in the sugarcane field?"

Laila's nearby voice startles me out of my bitter thoughts.

"Since the other two were killed, I believe your brother would've perished, too." It's odd to me that she would ask such a question. Especially considering how clear it is that Jumare would have died if we had not found him.

It's Laila coming to grips with everything that has transpired during the last two weeks. I can empathize since I came home for a fishing tournament not too long ago, and my world turned upside down and has continued along that track ever since. For Laila's sake, I pray this is a one-off situation and that her life can return to normal soon.

Mine? I am at peace that I will never be normal again, nor will I be able to lead the type of life my friends from high school and college will experience.

"It's okay, though. We found Jumare, and he is safe." I turn over a chunk of charcoal with the toe of my shoe. "And if we can find that creepy little blue dude, we'll end this for good."

She snorts and smiles. "The governor doesn't want any part of this impromptu coven."

"Oh, you know it."

Laila scans the four-thousand-square-foot ruined foundation. "It seems too obvious for him to be here."

I follow her view. "That's why he is not." My gaze settles on the two women continuing to argue. "Are they going to be all right?"

"Gramma and Ade?"

"Yes."

Laila blows a dismissive breath of air between her lips. "Never mind them. They're thick as thieves but argue like an old married couple. Gramma is just salty about Ade not sharing with her. Gramma's always been an open book, while Ade can be sketchy sometimes. She likes her secrets."

"Clearly."

Trisha is to our left, twenty feet away. She's picked up a long straight stick and is pushing debris over with it. Her intense expression tickles me for some reason.

"Leaving no stone unturned, I see, Trisha. Excellent job!" I call out.

"Yeah, well, I found the magic staff, but the darn thing is either out of juice or I don't know how to use it," she says dryly.

"She better not let Ade hear her make fun of that. She believes in the rug and the rod and will give her an earful," Laila whispers.

"The only thing I believe in is Atlas, the governor, and the need to neutralize both. Sorry, I'm a hard-facts girl. I *know* they exist—rug and rod, meh."

"Don't apologize. I'm that way myself. Still, finding the graves of the Silent Coven, and knowing it made me tingle all over, has changed my perspective on what I assumed was the Geechee version of Greek mythology."

"I'll second that. There was an awfully strange juju in the air inside the rectangle."

Trisha steps off the foundation and continues north into the weeds. She whacks the tall grass with the stick, swinging it like a scythe, back and forth.

"Where are you headed now?"

"I'm looking for something," Trisha hollers without turning.

"No joke," I mumble under my breath. "Come on. We better go with her before she gets lost."

Laila steals a furtive glance in the direction of the two older women still arguing at the foot of the ruined stairs and sighs. "Sure."

We jog to catch up with Trisha. I pull behind her and ask, "Where are we going, boss lady?"

"*What* are we looking for, not where."

"All right, what?"

Trisha stays focused on the ground as she slays bunches of tall grass and continues forward. I'd be lying if I said it isn't annoying that she doesn't stop to tell me what motivates her.

"Ade says there was a tree."

"Pardon?"

"She did. She said there was an oak tree in her dream," Laila interjects.

"I'll remind you it was a dream. Ade even said it was because trees like that can't grow so large on the island."

"Oak," Trisha says robotically.

"Oak shmoak... She said they won't grow on the island."

"And I saw the graves of five witches a couple of hours ago, too. I wouldn't have thought that possible either," Laila reiterates.

"Not helpful." I turn and glare at Laila. She arches her brow.

"Fair." I sigh.

Really, it's not. I'm supposed to be lounging on a beach, preparing my mind for the next step in my life.

Instead, I'm hunting for a murderous ghost and his sidekick demon minion, and all of it deals with unfamiliar magic.

So sue me if my thoughts have begun to wander. If I knew a vacation with Trisha would be like my brother's investigations, I would have turned her down. Regardless of how desperately I needed a distraction from my breakup with Lee.

I genuinely want to help Laila. During this brief trip, I enjoyed her company and have been quite impressed with her skills. It is comforting to know that there's someone my age afflicted with "gifts" more substantial than feeling the heebie-jeebies or occasionally catching a glimpse of a ghost.

Still, enough is enough. Whenever I think this hot mess is concluding—finding Jumare, chasing the governor off of Laila, or expelling Atlas from Ade—I only slide deeper into the quicksand of this drama. A supernatural situation that is far more complex than what I ever could've imagined. The island has its own history of magic and metaphysical beliefs that I couldn't even fathom when I first hopped off the ferry.

No, it's not more complex than other events I have been involved with. The Imperial Theater in Shelbyville and the Sloss Furnaces in Birmingham come to mind.

The issue is that I needed to prepare for this, and I'm not sure I'm in the correct mental state for a ghost hunt. Not to mention having Trisha in the mix when she has no prior experience with the supernatural, and a teaspoon of talent is most unsettling.

I am still figuring out how it will affect me if we cannot find the governor and remove the hostile entity from the island. In contrast, I know precisely how devastated I would be if something happened to Trisha.

And I found the kernel of power that would drive me forward. There is no way I can talk Trisha out of continuing with this wild goose hunt. Yet, if it turns into something tangible—something dangerous—I will be present to extricate her.

That is enough reason to push forward.

I knock aside the lackadaisical attitude taking root in my soul and fully lower my mental partitions. As I do, faint voices of the long-deceased plantation workers begin anew.

A nasty ozone scent travels to me, causing me to wince. "Do you smell that?" I ask Laila.

She swallows hard as she squints her eyes. "I don't smell anything. But I feel like something oily has been draped over my shoulders."

"Yes." Working with Liza, who also has a different skill set than I do, I'm aware we may experience varying stimuli reflecting the same entity. Both symptoms lean toward the negative and put me on guard.

Trisha has managed to get fifty feet in front of us, and suddenly I feel like I need her closer to me. "Trisha, slow down."

She whacks another clump of grass to the side. "I feel like we're getting close to the tree."

Tree … or ghost. I'm sure something is ahead of us, but I don't want her stumbling onto it first.

"Trisha! Slow your butt…"

I take a tumble as my left toe strikes something unmovable. As I move to catch myself, my right foot also hits the solid obstacle. I put both hands in front of me as I slap rudely onto a jagged section of ground. "Peaches!"

Laila runs toward me and pulls up. She stares, gaping at me as I try to roll over and check my hands, which feel like they have been punctured several times.

"You can quit gaping at any time," I snarl, reflecting my now-soured mood.

The palms of my hands have red welts on them, but nothing is bleeding. I look up and find Trisha also gawking mutely.

Putting my sore hands behind me, I rise to my feet. "No, I'm okay. Thanks for asking."

"April, you found it."

I barely keep from another snarky retort and follow their line of sight. This leads me to examine what exactly I tripped and fell onto.

Now I'm gaping, too, as my mouth falls open. I assumed I landed on a rock or a stray foundation stone. Instead, the surface, which is fifteen feet in diameter, is oblong with hundreds of tiny valleys.

Pushing up to a standing position, I closely examine the surface. Though turned a muddy black from years of decay, the rings of the tree stump are visible.

"Well, I'll be darned."

"Ade was right," Laila says.

"Let's not get ahead of ourselves. The whole point of the tree was that there was a distillery behind it." I gesture with a wave of my arm. "Unless it's invisible, we still haven't found anything that would be a suitable hiding place for our governor."

"Honestly, April. Quit being such a naysayer. If we found the tree, we'll find the distillery. You need to remember that everything has changed because of time," Trisha says. A wide grin creases her face as she examines the stump closer.

"What?" I turn my hands palms up. "We're looking for a suitable place for the governor. There's not even a pile of rubble indicating a distillery here."

Trisha dives into a section of grass nearly as tall as she is, whacking merrily as she goes with her powerless magical rod. Her sprint slows to a struggle as she flounders forward, her shoes sinking into the swampy area.

I roll my eyes and follow her. I'm convinced she will not relent until we find some magical distillery in the weeds or she is bitten by a poisonous snake. My thoughts are the snake is a much higher probability.

"Trisha, stop!" Laila yells and grabs my arm.

Trisha does as Laila asks. We gawk at Laila, waiting for an explanation.

"Do you feel that?"

As she asks, I open myself up entirely to the area. I feel sweaty and as if I've been bitten no less than five hundred times by vicious insects. Still, that's different from what I believe Laila is asking about.

I don't receive the slightest niggle of paranormal sensation. Which in and of itself, given the high ambient supernatural energy of the island, is odd. "No, I..."

A boisterous laugh fills my mind. It's a laugh as if I am at a bar, and someone leans over and chortles in my ear. Except it's not in the real world. It's a cutting laugh from the other side of the veil, and it makes my skin crawl.

"I need to keep moving. I think I'm sinking in this mud."

I favor Trisha with a come-hither hand motion. "Trisha, come closer. You need to be within arm's reach."

"You two sure have gotten bossy all of a sudden," she complains as she wades side to side, returning toward us.

Watching her struggle out of the mud's suction, the path to my right catches my eye, and I wish it had not. Undoubtedly, it looks as if it were made by large livestock. Or, more accurately, an oversized one.

The charred sections of grass on either side of the path further confirm my suspicions. This is the path that Atlas uses. Not in the black oily substance that flowed from Ade's mouth last night before turning into a snake. He travels this path when he is in his favorite flaming boar form.

"You see that?" I point out the path to Laila.

"That looks promising."

It's not what I would've said. Truthfully, it looks scary to me.

"Come on. Let's go check it out."

I follow Laila out of a sense of duty toward the opening between the tall grass. Without a word, Trisha falls in line with us.

The hysterical laughter explodes in my mind again. I cringe from both the volume and creepiness of it.

The dirt between the paths of laid-down grass is torn up with hundreds of hoofmarks. The grass on either edge is singed black, and residual power swarms busily around us. An unmistakably evil force.

In the lead, Laila turns and says, "I wish Ade had been a little more precise with how far the distillery was from the oak."

"She made it sound as if it were directly behind the tree. Not far," Trisha says.

The smell of burning fat and sulfur rises, making me gag. The laughter rings out once more, feeding my dread. It can't be a good omen for things to come.

"Maybe we should get Gramma and Ade up here," I offer.

Laila scoffs, "I would if we found anything. But until then, there's no point."

Oh, there's a point. That would be that there is safety in numbers. Currently, given Trisha has no defensive powers, it's definitely two against two if we meet up with the governor and Atlas. Given that neither Laila nor I genuinely understand how to use our powers, and I'm sure our resident evil spirits do, we are at a severe disadvantage.

Nevertheless, arguing the finer points of attack strategy with Trisha or Laila is pointless. They've both worked into a frenzied status that I often see from members of our ghost-hunting team. Travis is the most recent example of a partner becoming so excited about the chase they are willing to disregard obvious signs urging caution only to continue running merrily into the danger zone.

I should be on a beach lamenting my failed relationship with Lee and deciding how to get Snow and Associates back in business when I return to Guntersville. Instead, I'm following my cousin and our new best friend into what feels more like a well-laid ambush with every passing second.

Laila grunts and falls back onto her butt. "What the heck?"

She clutches at her nose as if someone popped her in the face. In my periphery, I see a momentary glimmer of silver and blue.

Hideous, roaring laughter booms in my mind.

Chapter 43

I extend my hand to Laila. "Are you okay?"

She pairs her hand with mine, and I pull her to stand. "I don't know what happened. It's as if I ran into a wall."

Despite the overpowering odors of sulfur and burning fat swirling in the air, indicating the evil before us, I lean forward and rap my knuckles against a transparent barrier. "You found what you're looking for."

"It's invisible?" Trisha asks.

"It is charmed in some manner." I lay my palm flat against the structure to ascertain what manner of magic we are dealing with. As if responding to my touch, the surface turns dry-ice cold. I yank my hand back, but it is too late.

"Peaches, that smarts." I examine my palms and find scarlet-red welts bubbling fiercely as the skin protests the shocking cold contrast against the balmy air.

"What now?"

I sigh at Trisha and add a shrug of my shoulders for good measure.

Laila groans, doubles over, and falls to her knees. I drop to the ground to support her as she convulses and teeters to the side.

"Laila! What is it?"

"What's wrong with her, April?"

It's as if she has been struck by a weapon, but I didn't see anything. Perhaps, like the barn, the governor can make himself invisible to attack his enemies. I pull Laila into my arms, attempting to shield her with my body from her unseen attacker.

As I squeeze her to my chest, I sense another surge of supernatural power. This one differs from the evil, foul-smelling energy I have experienced in the last two minutes. While I can't describe it as strictly altruistic, this energy is much more balanced than the other power. It feels at equilibrium between evil and good.

Laila continues to shudder as I press her tightly into my arms. It's the most helpless feeling since I have no idea what is happening to her. I don't understand the magic I encountered during the failed experiment with my hand. Despite my exponentially higher level of abilities, I am as useless in this environment as Trisha is.

"Gramma, Ade, come quick. Something is happening to Laila," Trisha hollers while pointing.

I close all my focus around Laila and the two women's voices as they come to render aid.

Since I have no idea what I'm doing, I should step aside and let Ade and Gramma have a go. As I decide that's the best of all options, Laila stops shaking and pushes against me.

"I can open the door for your coven. But I cannot help you any further."

I swallow hard and rock back on my haunches. It's Laila's, but the inflection of her voice and the glassiness of her eyes indicate it's not entirely her. "Okay."

As soon as I say it, I realize I should be asking the sister from the Silent Coven that has taken over Laila all sorts of questions. What lies on the other side of the barn door? How best to eliminate the threat from the island?

Instead, I scramble to my feet and gawk at Laila as she stands. She raises her arms, and her chest expands as she draws in a breath. Laila jerks as she brings her arms down in a rotating motion, and a mirage appears before her.

As the light bends and shimmies, the angles of the structure take on a silver glow, and the flat sections begin to glitter blue. It never fully culminates into a solid form. Still, it is a massive, wooden structure that would be excellent for storing items. Specifically, barrels of rum.

The center of the structure splits, and two large sections of the wood slats slide toward us in a fuzzy illusion—in triplicate exposure of the walls. I jostle my head, and the vision clears into one transparent image of the barn doors opening. The structure's interior is revealed as the doors part, exposing blue-and-gold speckles of chaotic energy that produce a swirling mass at the entrance.

"You must go quickly. I can only hold it open for a fleeting time. The governor's magic is much stronger these days."

Ade pushes past me. "We need to get Adeline's rod and the rug as soon as possible."

Gramma and Trisha follow her quickly through the opening as my concern about Ade's motives grows. Rather than articulating the need to end the governor and Atlas, she focuses on recovering the powerful magic items Esther told them about as children.

Then again, she may want to garner the objects to aid in the battle against the governor. Both items could be handy in a fight with a powerful entity.

Laila gasps and falls to one knee as the sister's spirit leaves her. The doors to the barn commence sliding shut.

Even though it might be better for Laila to remain outside, given she has endured so much, it seems equally dangerous to leave her here alone. I help her to her feet, and we sprint toward the closing door in an awkward, falling run. A wood frame bounces rudely against my side as we enter.

The doors close with a resounding thud directly behind us.

Ade and the other two wasted no time. They're on the far side of the barn, looking down at something.

Realizing that we may have a tremendous fight on our hands

if the witch that was inside Laila is correct, I absorb as much of the chaotic energy floating freely in the barn as possible.

"He's here."

I know she's talking about the governor. Yes, this invisible distillery is undoubtedly a suitable location for him and Atlas to hide. Still, I ask the question. "How do you know?"

She frowns and looks toward the ground in shame. "I didn't want to mention it, but ever since the governor fed on me, it is as if we're somehow connected."

I can't help but be alarmed. "Like you feel his pain?"

Laila blinks her eyes as she shakes her head. "No! Gosh, no. Thankfully not. I'm just saying that I feel his presence. He's near."

The horrendous laugh rattles in my mind again. It is followed by the squeal of a familiar entity.

"Ade, no!"

I turn at Gramma's yelled warning. Ade has mounted a ladder that appears to lead down an access hole.

"Can you tell us anything more exact? Like where he is or even what we can do to defeat him?"

Laila shakes her head. "I'm sorry, it's not that specific."

Me too. I'm into this too deeply now not to help. But I still have no clue how to improve our survival odds. This search is crescendoing my anxiety to the point where I don't even know if I could perform what magic I believe might help.

"Ade, stop!" Gramma screams again.

Ade's head disappears into the hole. I'm not surprised when Trisha steps onto the ladder and starts to crawl down after her.

I would scream for her to stop. But like the ghost lust Travis experienced in the Murfreesboro tunnel, I understand Trisha will not stop until her curiosity has been satisfied.

"Can you come with me, Laila?"

She nods her head as her eyelids droop.

I doubt we will survive the next few minutes. But at that moment, as Laila shows her resolve and bravery again, I know that if we do make it out of this, she is someone I want to keep as a friend. She is both a calming as well as an inspiring person to me.

"All right then. Lean on me, and we'll see what deadly trouble Ade is getting us into."

She scoffs, "The worst, I'm sure."

Gramma throws her hands up in frustration as we approach. "I'm too old for this. I can't believe I must chase those two down into that basement."

Unfortunately, navigating the ladder into the basement is the least of our concerns. "Do you want me to go first?"

"No. You help Laila, and I'll see if I can catch up with Ade and Trisha." With agility that belies her statement about being too old, Gramma swings a leg onto the ladder and quickly makes her way down the hole, leaving Laila and me to follow.

As Gramma slips out of sight through the hole, an elevated level of foreboding crashes over me. It's painfully apparent that we're doing precisely the opposite of all the precautions we should take.

The universe is trying to teach me a critical life fact in simulation mode, and repeatedly, I fail. The lesson is simple: don't follow a hostile entity into its lair.

It seems simple enough. And I'm an intelligent girl. It's even intuitive.

Yet, here I am again, allowing my team to endanger itself by going exactly where it shouldn't into the lair where, in the best case, the spirit has all the advantages and, in the worst case, has laid a trap for us.

"I guess we should go," I whisper.

Laila clicks her tongue. "Hey, April. Before we do, I need to tell you something."

I look her in the eye. Her odd expression forces me to swallow my complaint about us not having time for further discussions.

"I want to apologize for being so ungrateful when you and Trisha arrived. I think you understand that the magic on our island is different than in other places." She rolls her eyes. "I didn't even know if it was true that you had the abilities your uncle told Aduwa you had. I was suspicious about that, too. I'm sorry."

"You don't have to apologize for..."

She raises her hand. "Wait a second. I just need you to know how much I appreciate you putting yourself in danger for strangers. Not everybody would do that, and I need you to acknowledge that I appreciate your staying to help us." Laila shrugs. "I want you to know, just in case."

Laila opening up so thoroughly to me is as important as her words. Her need for me to acknowledge her appreciation makes it all that much more heartfelt in my mind, causing my face to heat. I could go into a long explanation about how I admire her and now consider her my friend. Still, I know that will only embarrass her and make the interaction more awkward. And the rest of our team is likely walking into a deadly trap as we speak. "Thank you for saying that."

Laila smiles. I watch as it fades, and I understand her final words. "You don't think we're going to survive this."

"I don't."

"There's not much good you can do in your current condition. Why don't you stay up here?" I'm desperate to allow at least one of us to survive and let our families know what happened to us.

"And let you have all the fun?" she scoffs. "Besides, I'm the one who is supposed to be down there. This is my fight."

I open my mouth to argue but shut it. As much as I would like to save her, this *is* Laila's fight, and I can't hold her from it. Just like Trisha is my responsibility to bring home in one piece or die trying. "Then let's do this."

I motion toward the ladder. "I'll go first and try to steady you on the way down."

The first breath of the air from below has me momentarily reconsidering my unconditional love for my cousin. The all-consuming odor is a sickly concoction of soured rum, gunpowder smoke, burning flesh, and sweaty jockstraps.

I recoil. My mind refuses to allow me to mount the ladder. Everything about the offensive, hot damp smell screams, *You're a fool if you continue, April.* But then, my foolish tendencies are legendarily known.

"I'm sure it's one of those smells we'll get used to," Laila says.

Her ludicrous comment is enough to steel my resolve to continue going forward. "I hope we're not down there long enough to get used to that."

"I like your way of thinking better."

We struggle our way down the ladder. I realize that Laila is in worse condition than I first thought, as she can barely grip the rungs, and her feet continue to slip. Despite the increased veracity of the stench, which now includes a male-locker-room, sour-sweat stench, I'm relieved as she finally steps onto the lava-like floor of the basement.

We scan the small, circular room we land in. It's as if it has been chiseled out of a single rock section.

"Is this real? I mean, was it real?"

"It doesn't matter. Let's find the rest," Laila says as she slides by me.

Sparks of hope flitter through me as I see her again transform into a woman of purpose. I'm comfortable being her wing woman on this excursion. I just can't be in the lead.

We walk down the narrow tunnel, and the remaining light fades. As a force of habit, I flick a small flame into existence on my right palm. The blue-white light dances brightly on my skin.

"Put that out," Laila hisses.

Obediently, I close my palm and snuff out the flame.

"He felt the energy draw."

The significance isn't lost on me. If we ever had the element of surprise, I have now messaged the governor that a magical being is in his lair.

"I'm sorry," I whisper.

"Don't worry about it. Let your eyes acclimate."

That's easier said than done. Besides an odd, pale-orange

glow from the floor and the lower third of the coarse stone wall, it is pitch-dark in the tunnel. I focus on watching the faint silhouette of my feet as we continue.

The more information I gain about the island's hauntings, the less everything makes sense. This is supernatural, which typically makes zero logical sense in the strictest terms. Still, why would there be a tunnel snaking below a distillery? What possible use could there be for constructing one? And how would it even be possible when Trisha's feet sank into a swamp-like field right before we entered the invisible barn?

The spirit who momentarily shared Laila's body was one of the witches from the Silent Coven. I'm sure of that much. It makes sense that Laila became a vessel for the spirit since she ate one of the dates from their gravesite.

Goodness. Suppose Laila does have a direct mental feed to the governor, as she claims, because he fed on her. And she is subject to temporary possession by one of the Silent Coven witches from eating the date. In that case, I feel guilty for my occasional outburst that makes it seem like I have some bipolar, Southern-princess disorder. Her situation truly sucks, and I am awed by her ability to hold her emotions in check for the sake of our mission.

I'm consumed with worry for her and concentrate on any way I can help her cope. Nobody should carry that many burdens alone.

She stops, and I'm a beat too slow to stop my step, forcing me to put my hand on her back to not run her over. "Sorry."

I wait silently in the darkness for as long as my patience holds out—which is never long—for Laila to explain why we stopped. I look over her shoulder and see nothing ahead in the darkness. "Why did we stop?"

"We're at an intersection."

That is *an* answer. I had hoped for it to be more complete. "And?"

"I'm deciding."

My silly hopes of finding Trisha and the older two women

quickly evaporates as I understand our predicament. Of course, there's an intersection. Why wouldn't there be a sixty-six percent chance of us taking a wrong turn, losing our way in this labyrinth, and never rendezvousing with the rest of our impromptu coven?

"I vote straight ahead," I blurt. I need to do something, and standing here at the intersection doesn't seem fruitful.

"Shh…"

I sigh on a sulk, fidget with my hands for what seems like an eternity, and cross my arms while I take to swaying on my feet. There's something about standing in pitch-darkness with no sound that makes time crawl. I'm sure it's been less than a minute, but I am slowly losing my mind. "What are we doing?"

"I can feel him. I want to be sure I'm correct on what direction will take us to him."

I feel marginally better. We're not merely playing Simon Says and standing frozen in a permanent state. Still, I wonder if Laila plans to get a bead on the governor today or tomorrow. In the meantime, with the help of Ade, I'm sure Trisha is managing to get herself into all sorts of danger.

Losing my patience, I reach out to tap Laila on the shoulder. A trail of light illuminates the distance. The light snakes toward us in a leisurely, strobing motion.

"What is that?"

"He knows we are in his sanctuary."

I want to ask who, and realize the stupidity of my question. The governor, of course.

As the light nears, I recognize the floor is illuminating. This amuses me as it is reminiscent of the yellow brick road. Of course, Dorothy would've been smart enough not to follow this road and recognize that it leads directly to the wicked witch.

"Straight ahead like you thought," Laila says.

"Never underestimate my talent for finding trouble."

We cross the intersection and follow the lighted trail for blocks. I see the end of the light but am disappointed as the trail veers wildly to the right, and the light continues ahead for hundreds of yards. It's unfathomable that we can travel this long underground on an island. Somewhere along the journey, we've got to encounter water. It would only make sense.

"How could they have gotten so far ahead of us?"

"Maybe he sensed them sooner than us and showed them the way as soon as they came down the ladder."

"Felt who? You're the one he fed on."

"Atlas wore Ade's skin for a few months."

"True that. That small detail slipped my mind."

The trail swings crazily back to the left, and I have the strange sensation that we are now double backing toward the small chamber where we came down the ladder. Because of our confined space, and lack of illumination higher than our knees, it is difficult to determine how long we have walked. Still, if it is less than two miles, this vacation has set me further back in my cardio training than I could have imagined. My lungs can't pull in enough of the foul air, and my hamstrings have begun to burn uncomfortably.

A shrill squeal of laughter echoes down the hall, followed by wet snorts. This time, unlike earlier, the noise is natural, not manufactured in my mind.

I reach for Laila's shoulder. Since we are so close to our nemesis, I suddenly need to revisit our action plan. It seems … well, inadequate.

She pulls free of my grasp and hurries forward, leaving me with one final opportunity for a decision.

Duty calls me to be brave and save my friends and Trisha. Still, I know intrinsically that I have no place in this world and can do nothing to change the events prepared to spring into action. It is, in effect, an act of suicide if I move forward.

And if I were to turn and run? If I could save myself, it's not an absolute that I can. What then?

How would I live with myself over the years? How would I explain to my uncle that I turned tail and ran when Trisha needed me the most?

I absolutely loathe the fact that I am a Snow. First, because of these wackadoodle paranormal skill sets I inherited from my grandmothers. Second, because everyone in my family is fearless. In fact, if it weren't for my supernatural abilities, I would believe my parents stole me from the nursery. I am nothing like them. I missed out on the abnormal gene that is supposed to give me the desire to put myself between people I care for and mortal danger. For the rest of my family, endangering themselves to save someone else is just another day in the life of a Snow.

There is no decision to be made when it comes down to it. I sway my head from side to side as I trudge forward. "Who's stupid enough to chase a ghost into a tunnel?"

I creep toward the distant opening, and my eyes acclimate to the light, revealing the hopelessness of our quandary. The three-foot-tall blue ghost sits at a massive three-section desk in the middle of a cavernous room. The governor has propped his abnormally large blue feet onto the desktop. He leans back in the wooden executive chair, sucking on a torpedo-sized cigar.

The walls in the room glitter golden as if they are electrified filaments, leaving spots on my eyes as I try to adapt to the differing intensity of light in the chamber room. Complete with flames dancing along his backbone, Atlas prances back and forth in front of the desk.

"Do it again! Do it again!" the governor yells with a laugh.

Atlas raises his right leg, strains, and emits a fireball out of his butt that shoots rapidly across the room. From my view to the right, the flaming sphere disappears, and an explosion reverberates throughout the cavern.

The governor squeals with a raucous laugh. Atlas, quite pleased with the attention, snorts his pleasure as well.

Besides the cleared area for the desk, the room is filled with rows of barrels stacked three high. I squat down and duckwalk toward the entryway, hoping to remain concealed from their view as long as possible.

Concern bubbles up in my stomach as I realize none of my friends are in view. I squash my fear down as I tell myself they are simply hidden from my line of sight behind one of the rows of barrels. That's it. I'll make my way to the barrels and reunite with the rest of the team, and together we'll devise a plan to end the governor's reign of terror for good.

I reach the edge of the tunnel. My blood chills to ice in my veins, and I am paralyzed with shock and bewilderment. On the far wall to my right, Trisha is chained spread eagle. Countless black holes pock the stone surface around her.

Atlas has been using her for target practice.

I shake off the initial shock. Rage fills me from the edges of my toenails to the tips of the hair on my head. My ears could be no hotter if Atlas were to hit me in the face with one of his fireballs.

How dare they do that to my cousin!

I scan the room again for the other three women. They wouldn't have left Trisha in this evil spirit's hands if they were here.

I fail to find them and step into the chamber, hugging up against a barrel while keeping Trisha in sight. Her bewildered eyes stoke the fire of retribution in my gut even further.

The governor will pay for his transgressions.

The governor pleads for Atlas to do his fireball trick one more time. Atlas prances into position and steps over the walking cane that Trisha used to separate the tall grass on our approach. I measure the distance between where I am and the makeshift club lying at the end of rows of barrels a few paces from the governor's desk.

Atlas raises his right leg, his face tightens with immense strain, and the locked prison door where I keep my crazy safely stowed blows off its hinges. I run toward Atlas. My rebel yell echoes throughout the chamber. The governor drops his cigar and flips his chair over as he tries to catch it. Atlas's fireball fails to launch. He makes a noise like a sad party favor from below his raised tail.

I grasp the stick before they recover and swing it behind me in preparation for clobbering Atlas into next week. As I bring the walking cane around with ill intent, the arc of its path halts, and I freeze in place.

I flit my point of view from Atlas to the governor's outreached hands, veins bulging and fingers squeezing as if choking my imaginary neck. An excited cloud of silver-and-red energy swirls around his grasp. "You won that bet fair and square, Atlas. You're right. Baiting the big fish with the minnow did work."

Atlas hops into the air, completing a one-eighty, and commences to prance around me.

I struggle against the governor's magic, but it is not like the binding spell that Atlas used. Instead, the paralysis worsens with time as I feel the magic seep into my muscles and undo them. The real fear of falling to the ground without being able to break my fall consumes me as it is impossible to even blink my eyelids.

The governor steps from behind his desk. He continues holding his tight grip while the particles of chaotic energy funnel from his grasp, swirl around my neck, and consume me in a glittering bubble. "Oh yes, Atlas. You were right. I knew of the Washington girl. And I still want to consume her. But I believe this witch to be enough to complete my transformation, too. You have done well, my faithful servant."

Atlas squeals his pleasure so loudly my ears ring.

The magic flows deeper into my muscles, my hand relaxes, and the stick clatters to the floor. The insanity of attacking two demonic beings with a simple stick irritates me. *Foolish, foolish girl.* How apropos that my foolish decisions have finally caught up with me and caused my doom.

The governor drops his right hand to his side. His left is still up, and only two fingers point toward me. I realize those two fingers are all that hold me from a nasty face plant onto the lava floor at my feet.

As he approaches, he grows taller, and his hair grows across his bald crown, the gray curls darkening as they spread. He steps so close that his fingers form cool spots on my chest as he crowds me.

He leans forward, angling his head so that his nose, now appearing strong and aquiline, rests near the crook of my neck. He inhales. "Hmm ... you will be more than enough to make me whole. So sweet-smelling yet potent. Quite the exotic blend you are."

He pulls back and squints his marbled blue eyes. "You're not from here."

Preposterous giggles bubble up from inside me. While I've never taken the time to seriously consider how my end will come, I had to believe and hope that I wouldn't have to listen to what sounds like a weak pickup line from a cowboy wannabe from some Podunk town.

"Are you laughing?" the governor asks.

Honestly, how does he expect me to answer while he holds me in a state of suspended animation? Despite transforming himself from a grotesque caricature into a rather attractive thirtysomething male, his intelligence must be directly inverse to his handsomeness.

The governor slides in front of me, his nose tip to tip with mine, and wrinkles his brow. "Nobody belittles me. Least of all, a woman. For that, your death will be long and torturous. You won't enjoy it, but I will." Leaning forward, he kisses my lips.

The cloying aroma of a July sixth dumpster after a Fourth of July fish fry assaults my nostrils. In auto-response, my body eager to hurl anything so rotten from my vicinity, I projectile vomit through the governor's opaque face. The primarily liquid expulsion makes a rude splatting noise behind him.

"You witch!" the governor screams. He slaps me with cat-like speed in a well-practiced move and knocks me to the floor.

My shoulder strikes first, followed by the side of my head. Darkness and tiny blooms of too-bright light fill my vision as pain radiates through my brain. My hand goes to my ear, and I realize the governor's spell is broken.

"Atlas, give her something to think about."

I can't see him from my point of view, but Atlas's hooves click in a rhythmic tap dance-like routine across the stone floor as he approaches me. If I plan to survive, I must get to my feet and create a defensive shield. It is all that comes to mind to protect me and allow enough time to solve how to release Trisha from the manacles.

But my head still hurts. And my muscles are cramping as if they have been injected with gallons of lactic acid. I manage to stretch my hands in front of me, but I can't even force myself into a crawling position. I look up and consider Trisha hanging limply from the wall.

I hate that I allowed her to be involved with this. Trisha is an innocent who made the mistake of trying to help. She had no idea how dangerous the supernatural could be for the living.

Me? From the first, when the Old Man in the Lake held me underwater, I knew that if I didn't avoid all paranormal events, I would be doomed to die by one. Yet no matter how hard I try to separate myself from the supernatural, I can never escape its gravitational pull. I have always believed I would die precisely in this manner.

A loud *crack* thunders behind me. A heavy weight falls, pinning my lower legs to the floor.

Did they throw a stone across my legs?

"That's what you get for hijacking me!"

I don't believe the woman is screaming at me, but it still scares the bejesus out of me. Given I have accepted the fact that I'm about to be murdered in an invisible underground cave, that's saying a lot.

Twisting my body, I change my point of view. A terrifying version of Ade is standing over me with a stake. It's not a stone on my legs, although it might as well be. It appears that she has finished the job and knocked Atlas out. His dead weight is sprawled across the back of my calves.

"That was the staff of Adeline," the governor says as he peddles back toward his desk. "You broke it, you ignorant woman. Everyone knows you should never use an artifact without knowing how to wield it properly."

"Maybe I meant to break it, you tiresome little boy." She shakes the broken handle at him. "I still have half of it to stake you and send you back to where you came from," she screams as she chases him around the desk.

I'm further alarmed by a grunt behind me, and I fear Atlas is waking up. I look over my shoulder toward my legs. Laila and Gramma are pushing against Atlas's ribs, attempting to roll him off of me.

A black, oily substance pools around Atlas's head. I believe his days of shooting fireballs are done.

"Do you recognize this!" the governor screams.

Atlas's dead weight rolls off me, and I work up to a crawling position. "Thank you," I say to Laila and Gramma.

Neither of them pays me any heed. I rotate my view to their line of sight and am amazed at the intricate quilt I had not noticed behind the governor's desk. Easily thirty feet by thirty feet, the quilt is constructed with hundreds of colorful panels of letters, numbers, and everyday items such as trees, birds, and knives.

The governor holds his hand a few inches below the quilt. A red flame burns in his right palm. "It's been quite a day, Ade. You've already destroyed one artifact you have searched for your entire life. Would you like to make it two?"

"You wouldn't. You need that power, too."

"No, Ade. I already have all the answers I need. The only thing I want is to have my corporal self back. Well, that and immortality. And you see, I already have both answers from the quilt."

"It's not yours to destroy. It belongs to my people."

The governor chuckles. "Your people? Who, Ade? The five dead witches on the hill?" He gestures in front of him. "The sad excuse for a coven that you attack me with?" Making a *tsking* noise, he adds, "Ade, your people are all gone." He blows on his left palm with a dramatic flair, and a powder-like substance takes flight into the air. "Your people are nothing but dust, Ade."

"No. You're dust. And if I have anything to say about it, you will remain that way."

The flame grows higher on the governor's palm. "And you will lose your precious quilt."

The one thing I could use right now is some answers. Specifically, how to put an end to the governor. If there's any truth to the quilt's ability to provide solutions, it's imperative I take advantage of it post haste. Before the governor sets it to flame.

Of course, I have yet to learn how the island magic works with the quilt. All I can draw on is how I usually generate magical abilities. So, I collect a fair amount of random power floating close to me and project my thoughts toward the quilt. In my mind, I continually repeat, "How can we eliminate the governor?"

No answer comes, and I redouble my effort to concentrate. Despite the train wreck around me and our inevitable demise, I focus all my attention on the quilt. Beads of sweat pop up on my forehead as I try to will the letters and symbols to move and reveal a coherent message.

Exhausted from my efforts, I stop and pant.

It must be the differences between the magic. My mainland magic will not work on island artifacts.

Laila and Gramma move to the right in my periphery to flank the governor. Dismayed by my failure, I struggle to my feet. I might be as useless as tits on a boar in this fight, but maybe I can distract the governor for the rest of the team.

Who knows? There may even be a possibility for me to free Trisha so that she can escape and notify our loved ones what happened to us.

"Even if you gained your body back, you would never be able to leave the island alive," Ade taunts.

"You have fully underestimated my abilities. Of course, you have done that from the start. You didn't believe Atlas could take hold of your body. Did you?"

That gains my attention. Gramma and Laila also favor Ade with open-jawed expressions of disbelief.

Ade pleads to Gramma, "It's not what you think, Beulah."

"Ade, what did you do?"

The governor smirks. "The most common transaction made in history."

"You tricked me!"

"Ade, Ade, Ade, you believed what you wanted to believe. Poor Ade. No family, no money, but the truth is, Ade, you have always been a power-hungry, sorry excuse for a woman."

"No, I'm not!"

"Oh, really? Is she now? Then what are you?" Beulah says as she strides toward the governor.

He looks tentatively between the two women, his eyes growing wider.

"What right had you to return to the ancestral home and use it for illegal purposes? What deal did *you* cut?"

"This isn't about me."

I asked the quilt too complicated of a question. I change the question in my mind to "Will we get out of this alive?" and focus my conscious stream on the quilt's letters.

Thrilling excitement courses through me as the quilt shimmies. Letters tumble and shift on the surface like part of some Rubik's Cube falling into place. I grin triumphantly as the letters across the top of the fabric spell out "Most likely."

Much of my anxiety dissipates as if an internal steam valve released my stress. I now know the fix is in on our bet. The quilt, a revered, ancient artifact of the island, has determined that we will survive this event. We will put an end to the governor and escape his lair.

I double over, placing my hands on my knees as I steadily try to regain my breath. I don't know what will be required to dispatch the governor, but knowing that we will survive gives me the ability to dig deep down into the well of reserves and prepare for the final battle.

I straighten my back like a ramrod and take one more look at those beautiful words saying we will survive. "Most likely." Then directly below it appears "Not."

Well, fudge nut.

"No!" Ade's scream draws my attention. She's running toward the quilt, but it's too late. Flames scale the face of the fabric, engulfing it with incredible speed.

As she closes in and swipes at the quilt, ineffectively trying to put out the flames, the governor wraps his arms around her. He squeezes her so tightly that her back arches as she gasps for air.

"Stop him!" Gramma screams. "If he steals her power, he will be whole again."

I must still be concussed from the slap and bouncing my melon off of the stone floor. I'm watching everything transpire in spectator mode, yet I'm leaning in toward the melee. I'm not trying to escape, it's just that I can't think of what to do.

A defensive shield will not be helpful because the governor already has hold of Ade. Fireballs and concussion explosions are the last things we need, given there is a higher probability of them hurting my team rather than doing any damage to the governor in such closed quarters.

I stand, slack-jawed, as I watch the craziness around me. There's a massive quilt on fire, and some of the flames have already leaped over to the barrels stored in the room. I'm not an expert on the flammability of eighty-proof liquor, but something tells me that it can't be good.

Meanwhile, Trisha has opened her eyes, which at least tells me she's alive. Her thousand-yard stare is unsettling. It makes me think that if we survive, she will have the worst case of PTSD ever.

What's going on behind the desk? I'm familiar with entities stealing energy, but stealing enough to become alive again? I've never heard of such things. That couldn't be true.

Ade convulses within the governor's grasp. Slowly, his ghostly vision becomes more solid while Ade's body prunes up as if she is having all the liquid sucked out of her.

Gramma reaches Ade first. She grabs hold of Ade's shoulder. A loud explosion claps against my ears, and Gramma is blown six feet away from Ade, landing on her back.

I start toward her, finally glad that my skill set will be helpful for once since I can check if Gramma is injured.

A loud mewing sound draws my attention back to the governor's embrace of Ade. Her eyes sink into her skull as she gasps ineffectually for breath. The governor releases her, and she collapses to the floor. He opens his arms wide, giving an exaggerated shoulder shake while wrinkling his nose and smiling.

"Golly, that feels good." His eyes settle on Laila, and he points at her. "You're next, junior."

Laila puts her hand to her mouth. She neither moves forward nor retreats.

"That's right. You know it's pointless to run."

I'm helping Gramma to her feet and yell at Laila, "Come on. Let's get Trisha down and leave."

Laila looks over her left shoulder at me and winks. She turns her attention back to the governor as she steps toward his desk.

I'm definitely concussed. My vision of Laila is shimmering left to right as if she is in multiple exposures laid cattywampus on top of one another.

"You wish to be whole again?"

"It's what was promised to me."

"If I make you whole, you have to leave," Laila says as she closes the distance between them.

"I don't have to do anything."

She pulls to a stop. "If I do this for you, you must leave. Agreed?"

The governor shrugs. "Sure," he scoffs. "It's not like there's anything to keep me here."

"Good. Take my hand."

"Laila, no!" I scream.

I don't understand what she's doing. I need her help if we have any chance of escaping. Gramma is writhing in pain, and Trisha is chained to the wall and catatonic. I feel like every muscle in my body is cramping, and Ade... I'm afraid she may not feel pain anymore.

If Laila thinks she can buy enough time for the rest of us to escape, she will be highly disappointed. I fear if she sacrifices herself now to the governor, we'll all still be dead in the cavern because I cannot get all of us out. Desperate to prevent Laila from needlessly sacrificing herself, I try to do what I can to improve our odds. I quickly gather energy and form a protective shield around Gramma and me. If I can manage it, I'll help Gramma toward the wall Trisha is hung on and envelop her in the protective, powder-blue cocoon, too.

I know it is a fool's errand in the marrow of my bones. As powerful as the governor is now, there's no way my simple defensive shield will be sufficient to turn him away after he has drained Ade and Laila of their energies.

"Please, Laila, don't."

Rather than turn to acknowledge me, she extends her right hand toward the governor. The narrowly built man with an attractive face licks his lips. He stares at her proffered hand with immense curiosity and hunger.

From my vantage point, my perception of Laila momentarily becomes two separate visions, like a projection jostled by someone hitting the table it is set on. The two fuzzy images slide side to side on each other as an intense light shimmers a halo effect around her.

"Don't you want to be made whole, Ricky?"

"Nobody calls me that." He snarls. "I'm the governor."

"No. The governor was an exceedingly cruel man with the aspirations of twenty men and the highest political and capitalistic abilities. You, Ricky, are not a governor. You are merely a scrap of discarded DNA, only a poor photocopy of his worst traits. You are a petulant, spoiled little bastard."

Ricky swings his right hand at Laila's face. Her arm is a blur, and I flinch at the smacking noise when his fist contacts her.

But Ricky did not hit his intended target. Laila holds his balled fist in her right hand. His eyes fly open in alarm, and he jerks backward.

Ricky is unable to free his fist from Laila's grasp. He pulls and tugs, but it is as if she has planted his hand in concrete and allowed it to cure overnight.

"Let me go!"

"But, Ricky, you said you want to be whole."

"Let me go!"

"Can't you feel it, Ricky? Can't you feel my powers surging into your body and making you whole?"

The pathetic powder-blue defensive shield I had brought to life shudders and evaporates. Blue-and-silver specks of chaotic energy jet toward the center of Laila's shoulders with such speed that it's as if they are tiny comets streaking past me in supersonic flight, all lighting her back.

Laila vibrates like a tuning fork. The halo around her intensifies so intensely that I squint and turn my head to shield my eyes. The coolness of the cavern has been replaced by dry heat.

"Stop!"

"Be brave, Ricky. I'm giving you what you've always wanted."

"This isn't what I wanted."

"It is what she wants. I'm only providing it to you because I can. Consider it my family's last gift to your family."

"I don't want it anymore!"

"Too bad, Ricky. Truly, I would rather repay the *real* governor for what he did to my four sisters and me, but you are all I have left to unleash my vengeance against."

Ricky closes his eyes and groans. He doubles over and screams in agony.

Laila releases his hand. The brilliant light surrounding her disappears, leaving only a calm, steady halo surrounding her.

The lighting in the room remains as bright as it was when I entered, but it is no longer like looking into the sun.

My gut turns as I watch Ricky stand straight and pat his chest and stomach with both hands. "You did it."

"My powers are great."

I'm gobsmacked. First, I wouldn't have even imagined it possible to bring a ghost back and give them a physical body. Second, considering how disgustingly grotesque Ricky was in his ghost form, he is a handsome man over six feet tall.

A man who used to be a ghost with a sidekick demon and recently killed people for their power. My vision goes to Ade, still limp on the floor while I say a silent prayer that she is all right; I fear she is another one of his victims.

"Is he real?"

I was so busy watching the spectacle that I didn't realize Gramma had checked back into the game. I open my mouth to answer but shrug my shoulders as I return my attention to Laila and Ricky. I shake my head in bewilderment, realizing that Laila has possibly saved us, but at what cost?

Ricky laughs. "I have to tell you. I didn't think there was any way that you could do this for me. I didn't expect you to keep your word."

"I did it for my sisters and me, not you. And you should know, Ricky, I always keep my word."

His eyebrows knit as he crosses his arms. "I appreciate that. But understand that the entire reason for being whole was to regain my status on the island. Just because you keep your word, don't expect I'll keep mine by leaving the island."

Laila steps closer and puts her left hand on Ricky's shoulder. "That's okay. I figured as much, and I will ensure you keep your word."

Ricky chuckles. "What are you going to do? Teleport me away from here or something?"

Laila's hand moves forward in a blur. The sickening sound is like a head of iceberg lettuce cracking apart, and it causes me to wince. The sucking noise as her hand returns toward her chest has an even more visceral effect on me.

Ricky's beating heart spurts blood into the air. The large

muscle convulses in Laila's hand.

"But—you—promised." Ricky gurgles, blood spewing from the right side of his mouth.

Laila releases his shoulder, and he falls to one knee before her. "I understand how difficult it is to travel away from home and not leave your heart behind."

I lose my balance as the floor bucks up, down, and to the side. A loud, low-pitched grating noise fills the chamber as barrels of rum fall from their perch, splitting and spilling their contents across the floor.

Ricky falls dead at Laila's feet. The ground rumbles, and I realize the error of our decision.

Chapter 44

"Get Trisha."

Gramma's raspy voice alerts me that I failed to protect Trisha—my cousin, best friend, and the very reason I was foolish enough to enter this mindscape world of Ricky's. The world that now crumbles around us as the last bit of oxygen is consumed by his brain. The best we can hope for is that he does not fall unconscious from the pain before we can escape his labyrinth creation.

The manacles chaining Trisha to the wall elongate as they melt like plastic held to a flame. I raise my hands as I bump into the wall from my sprint and hug Trisha's right thigh to guide her fall.

Distressed metal clanks and chains rattle. Trisha's weight knocks the air from my lungs as she folds over me, her stomach against my face. I struggle mightily to shift my hands, squat, and lower her onto the floor.

"No, leave her." Gramma's voice cracks from strain and draws my attention.

"No. I can carry her!" Laila insists as she struggles to lift Ade.

"She's dead, Laila."

"You don't think I know that!" Laila's voice rises several octaves.

Trisha is not in any condition to walk. My heart breaks as I survey the welts and abrasions on her. More concerning is that she remains as limp as a ragdoll and has a matching glassy-eyed blank stare.

I reposition myself into a squat and put my hands under her arms. I lift her up and secure her on my right shoulder.

"Laila, we've got to leave. We have a minute or two at best."

Laila favors me with a grim dip of her chin. She grabs Ade by the wrists and backpedals toward the exit. We meet at the center aisle as the earth lifts three feet into the air, shimmies, and drops.

My knees buckle under me. It is reminiscent of playing war on the trampoline as a child when my larger brothers would steal the momentum of my jump.

Gramma slides between us as we regrip our two coven casualties. "I'll lead the way," she says while bringing forth a glowing crystal sphere balanced between the space of her hands.

"We don't have any time to spare, Laila. I know it sucks, but maybe you should leave her behind."

"If we don't have time, shut your trap and get a move on. Given what Ade has done, she needs her proper burial rights more than any of us."

If we don't get out of Ricky's dreamscape before his brain shuts down for the last time, we will all need burial rights. Then again, it will be impossible for anyone to pray for us since we are Lord knows how many hundreds of feet under the ground.

We will have disappeared without a trace.

Laila drags Ade three more steps and stops. She stoops, lifts Ade into a fireman-style carry as I have Trisha, and turns to follow Gramma.

"Hurry!" Gramma yells from a pinpoint of light in the distance.

Laila speed walks toward the light, but as we both become accustomed to the extra weight on one side and the adrenaline levels explode through our nervous system due to our impending demise, we jog.

The stone walls shudder as they crack and break along the path that no longer offers pleasant lights to direct our way. Fissures form along the ceiling, and steam full of sulfur spews wildly in all directions.

Blue-and-silver specks of chaotic energy speed past us as if released from a gas canister under pressure. As we labor over the rock-strewn path, I realize the energy particles must also move toward the exit of the fantastical creation as the tiny bits break off from the whole.

Ricky's dreamscape is disintegrating atom by atom.

Once released from their bond, the particles must float back from whence they came. Returning to their natural state and location before Ricky harnessed them to create his labyrinth.

The fissures of the wall open, forming a vast void in the wall, and our path fills with flowing water. Stones the size of baseballs shake loose from the ceiling, making disconcerting plopping noises as they fall closer and with greater regularity. It is only a matter of time before one knocks me silly, and I drown in the rising, frigid, black water circling my ankles.

The struggle to progress forward is real as the water reaches knee-high depth. The only positive is that the incredibly brisk current runs toward the shimmering blue-white light Gramma holds up as a beacon in the distance.

My left hamstring cramps, and I fear it may fail me. Of course, it will be a photo finish, whether my hamstring will betray me first or my lungs will simply incinerate from the dearth of oxygen mixed with the harsh sulfur fumes I inhale.

"Just a little further."

If I had the energy to laugh, I would. Laila's positive outlook is going to remain intact until the end. Gramma's light looks so far in the distance. If it was only me, if I didn't have Trisha counting on me to bring her home, I might lie down and accept the end.

"Girls, you must hurry!"

A jolt sends a shiver from my stomach to my neck and

halts my progress as the frigid water reaches my crotch. I hate myself for wondering why we hadn't encountered water during our entry into the tunnel. It's as if I brought the water into the equation through the power of suggestion. Now it, as much as the time limit of Ricky's brain shutting down, is a significant obstacle to our escape.

With every inch the water creeps higher, it gains momentum and strength. I'm forced to lean back so the water does not bowl me over, sending me into the black tide. Still, Trisha's weight will topple me into a seated position if I lean too far back. It's a formidable balancing act, and with my energies already spent, it's becoming increasingly more challenging to manage.

The stone wall to my left splits open wide enough to change the water flow into the cave. Steam blows out from the crack, and the water around the cavernous void boils violently. The water surrounding me heats to an unbearable temperature. I lean precariously forward to allow myself to move more quickly.

I huff and puff like a sickly locomotive but continue lifting my feet and stomping them purposefully forward until the water temperature enveloping me returns to a lukewarm.

I look up now that I'm sure I will not be boiled like a Thanksgiving turkey neck. Seeing Laila silhouetted by Gramma's glowing sphere elicits a sigh of relief from me.

Oh, thank the Lord. Laila made it to the ladder.

Invisible daggers stab both sides of my rib cage from lack of oxygen. With the prize being so close, rather than trying to control my breathing and relieve the stitches in my side, I change to short, quick pants of breath and power forward. My body is spent, and I am marching to the end of the tunnel on sheer stubbornness.

Trisha grows lighter on my shoulder as I approach Gramma and the ladder. Stupid me. Of course, she is. The water reaches my chest and lifts part of Trisha, pulling her toward the exit.

Dag nab it! A few more seconds, and she would have gone

underwater and drowned as focused as I am on getting us to the ladder.

I spin Trisha off my shoulder and tuck her under my right arm, her nose even with the top of my shoulder. I don't intend to bring a second dead body out of this God-forsaken hole.

"Give me Trisha," Laila yells. Even though I can tell she is screaming, her voice is barely audible over the earth rumbling, water rushing, and the steam spewing from the cracked walls.

My first reaction is to recoil. I don't want to give Trisha to anybody at this point. I want to pull her to safety.

But I am spent. Laila was the only one who was not further injured in the melee. To carry a body up a twenty-foot ladder while the earth bucks like a pissed-off bull at the state rodeo will require a monumental amount of effort.

Effort I don't have to give.

I push forward as Gramma takes Ade from Laila, holding her body above the flood of dark, brackish water. I shove Trisha toward Laila and help her position Trisha the best we can on her shoulder as she grabs hold of the ladder's rungs.

I know Laila is strong and, just as importantly, determined. Still, we may only be able to get Trisha out if we form a harness to lift her out from above.

Laila goes up one rung, stops, and shifts Trisha's weight. Laila pulls up the ladder a few inches with her left arm while tentatively shifting her weight; she moves her right foot and hand simultaneously to the next rung. Her pace increases as she gains confidence that Trisha is well-balanced on her shoulders. I watch the flex and strain of Laila's calf muscles with each lift until the light from the opening above transforms her into a shadowy figure, losing all detail.

I turn to Gramma. "You should start up now. We won't have much time left."

As if to punctuate my belief, a section of the ceiling, six feet long and three feet across, collapses into the water with a crash. It forms a surging wave that hits Gramma's chin.

"I don't want to be in the way when Laila returns to get Ade."

"If you don't leave now, we may not have to worry about Ade."

Gramma glares at me. I give her my obstinate mule stare, and she concedes reluctantly. She mounts the ladder. Her right hand's grasp comes free on her first attempt, and she compensates by leaning closer to the metal ladder frame.

Laila appears above and reaches her hand down. "Hurry, Gramma!" Her voice is distorted and muted by the cacophony of noise. She looks over Gramma's head. "Start up, April."

I struggle to position Ade. I intend to lift her to my shoulder and balance her body as Laila did with Trisha. I am overwhelmed by my lack of strength. My arms and legs burn with fatigue. I can barely stand. How can I climb with Ade's weight on a slippery ladder, too?

"No!"

Her voice is garbled. I peer into the light as the frigid water swirls around me. A bowling ball-sized stone creates a tremendous splash six inches from my right shoulder.

Laila, silhouetted entirely by the sun at her back, waves her arm. "*You* climb."

I don't understand. Laila was adamant about not leaving Ade's body behind. She said she would not be allowed into paradise if she didn't receive the proper burial.

Being the person responsible for Ade going to hell is not something I believe I can live with on my consciousness.

I tug on her shirt to try and lift her to my shoulder as I stoop until my chin is below the water's turbulent surface. My grip fails, and the water pushes Ade away from me. I reach out again, but as I try to close my hand, my fingers will only close halfway.

"Get out of there, April!"

I look up into the blinding light. Laila gestures a come here motion with a heavily shadowed arm.

Ade's body bumps into my shoulder. My eyes tear as my throat tightens. "I'm sorry, Ade. You deserve better."

"April!"

The cave's floor bucks, and as quickly as the water fills the chamber, it flows in reverse, pulling me away from the ladder. I lunge for the metal rods, slapping the side of my face rudely against one of the vertical runners.

But I am able to clutch the cold bar while the running water pulls at my legs. That's a win.

I struggle to place my feet on the first rung as the water drains from the exit. A tremendous sucking noise rattles through the tunnel as if a giant of ridiculous proportions is sucking on the other side like a straw in a chocolate malt.

Bless it, Lord. Please give me the strength and the time to climb this ladder. I promise I will change my foolish ways if you only grant me the ability to complete this task.

"April, please."

Laila hollering at me isn't helpful. Especially when I'm asking God for a favor.

An inappropriate giggle bubbles out of me, and I cup the next rung with my treacherous, "will only close halfway" hand and push upward as both calf muscles decide to cramp.

"Fudge!" I scream.

Laila stops waving and turns her body as if she will come down after me. That won't end well.

"Don't! I've got this." Maybe not, but I don't want her dragging me the rest of the way out of this hole by my collar.

I laugh hysterically as I force my screaming legs to push up to the next rung and then the next. It's partly the absurd level of pain racking my body and Granny's preposterous claim that God will never give me more than I can endure.

If that's true, I believe God has way overestimated my abilities.

The conflict in my mind is monumental. The difficulty of the task at hand is juxtaposed with my strong survival instinct versus the failure of my body to respond to my brain's commands. My body is shutting down. It's not my choice, but between the fatigue of injury, stress, and physical exertion, the tank is just that empty.

Yet as I hang on to that wet, frigid piece of metal, visions flash in my mind's eye. Mama, Daddy, Dusty, Chase, Granny, Nana, Puppy, the lake house... They keep flashing in quick succession. I realize how fortunate of a woman I am and how I want to continue in that bubble of love that is my life. I refuse to let a hundred-year-old ghost steal that from me.

"Mind over matter, it just doesn't matter," I growl as I pull myself up the next rung. I command my brain to shut down all stimuli and focus only on the mechanics of forcing one side of my body to move up, grip, and step, then the other side grip and step, and I build a piston-like cadence.

"That's it, April. Keep it up."

That encouragement is helpful.

The left shoulder of my shirt pulls up awkwardly, and I take my eyes off of my surroundings, focusing on my hands. The sun hits my face. I climb a rung and lunge out of the hole. Brush and leaves crash into my face as I land on my stomach, wheezing for breath.

The rumbling below the ground grows louder. Our group is strangely quiet, and I roll to my side. Trisha lies on her back, Gramma cradling her head in her lap. Gramma peers down into the hole I just escaped.

"Where's Laila?"

Gramma favors me with a worrisome look and points into the hole.

I pop up on all fours and crawl toward her. "Why?"

"Ade."

"Why didn't you stop her?"

"I couldn't," Gramma croaks.

I peer into the hole and wait for my eyes to adjust. I'm convinced that Ricky has died. The barn that once sheltered the entrance to the tunnel is gone. The dreamscape labyrinth has deteriorated significantly in the seconds I've returned to the surface.

The water drains out of the crevice that opened earlier, exposing the floor, which bubbles with volcanic activity. As it releases vast volumes of steam, it's difficult to see what is happening below.

Closer to me, I watch parts of the wall explode, shooting shrapnel across the path. The bits of rock incinerate into dust as the atoms of kinetic energy explode up and out of the cavity below.

"She won't make it," I say, instantly regretting that I did not keep the thought to myself. I momentarily forgot it was Laila's grandmother I was speaking to. "Without help," I add, hoping it will assuage her feelings.

Yes, the entire constructed labyrinth is disintegrating, which is the root issue. Still, perhaps I can turn the negative into a positive. I know that on my own, I would not be able to harness enough energy for what crosses my mind, especially since I don't have my amulet with me. Still, the voracious flow of power escaping the cavern can be harnessed.

I spin around onto my butt, shove my feet over the lip of the entrance, and lay my hands on the opposite side of the opening. There's no need to pull the bits of metallic-colored energy into me. As it escapes the confines of Ricky's illusion, it is forced to flow through me. I open my core being to the flow. The surge of force expands inside me like I am a parachute opening after a long fall. The penetrating, thrusting motion inside me threatens to tear my organs through my back and knocks my breath out.

I scream as I fight to gain control of the flow and turn it. As the light blue illumination in the tunnel begins to form like a tiny bubble coming out of a bubble ring, I let myself have the first bit of hope that this may work.

My bubble creeps to the bottom of the ladder, now twisted with broken rungs at the base. I search for Laila in the apocalyptic scene below. I've been so focused on fighting to control the energy, I lost track of her.

Fortunately, the magic I cast creates a glowing hue at once, causing glare off of the smoke, but also moments of illumination into pockets where the smoke has vacated.

Thirty feet from the ladder on the left side of the tunnel, I detect motion. Laila attempts to drag Ade past a sizable boulder that blocks their path.

The wall to her right explodes a one-foot-circumference hole, hurling shrapnel across the tunnel. Laila cries in pain as several pieces strike her, knocking her down, and I nearly lose hold of my magic as I jump forward in my mind.

Regaining my composure, I will the previously asymmetrically formed bubble to elongate toward Laila down the left side of the wall. My concern builds. She has not moved since being struck. It causes a momentary lull in my abilities as profound sadness decreases my magic, which any thought of losing Laila would bring on.

So, I visualize Laila eating dinner with Trisha and me. I imagine Laila visiting me in Guntersville. I even envision Laila deciding to work with me in Guntersville as my law firm partner. What would it be like for her to travel with my brother's paranormal team on our next research project?

The happiness of those ideas allows me to regain control of my magic. Methodically, I organize each blue-and-gold speck of energy, using it to the highest efficiency. The bubble stretches, elongates, and finally bloops over her body.

Immediately, the essence of my coven sister flows to me, and I know she is still alive. I hold the protective bubble steady as another fissure on the right side of the wall explodes. The bits of dirt and rock strike the defensive shield and are simply absorbed as added fuel powering the effectiveness of my magic to an even greater level.

What now? I have her shielded, but if she can't stand to get herself to safety, what then? How long can I hold the protective spell? Even if I can for an extended period, the last of Ricky's dreamscape, which hasn't already decided to crack into thousands of atoms of energy, appears to be folding in on itself.

Laila, come to me. Come to me now.

My message rides on the flux of the energy wave. I don't know if she can hear my call, but it's my last hope.

This one, Laila's going to have to do herself. Even if I had the physical energy to descend the ladder and carry her out, I doubt there is enough time to reach her, much less for the return trip up the ladder.

Hold it open for me. I'm coming.

My face stretches into a wide smile as I hear her voice in my mind. My heart leaps as I watch her stand and squat in equal portions when she retakes hold of Ade.

I would tell her to leave her. But she's not going to, and I must trust she wouldn't try if she couldn't carry Ade's body out. I understand she wouldn't be able to continue living with her joyous outlook if she were to leave Ade behind.

Every step she takes is treacherous. The floor is littered like a moonscape now. Equally disconcerting is that the area where Laila rose from seconds ago has disappeared.

It simply is no more. Only an expansive, black emptiness exists behind Laila, drifting closer as she stumbles and jogs.

The dreamscape is dying.

Laila requires a moment to situate Ade on her shoulder. She grasps the bent rung on the crooked ladder.

I can no longer see anything past the small landing chamber. The random, chaotic energy that once flowed so forcefully out of the opening slows to a trickle. My protective bubble extends only to the back of Laila's heel. Halfway up, the bottom of the ladder deteriorates into electrically charged dust that floats lazily toward me in a glittering cloud.

"Give it everything you've got, Laila," My hoarse voice startles me. I thought I sent the encouragement via our psychic channel, but I yelled it instead.

She pushes up the last five rungs as if she can feel the icy void touching her shoes, ready to swallow her whole. I grab Ade by the shirt, pulling her body onto me as I fall backward to release the weight from Laila.

She dives in a bellyflop in my periphery and slides across the sawgrass.

I barely hear Gramma's cries of joy over Laila and me

panting as we struggle to catch our breath. The noise from inside the hole ends with a whoosh.

Chapter 45

With my newfound perspective on life and a heart full of gratitude due to all my unearned blessings, vacation time has suddenly lost its appeal. I need to return home and get busy. Lord knows when I arrive in Guntersville, I already have more on my plate than I can say grace over.

Still, it would have felt wrong to leave Turtle Key before Ade is laid to rest. Especially since Ade saved me from Atlas and because she meant so much to the Washingtons.

The decision to stay was made easier when I learned Ade would be buried two days after we extricated her from Ricky's grand illusion. Staying and saying those awkward words we share when someone important to a friend dies or sitting in silent companionship seems the least I can do for Laila and Gramma.

Guntersville will wait. Impatiently. Thelma went into full-blown ice queen mode when I informed her it would be a few more days before we could meet. And I'm sure twenty other equally important things are not reaching my mind due to the bruises, cuts, and abrasions needling every nerve ending in my body.

I'd be lying if I said I'm not considerably worried for Laila. Yes, she is intelligent and in tune with her surroundings. Still, when she tells me she called Adeline, the leader of the Silent

Coven, to use her as a vessel, her decision seems reckless even by my standards.

She explained she had palmed spare dates from Adeline's gravesite. The second Laila tells me that, I remember the odd motion when she put her hand to her mouth while negotiating with Ricky beside his desk.

Moments before she made him corporal and then killed him.

I understand why Laila gave herself over to Adeline willingly. Still, that makes it twice in short succession she was possessed.

Before this trip, I believed my veil to be a thin gauze. Considering Ade was taken over repeatedly by Atlas, and Adeline's easy use of Laila's body, I don't believe mine to be nearly so fragile. The Turtle Key inhabitants are far more susceptible to possession.

All things being equal, I'd much rather see a ghost than them inhabit my body.

Another positive has come from staying for a few more days. Although it could've been accomplished without me, Trisha needs the rest. Honestly, it still spooks me to know how close I came to losing my cousin.

I try to tell myself it is a good thing, but I'm intrinsically aware that it is a form of shock that is never a blessing. Trisha remembers nothing but walking through the weeds looking for an oak tree.

When I ask her about the rest of the day, she says we didn't find the giant tree and that oak trees can't grow so prominent on the island. It's as if she's missing half a day of her life. It is as complete of an erasure as if her mind is a videotape and someone recorded white noise over the day we nearly died. Those hours simply don't exist for her anymore.

Aduwa leads the service. His forehead glistens with sweat as he tugs at the blue necktie restraining his thick neck.

What a difference a few days makes. Jumare, who has easily put on fifteen pounds in the last few days, stands beside Gramma, supporting her with his arm around her waist. He insists that she sit during the service due to the contusion on her hip.

She won't have it. Gramma claims that standing to honor her life-long friend is the least she can do, and the pain in her hip takes her mind off the despair in her heart.

Gramma sheds no tears. But I hear her mournful cries echoing dolefully inside her mind. The power of her sorrow is so intense I cannot raise my partitions high enough to leave her anguish in private.

Despite the terrifying intensity of Gramma's grief, I'm in awe at the blessing it must be to have a friend you love so wholly who isn't blood to you.

As Bucky unlocks the ratchet on the hand winch to lower Ade's coffin into the grave, Gramma releases a heart-wrenching sob that shakes her body and unbuckles her knees. Jumare catches her fall and folds her into a hug.

Three women I have not previously met sing a song foreign to me. Even though the language is some form of English, I do not understand it. Still, it has the effect of drawing tears to my eyes.

Ade's coffin's lid dips below the surface. Laila strides forward, dropping something into the grave. She stands watch as Bucky lowers Ade to the bottom of the grave.

Chapter 46

Two women who sang at Ade's funeral, Beth and Maude, bring a meal to Gramma's house and encourage her to eat. She is inconsolable.

They realize their presence only makes it harder for their friend, so they leave. Laila urges Gramma to lie down and rest. She resists until Laila tells her she will stay with her until she falls asleep.

Aduwa and Norman slip outside to have a smoke.

That leaves me in an awkward position. Jumare, Trisha, and I sit in companionable silence. We are quite content, not to mention the elephant in the room.

Earlier, I called Nana about Jumare and Trisha having a massive hole in their memory. She suggested that it's not an unusual coping mechanism for non- or low-magicals when faced with overwhelming supernatural events. Still, it is troubling to me.

Jumare remembers talking to Ade and then waking up sick at home in his bed. Trisha remembers us running with Laila to Ade's house the night I was attacked by Atlas and says that she vaguely remembers something about a graveyard, but that's as far as her memory goes.

"It seems weird to think she's gone," Jumare says.

Trisha narrows her eyes. "What did you say she died of

again, April?"

I bite my bottom lip. "They're not sure, Trisha."

"It seems so odd when we spoke to Ade on her porch just the other day."

"That's how it happens sometimes. People are here one day and gone the next."

Her expression sours. "I know people can die unexpectantly, April. I'm just saying I haven't ever experienced it where I have recently seen somebody one day, and the next minute they are gone."

"Yeah. She even seemed like she had more spunk lately," Jumare says.

It might not be fair that neither of them will ever know precisely what happened to Ade. But it is our uncles' decision. They understand that magicals walk the earth despite having no magical skills themselves. Still, they feel it best to hide the knowledge from their wards who were gifted with low-level abilities.

Not that I have a say in the matter. Still, I feel it is a grave mistake. I can only compare how my parents kept the Lock Witch prophecy from me. It disturbs me not to fill in the voids in their memories with the truth, even though they may not fully understand or believe the details' veracity.

It remains difficult for me to comprehend that I am, according to my family, part of a legend that holds evil from overrunning North Alabama. As weird as all the tale's details may be, and as small of a chance that they involve me, I can strictly vouch for knowledge being better, even if it is discomforting.

But I remain mum about the topic per Norman's request. In his mind, the fact that Trisha does not remember the supernatural events confirms her ill-preparedness for an extended walk on the weird and spooky side. He does not believe her psyche is of the nature that could handle it.

"Gramma is really sad," Jumare whispers.

"Yes. She buried a dear friend today. But I'd like you to

promise me something, Jumare."

"What's that?"

"She can't see it right now because of the clouds from losing her best friend, but I know she is so grateful that you returned to her. Please smile a lot and talk to her during the next few weeks. I know that will help her deal with the loss of Ade."

Jumare sets his jaw, nodding solemnly. "I can do that."

"That's good advice for all of us," Trisha says blankly. "We all need to be not just present in the lives of the people we love, but *actively* present."

∞ ∞ ∞

I feel like I'm playing the princess part in *The Princess and the Pea* tonight, only potatoes are under my mattress. I flip over on my side for what must be the hundredth time. Even though I know she is comforting her grandmother tonight, Laila's empty bed is disconcerting.

I suppose, subliminally, the recent events are settling on me about how close we were to Laila's bed being empty forever. It still baffles me that she risked so much so that Ade could receive a proper burial with her pointed toward Mecca.

Then again, I must continue to remind myself that I don't know the totality of the relationship. I had only a few days of experience with the woman while she was being controlled by a low-level demon. I suppose I should extend the deceased woman a pass for that point alone.

Regardless of how unwelcome Ade made this outsider at the start of our visit, she more than proved her bravery when she destroyed one of the artifacts she spent her life searching for to stop Atlas from killing me.

If I'm being fair about my assessment, I'm still shocked about what transpired with the five of us. Yes, we lost Ade, and we mourn her death, but it is nothing short of a miracle that the other four of us escaped. It's as probable that we would have disappeared into the void once Ricky's constructed reality folded in on itself.

I have risked that manner of dreadful death often while traveling to different periods and alternate realities. The blank void thrills my soul every time I travel through it, but those other times it was only me at risk. Knowing that four other people in our impromptu coven were in jeopardy if I made a wrong decision made it much more stressful.

Oh, fudge nut. This is pointless.

I punch my pillow, sit up, and scan the floor for my tennis shoes. Not finding them, I decide to go barefoot. As quietly as possible, I tiptoe past Trisha's bed.

Bless her heart, she passed out the moment her head hit the pillow. It's been that way with her the last two nights.

Ignorance is bliss. Or at least it gives you a better opportunity for a good night's sleep.

I slip out of Laila's room and across the kitchen. I can enjoy the last few minutes on the island at night and take in the summer constellations in peace. The screen door squawks, and I freeze halfway through the doorway. My stomach muscles tighten as I glimpse a red ember glowing to my right. I suck in a breath with a gasp.

"You can't sleep?"

"No, sir."

"I gave up about an hour ago."

I sigh as I close the screen door slowly behind me. "I should probably have given up two hours ago."

Norman scoots from the middle of the metal sofa glider to the right side. I take the seat next to him.

"I thought you only smoke those during an emergency now."

Norman extinguishes the cigarette in the small bowl in his hand. "This week has been one long emergency. At this rate, I'll be smoking four packs a day."

I snicker. "I guess it's good that we're leaving this morning."

"Hmm." Norman lifts his chin in agreement. He slides his

legs out further and crosses his arms.

We sit in companionable silence, staring at the stars.

"You know, you'll need to talk to her at some point about it."

In my periphery, I study Norman. He diverts his eyes back to the sky and crosses his legs. "I don't think so."

"It's getting stronger with her. Plus, she's naturally drawn to it."

"It only gets stronger when she is around you, April. It's the only time she's exposed to it."

I swallow hard as his words sting my feelings. It's a true statement. Trisha is only exposed to paranormal events when we get together. She refuses to take precautions when I tell her to.

My throat becomes unnaturally dry. I don't want to float the question to my uncle, but I must ask his preference. "Do you want me to stay away from her?"

He turns his focus to me as his eyebrows knit. "As if I could keep Trisha away from you. You are her favorite person, April. Even if you tried to avoid her, she would still come to visit."

"Then why don't you let me explain to her why she is drawn to paranormal events. Please allow me to demonstrate to her the abilities she does have, Norman. Don't let the skills come to life unexpectedly and make her feel like a freak of nature."

Norman shakes his head and groans. "This is precisely why Nancy insisted we move away from Guntersville."

The name of Trisha's mama, who died when we were children, and Norman's combative tone jolt me. "What is that supposed to mean?"

"After what happened to Dionis, Nancy insisted we move to Nashville. She wanted us to be as far away from the paranormal influence of Guntersville as we could."

"Why is Aunt Dionis committing suicide a reason for y'all to move away?" This is all new information to me.

"Not only that, but what happened with Rodney. Nancy was fearful that because I was there that night that I might end up being charged with a crime if he was ever found."

I turn sideways to face Norman. "If who was found?"

Norman's expression becomes highly agitated. "Rodney."

"Rodney left town. That's why Dionis was heartbroken."

Norman squints his eyes, grunts, and turns away from me.

"Am I missing something?"

I wait for him to answer me. He recrosses his legs and leans away.

"What do you mean by that?"

"It's not my place to say. I shouldn't have said anything."

"Well, you have. Now tell me what you mean."

"I'm sorry. I had been told Viv spoke with you about everything this spring."

"Mama told me about the legend of the Lock Witch and the possibility I may be involved with it if it's true."

Norman drops his chin to his chest and rubs his forehead. "Oh, April. You're telling me to talk to my child about her limited ability to sense magic. But there's so much that you don't... You know, you need to talk to Ralph."

"What does my father know that my mama wouldn't share with me?"

Norman pulls a cigarette pack from his shirt pocket, taps the box on his thigh, and pulls one out. "Obviously, quite a bit."

"Like what?"

Norman lights the cigarette and takes an extra-long drag. "Ask your dad, April. I've already said too much."

Chapter 47

I step off the plane in Huntsville, and all the stress leaves my body. It's as if I turn into a massive block of Jell-O, and I nearly slide to the floor. If it weren't overdramatic, I would kneel and kiss gate number four's filthy, low-cut carpet.

Practically skipping, I rush to the baggage claim. I miss my bag the first pass around the carousel because I am pinned in by so many people, and rather than swear, I laugh. Nothing can pop my bubble of exaltation today.

I drive out of the airport parking lot, thrilled to pay the obscene parking fee for two and a half weeks.

The brilliant colors of the world envelop me as I crest the hill on Highway 431, leaving Huntsville.

The trees look to be more than four hundred vibrant shades of green. As I cross it on the south side of Huntsville, the river is the deepest shade of blue I ever recall. The water calls me playfully to pull my car over, strip, and take a dip in the refreshingly chilled waters. I only ignore the call of my waters because I am eager to be home and visit with my family.

It's not that Turtle Key was not a lovely place. I'm sure to many people, it is paradise personified.

Still, I've never been quite so glad to leave a place behind. My only regret is that the distance between my new friend Laila and I means we must make a concerted effort to remain in touch.

That, I regret. The rest of Turtle Key, I leave gladly to the Gullah Geechee and the wealthy mainlanders moving in who have zero supernatural skills.

Again, proving that ignorance is bliss.

Dusty will be highly disappointed the next time he tries to talk me into a trip with the team. Unless we stay local in Marshall County, he will be hard-pressed to convince me to participate. I'm ready for an extended stay in my hometown.

Besides, if I do what I intend at Snow and Associates, it's not like I'll need the extra money from the supernatural research trips anymore. Life is simpler at home and, most importantly, less expensive.

I'm giddy, considering the proposition of setting roots down in Guntersville. Sure, it would be more enjoyable if I had a life partner to share in my future. But not at the expense of what I want to accomplish and experience.

I loved everything about being *with* Lee. Yet the idea of having to forgo my ambitions to be everything he required me to be as a player's wife... Well, I'm not that girl.

In fact, I need a man who is there for when *I* have time— when I want his attention—but is equally okay if I must leave for a few nights to take care of a case.

That's not realistic. I would be less than thrilled if my husband had that exact requirement of me. So where does this leave me?

Better off alone and doing what I love until I don't love it anymore. And that's a fact.

I've convinced myself I must go through life alone to be happy. Still, I remember there is a man who fits my unrealistic description. Someone who I last heard from quite a while ago.

I need to call him. I *need* to get his number.

No. He has my number. He would have called if he wanted to talk to me or thought about me.

But he thinks I'm with Lee. And he is respectful enough that he would not interfere if he thought I was happy with Lee.

This is an awful idea. A better plan is no guys for six months, and then if he is still on my mind, I'll call Vander and force him to give me Jacob's number.

Of course, the way Vander can drop off the grid for months at a time, it may take me six months to locate him when I decide I am ready to call Jacob. I should get the number now, so if I want to, a few months later when I've proven that I can be self-sufficient and have started to build my business back, I can call him. Then I won't be forced to waste time chasing Vander down for the phone number.

That sounds reasonable.

Pleased with my pretzel logic, I dial Vander.

"Is everything okay, April?"

Vander's tone is so commanding that my thighs and stomach muscles draw taut. "Hey." I roll my eyes at how stupid I must sound.

"Hello." Vander's voice is low and contained.

"What are you up to?"

"Working."

"Have you been doing all right?" I'm caught in an internal debate about whether to hang up or slap myself.

"Yes."

An awkward silence ensues. Who knew my bottomless well of stupid things to say could run dry.

"April, I don't mean to rush you, but I have an agenda today. Can I do something for you?"

"Funny you should ask. Could you send me Jacob's phone number?"

"Hurley?"

He's toying with me. There's only one Jacob I would be calling him about. "Yes."

"I thought he would have your number."

"He does."

Vander sighs heavily. "But he hasn't called you."

"Yeah."

"Yes, he has called you, or he has not?"

"Are you not going to give me his number?"

"I'd prefer not to. And given that he hasn't contacted you, I believe he prefers you not to have the number."

"Rude."

"April, it took him a full month to get into a groove once he left Guntersville. You last talked to him six months ago. What do you need with him now?"

"What are you, the phone monitor?"

"No. I'm his concerned manager trying to keep his mind in the game so he doesn't come home to Guntersville in a casket."

Vander's comment, coupled with his harsh tone, makes me ill to my stomach. Nobody tells me what Vander does for a living, especially Vander. By no means do I believe it to be something illegal. However, I do consider pursuing high-level criminal syndicates as highly dangerous.

We used to be moderately friendly business associates. But since he talked my best friend into leaving town and ghosting me for some hazardous job, Vander has moved permanently onto my do-not-trust list.

"He is an adult, Vander. He doesn't have to pick up the phone if he doesn't want to talk to me."

"But he can't help himself when it comes to you."

"What have I done to deserve this?"

"You're seriously asking that question?"

I snort. "Yes, I'm asking why you're more obstinate than usual."

"You must be the least self-observant person I have ever met, April Snow. Don't you have a fiancé to play mind games with?"

"Lee and I ended it."

Vander groans. "Oh, blow me. Of all the lousy luck."

"What?"

"So, what? Do you need validation from a male now? Is that what this is?"

"What crawled up your butt and died, Vander?"

"You know what? I'm double booked and don't have time for this drama fest. I'll text you his number. If he wants to talk to you, he will pick up."

"See. Was that so difficult?"

"You're welcome. Bye, April."

The line goes dead.

My ears are on fire when my phone dings. Vander excels at being a royal prick, but he can always be relied on to keep his word. It's not chivalry but some other paramilitary code he lives by.

I glance at the number in the text and set my phone down. Not that I would ever take relationship advice from Michael VanDerveer, considering he is the definition of a lone wolf. Still, his words convict me.

Last Christmas, I had the advantage of visiting Jacob at his apartment while in voyeuristic-ghost mode. That was my first hint that he had designs on us one day being more than friends. To his credit, before he took a position with Vander, he laid it all out on the line and told me how he felt.

The timing was poor, considering that Lee and I had recently found each other again. And at the time, it seemed like we were destined to be the next power couple in Baltimore, Maryland.

It wasn't just that, though. It's also the fact that even though I recognize Jacob is a handsome man and good as gold, I don't see him as a romantic partner. I mean, he's my best friend. That's awkwardly weird. Right?

It doesn't matter today. I've got plenty of time to work through this. And even though I don't want to admit it, Vander may have the right of it. Jacob is doing what he has always wanted to do, and I need to build Snow and Associates back up and do something else grown up ... like consider moving out of my parents' home.

That isn't a particularly good idea, and it's not only the financial reasons. Chase once said, when I asked him why he was still living at home, "The people I care about the most live in this house, and I get to have dinner with them every night." It seems foreign to me to agree with that bit of Chase logic, but

I do.

Moving out, even if I stay in town, changes the dynamic of my relationships. I know this from the half-year I lived at Lee's home in Guntersville.

I raise my phone and stare at the text from Vander. *Area code 812?*

I ask Siri where area code 812 is located. *Southern Indiana? What in the world is there?*

If Vander never shows his face in Guntersville again, that would be wise on his part. I have wanted to throttle him the last few months for having convinced Jacob to take this position and leave home.

It's not like Jacob can't handle himself. He did two tours with the Marines in Afghanistan and has been a police officer for several years. Still, Vander gets into that super-macho, shady-government stuff. Going after those types of folks isn't intelligent. They hold grudges forever and will ensure you will get your payback when you least expect it.

My phone's screen lights up a second time, displaying Jacob's number once again. My phone mocks me.

Chapter 48

Dusty's car is the only one in the driveway. I lug my bag to my apartment and unlock the door. Pulling the bag inside, I scan the room. "Puppy?"

He doesn't answer, but that doesn't mean anything necessarily. I check under my bed and in the closet for a sixty-pound furball. I come up empty.

I walk to my parents' porch and open the sliding glass door, careful not to slam it on its track. "Honey, I'm home."

Crickets. It is a wasted line.

I march to the stairs, and the door is open to Dusty's office-slash-bedroom below. I take the stairs two at a time, holding onto the handrail as I go. AC/DC's "Back in Black" surrounds me.

Dusty sits at the terminal on the far wall editing a video. I stoop over him and hug his neck.

"April?"

He tries to turn, but I squeeze him tighter around the neck. "I missed you, you big lug." I release my grip.

"I missed you, too." He swivels his chair toward me and angles his head to the left. "Wait a second. Why aren't you in Baltimore?"

"Mama didn't tell you? I cut Lee loose, and I'm flying solo again."

Dusty squints his eyes as he recalibrates my situation in his mind. "Did you two have a fight?"

"Nah, it became painfully evident that we would not be able to give each other what we needed."

"And you're okay with all this?"

I shrug my shoulders because even though I know it is the correct decision, there is still a sore spot in my heart. "It seemed like the right thing to do. Lee is a great guy, and if I can't be what he needs, it only made sense to walk away now."

A faint smile grows on Dusty's face. "A rare moment of mercy from my kid sister. Give me a moment while I savor this."

"You're a jerk."

Dusty laughs. "I didn't think that was a secret. But still, this is about you. You went all the way up to Baltimore to set the boy free?"

"Well, it didn't exactly happen that way."

Dusty raises his eyebrows and waits patiently for the rest of the story.

"He was upset because I missed his playoff game."

"Oh, April." Dusty leaves his mouth gaping open to punctuate his groan.

"It wasn't my fault."

"It never is, is it?"

My ears flame hot. What is this? Pick on April day? I cross my arms and glare at Dusty.

He makes a rolling gesture with his finger. "Come on. No commercial breaks. Give me the rest of the story."

Realizing there will be no safe harbor among any of my male friends or family, I've lost interest in sharing. Still, if I don't finish, I know Dusty will wear me smooth until I give him every gory April-misstep detail.

"Anyway, we had this huge blowup... Well, no, I think I was the only one that blew up because there was this girl at his place."

"He hooked up with somebody?"

I shake my head. "No. He's not like that. *She* wanted to hook up with him, but that was not happening. Of course, I had no way of knowing that."

"Did they both have their clothes on?"

I stomp my foot. "Yes. Do you want me to finish the story or not?"

"Yeah, but I also want to understand what happened when you finish it."

I want to understand, too. But I doubt I'll ever grasp how I let myself—our relationship—arrive at that moment and know that Lee was absolutely correct. Our once-promising romance, for all the positives we had shared, was terminal.

"The girl is his marketing manager. She wanted to line up some advertisements because he was the game's winning pitcher. I suspect she had a mind to line up some personal sessions, too. Lee wasn't buying her pitch for some one-on-one time, so she is less savvy of a marketing manager than she thinks. Still, once he made her leave and the door was shut, he didn't mince words about our relationship not working for him anymore."

I favor Dusty with a droll stare. "Okay, you can ask all your questions now."

Dusty narrows his lips as if clamping them shut to prevent him from saying what is on his mind.

I raise my hand palms up. "No questions ... no comments?"

"No, it's perfectly understandable."

"Really?"

"Yes. April, take it from someone who has some experience with this. Marriage is a challenging, long marathon. The only way it works is if you're like Mom and Dad. They have their own lives, but their priority is always their relationship. Neither of them lets their passions take them away from the needs of the other.

"In the case of Bethany and me..."

"Do not even begin to compare Bethany to Lee."

"As I was saying, Bethany was never more important than

my books. Never, ever, ever, and she never would have been. That's on me, and I know better now. If I ever marry again, it will be because that woman is above and beyond my passion for my career, or she participates in my career, which would be the best of both worlds."

The gears in my head click into motion, and I must catch my tongue not to share Liza's secret with Dusty. One day I'll need to break Liza's trust and nudge the two together. But right now, as he recollects the apocalypse known as Bethany, it doesn't seem like the best time.

"When you consider that Mom is a real estate broker and still acts as a mentor for Chase at the marina, while Dad works for Redstone, teaches his classes at UNA, and has the perpetual energy machine that he tinkers on, they are very, very busy people." Dusty smiles, and his eyes turn liquid. "But none of us kids can ever doubt that those two always have each other's back. Plus, how often do we catch them showing affection? I mean, it's gross because they are so old, but it's nothing to see them cuddling on the couch, Dad slapping Mom on the butt, or her cornering him in the kitchen and laying one of those suck-face kisses on him.

"Only people who put each other first do that. And do you know what? I'm jealous. That's what I want."

I purse my lips as I consider everything Dusty says. "Yeah, me too," I whisper.

"I mean, without that, what's the point?"

We stare at each other long enough that it becomes awkward, and I point at his monitor's screen. "What are you working on?"

"It's the footage from when Miles, Luis, and I went back up to Murfreesboro to talk to the officials about the haunting in the tunnel and to discuss how to seal the tunnel off."

I pull up a chair. "And you got some new footage?"

Dusty scoffs, "Not hardly. None of our equipment picked up any paranormal energy this time."

Considering what I experienced in the tunnel, the forcible

sapping of my magical energy as if that was how the entity survived, I'm not surprised. None of those team members have a powerful energy signature. It is most likely that the spirits became animated from their proximity to Liza's and my energy that night, or they were drawn out by us.

With this latest information, the tunnels will be safe for almost anyone wandering into them. Which puts my mind at ease.

"Then what are you working on?"

"There wasn't any spectral energy, but I found the creepiest thing when we went through the tunnel. And it will be awesome on a trailer." Dusty runs the footage back, and I'm looking at a crooked stick with hundreds of pebbles around it.

"Oh, that's scary." My sarcasm is so heavy that I tickle myself and giggle.

Dusty flits his eyes from the screen to me. "You don't see it?"

I grin and shake my head.

"Then it is fortunate that you saw it before I uploaded it to my website. I need to lighten this up and zoom in closer. I tried to keep it spooky and made it too difficult to see." Dusty taps his mouse several times, and as the image clears, the hair on the back of my neck stands on end.

Dusty jabs his finger at the screen. "See, I think this is some sort of weird-looking stick, but tell me it doesn't resemble a giant spider leg. What makes it even spookier is all those pebble-looking things around it. Those are dried-up black widows, about three hundred of them."

I have never been one to fear spiders. But I'm still young enough to learn.

Chapter 49

I have an overwhelming need to see Mama. Even when Dusty informs me she is working on a project at the women's shelter, I am off in a flash.

Pulling into the parking lot, I realize my decision's error. Since Mrs. Wanda Neil can't stand my guts, I should have waited until Mama gets home.

On second thought, forget Mrs. Neil and her judgy attitude. That's her issue, not mine, and I don't care what she thinks about me.

I straighten my posture and stride into the women's shelter.

Monica Larson is on duty at the front desk. She smiles as she recognizes me. "Hi, stranger. I thought you had left town to be with your ball player."

Monica's husband manages the Piggly Wiggly grocery store in Scottsboro. Her daughter is in high school, and Monica volunteers at the center sometimes during the day.

"My plans changed on me, and I'm back in town for a while."

Her eyebrows draw together. "Really? Is that a good thing or a bad thing?"

"I think good. Very good."

Monica's lips twitch into a faint grin. "Well, I'm glad it's working out for you."

I want to ask where my mom is, but I am back home, and there are specific rules of conversational engagement when you live in a small town, so I ask, "How is Lindsey?"

Monica rolls her eyes. "I swear these days I have to keep her separated from Curtis. He doesn't like her new boyfriend, and she doesn't think it's any of his blessed business. I can't tell you how much I appreciate getting out of the house and forgetting about them some days."

"Oh, I'm sorry."

She waves her hand at me. "It's just a thing. Don't you know she was a daddy's girl her entire life? It was always 'Daddy this' and 'Daddy that' in our home. It was a real splash of icy water to the face when she took to calling him Curtis. And you know there's nothing wrong with Mickey. I mean, he's just a kid. But it's like Curtis thinks that if Mickey doesn't already have a job and a house, he's not good enough for his baby girl. I mean, the boy is sixteen years old! He's just darn proud he has a truck to drive her around in. You know what I mean?"

I can't help but giggle at how animated she's getting, and when I do, she begins laughing. "I mean, like, get a clue."

"I'm sure they'll work it out."

She rolls her eyes. "They better, 'cause I might have to take out the frying pan and brain both of them if it doesn't get better soon."

"I hope it doesn't come to that."

She waves her hand again. "Honey, I'm just kidding. Hey, are you here to see your mama?"

"Yes, ma'am."

"She is in the conference room meeting with Wanda."

"Should I wait? I don't want to interrupt them."

"Honey, you'd be the only one that didn't interrupt them when they needed something. Go on back there. I'm sure they won't mind."

Walking back to the conference room, I notice that the hallway and the rooms where the doors are open have a fresh coat of paint on them. I pay attention to these things because

I absolutely despise painting, which means no one will ask me to help with that anytime soon.

I hear my mama's voice … and that of the woman who can't stand me—Wanda. I knock on the door and stick my head in the conference room.

The two women are sitting together.

"Well, isn't that apropos? Just mention the word lawyer, and one pops up," Wanda says smugly.

I have no idea what her barb means, but my face heats since I know it's most likely not complimentary.

"Hey, baby. I didn't realize you were already home."

I favor Wanda with a quick "somebody thinks I have value" glare and smile at Mama.

She extends her hand in that familiar Mama gesture, and I take hers in mine as I stoop over and squeeze her around the shoulders.

She sighs. "It's so good to have you home. I was worried about you."

That would make two of us. "No need to worry, Mama. I always manage to take care of myself."

She raises her eyebrows with an expression of amusement. Mama values actions over words, and she knows her daughter well.

I know it's unnecessary. Mama will know I came by simply to confirm that she still exists because she is my touchstone. Mama is home to me.

"You're in luck, April May. We finished remodeling last month."

I ignore Wanda's snide comment as I scan the paperwork in front of Mama. I point toward the documents. "Unfortunately, I am better at budgets and schedules than with a paintbrush, Wanda. It's just the way God made me."

Wanda straightens her back as her chin drops to her chest and her eyebrows draw together. "I didn't mean to offend you, April May."

I don't believe that for a second. It occurred to Wanda she

was taking the browbeating a bit too far, and it was best not to do that in front of my mama.

"I apologize. I am only frustrated because our group counsel for the women recently retired, and our budget is already strapped covering rent, utilities, and food. Folks don't donate like they used to either."

I'm processing what Wanda has said when Mama taps my leg. "Baby, why don't you sit down. We could use another set of eyes. You may even see something we've missed since you have a different paradigm."

I pull the chair next to Mama's back. "Counsel?"

Wanda tilts her head. "Sure. When the women arrive, they need four things—almost equally. They need a safe place to stay, food, someone to listen to them while deciding what is best for them and their children, and legal counsel. The women who arrive here often arrive with only the clothes they wear. They have no resources for the legal actions they must take to improve their lives."

I clasp my hands on the table and lean forward. "Like custody hearings?"

"That's the tip of the iceberg," Mama says.

"There's a whole myriad of things that must be taken care of," Wanda says. "Restraining orders, child support cases." Wanda's lips curl. "Even kidnapping charges."

I'm chagrined that I have never wholly thought through the process of what their organization does. I've always considered it where Mama went when disappearing from our home, and women went when transitioning through a rough spot in their failing marriages.

And I think of Jax's mom. Gemma, my best friend in high school, who pulled herself up by the bootstraps to become a nurse, only for her estranged husband to murder her.

Gemma had a restraining order against her husband. Because of her line of work, she could provide her own shelter and food. But did she have someone to talk to about how best to manage the situation with her husband? Was everything that could've been done to protect her from a man who had a high probability of becoming violent enacted?

The one deep, piercing thorn in my heart for the last two years is how I wasn't there for Gemma. I tell myself that I couldn't have done anything to prevent what happened to her.

While that may be true, the fact remains that I wasn't there. I never even tried.

It's coming to me shamefully late, but life isn't a simple ledger of wins and losses. Because if it were, it would be too easy not to try if you don't see the opportunity to succeed.

No. Life is about trying. It is about doing your best with all of your skill sets and the deficiencies you bring with you.

I understand that the most significant expression of faith is to try even when you see no way of winning.

"I do family law, Mama."

My statement hangs in the air for an eternity. It's as if I have cast a freeze spell, and time has stopped.

"Mama?"

"I know. But this work's pro bono, April."

I shrug. "I expected that."

"You're just getting started and have a lot of responsibilities, April."

I know she's referring to my student loans. Still, given my lifestyle and the two jobs I've been fortunate to have since moving back to Guntersville, I've already put a significant dent into the principle.

"I've got a handle on things. And besides, since my engagement status has changed, I'll have a few more hours a day to work on cases for the women."

Wanda's expression has softened considerably. If I thought it possible, she might be looking appreciatively at me. "April May, that is really sweet of you to offer. But these are less-than-desirable cases because of their nature, and like your Mama said, there's no money involved."

"But your counsel has already retired. Correct?"

"Yes, Beatrix found out last week that her partner has

stage four cancer. They spent their lives planning for their retirement on the beach. She wants to move her down there so they can spend the last few months where they always planned to be."

"Wow."

Wanda stares at her hands on the table. "Yeah. Wow."

I lick my lips as I consider the obligation. Wanda is correct. It's not only the hours of volunteerism. It's what goes on during those hours.

I already know this from my experience with Uncle Howard. When you're an attorney, you see people at the worst time. Like when they do something foolish such as start a fight or steal a car. Or, in this instance, allow what was once a beautiful, loving relationship to eat itself from the inside out while filling both parties with poison that will never leave their bloodstream.

It's true. It does wear on me to regularly know and see how awful people can be to each other. Few people can be as fortunate as I was with my relationship with Lee. Being with someone who could end the relationship in a healthy, adult-like manner was a blessing.

Do I really want more of this? Do I want to wade through more of the hurtful garbage people throw at each other when they've decided a relationship doesn't work?

Heck, if I wanted rainbows and unicorns, I should've been a wedding planner.

I am a lawyer, and a darn good one at that. It's my *job* to help people.

"Let's do this. Let me take care of the most critical while y'all take some time and see if you can find a replacement for Beatrix. Or your budget could improve, and you could do something different."

Wanda opens her mouth as if to protest.

"It's not really negotiable. I can't paint worth a darn. Let me do this for you."

Wanda snorts loudly and releases a hee-haw laugh. I draw

back because it's such an alarming noise. The laughter, not the snort. I don't believe I've ever heard her laugh before.

"You are right awful with a paintbrush, April May."

Mama reaches over and squeezes my hand. It makes my heart swell as if it is doubling in size.

Chapter 50

The acrid smoke, stinging my eyes, keeps my attitude on a nasty, mean knife's edge. I am hunting again, not for blood, but to mess with his head.

Austin believes he is eluding me. He thinks he's clever and covert.

He has no knowledge of my journey to Turtle Key, nor how that trip transformed me.

Austin failed to keep tabs on me when I left for Baltimore. That's his error in judgment. He will pay dearly for the oversight.

He watches me on shaking knees behind what's left of the Fant's General Store façade. A disgusting man-creature whose magical silhouette imprint shows through the brick wall as if he is hidden behind window shears.

This is my new reality he has no knowledge of. Since being force-fed more energy than any witch should be able to hold—and much less control—I can extract power with a minuscule portion of the effort required previously.

The improved harnessing skill does not only exist in Austin's apocalyptic dreamscape, where my powers usually surge. It applies in the Guntersville of my reality, too.

I discovered this quite by accident. Anxious to return home from Turtle Key, I aimed to quell my fidgets with one of my favorite parlor tricks. Despite knowing it was a mark on the dark side of the magical ledger—using my magic for amusement—I opened my hand to form a glowing sphere. I envisioned creating one like Gramma used to lead us out of Ricky's labyrinth. I only planned to keep it a discreet, dimly lit globe the size of a marble.

A rotating platinum bowling ball appeared above my hand. I darn near blinded myself when it lit up like the sun.

Not knowing the amplitude of my divinations helps me refrain from using my powers for entertainment. There's nothing like wanting a Snap and Pop, only to have someone toss me a stick of dynamite to suppress my appetite for such novelties.

One more quirky trait to add to my growing list of items I need to practice controlling in my life.

Austin skulks to the opposite end of the ruined wall. I spy his swirling, metallic-blue-colored eye peering through a hole in the brick's mortar. I can send a single pinpoint of energy in his direction and permanently maim his supernatural being by obliterating his eye. I also could explode him back to the pit he crawled from with a concussion blast.

But I won't. And I can't … or at least I shouldn't. I am not prepared to take a permanent walk on the evil side.

When balancing the scales between good and evil before my amped-up skill set, I sprinkled grains of sand on either plate when I used my powers. Now with the striking force at my disposal, it may take only one hostile, overly aggressive action on my part, and it will be as if I dropped an eighteen-wheeler on the evil scale. Thereby casting me onto Team Darkness forever.

Still, Austin is unaware of this change in our game. And while I am not free to do any severe damage to him or his witches without losing my soul, it is still amusing to mess with his reptilian mind.

What's that saying? Payback is a witch. Well, she's here and sashaying the streets of your dream like she owns them, buddy.

I furrow my brow. Austin's telepathic commands to his witches echo in my mind.

Another thing he is clueless about is I hear his communications.

He directs his scraggy entourage to flank me. The same tired, tactical strategy he employed last time with his six—no, he now has a seventh scared witch in his platoon.

I must give him credit, though. After I decimated Austin's two-hundred-strong rank of twilight witches in the spring and burned him to a crisp, he slowly and methodically rebuilt a platoon and mostly healed himself.

But you can't fix stupid. Austin holds doggedly to the belief he can capture and harness my power for his use. That only illustrates his level of ignorance or arrogance. I'm yet to determine which of the two characteristics allows him to proceed with hunting the alpha predator I have evolved into.

If Austin were to trap me—given I am ten times more potent than him—and make his witches look like they are releasing static electricity charges, it would be a ruse on my part, albeit an amusing one. How I would love to see the expression on his face when I break his chains again.

I've considered if my transformation would have come sooner if I had worn the amulet Dionis gave me rather than stored it in ice. It would have. The one thing holding true throughout my paranormal growth is that the more I am exposed and take on, the greater my powers expand.

The witches, three on my left and four on the right—although the new one is scared and refuses to move forward—close in on me like I am prey. Austin moves from behind the jagged edge of the wall onto the buckled sidewalk.

"Have you considered my offer, April?" Austin steps off the sidewalk to cross the road in his charming, human form.

"The one where you renounce your standing with your maker and return to your grave?"

His smile is genuine. We've developed a perverse, snarky

relationship during these hunting sessions. Perverse because, in the end, he will perish.

"That would be the less attractive of the options." He sighs dramatically.

"If you join forces with me now, you receive all the prizes behind door number three." He waves his hand with a flourish, stops, and puts his finger across his lips as if in deep thought. He smiles and opens his arms wide.

"Forget that. I'll give you all the prizes behind door number one, two, and three because that's how much I believe in you."

"Oh, you make me feel all warm and fuzzy inside, Austin."

He laughs, open-mouthed and genuine.

"And I can make you feel that way for all eternity. You only need to say yes."

"You didn't get the news flash. I've taken a break from men. But I really do appreciate the offer."

The specks of chaotic energy swirling around Austin change from a blue-and-silver hue to crimson and gold. His expression continues to be playful and flirtatious, yet its edges crumble. He's wrestling with his emotions. "April, you know it's only a matter of time before you are on the losing side of this battle. You belong with the winners. You are a winner."

"Austin, please, move along for your safety and my sanity. Find someone else to bother."

He steps closer to the curb and makes an imploring gesture with his hands. I form a blue shield in front of me the size of a dinner plate, and he stops.

"Look all around you. Don't you see it? Love and light have lost the battle. Fools hate each other for their *thoughts*, not just their actions. The most common question humans ask when something needs to be done is, 'What's in it for me?' You don't want to be the last power standing on the wrong side when the game ends. I promise it will not end well for you."

This is not the first time he has used this argument with me during our parlays. I would be lying if I said there aren't specific points he makes that leave me feeling raw and vulnerable. Still, in my heart, Austin has severely overestimated the lead his Team Darkness currently holds. As for me, my daddy always taught me to only look at the scoreboard once the game was over.

"It baffles me why you can't take a hint. You don't seem like an exceptionally dense man other than for this one example."

Austin lifts his right foot onto the curb. As the toe of his black, lizard-skin cowboy boot rests on the sidewalk, he puts his hands on his hip. "Do you think I like having to convince you to do the right thing?"

I shrug. "I don't know what you like. I've told you dozens of times that there's no way I am converting to serve your master. Surely there is someone else you can spend your time on."

His sardonic expression tells me he thinks I've lost my mind. "You're the only Lock Witch at this portal. By Satan's horns, if I had a choice, I would rather not deal with your stubborn, redneck logic. I swear you go out of your way not to do what's in your best interest…" He jabs a finger at me. "In your family's best interest, only because it isn't your idea."

My skin heats to an unbearable temperature as my power surges to the surface. I step forward as the area around me abruptly glows as if a high beam of light hangs directly over me. I struggle to grab hold of my powers by the tail with one hand and the hair of the redneck, Southern girl coming out for a fight in the other.

"If I told you once, I've told you a hundred times not to bring my family into this. You will be sorry if you dare mention their names again."

Austin stands firm, but I sense his fear by how the energy swirling about him slows to a crawl. The most devious and deceptive plan comes to my mind.

I doubt it will be successful. Austin does work for the king of deception, after all.

"Perhaps that's why you were selected. You may be uniquely qualified due to your annoying persistency and, most importantly, expendability."

"What do you mean?" Austin stutters.

I mustn't share everything with Austin, but seeing him considering my words so wholly and being shaken by them is delightful. "You know from first-hand experience that I can do damage to you. I might not win, but I can hurt you. Consider it. Why would your leader want you to consistently put yourself in danger when even you know I'll never change my mind? The only thing that can possibly come from this is I lose my patience and injure or kill you."

Austin swallows hard and scoffs, "I'm indispensable. You're delusional."

"*Nobody* is indispensable."

Austin recovers his composure as he does what gives him the most joy. He collects the energy around him and pushes his hands out in either direction. It's as if bulldozers have dropped their blades on either side of him, and large chunks of asphalt and soil push away, building ten-foot-tall berms on either side. "My ability and appetite for destruction are second to none."

Magic flexing bores me. And I'm none too happy that he tore yet another hole in Gunter Avenue. Careful not to overheat my magic, I draw in the ambient powers while holding a vision of *my* Guntersville. My glow intensifies, and Austin raises his hand to shield his eyes.

The sidewalk, in a three-foot circumference around me, repairs itself. The glowing circle of healing steadily creeps outward.

I stand next to the ruins of the men's store, and the bricks stack themselves in an orderly manner as mortar appears in their seams. The shattered glass pane strewn across the street pulls together as the transparent sheet becomes whole again.

"Stop! You can't. This is *my* vision."

"No. It's my town, Austin. It always was and always will be."

He steps back and forces his hands toward the growing circle of repair. My bubble of magic absorbs his blow, turning the energy and adding it to my power, increasing the speed with which the ring of repair spreads.

"You can't alter my vision!"

"Love has always been stronger, Austin. Change your ways or leave. Those are your two options."

Austin flexes and strains as if he will try another attempt at piercing my bubble of brightness. He stops and reconsiders.

His call to his witches, echoing in my mind, is unheeded. They left minutes ago to the far corners of his constructed reality, seeking safety.

"Blasted redneck witch! I promise you will rue this day, April May Snow. He'll come for you, and when he does, you'll regret not accepting his generous invitation."

"Well, he knows where to find me. I'm not going anywhere."

Austin favors me one more death glare and transforms into the disgusting hell kite that is his beast form. He expands his massive leathery wings, still pocked with holes from our battle in the spring, as he whips his dark, rat-like tail with its dripping stinger above his head. "You have not seen the last of me."

"I have for tonight." I wave goodbye with my right hand. He flaps his wings and takes to the air. Austin circles around the fifty-yard radius my magical light has repaired.

I smile as I watch him fly across the river's dike to the far side of the lake. He lands, turning to watch as I continue a slow walk down Baker Street. The buildings pull themselves together as I stroll toward the lake.

It is in my power to pull in enough energy to make his nightmare illusion of Guntersville disappear. I could also track down his witches and push them out of his reality as I corner them and change his false vision to reality.

I won't. One, because it's Austin's vision. His idea of what Guntersville should be. It won't change anything significant if I change it by force. His desire will remain the same. Second, by my current display, he already knows I'm considerably more powerful than he believed.

As I reach the water's edge, peering across the lake at his dark figure, I decide I'm done with our fun game for tonight.

I'll return to my bed in the real Guntersville. I may not even seek out Austin for a few weeks. And then only to ensure his army of twilight witches has not grown too quickly.

"Is it true?"

The unexpected voice startles me, and I release the bubble of light I created. I scan the area around me. Nobody is present.

A hand comes out of the lake. It claws at the earthen-mound dike, and a second hand appears a foot below the first. I gasp as the crown of a blond-headed human comes to the surface.

My thoughts reel as I try to understand what I am witnessing while remembering that I am in Austin's vision. This could be a trap.

The arms' muscles exhibit great strain. As if the being realizes it lacks the strength to pull itself from the water, the grip releases and the body slides back toward the lake. I dive forward onto my belly, seizing a hand as it dips below the water's dark surface.

The familiarity of the hand courses through me as I grasp it. My first response to let go and get as far away as possible is difficult to override. Still, I manage to pull until I can rise to my knees.

I bend forward, clutching the back of the man's belt, and tow steadily until we reach the dike's top.

I release him and fall back into a sitting position.

His expression is pained as he pants for air. His eyes remain closed, but I've seen enough pictures to identify Randolph from his profile.

He pushes against the wet fescue, rising onto all fours. Water drips from his golden-blond hair, and a single drop hangs from his nose. He opens his eyes—a startling shade of blue—and sighs as if a great wind has been released from his chest.

"Thank you," he whispers.

I choose to say nothing. I still need to be convinced that this isn't a ploy of Austin's. Letting things play out before making assumptions about this odd occurrence is best.

In turn, he leans back and sits on his butt like me. He extends his long legs, crossing them before him. "I'm sorry," he says, punctuating it with a chin dip.

My prudent decision to remain silent escapes me. My curiosity reigns supreme. "For what?"

"For scaring you." He makes a circular motion with his hand. "When you were younger." He shrugs his shoulder. "Last year, when you returned. I'm just sorry in general."

We sit in silence. Randolph stares at his hands as if waiting for absolution. I gaze at the handsome man and wonder if he loved my Aunt Dionis or if only a desire for power drove him into her arms.

"I loved her dearly."

His answer to my unspoken question startles me. How odd. Is it possible he had psychic abilities while Dionis possessed magical skills? How awful for the cousin I don't know—their orphaned son. He would be more messed up with his inherited DNA than me.

"Yes. I can read your mind and hear your thoughts. I've always been able to."

That revelation is at once highly inflammatory but also answers a lot regarding how the Old Man in the Lake always was able to appear at my weakest moment. "I don't know how I feel about that."

He looks up with his hypnotic blue eyes. "You should feel angry. I shouldn't have been listening."

"Is there anything else I should know?"

Randolph clasps his hands in front of him, cupping his shoulders forward. The silence continues, and I wonder if he will answer me.

"I'm a hell kite."

It takes considerable effort not to crab crawl away from him. I pat down my fears as I remember I can protect myself. "Like Austin?"

"Yes, but for different reasons."

My curiosity returns full force, and I lean toward him.

"Different, how?"

"Austin is a hell kite by his choice. He has selected that form for greed or a promise of power."

"And you?"

"I was born into the Lock and Key prophecy."

Randolph says it as if it explains everything. And that's what I've come to expect with how the information about the prophecy comes to me. So many riddles and so few answers.

"So, all hell kites are part of the Lock and Key prophecy?"

Randolph's face twists into a sour expression. "No. All key warlocks are hell kites, but not all hell kites are key warlocks."

"Yet all hell kites are of the dark."

"Who told you that?"

I scoff. "It stands to reason. Doesn't it?"

"Do all witches serve the darkness?"

Well, peaches. That's an interesting question. I've been struggling with that mystery myself. "Maybe you can enlighten me. It seems you might have an information advantage over me."

He chuckles. "I have truly always found you amusing."

"Well, I'm glad you found me entertaining. Although it is in some sort of creepy, voyeuristic-uncle manner."

He sobers. "Yes. Again. I hope you can forgive me someday."

We again enter a long silence as if he expects me to pronounce my forgiveness. Something I'm not prepared to do as of yet.

He favors me with a slight smile. "Those born with these abilities have the same choices as any other person. We can choose to use them for good or for bad."

"And you chose for bad." My voice sounds more accusatory than I intend.

The faint smile again. "Yes. I made a terrible mistake."

"Why."

"Because I'm an insecure idiot... *Was*."

I shake my head. "Not good enough. You tormented me all these years and brought on my aunt's death. You owe me a real answer."

His eyebrows knit together as his eyes turn liquid. "And my son's. I destroyed my little boy's life, too."

"And for what? What drove you?"

"Have you ever heard of the phrase 'all hat, no cattle'?"

"Are you talking to a Southern girl?"

He smiles, the joy reaching his eyes, and he swipes away the tears. "Yes, so I am." He crosses his arms. "I was bowled over by Dionis's beauty. The funny thing about it was that, as unmistakably gorgeous as she was, she was even more beautiful on the inside. She was vivacious, with a biting wit that constantly surprised me." He licks his lip and makes a circling gesture with his left hand. "It was like tasting sugar for the first time. Everything consumed me with how to be closer to and spend more time with this incredible person. You can imagine my surprise when she returned the interest." He points at his chest. "She began to like—no, love—me."

"And this made you turn to the dark side because, what?"

He guffaws. "Because I was a complete fraud, a shyster, an imposter. I had nothing to offer her. I was only in town because they ran me out of Enterprise. I came to Guntersville to look for another mark. I never intended to meet a girl, much less fall in love with one.

"And then the Snows. Have you seen your family? What the heck? Everybody works their tail off and is nice to everybody regardless of social status. I knew my goose was cooked when Dionis took me home to meet Loretta and Leonard. Her parents gave her so much more than I could, and she had such a strong bond with her brothers. I don't even have any siblings."

"But she loved you. Not your family or what you could give her."

"Yes, true. Thirty years on the bottom of the lake gives you plenty of time to think about the errors of your way and gain clarity regarding such matters."

I'm not the only sarcastic person in this conversation. "So, you made a deal."

"Answer my question first."

I shake my head. "What question?"

"Is it true? Can I be released from my bond?"

I favor him with a wry smile.

"Are you grinning at me?"

"I find it ironic that a key warlock doesn't understand that the key to releasing our heart always resides with us. Yes, you can be released from your bonds."

The burst of light blinds me. A crack slaps my ears as the scent of burnt ozone engulfs us. I scramble to my feet and form a protective bubble.

A second bolt of lightning strikes my barrier. Another brilliant bolt appears across the lake, illuminating Austin's wings on the opposite side of the lake. I track the bolt as it strikes my bubble.

Water slaps my left cheek.

I close my eyes, shaking my head as I push more power into the shield. I open my eyes, and the surroundings have darkened considerably.

Something wet strikes my left cheek again, and I roll over to find Puppy staring at me.

"What the heck, dude?"

He emits a low-pitched whine as if to tell me I should know.

I grab his furry, barrel-shaped chest and pull him tight against me, pushing my face into his cotton-like neck. "I missed you."

Chapter 51

"It would look good in my kitchen. Once I paint the cabinetry white," Granny says.

Granny holds up a lithograph of a bunny in a garden. It's not a cute bunny, just a regular old buck munching on dandelions. The frame—I'm assuming that's why she picked it out—is white but crusted with years of dust. "I suppose if you clean the frame."

She examines the frame, inspecting it for defects, and runs her finger along the edge. "It's nothing some Murphy Oil Soap won't cure." She favors me with a blank stare.

I consider apologizing for being rude. To each their own and all that.

She bursts into laughter. "I suppose I shouldn't buy it for the frame alone."

"People have bought cars before based on the color."

Granny puts the gosh-awful picture back, replacing the tag that reads "75% off," which I have a keen suspicion is what convinced her to pick it up in the first place.

No, I'm still not partial toward antique hunting. But I do love spending time with Granny.

The disastrous trip to Baltimore and the near-deadly excursion to Turtle Key knocked my visits with my grandmothers off schedule. It is humorous that I regard it as "off schedule," considering I moved out of state two weeks ago for a hot minute.

It confirms Lee's assertion. If only subconsciously, I never intended to move away from Guntersville.

Because it's already been too long, I agreed to accompany Granny to church today. After all the evil I experienced in Turtle Key, I figure the least I can do is make an appearance in church and tithe, given I still believe we had some higher force of protection on our side when we were escaping Ricky's collapsing dreamscape.

I like church simply fine. I've never been against it. Jesus and I aren't as close as we used to be. My fault, not his, but we are still on friendly terms.

The sermon was disconcerting. It was as if Reverend Peak looked into my soul and knew I needed reaffirmation about using the skills God gave me. Although I had previously heard the sermon about the servants who were given gifts by God, their master, and asked to multiply them, it has never convicted me as it did today.

It did not help that Reverend Pike stared at me during the sermon. Still, I'm positive if he was gazing at me too long, it was because he was shocked to see me on a Sunday.

After church, Granny wanted to go to the Frontiersman Buffet. My brothers and I refer to it as the "old folks" buffet. While everything looks normal, the Frontiersman has an unwritten rule that they cannot use any seasoning.

I chose the turkey and dressing. At least, that's what the placard said. I'm still determining what part of the turkey they used. I've never seen turkey patties, perfectly round and brown —not white, but not exactly dark meat either.

Since I'm in an indulgent mood because I have missed her so much, I allow Granny to talk me into going antique hunting off Highway 72. It has been a while since we've done that, plus I try to be a good granddaughter these days to overcome my past inadequacies.

When we enter the store, Marjorie's Menagerie, the third

stop in the last hour, I notice something about Granny that makes me sad.

While her mind is still whip-smart, her humor is ever-present and good-natured, and the exuberance of her personality is often like a child on Christmas morning, Granny is getting old.

It's not like it's a mystery. Heck, I'm approaching thirty, which seems so old to me. But it isn't until I notice Granny limping slightly and how she leans against furniture items to take a deep breath as if catching a covert respite that I become painfully aware that time is taking its toll on her body.

I try to push it out of my mind. Knowing that the clock is ticking on all of my relationships only makes me anxious.

"That piece has seen better days."

Her emphatic statement brings me out of my thoughts. Which is good. There's no point in borrowing trouble when I should live in the present and soak up these visits.

The dull-walnut armoire towers over her. One of its double doors hangs askew on the face, and all of the handle hardware is missing from the piece.

"Narnia," I whisper.

Granny tilts her chin down with an expression of skepticism. "Hardly. If you went through that cabinet, you'd end up in a junkyard. Or some suspicious speakeasy in 1930s Chicago."

I step forward and rub my hand along the rough, long-neglected surface. "It's beautiful."

"April, you just got done giving me a hard time about the dirty picture frame."

I favor her with a droll frown. "The picture was hideous. It wasn't only the frame. This is gorgeous."

I try to open the three-foot-tall doors. One is stuck, and the other comes off the armoire in my hand.

"It was beautiful. It's not even fit for firewood now."

"Daddy has the wood shop."

"He does. But I don't see how that matters unless you want

to create this from scratch."

I wiggle my eyebrows at her. "You're losing your game. You don't recognize a real value when you see it now."

Granny pointedly grabs the tag and flips it over. "I've lost nothing. Eight hundred dollars for garbage is eight hundred that you might as well have lit for heat."

"I wonder if they would take seven hundred?"

Granny chuckles. "If they take more than seventy-five cents, they're thieves.

∞∞∞

Granny backs her truck into my parents' driveway. It was meant to be, as Daddy sits on the dock while we park.

"Ralph will not be happy I couldn't talk you out of this."

"Daddy loves doing woodwork. This will be fine."

Granny shakes her head. I roll my eyes and shut the door.

If there is one man in the world I can count on explicitly, it's my father. I wouldn't exactly say he spoils me. But I can get him to do anything I ask him to.

The piece twisted precariously when we loaded the armoire into the back of Granny's truck. I feared it would fall into pieces if we weren't exceptionally gentle. I won't tell her, but Granny may be right about this once beautiful armoire being beyond help. What kept my faith in reviving the work was that I have an excellent carpenter to help me resurrect the whimsical furniture masterpiece.

"Are you busy?" I ask, skipping down the path toward the dock.

He watched us while we backed the truck up to the garage, yet he acts like he's surprised.

"What are we doing?"

I stop at the edge of the dock and shield my eyes from the sun with my hand. "I've got a piece of furniture for my apartment that I want to repair."

Daddy takes the cigar out of his mouth with his left hand while scratching his head with his right. "Repair like how?"

"Like new?"

He chuckles. "Okay … but what's wrong with it?"

I decide honesty is the best policy. "According to Granny, pretty much everything."

"Is Hancock Furniture store out of business?"

I favor him with a wry smile. "They don't make pieces like this anymore."

He moves toward me, which is a positive sign, and squeezes the lit end of his cigar. "All right. Let's see what you got. Hopefully, you didn't buy a pig in a poke."

Granny was right. I bought a pig in a poke.

According to Daddy, and he seems to know what he's talking about when it comes to furniture, the piece was probably stored outside in a barn. While that kept it out of the rain, it did not protect it against the dramatic temperature changes from one hundred degrees and one hundred percent humidity to thirty degrees and one hundred percent humidity we experience in Alabama.

Every drawer is off-center, and worse, the drawer bottoms are so warped they are falling out as we attempt to sand and correct the other issues.

"Baby, we may have bitten off more than we can chew here."

"We can rebuild it bigger, faster, and stronger than ever before…" I say.

He turns and stares at me as if I've lost my mind. He cracks a grin. "Well, I must appreciate your optimism, if nothing else."

"But it can be repaired?"

He turns his attention back to the runner he is attempting to straighten. "No. I said I appreciate your optimism." He grunts. "Ugh … this is going to have to come off."

"What can I do to help?"

He grabs the power screwdriver and removes the runner from the inside of the shelf space. "You can take that optimism and start sanding the front of the armoire doors. Assuming that we can salvage the rest of the piece."

I hop to it. I don't want him to become discouraged with the project. "Do I need two hundred twenty or sixty grit?"

He chuckles. Daddy has his amusement button permanently pressed today. "Take the sixty across it *lightly*. If you start at two twenty, it'll be Christmas before you get it smooth."

"Right."

I work the sandpaper with the wood grain as Mama taught me. The light strokes I'm taking don't make much of an impression, and I push a little firmer, ever mindful not to strip more than what I have to.

"Did Norman mention anything about what took place on our vacation?"

"Not much other than to say it was more of a working vacation. I swear that man works more retired than most people do during their career."

"Yeah, it was pretty intense."

"Blast it."

"What's the matter?"

"Nothing. The runner just crumbled in my hand. I'll have to cut some new ones." He stands up, holding the broken piece in his hand, and stares contemplatively at the armoire. "It's best to go ahead and replace all of them. There's not much here worth saving."

"I'm sorry. If I had realized it was so much work."

"Nah. It's okay. It'll be a beaut once we get done with it." He shrugs. "Assuming we get done with it."

He measures several one by four sticks in preparation to cut them before shaping them with a router bit. "Y'all did a good thing, though. Saving that young boy. It was a shame about their neighbor," he says.

"I feel bad that I initially didn't like her. In the end, I came to realize she was a courageous person."

"I know someone else who is brave."

Daddy turns on the table saw and makes his first cut.

I appreciate the compliment, but it wasn't earned. That day, everyone in our makeshift coven outshone me for bravery. I only did what I had to do to survive.

I hope if I keep trying and believe in my abilities—*all* of my abilities—I, too, will be able to react as quickly and fearlessly as others.

As fearless as I feel when I visit Austin in his vision.

Thinking of Austin's version of a Guntersville devastated by evil powers reminds me of my interaction with Randolph. The cascading thought pattern that is my world leads me to Norman's statement about asking Daddy about Randolph.

"Daddy, Norman said I should ask you about what happened the night Randolph left Guntersville."

The whine of the sawblade changes pitch.

"Son of a monkey's uncle!"

Daddy jerks his hand away from the saw blade. Blood splatters onto the wall behind him.

Chapter 52

I spring into action and clasp his hand in mine. He pulls away to look at his hand, nearly pulling me off my feet.

"April!"

I pull his hand against my stomach. "Chill! Let me see how bad it is so we know if we have a trip to the emergency room in the near future."

"Yes! Yes, we do. I'm surprised it's still attached."

"Hold still so I can keep pressure on it before I check how deep it is."

"Why are you being so odd?"

"Hush."

"Near sixty, been cutting wood my entire life, and the first time I cut myself."

I let him ramble on as I steal a peek at the damage and nearly add to the growing mess on the floor as my gorge jumps. His right pinky is held on by the thinnest string of skin.

But I've got this. Assuming I don't put my father's finger on backward. Always a critical point to be sure of before I attempt to heal a finger.

"How bad is it?"

"Surprisingly, not too bad. The saw must have knocked your finger out of the way when it came into contact with it." I keep my eyes on his hand to pass the lie.

"Bull. Let me hold it so you can drive me to the emergency room."

"Hold on." I use my softest, most patient voice possible to stall for more time as I force healing energy down my arm and into his finger. "Let me see if, by keeping pressure on it, I can get the bleeding to stop. It would be much better to close it with super glue rather than have a bunch of stitches in your finger."

He guffaws. "It feels like I cut the darn thing off. I think super glue is out of the question."

"I really think it startled you. Hold still while I check if it stopped bleeding."

I watch with extreme intensity as I open my right hand. I'm sure Daddy is praying that it's not cut off. Me? I hope I set it straight, and it's not backward.

I breathe in relief. His finger looks fully repaired despite the copious blood pooling in my palm.

"Well, I don't understand," he stammers. "I would've bet I cut that clean off."

"I'm sure you did. It had to be scary."

"I can't believe... I've never cut myself before."

"Well, I should know better than to ask you something while you're operating a saw."

His expression turns into a frown.

He doesn't want to talk about it, but it's best to motor on through. "So why would Norman tell me that?"

Daddy scratches his chest absently with his left hand. I can tell he's contemplating whether he can float a lie, and then considers it best to tell the truth. I can pick up on his thoughts if he becomes nervous while lying.

"Do you want a beer?"

"If you think we both could use one."

"I definitely could, and I feel you'll want one after my story."

"Fair."

He rummages around in the workshop refrigerator. "Bingo. Even better." He lifts half a liter of tequila from the fridge and grabs two tumblers from the cupboard above his workshop sink.

"That bad?"

"Worse.

Angst grips my stomach, and acid flows up to my tongue. I have an ominous feeling that whatever I asked could change our relationship forever. I no longer want to know.

Daddy hands me one of the tumblers. I take it and say, "It's okay. We don't have to talk about it."

"No." Daddy grabs a lawn chair and unfolds it. He directs me to sit as he opens a second one for him. "April, maybe I failed you, but I want you to know it's not because I was afraid to talk to you about it. It's because I thought it best."

I repeat. "We really don't have to discuss this."

He stares at his drink. Then he levels his eyes and asks, "How's that drink?"

I'm obstinate, but I can take a hint and sip the chilled tequila. "Good." It's Patron. Of course, it's good.

"There is a lot you don't know. And frankly, if I had thought you would make your home here, your mom and I would've discussed many things sooner. Despite what your mom wanted."

He leans forward and favors me with a chilling expression I have never seen from him. "You need to know that Norman, Howard, and I are the only ones who know what happened that night. I need you to promise that you will not breathe a word to anyone."

I put my glass tumbler on the concrete floor. "You're spooking me."

"Promise!"

The horse is already out of the barn on this one. No matter how I would like to end the conversation, he plans to share it with me and, in doing so, pull me into the conspiracy. "Yes, sir," I croak.

"I need you to also understand that while I've been exposed to all manner of paranormal abnormalities in my life, I don't have any unusual skills like you, Dusty, or your mom."

I feel my face twist into an expression Buckwheat from the Little Rascals made famous. No one's ever mentioned Mama having any supernatural abilities. "Our mama?"

Daddy takes a sip of his tequila and makes a waving gesture. "We can talk about that another time. This is about Randolph and what happened to him."

I nod in agreement. As much as I don't want to hear something that troubles my father so thoroughly, I must now know.

"When Randolph first appeared in town, Norman and I liked him well enough. Howard couldn't stand him. He said he was full of it and that he was a shyster. It was more like Howard didn't think anyone was good enough for his little sister.

"Things progressed, and we knew Dionis was falling increasingly in love with Randolph."

He takes another sip of the amber liquid in his left hand and rests his forehead between his forefinger and thumb, his elbow propped on his knee. "Your aunt began to show, and Howard insisted that we have a talk with Randolph."

"So, shotgun weddings were a thing?"

He emits a cynical laugh. There's no humor in it. "Very much a real thing. And it was one shotgun and two shovels. We were trying to make a point."

I'm searching my dad's face. I'm waiting for him to crack a smile so that I know he is pulling my leg. There's no way those three men I know so well could do something to hurt somebody or scare them in that manner.

"And the point was made. It just didn't have the results we anticipated. Randolph grabbed the shotgun and caught me by surprise. Howard wrestled it away from him before he could turn it on us."

My face stretches into an expression of horror as I shake my head from side to side. "Y'all killed him because he grabbed for the gun?"

"Lord, no. We outnumbered him three to one. It's not like we couldn't have handled him. But it wasn't him."

I stare at my dad blankly. His syntax is so jumbled I don't even know what to make of it.

Dad grimaces. "He changed April... Randolph changed into something grotesque. Not normal."

The pieces fall into place for me. I understand what my father means by "changed."

"Howard was wrestling with him, and suddenly he grew two feet taller and sprouted wings and a tail. Lord, help me. I didn't even think about it. He wasn't even human to me at that point anymore, and I swung my shovel."

My father runs his hands through his hair. His expression makes him look twenty years older. "The blade stuck in the side of his head." He makes a slashing motion with his hand. "It just stuck there for the longest. He was still standing, and he transformed back into Randolph and fell."

If coming clean was supposed to give him relief or closure, it failed. I hope to provide him with some solace.

"You were protecting your brother. You were scared by his beast form. I get it. Demons can be scary."

My father looks up at me with imploring eyes. "I don't know what you mean by 'beast form.' But I know that night *we* were the beasts. As we discussed whether we should bury him or call the police, he transformed again into that thing with the tail. His tail struck out, and the stinger caught Howard in his left arm. Immediately, he was paralyzed on the left side of his body. This time Norman and I hammered him on the head with our shovels until he returned to Randolph's form."

Daddy stands, inadvertently kicking his chair over behind him. "All we wanted him to do was do the right thing by Dionis and not leave her to raise their son alone. If he had already made his intentions known, there would have been no need for us to bother him that night. He and my sister would still be alive."

My father paces back and forth. He's no longer speaking to me.

"And for their son, given the prophecy, there was no way he could remain in our family. My mom wanted to raise him so badly that she was heartbroken."

He leans against the refrigerator, tears streaming down his face. "We were only trying to keep Dionis safe. Keep her happy. Ultimately, we did exactly the wrong thing."

"You didn't know."

He releases a bitter laugh. "That makes it better? That makes it all right? We killed her. We drove her into the lake. Why did we ever think, with her abilities, she wouldn't know where he was and what happened to him."

"So y'all hid him in the lake."

"Oh, if it were that simple." Dad downs the rest of the tequila in his tumbler and laughs. "Come to find out, we couldn't kill the darn thing. And we couldn't rightly let it go. If the roles were reversed, the first thing I would do is kill the three hotheads that came after me."

My father's tale goes from awful to monstrous so quickly I genuinely wish I had never asked the question.

He refills his tumbler and mumbles, "Well, in for a penny, in for a pound. We three had the bright idea that we were dealing with some demonic force. We all believed in the power of crucifixes, so we knocked him upside the head until he became Randolph again. Norman attached his crucifix around Randolph's neck. Howard and I attached ours around his ankles. We proceeded to take rebar and form solid concrete shoes for the man." Dad makes a flustered gesture with his right hand. "The whole process took the better part of the night. Then right before dawn, we dropped our boat in at the ramp and found a quiet inlet to drop him over the side."

Dad favors me with a sardonic smile. "Of course, it's only apropos that the house your mom fell in love with fifteen years later is in the same inlet."

All these years. I wanted all this information, and now that it's coming to me, it feels like I'm drowning. It's as if someone has opened the dam, and I'm reaching wildly for the valve to stop my father.

And yet I still have questions that pop out of my mouth.

"What happened to him?"

"As far as I know, he is still on the bottom of the lake, twenty feet from our dock."

"No, Dionis and Randolph's son. The cousin I never knew."

My father downs the rest of his second glass of tequila and turns away from me as he rinses his glass. "It didn't go well for him. Because of the prophecy, and the possibility of him being a key warlock, we thought it best to place him in a home far away from Guntersville."

"What town?"

"Birmingham. But the couple we placed him with was killed in an accident. He only lived there for a short time."

"Where is he now?"

My father shakes his head. "I have no idea where he is."

I glower at Dad. "You're lying to me."

"No, I'm not, April. His work requires him to travel a lot. I don't believe he's had an address for the last ten years."

"What's his name?"

"Why?"

"Because I want to meet him. And I'm good at finding people, but I'll need his name to start."

Dad points at my armoire. "Can we pick this up when you get off tomorrow evening? I've lost my fancy for doing woodwork tonight."

"Don't deflect. Answer me."

"I can't, April. He asked me explicitly not to ever reveal to you who he is."

Chapter 53

I wish I had made better choices and come into the office to work late yesterday instead of messing around with an old, filthy, dilapidated armoire. It would have saved me from uncovering equally old family dirt. I understand the adage that everybody has skeletons in their closet. Lord knows I have made my fair share of poor decisions in my brief life.

Still, I don't have *real* skeletons in my closet, as do my uncles and father. The level of disappointment toward the men in my life that kept me safe as a child made for a thoroughly restless night of tossing and turning.

Neither the lack of sleep nor the knowledge that I come from a family of murderers is helpful in cleaning up the mess I made by stopping and now restarting my business. It is an understatement to say it will take considerable focused exertion. I've spent the first part of the morning working on the budget, which is a complete disaster considering that I'll need cash flow for utilities and lease payments to restart. I have no revenue streams other than the cases with Andy and Kat.

Most aggravating of all, I forgot that I had removed the remaining coffee when I locked up last. Still, I focus on the positive.

First, my call to Lane was fruitful. He believes that

Lamar may be taking a position in Montgomery, leaving a public defender's position open again. Which means overflow business from the DA's office for April.

The second blessing, even though I am not happy with him currently due to what I learned last night, is that Howard was so busy with his pizza franchises he has yet to place the office with a real estate agent to lease out.

I lock the office door to make a quick trip to the Piggly Wiggly and pick up the much-needed coffee. There's a folded piece of white paper flapping in the wind on the windshield of my Z-28.

"What the devil? Does Lau have them handing out parking tickets for the business owners now?"

If this new police captain keeps it up, one of these days I swear we're going to mix it up. He'll be sorry he ever messed with me.

I stomp to my car and rip the sheet of paper from under the windshield wiper blade. Are the police writing tickets on college-ruled notebook paper now? I swear this town has gone to heck in a handbasket since I've been gone.

My curiosity piques as I unfold the white sheet of paper. I'm sorely disappointed on both counts if I was hoping for a long, handwritten love letter from a secret admirer. A simple message is scrawled across the sheet.

Butt out or die, girl.

What the heck? I despise coded messages. *Butt out of what?*

I surely don't want to die. It would have been most helpful if the writer had bothered to tell me what exactly they wanted me to butt out of. It may be of no consequence to me, and I'd gladly sidestep the issue and comply with their request. But now, with how they have left it, I have no idea what to do to keep myself safe from this less-than-accomplished wordsmith.

The letters *l*, *r*, and *t* have a leftward curl at the base and the letter *u* has a flare to the right. The letter *i* has a peculiar small *o* serving as the dot. In totality, it is the oddest print I have ever seen and has a distinctly feminine feel. Or a male attempting to change their handwriting to look more feminine. Given the overly exaggerated o dotting of the *i*, it must have been written by a man trying to cover his tracks.

Oh, fudge biscuit. Tell me Liam is not stupid enough to place a threatening note on the car of his girlfriend's lawyer.

Given he will not be recruited by Mensa anytime soon and has amply demonstrated his hotheaded nature, that's precisely what he has done. It's easy for me to deduce, given my ultrathin caseload. I only have so many folks who can be disgusted with me currently. It is either Thelma or Liam.

Maybe I'm projecting my disappointment with my father from yesterday. People making threats and bullying to get the outcome they want, whether they intend to follow through or if it's a bluff, really makes my butt itch.

I get into my car, slam the door, and start the engine. I may not like Captain Lau, but even he will want to act on this letter threatening a defense attorney.

Riding the four blocks over to the police annex, my heart rate rises. It may be time to finally take the P365 9mm I bought for myself during the summer out of its case and load it. If Liam decides to do anything stupid, I plan to be prepared.

I march into the police station and make a beeline for Captain Lau's office. One of the plainclothes detectives leaves Lau's office as I approach.

I tap on the door case. "Do you have a moment for me, Captain?"

He furrows his brow, making a come-hither motion with his finger. "Morning, Counselor." He motions toward the chair in front of him. "To what do I owe this honor?"

"I can't stay." I approach and hand him the letter. "I found this on my car windshield this morning."

He reads the note and sucks in his lips.

"What can we do about it?"

His brown eyes meet mine. "Do you have any idea who it might be?"

"Liam."

He sighs. "Remind me never to get on your bad side, Counselor."

"What does that mean?"

Pete pauses and measures his words. "I understand how you feel about him. I think domestic violence is one of the most perverse crimes there is. I cannot understand how an individual can hurt someone they claim to love. But I would like to remind you that nothing has been proven yet. We don't know what transpired in that household."

I scoff. "We know exactly what happened in that trailer. We also know that with this town's good old boy system, it'll be covered up and laughed about next week at the bar."

Captain Lau raises his eyebrows while favoring me with a wan smile. "And if that were true, that would be both a crime and a tragedy."

I angle my head as my jaw muscles flex. His comment surprises me mildly, but it still doesn't fix anything for me. "So, you're not going to investigate this?"

"Of course, we will. We have an ongoing investigation, and this will be considered duly, as will all the evidence. Also, if you are equally concerned for your client's well-being, we have a police cruiser scheduled for the periodic drive-by of Kat's trailer. What more would you suggest I do?"

"Bring him in for questioning."

"About a letter on your car with a threat from someone we can't identify?"

It sounds silly, but I have decided this is the hill I will die on. "Yes."

"No."

"But—"

Pete makes a shooing motion with his hand. "Counselor Snow, I have more investigations open than I can shake a stick at. If you don't mind, I need to get busy."

"Well, I'm gonna go tell Kat about this letter."

He returns his attention to his PC screen, feverishly tapping the keys on his keyboard. "It's still a free country, Counselor."

∞∞∞

I am not a woman of idle threats. It would have been helpful if I had checked my schedule before I declared my intent to warn Kat that Liam left me a threatening message.

My car slides on Kat's gravel drive as I arrive. I jog to her door and ring her doorbell.

I glance at my phone, noting that I have time for a five-minute conversation—tops—before I'm due for the meeting with Thelma and Andy.

"Kat? Are you in there?" I holler as I beat on the metal screen door with my open palm.

"She ain't in there."

Turning, I see a woman in her fifties sitting at the base of the stairs of the trailer to the side of Kat's snapping pole beans.

"Pardon?"

"If you're looking for Kat, she's over at her mama's." The woman points over her shoulder and returns her attention to her chore.

"Thank you, ma'am," I say as I step off the porch and duck around the corner of Kat's trailer. There are three trailers behind Kat's, and I'm amazed that I did not take note of them on my prior visit.

The doors are shut on the two flanking trailers. The screen door is open on the one in the center, and a TV show blares into the gravel courtyard.

I don't know which one belongs to Kat's mom, but I know an open door is better than a closed one. Still mindful of my game of Beat the Clock and not looking forward to another scolding from Thelma if I'm late, I rush to the door.

"Hello?"

Inside the trailer, the noise drops precipitously. I realize only half of the loud voices from the trailer are from the television. I interrupted an intense argument between two women.

A tall, willowy woman appears behind the screen door. She takes a long drag on her cigarette and blows smoke through the screen. "We don't want none."

"Is Kat here?"

"Who's asking?"

"Her lawyer."

A smirk forms on her leather-like face, and she opens the door. "You're the woman who's gonna make sure that Liam doesn't hurt my girl."

Kat hops off the sofa against the opposite wall. "April? What are you doing here?"

I try to ignore it, but a thick, oily sensation covers me as I move into the trailer. It knocks me momentarily dizzy, and I place my hand on the wall to steady myself. The stickiness of years of cigarette smoke residue clings like adhesive tape to my fingertips.

"I came to warn you. Liam left a threatening message on my car. He told me to stay out of your business, or he would kill me."

Kat recoils in horror and covers her mouth. "Oh my." Her eyes open wider. "I know he can have a temper, but I can't imagine him threatening you."

"Yeah, it's sort of a first for me."

"I've been saying it all along. That boy is like a rabid dog. There's only one thing to do, and that's to put him down," Kat's mom says.

Kat points in my direction. "That's exactly what April said she would do. She said if a boy ever laid a hand on her like that, he would not be breathing."

The shock that Kat took my flippant conversational remark to be the gospel steals the air from me. I do an excellent job miming a goldfish that accidentally leaped from its bowl.

"Mm-hmm. That's exactly right. Little boys that want to hit girls... All they are good for is target practice. That's the God's honest truth."

Kat's mom moves closer and lays her hand on my shoulder. I try not to flinch as her sour darkness flows across my shoulder.

"I'm glad my little girl has a lawyer who understands what side she is on. If you ever need something, April, you just tell Maude, and I'll repay the favor."

"Th-Thank you," I stutter as I backpedal toward the screen door. "I'm sorry, but I have a full day booked since I only just arrived back in town. I really must be leaving. I thought you should be warned, Kat."

"Bless your heart, April May. I sure do appreciate you taking care of me like this," Kat says with a much-practiced rhythmic sway of her head as she favors me with a pleasant smile that doesn't reach her eyes.

Chapter 54

I have a complete and total train wreck on my hands. And that's a great analogy, too. Two obstinate, stubborn, intelligent people are traveling in opposite directions on the same track. Rather than use their brakes, they're throwing more coal in the boiler to increase the speed toward their mutual destruction.

Boom! Hundreds of railcars strewn like flaming sticks across the single track. Blooms of mushroom clouds tower into the sky, releasing deadly toxins.

Okay, I'm being overly dramatic, but my head hurts. Andy and Thelma have obviously decided that neither is willing to compromise. Both are willing to destroy the company to save face.

While a scorched-earth strategy may be acceptable when ending a relationship, albeit not adult-like, it's shortsighted—no, it's stupid—when a business is involved.

The business was initially Thelma's. She pulled Andy in to help, and together as a team they grew the company ten times larger than it would've ever been if they had done it on their own.

They should be thankful for the years that they worked together. They should be proud of how they built such a prosperous business as a team.

Instead, they act like they no longer care about the

business's health. It's all about making the other person pay financially and emotionally.

Because I worked closely with both in the past, this is particularly troubling to me. I've seen them at their best, and how they conduct themselves today seems like sheer madness. These two people differ from the pleasant, professional team I worked for earlier.

"This is how we conclude this negotiation. There are two proposals on the table. Claude, you and your client can accept one of the two, or we can defer the decision to arbitration. I have no interest in arguing anymore over this. It's not getting us anywhere, and these two fine people have a business they need to figure out how to run and keep healthy."

"Agreed," Claude says.

"These numbers aren't even right," Thelma grumbles.

The numbers are spot on. I may not be comfortable with this partnership dissolution, but I have complete faith in the accuracy of the numbers since Elsa provided the report. Her thorough breakout of the financials is quite enlightening.

Thelma is not complaining about the report as much as what the report reveals. The vast majority of the revenue is generated from the commercial accounts. A side of the business that she needs to gain more knowledge about and stands no chance of running successfully solo. It's a relationship business, and Andy has all of those relations.

Despite the disparity of the income flow, the partnership has remained fifty-fifty, and Thelma has enjoyed inflated earnings for many years. Until recently, Andy had been more than happy with the arrangement, as having someone he trusted overseeing the finances allowed him more time to develop accounts.

It was a beautiful arrangement while it worked.

"You have the books, Thelma. You're more than welcome to present your own analysis. But I'd appreciate you not slandering the thorough workup my CPA provided us."

Thelma narrows her eyes at me. "Haven't you turned into

the little miss high and mighty."

"I beg your pardon?"

"I gave you a chance when you were brand new to this town. Andy didn't want you. He wanted Howard to manage our account. But I said, 'No, let's let the young girl have an opportunity.'"

Thelma blows air between her teeth as if she's about to spit. "If I had only known you would turn into a backstabbing, money-grubbing, privileged princess who has never had to earn a living, I wouldn't have wasted my time with you."

"Whoa!" Andy says as he leans back and throws his hands into the air.

Claude places his hand over Thelma's. "Thelma."

I focus on controlling my breathing. It's difficult, but I maintain my poker face. "Thelma, I understand this is disappointing to you. Still, this is an equitable dissolution of your partnership with Andy. I wish you would take the time to consider it."

"How about you consider this?" She jabs her finger at me. "I'm buying Andy out."

"With what?"

I place my hand on Andy's shoulder so he does not have another unhelpful outburst.

"Why don't you put that in your hat and smoke it, missy."

I've known Thelma most of my life. I believed I had gotten close to her in the last year and a half and knew her well. I only knew part of her, as I had never seen this side of her before.

This version of Thelma is incapable of negotiating. I turn my attention to Claude. "Claude, since I haven't seen it yet, I'm guessing you need to compile a counterproposal?"

He twists uncomfortably in his seat. "Yes. I'm sorry. I wasn't aware."

"You weren't aware because I didn't think I'd have to go there," Thelma rants. "But I never expected this spoiled witch to try and steal everything I built."

Chapter 55

I am not responsible for the sins of my father. Or any other man in my family tree. However, since I am endowed with the ability to set matters right, as much as they can be, it is incumbent upon me to try.

It should concern me and strike fear in my heart. It's something I've never tried before and never heard described. There is little reason to believe I will be successful.

Instead of fear of failure, my spirit has been buoyed all day by the opportunity to try. The flame of hope in my nature refuses to die, and I will succeed.

Puppy pops out of his doggy door from my apartment to meet my car. He has long since learned the unique sound of my car's engine.

I squat, and we hug each other. "Do you want to help Mommy? Would you like to go for a boat ride?" I ask him.

He barks in my face, which elicits a laugh from me, and I give his mane one more rough scrub as I stand. "Give me one second."

Puppy follows me inside my apartment. I don't bother to close the door.

I change into my swimsuit and grab a towel. I move to my kitchen sink, taking a moment to center my energies.

The white, plastic container on the counter has remained in

my freezer for two years. This morning I set it out so the block of ice would melt and release the amulet.

The amulet's gem senses my presence and glows a vibrant violet as I approach. I reach into the cool water and grasp the sterling chain. The sensation of grabbing a live wire works its way up to my elbow before stabilizing.

Puppy's nails tap the old, wooden floors of my apartment. He pistons his legs nervously up and down.

"Are you hungry?"

He yaps and spins in a circle.

"How about we share an apple?"

He freezes and cocks his head. Puppy *will* eat apples, but they'll never be his first snack food choice. Puppy also has been scamming too many scoops of ice cream from Chase lately and can use a lighter snack. Not throwing shade or anything.

I clasp the chain behind my neck and tuck the amulet into my shirt. I grab a Granny Smith apple from the fruit bowl on my dinette, a knife from the counter, and speed walk toward the door. "Let's go, boy."

Puppy feeds off my energy and excitement. He has no clue what we're up to, but it must be fun if I'm happy about it. He races past me to the dock.

That's the easy part—the preparation. Now comes the execution of the plan, and despite a moment's worth of doubt, I push the negative thoughts away quickly.

I walk to the end of the dock where my father often sits and contemplates the meaning of life. How awkward must it be that Randolph was only a few feet off the end of that dock all these years?

Carefully, because the boards are aging and I don't want to end up with a splinter the size of a toothpick in my kneecap, I lie flat at the end of the dock with my head and shoulders hanging off the edge. I center myself, waiting for the butterflies of excitement to calm down and my heartbeat to slow.

Puppy shoves his nose against the right side of my ribcage,

and I push him away. "Okay, Mr. Patience, give me a second. I'm thinking about how best to do this."

He growls and goes into a crouching-dog position, mocking me.

"Okay, already."

I hold my hand above the lake's black surface. With minimal effort, I pull random energy to me and dip my right hand, breaking the surface. "Randolph, can you hear me?"

There's no answer in my mind and no vision in the water.

I swirl my hand slowly, enjoying the familiar feel of the lake water. The density and sensation of it are so different than bathwater or seawater.

Puppy moves closer to me and swings his butt until he's flat against my side. He peers into the water, too.

"Randolph, remember what we spoke of the other night?"

I'm not sure that the vision I saw in my dream that night was as straight of a line for him as it is for me. I know time is funky on the other side of the veil. And then there is always the fact that what I met the other night may have been a figment of my imagination, not Randolph. It could be an ordinary dream from a girl whose guilt regarding her father's terrible error was troubling her thoughts.

Still, I have hope.

"Randolph, it is time to free you of your binds."

Puppy growls a low, rumbling noise.

The gray-mottled face of Randolph appears a foot below the lake's surface. If I were not prepared for him and had not called him, it would've scared the living daylight out of me.

"Randolph."

He raises his hand toward mine in the water. I debate if I should remove my hand but leave it in the lake. Randolph runs a decayed finger down the side of my wrist.

It's a gentle gesture. Still, it sends chill bumps from my tailbone to the base of my skull.

"I want to take you to Dionis."

I cannot free myself from the bonds.

His voice echoes in my mind, convincing me to change my mode of communication.

I will release you from your bonds.

How?

How indeed. If I can locate Randolph's body, I can obliterate the concrete holding him fast to the bottom.

You will guide me.

All day I have thought of this moment. When I received the threatening letter from Liam, I was considering the best way to find Randolph. As Thelma was calling me every ugly name she could think of, I was considering how to communicate with Randolph.

Now, when it is most crucial that I be brave and be a woman of action, I stand and dive into the water. It is imperative. Any more thought on the subject would be detrimental to my execution of the plan.

Randolph.

Over here.

I twist my body and make a ninety-degree correction to the right. I took a full breath of air when I dove, but the coolness of the lake water constricts my lungs, and they burn from a lack of oxygen.

Randolph.

I'm here.

We continue our game of Marco Polo as I stroke as efficiently as possible under the water. My lungs, now acclimated, do not burn as I continue to push toward the center of the inlet.

The greenish-white cap comes into view through the murky water. I know I have found him and pop to the surface for air.

I take my time, allowing my breathing to normalize. I don't know how long this second part of the operation will take, and I need maximum air for my dive.

Satisfied I have as much breath as possible, I flip over and dive straight into the murkiness. Randolph's skull comes back into view, and I push past it until my hand strikes the lake's muddy bottom. Quickly I feel for what has held him to the bottom all these years. I can use the weight to my advantage.

The back of my left hand strikes something hard and rough. I grasp the concrete slabs, one in each hand, as I pull all the chaotic energy in our vicinity toward me. I release the power in a targeted cone shape that will be a small, well-directed concussion blast targeting the concrete slabs on either of Randolph's legs.

The blast knocks me backward through the water, crushing the remaining air out of my lungs.

I scratch for the sky, desperate for more oxygen. The surface takes forever to reach. As I break through, I gasp in the air greedily.

Puppy has lost his Jesus at the end of the dock. He barks loudly as he paces back and forth at the edge. He tenses in preparation for diving in the lake.

"I'm okay!" I holler at him.

Bless it.

I will either get used to my increased power or accidentally kill myself with it. I'm not confident enough to lay down any bets on the matter yet.

Taking a moment to ensure I haven't concussed myself, I tread water. I've had enough experience with blows to the head recently that I feel I'm still good to go.

Randolph.

He doesn't answer me, and I'm growing concerned that I may have blown him into infinity. I was worried about what damage I caused myself. I can only imagine if I were a waterlogged corpse on the bottom of the lake for thirty years.

Randolph, are you still with me?

The sun is dipping below the horizon. Darkness creeps across the lake's surface. The rhythm of the lapping water against the boathouse and the mournful whine of Puppy on the dock are all that breaks the perfect silence.

Randolph, please tell me you're still with me.

You freed me!

∞∞∞

If anyone sees me driving Mama's boat, they will think I have lost my mind. Not because I'm driving erratically. I barely create a wake since I don't know how well Randolph can keep up with me. But I laugh manically as I shout encouragement to someone over the side of the boat.

And I don't care what people see … or don't see. I'm giddy that the first half of my plan has worked.

Now if I am only blessed with the same luck during the second half of my plan.

While I did not know the location of Randolph, I encountered Dionis in the lake previously. My expectation is that I will find her there today. The only fact I worry to death is that, unlike Randolph, Dionis can move about the lake and surrounding properties. Lake Guntersville is a vast lake, and to be honest about it, she could be anywhere.

I refuse to let that fact dampen my excitement. I have freed Randolph from his binds, and I should be able to rejoin the lovers.

The area where Chase and I struck the log two years ago comes into view. It has a visceral effect on me. The pain was real, and the subsequent growth of my paranormal abilities has been something I have struggled with since that fateful morning.

I kill the motor and allow us to glide where I believe we can call Dionis. Puppy follows me to the bow, and I drop anchor. Like on the dock earlier, I lie on the boat's bow and reach toward the water, my hand a foot short of touching.

Randolph, are you still with me?

Where is she?

His face, with a shock of blond hair, his strong jaw, and striking blue eyes peer up from below my hand. I pull back at the unexpected transformation. As my intrigue regarding his attractiveness builds, I relax and extend my hand again. I am pleased he has been able to convert into his former glory. That is how Dionis should see him.

I can't say for sure. I thought she would be here.

Despite him still being underwater, I watch the fret and worry lines increase on his handsome face.

Don't worry. If we don't find her today, we can look again tomorrow. I won't stop until we find her.

But what if we don't find her?

Don't do that, Randolph. I need you to remain positive for us.

Because I'm lying on it, the amulet is uncomfortable against my chest. I shift my weight and pull it up toward my neck to get it out from under my breastbone. A brilliant idea comes to me as the chain tangles in my hair. At least, I hope it is brilliant.

I untangle the clasp from my hair and lower the amulet into the water.

Randolph, this is yours to give to Dionis.

He reaches up and takes the amulet by the stone. It rests firmly in his masculine grasp, and I release the chain. The amulet's shining light goes dormant. The gem turns blood red and is barely visible below the water's surface.

Randolph sinks below my view.

I wait and watch. I try to raise communications with Randolph again. I receive no answer.

Puppy grunts his displeasure as we wait. I did promise him a bite of apple after all.

I push to my feet and return to the captain's chair. "Puppy, your mommy may have just thrown a priceless amulet to the bottom of the lake for no good reason." I shrug as I cut the apple into slices. "But if history is any indication, it'll just come back to me whether I want it to or not."

Shoving half a slice of the apple into my mouth, I cup the other half in my palm. Puppy takes it from me uncharacteristically gently and chomps on it, never breaking eye contact with me.

"Good boy." I sigh. "At least no one can say we didn't try." Another maniacal laugh escapes me, and the concern that this adventure has somehow cracked me returns.

Forcing myself to calm down, I take a bite of the next slice of apple. As I extend Puppy's portion to him, he breaks eye contact with me and runs to the front of the boat. He barks with such force his front legs bounce with each bark. I follow his line of sight and lie on the bow again.

The water boils and spews as white foam forms on the surface. A pinprick of lavender light reaches my eyes from the bottom of the lake's depth. The light increases steadily until it illuminates the lake floor thirty feet across.

I pull Puppy into an embrace and squeeze him with all my strength. "I think he found her! I think Randolph found Dionis, Puppy!"

The clouds above us separate, producing a shaft of golden-white light matching the circumference of the light purple light below. It columns directly down from the sky, lighting the lake's surface on the topside while the amulet's lavender glow illuminates the underside. This is an absolute impossibility from the angle of the sun.

The purple light and the golden column strobe once in unison and vanish. Dusk returns, and the water is still.

Chapter 56

Puppy and I turn the boat for home and take our time. There's no rush now. We share the rest of the apple. I talk to him about my day, and he adds his thoughtful grunts and facial expressions in all the right spots.

The happiness that fills my heart is difficult to explain. I know it's not a perfect solution. They are dead, after all. Still, the ability to help the couple move to the next plane is more satisfying than any recent activity I can remember.

For once, I was not simply reacting to life. Which is how I often feel. I recognized the need to correct something, devised a plan, and used all my abilities to help.

Yes. The greatest demonstration of faith is to try when you do not know if you will succeed. And faith feels good.

We reach the entrance to the inlet of our neighborhood when the light finally fails. It wouldn't matter if it was pitch-dark. I'm home now, and parking the boat at my parents' is almost an autopilot event.

A flash of light to my right catches my eye. It's the same eerie, blue glow that caught my eye the other night.

I break the straight line to our boat dock and set a course for the far side of the inlet. The heavily wooded vacant lot sits directly across the small body of water from my parents' home.

I drop the boat's throttle into neutral as we approach the

first pile-driven posts of what remains of the dock. I peer over the side, checking how far I can travel before I'm deep into the grass, even though the sonar indicates I still have ten feet of depth.

Mama had a fit the one time I drove the boat up on a sand barge. The last thing I need is another scolding because of my curiosity.

Tapping the throttle forward, I scan the water's edge for indications of the blue light. There is nothing out there. Just hundreds of shadows cast by the most giant cedar trees I've ever known.

Throttling the boat into reverse momentarily, I slide it back into neutral. I glide gradually toward the buckled gray dock, a few inches every minute.

"I guess it was my eyes playing tricks on me, Puppy."

My stomach rumbles. The apple has only increased my appetite.

Given the poor condition of the property's dock, it's best to curtail my investigation tonight. It will be considerably easier to ride my bicycle over here tomorrow for a closer inspection, and I won't have to worry about Puppy wandering off in pursuit of a squirrel, opossum, or mountain lion.

I grip the throttle handle to pull back, and the blue light strobes in my periphery.

Well, it's gonna be hard to see that light during the day. It's better to check it out now than later.

I go to the left side of the boat and throw out the bumpers, tying them off to the level I estimate the vacant lot dock will tap the boat's side. I'm satisfied that I have them at the correct height and that the boat is protected. I throttle forward another fifteen feet to the first badly buckled board and halt the boat's forward movement.

Puppy barks and paces frantically from side to side as he stares into the distance.

I grab the rope to tie off the boat, and he blocks my progress. "Watch out, Puppy."

He doesn't pay me any mind as he continues to bark uncontrollably. I jump the two-foot distance to the dock, intending to tie the boat to the post and help Puppy off the stern.

I loop the rope around one of the round posts, but Puppy launches himself from the deck before the boat touches the side of the dock.

"You're gonna break a leg doing that!"

My scolding has zero effect. All I see is my keeshond's furry butt as he scrambles up the dock barking merrily on his way. "I'll have to take away his boating privileges if he doesn't do any better than that," I grumble.

With the boat secure, I walk up the destroyed landing, careful not to step on any of the boards that look suspect— more suspect than the rest of the structure. I'm in a good mood, and the last thing I want to do is spoil it by punching my leg through a dilapidated board.

"Puppy!"

I'm not sure why I'm hollering for him. I can quickly find him by his barking; the lot has been vacant my entire life. It's not like he's causing trouble, even if he is loud enough to wake the dead. If I were to guess, he caught the scent of a rabbit or a bird. It is still his life goal to be a hunter, although his speed, or lack thereof, will likely prevent him from ever reaching his goals.

I step off the dock onto roughly rounded step stones that form a winding path. That's unexpected, given that it's a vacant lot.

The cedar trees, prominent while riding by in the inlet, are daunting. They are easily forty feet tall and twenty feet round at the base. The further I walk toward Puppy, it becomes plain he is not barking at a random occurrence. The trees are equally spaced. The grove must have been planted decades ago —probably before my parents' births.

Puppy's barking stops. Because I didn't hear a yelp, I'm not particularly concerned.

Even for Guntersville, this lot of land has an overabundance of chaotic energy swirling in the air. It causes my skin to hum and my heartbeat to increase.

"Puppy, where are you?"

He releases a single yap, and I correct my course to the left. I squeeze between two giant cedar trees and step into a large, circular area of tall grass. The site is surrounded by thirteen large sentinel trees, and a place where a fourteenth tree would form a perfect circle is left open. My breath catches as I note the opening leaves a direct view of my parents' home across the inlet.

In the center of the courtyard-like space is a mass of vines. Puppy sits near the mound of vines, looking through the gap in the circle of trees.

"Did you get lost, buddy?"

He whines and pats the ground with his front paw.

Looking behind him at the mound of vines, I note that an old wrought-iron loveseat has been overrun with honeysuckle. The blooms are long gone, but the tiny leaves are unmistakable.

I turn my attention to Puppy. "What are you looking at?" I ask as I approach him. I squat and rub his ears, turning to his point of view.

Across the placid lake, I watch two men grilling. Behind their grill is a large, glass picture window. A warm yellow light glows through the window. A woman and a man work side by side at the sink inside.

I place my left hand on the ground to balance myself as déjà vu causes me to become dizzy and lose my balance. No, I have never been here. Yet this point of view is highly familiar to me. I've seen this panorama in my dreams hundreds of times. It always leaves me with a nostalgic sensation of simultaneous inclusion and isolation.

Chapter 57

It was probably my imagination, but I swear I could smell the smoked chicken my brothers were cooking on the patio from where I sat across the lake inlet. Mama and Dad had created a scrumptious pasta salad side and collard greens with ham hock.

The meal was the same as the thousands we'd shared before. Yet the hour we were together had a different, almost celebratory, sensation. It may be believing that night Randolph and Dionis are at peace.

Or that the Norman Rockwell picture I enjoyed from across the lake inlet was as warm and inviting in real life as it was from a distance.

Primarily, it was knowing how blessed I am and my gratitude for my good fortune.

I help Mama with the dishes as my brothers and dad head to the mechanic shop to work on Dusty's car.

There is reason to hesitate because I know she may disapprove of my thought process. It does seem rash, maybe even foolish, but as I sat with Puppy inside the circle of those towering cedar trees and watched my family across the lake, I wondered, *Could it be a thing? Is this spot where I'm supposed to make myself a life in Guntersville? Could I be happy and fulfilled here?*

I can. And I believe I will. I have a burning desire to have a place of my own. But with my family always in view, the cedar tree lot fills all my needs.

"Mama, what do you know about that property across the lake? The vacant one with all the cedar trees."

"The Burger sisters' property?"

I point across the inlet, realizing it is too dark now to see. "It has the old dock, but it's fallen apart."

"Yes, that's the Burger sisters' property. They passed a few years before we bought our home."

"Why has it never sold?"

"They only had one living heir. She lives out west—Colorado. She's been approached several times but claims there are certain stipulations on who the property can be sold to. She turns down every offer, and folks have quit asking."

"Can you contact her and find out how much she wants for the lot?"

Mama frowns. "She won't sell, April. Why are you asking anyway?"

I huff and blurt out my statement as if it is a poison I am expelling from my body. "I want to buy it as an investment."

Mama's hands stop moving under the stream of water. She looks like she may choke. She recovers and asks, "Where is this coming from?"

"It just seems like it would be a great investment property."

"Hmm... As a real estate broker, I'm pleased my daughter has such an excellent eye for property. That said, as of two weeks ago, that same daughter is up to her eyeballs in student loan debt and was going to be living hours away."

I look her level in the eye and say, "So what's your point?"

Her jaw drops open.

Despite my best effort, I burst into a bout of giggles.

Mama flicks water at me. "I swear you will be the death of me."

"Seriously, Mama. Things have changed. I've learned much about myself recently and can make a good life here."

"April, I would be thrilled for you to stay in town. But I don't know what you want. I'm not convinced living here will make you happy long term."

"Mama, I'm not sure either. Today, it feels right. That's all I know. Today I walked that property, and it was the weirdest thing. It was like I'd been there before. Something about it speaks to me. I know it sounds crazy, but it feels like it was always supposed to be mine, and it has been waiting for me to notice it."

I know the tides are turning against me as Mama dons her "stern Mama" expression—one of her specialties. She becomes highly interested in rinsing the rest of the dishes. "Still, April, with your student loan debt, it is not smart to take such a risk."

"Mama, I don't want us to make a habit of talking about my money. I've worked hard since coming home and made a serious dent in my student loans. I need to find out how much that property costs. I can only run the budget once I know. Still, I've got a handle on it. I can do this."

"I feel like I will be setting you up for failure."

My ears heat, and my neck itches as my agitated blush rushes across my throat. "Mama, you wouldn't be doing anything except checking to see if she would sell and what it would cost me. The decision is mine, as is the success or failure of my choice."

"I just don't—"

"Mama, don't make me ask a different real estate agent to check for me."

We share a stare, and she nods her head. "Fair. I'll make the call for you."

"Thank you, Mama. You're still my favorite real estate agent."

She blows an exasperated breath through her lips and hands me another plate to put in the dishwasher.

"One more thing you can help me with. Do you remember Thelma Banks?"

"Sure, I do."

"In middle school, she always participated in the bake sale for the cheerleaders and football teams with you."

"We did."

"What cake did she usually bring?"

Mama guffaws. "That's a random question, April."

"Seriously, just tell me."

"You can act so odd at times." Mama rolls her eyes. "Thelma was always known for her red velvet cake."

The critical information stiffens my spine as the excitement of a plan coming together makes my mind thrum with energy. "Thank you."

An inquisitive expression forms on Mama's face. "Are you going to share why you asked?"

"Depends." I favor her with a cocky smile. "If my plan works, I'll be sure to celebrate with you."

Chapter 58

Mama is turning on the dishwasher when my phone rings. I look at the display and get a little hitch in my heart. It's Shane White, our local medical examiner.

"Mama, I got to take this. It's work." She nods, and I step into the den.

"Hello, Dr. White. To what do I owe this honor tonight?"

"Do you still have your clothes on?"

My cheeks heat as my stomach tightens. "Why?"

"I know how quick you are to get in your PJs, and if you're still dressed, I need you to come over so I can show you something interesting."

I fight back a nervous giggle. I'm trying to be mature, but everything Shane says sounds like a double entendre, tickling me all the same. "I can be at your place in thirty minutes. If that's not too late for you."

"Perfect. I'll see you in a few."

I would've asked what it was about if he had stayed on the line a little longer. Still, given both of our roles in town, Shane consistently has excellent information for me that keeps me ahead of the curve with my defense cases. Accordingly, when he calls, I make it a point to be grateful and go over there.

Plus, I enjoy Shane's company.

I walk back into the kitchen and open the refrigerator door.

"Do you mind if I grab a piece of this chicken?"

"That's what it's in there for, baby."

I pull a chunk of white breast meat from the Tupperware and drop it into a sandwich baggie. "I'm over at Shane's if you need me, Mama."

"Drive safe. Text me when you get there."

"Yes, ma'am."

Shane bought the medical examiner practice from Doc Crowder when Doc retired and eloped with Jacob Hurley's grandmother. The last time I heard, the two lucky ducks took up residence in Key West.

I was nervous when I learned Shane would be my professional work partner. I was unsure how the dynamic of Shane being the medical examiner and me being an often-time defense attorney for the city would affect me. I shouldn't have worried. While we are not a couple—strictly Shane's call—we have always been a dynamic team.

You see, Shane and I have a history. When my career crashed in glorious flames while living in Atlanta, and I was left homeless, Shane, a total stranger at the time, came to my rescue.

People who are that good and considerate are as rare as hen's teeth. If you are fortunate to call such a person your friend, be grateful and hold on tight.

As it turns out, I had nothing to worry about Shane moving to town. Expectantly, he is the consummate professional and highly proficient at his job. I like to think I'm skilled at mine, too, and with time, I've been able to squash down the sexual feelings that erupt below my navel when I am around him. I care for him as a person, so I will continue to struggle to not make a fool of myself.

Truthfully, our friendship has developed both socially and professionally to the point that if the opportunity arose to *accidentally* fall into bed with Shane, I would have to think twice. I might not think too long about it, but I would still have to pause and consider if it would ultimately damage the relationship we have forged together.

The automatic gate to his farm is open, and I drive through. My car leaves a dark grape plume of a dusty rooster's tail behind as I drive up the gravel road.

I'm surprised to see Shane sitting on a rocker on the wraparound front porch of his cute farmhouse. You would never guess a morgue and autopsy lab are hidden in the basement.

I open my car door, and a thick, black beast of a dog launches off of the front porch and charges me. I fumble with the plastic bag I brought and must double-grip it to open it in time. "Hey, Bubbles."

The Rottweiler slams on her brakes and stops inches from me. She eyes me suspiciously and whimpers her recognition of me.

"Have you been a good girl?" I ask as I pull out the piece of chicken. "Look how patient you are." I place the chicken in my palm and extend it to her.

Bubbles tilts her head to the side. I barely feel her muzzle graze my skin as she delicately lifts the chicken piece from my hand.

This is a trick when offering chicken that I would never try with Puppy. With him, I would be minus a finger or two.

I rub the back of her head with my other hand. "You're such a sweet girl."

Transaction complete, Bubbles trots off to the edge of the porch behind one of the boxwoods to eat in private.

"Are you spoiling my dog again, Bama?"

"She is too sweet to be spoiled. I still can't believe Doc left her to you when he moved to Florida."

"That over-fifty-five community he bought into has rules against dogs over ten pounds."

I step up the stairs onto the porch. "I think she's got that beat by a few pounds."

Shane smiles at me, and my stomach makes a loop-the-loop. "Ya think?" he says.

"It's a little chilly to be out here tonight."

"It's good for the immune system. But if you're cold, I can grab you a jacket from inside." He leans over and lifts a bottle of Wild Turkey. "Or you can have this to warm you up."

I can think of more than one way I would like Shane to warm me up. *Ugh… Stop it, April.*

"I don't mind if I do," I say, sitting beside him in the spare rocker.

He pours and hands me a tumbler. I take a sip of the smooth liquor. "Talk about spoiling somebody."

"Yep. A life like this definitely will spoil you."

I'm referring to the liquor, but I follow Shane's line of sight. "We're looking at trees, Shane. In the dark."

"I know. Doesn't it fill you with a peaceful feeling?"

I take another sip and angle my head as I look at the tall silhouette before us. "Sure."

Shane regards me out of the corner of his eye and chuckles. "Girl, you still haven't learned how to relax. Have you?"

"I'm relaxed."

"Sure, you are." He takes a small cigar out of his front pocket and lights it.

"I didn't know you smoked."

He holds the cigar out and turns it while examining it. "Sometimes. I think I'm playing with it more than smoking it."

We sit in companionable silence. I have another shot of Wild Turkey and continue staring at the trees. They're still not doing anything extraordinary.

The boredom has built to such a level my scalp itches. "So, did you just need a drinking buddy tonight?"

"Don't be like that, Bama."

"Dude. Some of us have live clients."

Shane covers his heart with the hand holding his cigar. "Ouch. That's a low blow even for you."

"Sorry."

"Do you want a puff?"

I shake my head. "I'd rather kiss Bubbles on the butt."

"I'm not sure how she would take that."

"Not well, I'm sure." I put my tumbler on the porch and stand. "Well, thanks for the drink. But I need to get home."

"Sit your butt down, Bama. I spent hours of my spare time working on something for you for the last six months. You can hang out for six minutes for me to give you the information."

I retake my seat on the rocker.

"The body in Dottie Castle's house."

"*The* body?"

Shane nods. "The body. As in confirmed, *not* Dottie Castle."

My shoulders droop as my jaw opens. "Get outta here."

"True story."

"Your suspicions were right."

"It seems so."

"I didn't think we got enough DNA to test anything."

"This kid's got some serious talent," he says. "I finally found a smidge of marrow that had not been destroyed. It was just enough to get a reading. It was enough to allow me to compare it against the hair fibers we found in her car."

I lean the rocker forward while grasping both armrests. "Then she is still out there."

"I can't guarantee that. Dottie was so old she might be dead. But the fire didn't kill her."

I shake my head. "Wow. All this time, Baker hasn't been able to find her."

"That old broad is slicker than owl poop."

"You can say that again. I wonder where she went?"

Shane grins and covers his lips.

"What? What are you not telling me?"

"That you won't have to necessarily pay Baker Diaz to find her considering he'll have a lot of help looking for her now."

I shake my head and shrug.

Shane grins. "The Feds get tense about capital murder across state lines."

"I don't understand, Shane. Do you know where she is?"

"No. But you are asking the wrong question, Bama. It's not

where Dottie is. The fascinating question is, *who* was the body in the basement."

"You've identified the body?"

Shane holds out his hand with the cigar and rocks it back and forth. "With ninety-eight percent probability and reasonable standard deviations."

I make a circular motion with my finger urging him on.

"I believe the body was Felicity Jefferson. The only daughter of the original owner of the car dealership the Castles owned."

Chapter 59

My mornings are too often filled with regrets for my actions the night before. Unfortunately, this morning is a prime example.

After the bombshell newsflash Shane broke, we spent hours drinking his Wild Turkey and hypothesizing how a Southern belle of an aristocratic, small-town family ended up in the basement of Dottie Castle. Especially when the story I heard was she had moved to Arizona, was happily married, and died in a tragic balloon accident.

One drink led to another, and it became later and later. Then Shane talked me into something I never had a mind to do. Of course, it will always be easy for Shane to convince me to do much of anything.

I smack my tongue against the roof of my mouth and gag. It's like someone used my mouth for a vast kitty litter box. As bad as the taste is, I might have to hunt Bubbles down and give her that kiss on the butt I joked about last night to get the taste out of my mouth.

And I know better. It's not like it was the first time I have tried, and I know I don't enjoy it. And still, I let Shane convince me to do it. Just like he convinced me to stay over because I had drunk too much to drive home.

His suggestion for me to stay over was a sound one. Him

talking me into sharing his cigarillo with him, not so much. Smoking has never agreed with me.

I slide out of his guest room bed and pull on my shorts and T-shirt. I make a solid attempt to make the bed appear as pristine as I found it last night, straightening the comforter edge level to the base of the box springs.

Meh. As my father would say, "It's good enough for government work." Bed making has never been my strong suit. Besides, as fastidious as Shane is, I expect he'll strip the sheets and wash them before the sun sets.

I carry my flip-flops out into the den. I don't want to wake Shane, and I must be at the bakery when it opens in thirty minutes.

Although the information Shane discovered about Felicity is the most exciting topic on the drama smorgasbord known as my life, it is not the most vexing. These days, I'm all about tending first to matters I can control that have a high probability of causing me pain. Even if they are not the most fascinating topics to fixate on.

Shane's bedroom door is open. He is gone, but Bubbles spots me, greets me, and escorts me to the foyer. At the door, I give her a vigorous shoulder rub, which seems to satiate her, and exit, locking the doorknob as I leave.

It's still unfathomable to me how Dottie Castle may have been a serial killer and went unnoticed for decades while remaining a prominent socialite within the Guntersville social circle. The two lessons I take from my dealings with Dottie Castle are that I should trust my initial gut feelings and that you never really know a sociopath.

I pick up the cupcakes I ordered from Petit Fours & Pimento the moment they open the shop. I keep the small talk to a minimum and hurry toward Thelma and Andy's rental store.

From my experience with them, I know Thelma is the early bird who likes to come in, set the schedule for the day, do the books, and make out the deposit. Andy often entertains his business account clients at night and might make an appearance at 10:30 before he takes more clients to a business lunch.

I shake my head as I consider how they justify nuking their perfect working relationship. Together, they make a fantastic team. Separately, they each lack crucial skills needed to grow a successful business.

Pulling into the parking lot, I am pleased that Thelma's Mercedes MX is the only car on the lot. My plan is working to perfection so far.

The front door to the counter area will be locked this early, so I call Thelma on her cell phone. My call goes to voicemail.

I get out of my car and walk to her office window. The blinds are open, and I can see the back of Thelma's head as she works on her laptop.

Shifting my cupcake box to my left hand, I call her again. I watch through the window as she picks up her phone and taps the screen with a flourish.

This is Thelma. Sorry I missed your call, but it is important to me...

Well, that just gets my goat. My call is important, my butt.

My emotions build with ill intent, and I grab them by the neck before they get loose. I already feel like I could melt her window with my glare.

Half the town has heard rumors I may have odd abilities. I don't need to prove my freakish powers to the rest of the city by accidentally doing something magical.

Me tapping on Thelma's window may scare the bejesus out of her. But if she tinkles on herself, it'll be her fault for not taking my call.

I rap my knuckles on the thick glass. Thelma jumps, and both of her hands fly into the air. She rotates her chair and backpedals backward, her desk stopping her motion quickly.

With immense pleasure, I favor her with my sweetest Southern-charm smile while I wave at her. "Heeey," I say, even though I know she can't hear me through the plate-glass window.

Ooh, she is madder than a wet hen with me. I smile and wave pleasantly at her, but I am secretly pleased that plate glass separates us momentarily. I also hope it's bulletproof because she doesn't look exceptionally stable this morning.

Thelma shakes her fist at me, and her mouth has not stopped since she recognized me. Of course, I can't hear a word she says, but I easily decipher a word by reading her lips that would make a sailor blush.

I continue to wave and lift the pink cupcake box to shoulder height. This doesn't have the desired effect of slowing her rant, so I lift my phone and rotate it side to side.

Thelma glares at me, and I wonder if we can stay like this all day. She turns and snatches the cell phone off her desk, and my phone rings.

"How dare you show your face here."

I hoped for a more pleasant greeting. But I cannot afford to let my feelings get in the way of our negotiation. The stupidity of this all has begun to irk me, and I need some answers. "We need to talk."

"I make it a habit never to talk to people that are traitors, you Benedict Arnold."

"Well, darn. If I'd known you would call me that, I would've brought you eggs Benedict instead of a cupcake."

"I don't want anything from you, you spoiled little brat."

"Thelma, let me in. We need to talk, and it would be better to do it before the rest of the team shows up."

"You obviously have a hearing issue. I'm not going to talk to you." Thelma makes a show of tapping the phone with her thumb and sits back at her desk.

I'm polite enough to allow her a moment to change her mind and be an adult. She forces my hand by continuing to work on her laptop, ignoring me.

I tap methodically on her window in five-second intervals. My administration of the mental torture is incredibly satisfying as I watch her shoulders creep slowly toward her earlobes.

Thelma stands up so quickly that her chair rolls back and slams against the wall. She turns around and throws her hands up in a questioning gesture, and I read "What!" on her lips.

I renew my sweet smile and rotate my phone again, inches from the window.

This earns me a scream of frustration from her that I hear through the glass. She calls my phone. "Get a hint and leave before I call the police."

"Call the police. When they arrive, you'll have to open the door to give them your statement, and I'll talk to you then."

"What can we have to talk about?"

The apparent discussion is the dissolution of the partnership. But that's not really why I'm here. I'm here to better understand Thelma's motivation because, given Andy's offer, it is not in her best interest to pass on the opportunity to sell.

There must be another motivating factor. I need to understand what concerns her before this matter can be resolved.

"Anything you want to. I know you're upset with me, and I have always looked up to you as a fellow female business owner. It might be lame, but I thought we could enjoy a couple of cupcakes together and talk just between us girls to clear the air."

"We girls could talk if we stuck together," she says sarcastically.

"Thelma…"

She huffs. "April, I appreciate the gesture. But there's already too much water gone under the bridge. Honestly, I've got way too much to do this morning to be socializing."

"Well darn." I add a well-practiced sigh to punctuate my disappointment. "I guess I'll have to find somebody else to eat this red velvet cupcake. I've never developed a taste for them."

"Red velvet?"

"Yes. I thought you liked that flavor."

The indecision shown on Thelma's face is comical. The

struggle to keep the façade of disappointment on my face is real.

"Hold on a minute."

The line goes dead, and Thelma leaves through her office door.

The autumn air is cool this morning, and I stretch my right arm across my chest. I wasn't expecting to be welcomed with open arms, but I never thought she would turn me away without a conversation.

The lock in the double-glass doors that lead to the counter turns over, and Thelma cracks the doors open. She peeps her head out the door. "Come on in, April. But I am busy, so this must be a short visit."

"I understand."

She holds the door open for me, and I slide by her. She locks the door behind us.

"Take a seat at the counter. I'll put some coffee on."

I take a seat on one of the barstools at the sales counter, where customers place their orders. I move the newspapers to the side and set the box down.

The coffee maker hisses, and the smell of dark roast fills the air.

"That'll be a minute," Thelma says as she walks behind the counter until she is directly across from me and opens the pink box. "Oh, these are pretty. Did you get these from Petit Fours and Pimento?"

"Yes, ma'am. Besides my mama and nana, I don't know anywhere else in town to get cupcakes like these."

Thelma nods as she lifts the red velvet cupcake out of the box. "Vivian always was a superior baker." She squints her eyes. "I haven't talked to your mama in ages. Does she still bake?"

"On special occasions. When she only had the marina, she had more time. Now that she has the real estate business too, she has very little time to bake."

Thelma's expression is vacant as she stares into the distance as if she's not with me. She pinches the bridge of her nose and walks toward the coffee machine. "Running a business can take away all the time for the finer things like baking."

"I suppose. Mama seems to get a lot of joy out of the real estate." I scoff. "Actually, I think she enjoys winning. When she sells a listing before the competition does. I suppose I got that from her."

"You did. Because of your coloring, you don't resemble your mama physically. Still, anyone who spends time with the two of you must know you are related."

Nothing could be further from the truth. Mama and I are only similar in the competitiveness department. Other than that, I'm nothing like her. But people say stuff like that occasionally, and it is just best to let it go rather than argue the point with them.

Thelma lifts the coffee urn. "Do you want anything in yours?"

"Black is fine."

She pours two cups of coffee and walks back behind the counter with them. "I don't get to bake much either these days. I don't have two companies like Vivian, but doing the finances of this one seems to be enough to take all my time these days."

"What?" I make a face at her. "I figured you'd be baking all the time. Don't Jason and Lucy have three kids?"

She smiles, and it crinkles the lines around her eyes. "Yes. Grandbabies are the best." She rolls her eyes. "But it's hard with my schedule to see them as much as I want. And they're growing up so blasted quick. If I could find growth-slowing dust, I would sprinkle it on their food at night."

I pick up my German chocolate cupcake and laugh. "Your grandkids would probably get pretty upset about that."

"I know. I just feel like... Time is speeding by so fast. And now this thing with Andy is another instance where my life isn't ending up how I pictured it."

"Hmm ... I understand that. Still, it's hard to complain too much. I mean, we are the successful ones."

She stares at me and cocks her head as if she doesn't

comprehend what I mean.

"Look at us. Two lady business owners, we've made a little money, and most importantly, we have family and friends who love and look out for us."

Thelma rests her chin on her hand, covering her mouth. She bobs her head. "It's easy to forget that sometimes and not be grateful."

"Amen, sister."

We enjoy our cupcakes and coffee in quiet. Being close and sharing a treat is an excellent salve for the ugliness that visited our relationship since the partnership issue has come to a head.

A broad grin overtakes Thelma's face, and she brightens as if she has a halo around her. "Loretta, did I mention that Jason and Lucy are pregnant?"

Being called by Granny's name takes the breath away from me. All I can do is raise my eyebrows.

"I declare, I'm so excited about being a grammy I can't hardly stand it. I've been waiting forever for those two to finally decide to have babies." She gestures with her hand toward me. "Just hearing you go on about Ralph and Vivian's kids has always made me jealous. And finally, I will experience what you've been talking about all these years."

I swallow hard as my throat feels like I have eaten a handful of sawdust. "Thelma…"

"When I complain about them not having any babies yet, Joe always tells me that he doesn't care one way or the other. He says, "Thelma, leave those youngins alone. It's their life to live as they see fit." But I always knew it was a lie. He might be more excited than I am about the news." She stares at me with an expectant expression. Waiting for me to congratulate her.

"Thelma … Joe has been dead for six years."

Thelma furrows her brow. Her eyes open wide, and she covers her mouth as if she has belched at church.

My heart falls, and my nose itches as if I'm about to cry. "I'm sorry."

Her eyes flit about the counter area. "I haven't been getting good rest lately." She balls up her napkin and cupcake paper. "That's all."

I lay a hand on hers. "Thelma."

She pulls her hand back and favors me with a smile. "It's nothing at all, April. Like I said, I'm just tired. And, like I told you, I have a lot to do today, and it's on my mind. So, if we can cut this visit short. I need to get some orders placed."

"Thelma, I'm not leaving until we talk about this."

"What would that be, dear?"

"You selling your portion of the partnership to Andy so you can spend time with your grandchildren."

Her face flushes beet red, and she trembles. "I knew better than to invite you in. I might as well have invited a vampire in, and now you'll suck me dry."

"You've known three generations of women from my family. I know you don't really believe that."

She glares at me with such contempt that I can only be thankful she doesn't have my abilities. I honestly believe that if she did, she might strike me dead now.

"Loretta and Vivian would've never turned on me. You're nothing like them. You're a hired gun to the highest payer. Andy has more money to pay you, so you sided with him."

I let her hurtful comment hang in the air and age as I nod and hold eye contact with her. "Did Andy tell you that I first told him I would not take the job?"

"I don't talk to that backstabber anymore."

"That's a shame, Thelma. He still respects you and wants the best for you."

She blows a rash blast of air between her lips. "Oh, please."

"I agreed to take this on to ensure the division was fair. It is more than fair, Thelma."

"No. It's not fair. I built this."

"Y'all built it together. And everything has a season. It's time for y'all to separate before you damage the relationship."

"You should turn your tail around and leave, missy. I'm not

changing my mind."

"Bless it, Thelma," I say with more force than I intend. "What is holding you back? You must know that you're having bouts of forgetfulness. There's nothing to be ashamed about. We're all going to be there."

"I am not."

"And you just alluded to the fact that you would like to spend more time with your grandchildren because they're growing up so fast. I know from earlier conversations that, inexplicably, even though you're over seventy, you still do not draw your Social Security check. Between that and what Andy is offering you, your lifestyle won't even change. What's holding you back from taking this generous offer? Please help me understand. Because from where I'm sitting, it's all, 'Oh please, don't throw me in the briar patch.'"

"You couldn't understand."

"For the love of God, please try me."

She lowers her eyes to her fidgeting hands. As the silence drags on, I work to bring my emotions back under control and lower my heart rate.

"Jason's a good boy."

I only know Jason and Lucy in passing. They are ten years older than my brothers. Still, I nod my head when she makes eye contact.

"But he doesn't have any interest in running the business." She sighs. "He doesn't have an aptitude for management or finances."

My mind spins furiously on what has the feel of a hamster wheel. This is the moment I'm supposed to figure out the genuine motivating factor for Thelma so that I can close this distasteful deal and get it behind my two business friends so they can go on with their lives and both feel like they won. Unfortunately, it's a lot like working on an algebra problem and needing more information to complete the equation.

"Jason concerns you?"

She smirks. "Your babies always concern you until the day

you die."

So much for my leading question, it felt like I was so close to victory, and it slipped through my fingers.

"Thank you for the cupcake, April," Thelma says, attempting to excuse me.

"Thelma, before I leave. I'd like you to help me with one more nugget of wisdom. I know you're unhappy with me, but I did it with the best intentions. Taking on the case with Andy. Still, I consider you one of my mentors. And I need a point of verification for future use."

She leans against the counter and tilts her head. "What would that be?"

"As much as I enjoy my job, I will want to retire one day." I shrug. "I don't know. The idea of taking a six-month cruise around the world has always intrigued me. I'd like to see everything the world offers before I head home to my maker."

She chuckles. "That sounds nice."

"I know, right?"

I pause. Thelma looks at me expectantly.

"But your question, April?"

"Tell me what prevents you from retiring so I don't get myself in the same situation. Because I want to take that cruise when I'm your age."

Thelma holds her mouth open. She guffaws and says, "Don't ever have kids."

Leaning away from her, I say, "Wow. That's harsh."

She laughs as she shakes her head from side to side. "Jason's a good boy, and I love him to death. But if I were to sell my part of the business, I don't know what he would do for a job."

Chapter 60

Andy is horrified on two counts by Thelma's concern about Jason's employment. First, Thelma has such a low opinion of her son's abilities. Andy considers Jason an invaluable associate, primarily because of his mechanical skills that allow him to fix almost anything with improvisation and how much customers enjoy him during setup because of his good nature. He is equally disappointed that Thelma believes he wouldn't be concerned for Jason.

While nothing is guaranteed in life, Andy and I work on redrafting the offer in a manner that lays out a path for Jason's growth into a trainer position for the newer staff and a guaranteed severance package that will allow him ample time to find another job if the rental company is ever sold or closed.

The whole project only takes thirty minutes to brainstorm and another hour for me to draft.

Thelma has been eager to review the reworked proposal ever since this morning when I informed her I would be able to fix this. It takes her only an hour to discuss with her lawyer, Claude, before he calls to notify me that Thelma has accepted the sale terms.

Claude's relief and appreciation are comical. It's good that Thelma is getting out of business and won't ever need an attorney again. She'd be disappointed that Claude would turn her down next time.

I never expected the parting gift from Thelma, but I hold it in the same esteem as the win. In a letter, Thelma apologizes for doubting me, which, given I shouldn't worry too much about what other people think as long as I'm doing the right thing, shouldn't matter so much to me. Still, it makes me feel ten feet tall and as if I am glowing.

I am the girl who got the extra golden star.

Then Thelma had to go and douse the flames of pride with her same comment from earlier. *You're just like your mama.* No, ma'am. I wouldn't mind being like Mama, but we are nothing alike.

The most vexing issue of my life being solved means April gets to do something that's been on her mind since last night. Full of anticipation, I turn out the lights at Snow and Associates, step out into the autumn breeze, and lock the door behind me.

I freeze on the way to my car and watch the folded, white paper under the wiper blade slap in the wind. "Oh, for crying out loud!"

I stomp to my car and yank the note free.

Unsurprisingly, the first thing that draws my eye is the same flourished, overdone lettering, like the threat I dropped off to Captain Lau earlier in the week.

You better not be sticking your nose into my business, or I'll make sure it is the last time.

Cute. The creator of the threat is obviously getting way too much fun from attempting to jerk my chain. Too bad his prose isn't improving with all of his practice.

I crumple the letter and am about to throw it into a nearby Guntersville waste basket when years of legal training finally kick in, and I think better of it.

Assuming that this ballless prick is man enough to back up his threats, I may need the letter during the interview with the police after I give the violent man his comeuppance.

You know how the interrogation will go.

"April, why did you shoot your attacker thirteen times?"

"That's easy, Officer. It's all the bullets I had in my gun."

I slide into my IROC, pull my P365 with the extended twelve clip and one in the chamber from my purse, and lay the gun in my lap. It's not the safest driving condition, but at the moment, I feel exposed, and the idea of having it within easy reach calms my nerves.

I put my car in reverse and grumble, "If you're coming after this chick, you better pack a lunch, buddy. Because it's gonna take you all day to finish me off."

It just gets my goat that some goon can decide to ruin an otherwise perfect day. Well, I'm not gonna let him.

Not to mention there's not anything I can do about it anyway. The goofball didn't bother telling me what he was talking about. It might be helpful to stay out of his business if I knew what business he was referring to.

Stupid people chap my butt.

As I catch the bridge out of Guntersville, I allow my mind to go to more pleasant topics. I watch the smattering of boats plowing across the dark, choppy water and congratulate myself on my choice to stay.

Baltimore has the vast Atlantic Ocean and the beautiful Potomac River, and there is an uber-sexy ballplayer I have a comfortable history with.

Still, Guntersville has its own beautiful sights for all the complications it brings into my life.

It also soothes my heart and mind because it is home.

Since I've returned, I better understand Laila staying on Turtle Key despite her having fewer long-term career opportunities on the island.

Her island is beautiful, and the people she loves are there. The world crams so many expectations and aspirations into our minds when we are young that it prevents us from seeing the slice of heaven we were gifted as a birthright.

I am grateful for Gramma and Laila and my time on Turtle Key, which taught me this great truism. It is an incredible gift to appreciate your home.

As I pull into my parents' driveway, Puppy saunters out of his doggie door from our apartment. He yawns and stretches while I feel a twinge of guilt. He won't be happy that I plan to ride my bike to explore the Burger sisters' property. I can make a concession and keep my friend happy.

"Hey, Puppy. Do you want to go for a boat ride?"

He tilts his head as if contemplating my question. He turns and walks back into our apartment.

Okay, so he's not as torn up about not getting to go as I thought he would be. I try not to let the sting of rejection linger too long and walk up to the garage to get my bike and Mama's pruning shears.

It's a big decision, and I want to ensure the feeling wasn't just a random déjà vu moment. Lord knows it wouldn't be the first time that happened to me.

Inside the garage, though, I already know that it's right. It's as if everything has led to this moment. It'll take time to explain it to my family and friends. But I'm no longer concerned with that. From their vantage point, it'll be one more cockamamie choice in a long string of haphazard decisions in April's hot mess of a life.

But it's not. This is what I want, and for the first time ever, I will allow my heart to do what it wants rather than try to force-feed it what the world tells me it needs.

The Burger sisters' property is only one hundred yards from my apartment across the lake. The bike ride to get to the property, because of the winding road on our peninsula, is closer to half a mile.

It's beautiful this time of year as the hardwood leaves change, leaving them in stark contrast against the emerald-green cedars and pine. A breeze comes off Lake Guntersville, putting an extra-wet nip in the air.

I appreciate the coolness as my exertion increases my core temperature. As I roll onto the sisters' property, I glisten. I lean my bike against a rotten post that I assume must have been part of a fence—long since destroyed by weather and time.

I move toward the towering cedars. My skin tingles as thousands of electrical shocks play across the surface, and gooseflesh pops up.

"Well, that's interesting."

The ambient energy levels in Guntersville are abnormally high, but the power on this lot is even more vital. The energy around me crackles with an incessant desire to be harnessed as I enter the cedars.

I scan left and right as I realize that it's not a random collection of cedar trees. It's a symmetrical grove.

Now curious, I walk the grove property to better understand the layout. Four rows, five across, and thirteen in front of the lake. Another prime number.

Coincidental? Nothing about this property is a coincidence.

Including the way it calls me.

A shiver slides up my spine. The call may be from the dark side. It's not as if I haven't felt a niggling in the back of my mind when I use my powers unwisely. Still, I don't get the impression of evil. Instead, it's a calm, peaceful sensation. A sense of belonging. A feeling that is so foreign that it surprises me that I even understand it.

As I move into the semi-circle where the bench sits, I jerk with surprise. I spy a home under the tangle of kudzu and honeysuckle to my right. I swear the house was not there a moment ago or last night.

It's in a terrible state of disrepair. The roof has all but given up the ghost to the weather. Still, the walls and the small chimney made of an interesting cream-colored river rock with blue swirls appear sturdy. The walls appear nearly two feet thick from the one corner where the roof has given way. The entire structure is smaller than a thousand square feet with a single, squat level.

Well, isn't that the darndest? All these years, I've never noticed the house is here. Of course, it's more like a mound of vegetation than a home.

Backtracking toward the building, I do not see the front door. Assuming it is on the other side, I circle the tiny structure while painstakingly surveying for the entrance. I arrive where I started and still have not found a door.

"Maybe I should try 'open sesame,'" I joke. "There has to be a front door unless this is Santa Claus's house, and he went down the chimney every night."

The setting sun glitters off of a lead windowpane exposed through the kudzu. A second window sparkles to life from the orange rays as if the setting sun is melting the vines away.

It's beautiful. The windows sparkle as if they are made of multifaceted diamonds. This shouldn't be possible. Even if the light could reach the windows through the heavy vine coverage, the glass should be covered with years of grime, given the disuse of the building.

The less dense section of the vines twinkles crimson and silver. As I move toward the light to give a closer inspection, I trip on a stone. I toe the slate stones covered by sawgrass and weeds that form a path. I grin as my heart rate increases.

A walkway is what I call a clue. I follow the stones in my line of sight, knowing they will lead me to the hidden door to the inside.

I had planned on cleaning off the bench with Mama's shears. It would have been suitable for that task. But as I work on the vines of the home, I find them to be much thicker, and I wish I had brought my father's battery-operated hedge clippers. If my curiosity could wait a day, I would return tomorrow with better-suited tools for this challenging task.

Instead, I struggle to clip through the voracious vines. A few runners fall free, and a small alcove is revealed. A door with crimson-and-white stained-glass inserts stands at the back of the nook.

The sun strikes the glass wholly, illuminating the alcove in its entirety. My chest tightens as my thinking mind catches up with my reckless curiosity.

Past the vines I cleared so I could peek my head in, the

alcove is utterly free of all debris. No dried leaves or even a speck of dirt are on the black-stone floor. Nor is there a single cobweb inside the arch of the stoop. It's as if someone cleaned it thoroughly with a broom this morning.

The thought of caution passes, and I set to clear a big enough hole to step through the vines. A large section comes apart, and I grasp the vines, giving a solid pull to take it down.

"Fudge nut." I pull my hand against my waist as I cup my shoulders. Grimacing, I watch the laceration across the palm of my right hand pucker and bleed.

Now I really should go home. That is precisely what I get for not being able to hold my horses until I had the right tool for the job.

But before I go, I should check if the door is locked. If I can get inside, I want to see what remains in the house. I am considering buying it after all.

With my right hand, I reach out to turn the doorknob, and blood drips on the floor. Rolling my eyes, I shift to my left and grab the knob. It opens without me turning.

Butterflies take flight in my stomach. I grin and look over my shoulder—as if anybody is watching me across the lake and through several large cedar trees.

Stepping inside, the scents of cloves, lavender, and ginger envelop me. Despite all the windows being covered with vines and the failing light, the inside of the cottage has a warm, yellow glow.

Intrigued, I scan the room I stand in and am pleased by how the chimney is positioned in the middle of the home. A fire would be visible on both sides. A double-worktop kitchen runs the length of the right wall, and a small bay window across from me would be a perfect location for a small breakfast table. The well-proportioned section to the left of the chimney makes an excellent sitting area for company.

As I envision different pieces of furniture set within the living area, I notice the small doorway to the left and, at once, track toward it. As I reach the threshold leading to the tiny Tshaped hallway, I see through the open door in front of me a bathroom that is unbelievably smaller than the one in my apartment. Two small bedrooms, one on either side, complete the cottage as a two-bedroom and one-bath home.

Or, as I like to think, a bedroom and an office. *How perfect is this?*

Thrilled with my good fortune, I step into the bedroom on the left. Dizziness overtakes me, and I am forced to balance myself with a hand on the wall.

Visions flow into my mind at a frightening pace—so fast it's as if watching a large-screen TV with my nose pressed against it, as the show is on maximum fast forward.

It is impossible to discern what the visions are. The pictures pass too fast to comprehend. The voices in the images have melded together into one loud, incomprehensible din. Still, I can glean the emotions: happiness, excitement, and sorrow.

My dizziness is now accompanied by nausea, and I turn to leave the room. As I exit, the dizziness dissipates, but I still feel like I will be sick. I quickstep my way to the exit and out onto the alcove.

The outside world has turned to a twilight violet, and the air has cooled further. I sit on the step and force myself to take a deep breath.

As quickly as it came upon me, my nausea disappears. Still, I don't want to press my luck, so I stay seated with my head tilted, and I watch a drop of blood strike the black stone below me and a second strike the grass beside the stepping stone. I examine the injury I had forgotten due to my excitement about exploring the tiny cottage.

Somebody touches my shoulder. I turn and look behind me. The front door thuds shut.

Nobody is there.

All I see is the impossible glitter of the crimson stained glass in the door I did not shut.

Chapter 61

I park my bike in the garage and put away Mama's shears. Walking to my apartment, I look toward my parents' front porch. The lights are out in the kitchen, and the blue haze of a TV shines through the living room window.

I'm sure there are leftovers in the refrigerator. But it feels rude to rummage through their fridge when I can't show up for dinner. Besides, my appetite has been replaced by the intrigue of the Berger sisters' cottage.

Okay, so I won't pretend to ignore that there is a presence in the house. There's also the oddity that when I touched the bedroom wall, I received readings as if it were a personal item. Still, these things don't concern me. Much.

I can only focus on how the house is laid out perfectly for my needs and has a high-energy signature. Something I would've avoided a year ago, but after the events in Turtle Key, I realize how important it is for someone with my skill set to have an abundance of energy at my beck and call. Primarily since I am still being hunted.

The home is in my present community, allowing me to remain close to my family. I can even look across the water and see if my brothers are grilling that night. It's the perfect property specially designed for April. Right?

I open my apartment door and scan the room as I frown.

"Puppy?"

My furry wingman is MIA. I check under my bed and in the closet in case he's done something destructive and decided it best to hide out for now.

None of my shoes have been chewed on, and my apartment has no unwanted doggy mess. There's also no Puppy.

"Where is that dog?" I love him to death, but sometimes I wish he wasn't such a … guy. He can disappear like smoke when he wants to like the best of them.

I won't be able to sleep until I know where he is, so I track over to my parents' and open the sliding glass door as quietly as possible. The scent of smoked turkey lingers, and my stomach rumbles.

I'm exasperated that my dog has forced me to be rude and intrude on my parents' peace. I scan the kitchen for him. He is not asleep on his bed in the kitchen, leaving me with a whole house to search.

Reluctantly, I admit it will be easier to enlist my parents' help and walk toward the TV's glow. Mama and Dad are curled up on the sofa watching *Ozark*.

"Mama, have you seen Puppy?"

Mama pulls away from my father's embrace and props up on her arm. She smiles and puts her finger to her lip. She points to the far corner where my brother's oversized beanbag is kept when Chase is not using it.

Puppy's legs shoot straight into the air. I move closer to the beanbag to get a better view. I roll my eyes and shake my head.

Mama giggles. "Chase cut up a turkey drumstick for him. He was in heaven."

"I bet. Chase spoils him too much," I grouse. Honestly, I'm more envious of Puppy scoring a turkey drumstick while I go without than of Chase spoiling him.

Mama points toward the kitchen. "I made you a plate. It's in the refrigerator."

She slips back into my father's embrace and returns her attention to the TV show. I've been summarily dismissed. But it's not all bad. I did get a turkey and dressing dinner.

I open the refrigerator, and it's like Christmas. My love and appreciation for my mama can't be adequately explained as I pick up the plate and take the measure of the hefty weight of what she has put aside for me.

It is a shame Puppy has already had his fill and tapped out for the night. There's plenty here for both of us.

Since I don't want to distract my parents' show-watching by continuing to rummage around in their kitchen, I exit through the sliding glass door, pulling it shut behind me and attempting to make as little noise as possible.

There was a time when Mama loathed me taking her dinnerware to my apartment. So much so that she even forbade it once or twice.

To be honest about it, she didn't mind me using her dishes in my apartment. It was the fact that I never brought them back.

Since Lee left for Baltimore and I moved back into my apartment, I am a stickler for washing dishes in my kitchen and returning them the following day once they're dry.

It only makes sense. If I wish for the magically appearing surprise meals to continue, I never want Mama to run out of plates.

My apartment is uncomfortably silent tonight. I'm minus Puppy snoring on my bed and the random call from Randolph echoing in my mind. Truthfully, it's not as if Randolph spoke to me all that often, considering how much time I have spent in the old boathouse party room. It is more the void his departure has left in the energy field here. The absence of his energy force pressing against mine leaves me feeling oddly lonely.

I am thrilled for him and Dionis. Their tragic love affair can now have a happily ever after, or at least they will be together in the peace they deserve.

As I enjoy my meal, the gratitude for what has been revealed as a perfect life swells my heart. It is as if the brutal and sometimes ugly transformation is finished, and the butterfly now emerges from her cocoon.

Maybe not a magnificent butterfly but a very interesting moth.

I received validation today that I am not in my career strictly for financial gain. Excuse me if I pat myself on the back. Still, only a lawyer who understands and cares for her neighbors would have been patient enough to solve Andy and Thelma's predicament.

This and how I've held Austin at bay in his reality and learned the secret of staying on the bright side of my magic have allowed me to become comfortable in my new skin. Before now, my self-confidence had been sorely absent since I walked into MMJ in Atlanta and my dreams were dashed.

They hadn't been, though. Instead, they were merely redirected to where they were most required and I needed to be.

Plenty of capable lawyers can go to Atlanta and fill the role I worked toward during college and law school. Maximizing your stock portfolio, real estate holdings, and social standing do not require a particularly unique skill set.

I am the only person who can fill my role in Guntersville. I am where I should be.

There is one itsy-bitsy wish I need to come true. I want to be fortunate enough to be the person who the sole heir of the Berger sisters deems worthy of buying the lot across from my parents. That would really dill my pickle.

I scrape the leftover turkey skin into the garbage, then wash and dry my plate and pad toward my bathroom. I take the time to peroxide the cut on my hand and dab some hydrocortisone on it. Satisfied I won't develop gangrene, I wash off the minimal makeup on my face, brush my teeth, and attempt to comb through my hair, which became extra curly today.

The comb sticks halfway through five times in a row. I don't want an act of futility to knock the shine off of my mood, so I set the comb down. *There is always tomorrow*, as Scarlet once said. I'll use a massive glob of detangler in the morning.

I strip down to my panties and pull on a yellow, 3XL Tybee

Island T-shirt I picked up when we were in Savannah. I sigh as the uber-soft fabric caresses my skin, and I slide into bed.

Before turning off the lights, I notice a small box on the corner of my kitchen counter. It's wrapped in nondescript light green wrapping paper. I smile. Baker's gift to me. I left it here, intending to take it when Lee came down to help me move. I knew if I had taken it with me, I would have opened it before my first day on the job. I suppose I'll have to give it back now.

With the app Chase installed on my phone, I turn off my lights, casting me into darkness.

Staring into the pitch-dark of my apartment, I am too excited to go to sleep. However, I recall reading that being still with your eyes closed will give you seventy percent of the rest sleep will. It could be true or total bunk, but it's worth a try.

Baker said to wait to open his gift until I started my new career. Technically, I began my new job today.

I fumble for my phone and turn on my lights. Earnest expectation builds in me as I rush across my cold, wooden floor and grab the green box.

What on earth could Baker have gotten me? I didn't even realize we were at the "gift friend" stage. But his thoughtfulness is adorable.

I tear off the green wrapper and open the box. The item is encased in styrofoam. I separate the two pieces and raise my eyebrows.

The bulbous, green sculpture elicits a cackle from me. I'm amused and horrified as the bullfrog sculpture is reminiscent of the football-sized toad that was "disappeared" by the unseen dinosaur toad in the sugarcane field on Turtle Key.

My initial shock passes, and I notice a placard at the sculpture's base. I lean in as I try to make sense of the letters.

Evry frog praise e ownt pond.
        —Gullah proverb

Tears pop into my eyes as I recognize the meaning. Yes, everyone does prefer their own home. That includes April.

It's all a tad creepy, in a good way. That Baker selected a

gift not only of something I would witness later but to have it inscribed with a dialect I had not been exposed to earlier.

I must share this with him when I tell him thank you. I'm sure he will get a kick out of it.

My mind spins with the probability of such a double coincidence as I slide into bed and turn out the lights with my phone. I giggle in the dark about the absurdity of the toad sculpture and wonder how a girl works that into the decor of her home. That is a problem for another day, assuming I get to buy the Berger cottage.

I close my eyes and slow my heart rate with measured breaths.

The bitter, tart scent of a Winston cigarette burning forces my eyes open. I suck in a deep breath and stop. It's not my imagination. The acrid smoke hangs heavy in my room.

That's impossible. I don't ever allow anyone to smoke in my apartment, and what's more, even my father knew not to smoke cigars in here when it was the party room. I reach for my phone to turn the lights on, my hand freezing as it hovers over the nightstand.

A single red dot glows brightly across the room. The glimmer dims, and there is a whoosh of air. The scent of the burning cigarette increases.

Forget the phone and light.

I jerk open my dresser drawer with my left hand as I struggle to my knees and reach in with my right. The top of my hand scrapes the lip of the drawer frame as I yank my Sig Sauer free.

Even over my rushed breathing and heart beating in my ears, the mechanical click near my kitchen sink sends icicles through my veins.

"I wouldn't do that."

I've already frozen as if I'm the thief caught entering a home. I can't move, and I struggle to draw my next breath.

"I would hate to blow that pretty blonde hair all over your bedroom wall. I wouldn't wish the task of cleaning up their daughter's brains on any mama."

My stomach turns over to the visuals his words elicit. Reluctantly, I have no choice, so I place my P365 back in my drawer, open my right hand, and hold it up.

"Good girl. I heard you were a smart one," he says. The red dot of the light grows brighter.

I tremble uncontrollably. Some of it is from the frustration of being unable to do anything, but mainly from the fear of what my intruder has planned for me.

"You really don't have to be afraid. I don't want to hurt you."

"What do you want?" I croak.

"Not much," he says and chuckles.

A whimper escapes me. It sounds foreign to me.

"Come now. I am a man of my word. If you give me yours that you will mind your business and stay out of mine, you and I won't have any trouble."

"I don't understand."

"Hmm... I think you do, but I'll spell it out so there's no misunderstanding. You will stay out of Kat's business."

Cautiously, I slide back until my butt is on the mattress. "Drop her case?"

"That and quit nosing around in what happens to her and Maude."

"I can't do that."

The red dot somersaults toward me. I dodge to the left and watch as it falls onto my bed. I curse as I slap at the burning cigarette stub until it is extinguished.

"Why would you do that!"

"To get your attention. I've had all I'm going to take from you, and either you get out of my way, or you get the same thing that's coming to them."

"What are you going to do to them?"

He scoffs, "Darn, girl. You can start by minding your own right now and not expecting me to answer you."

"Liam, don't do this. This will end poorly for you."

He clops across the wooden floor. I gasp as metal taps against my forehead.

"Promise me now!"

"Yes." I choke as tears flow down my cheek. "I'll stay out of it."

"Man. You are one hardheaded chick."

The hammer of his revolver clicks back into place, and I melt onto the mattress with relief and guilt. "Keep your word, or you'll be sorry."

I follow the sound of his footsteps to the front door. It squeaks as he opens it. I exhale as he slams it shut behind him.

I continue to shake and wonder if I won't have to vomit.

Chapter 62

I lie in bed shivering as my fear of having a pistol tapped against my forehead is replaced with shame for not being as brave as the moment requires. Gradually, the redneck in me pushes aside the guilt and becomes angrier than a wet hornet.

"Screw you, Liam Hoyt." I grab my phone and turn on my lights as I search for a pair of jeans.

"Put a gun to my head," I grumble as I yank my jeans up until they catch on the underside of my butt. "Aah!" My rebel yell releases my pent-up frustration and blunts the murderous thoughts coursing through my mind.

Taking measured breaths, I concentrate on controlling my anger. The last thing I want to do now is accidentally set off a magical firebomb and burn down my parents' boathouse.

I put on a sandal. *That's stupid.* I fling it across the room, where it bounces off of my kitchen cabinet as I hightail it into my closet. I push my meticulously organized shoes aside until I find my hiking boots. Yes, I'm gaining control of my anger. Still, a girl can't ever over-prepare. I prefer to be ready if I need to use my best physical strike and kick the living tarnation out of a guy.

I'm as suitably dressed for a physical altercation as I'll ever be. I shove my handgun into my purse and pick up my phone.

The damp, chilly conditions outside my door make me

shiver. Fog from the lake has crept up, touching my parents' porch.

I consider waking my brothers. Lord knows they would be helpful in a fight.

A single question pierces through the storm clouds created by my indignant anger. *Where am I going?*

That is an excellent question. I'm standing here as if I'm ready for a gunfight, or at the very least a butt beating, and my adversary, Liam, has long left the premises.

I hike my purse strap further up on my shoulder and cross my arms in defense of the cold. The movement causes my phone light to come on, drawing my eyes to the screen.

"Goofball," I mumble under my breath.

Why not take the novel approach and, for once in my life, do what a normal person would do and call the police. Before I do, in case Liam left me to go directly to Kat's, I dial her number to warn her.

I pace in front of my apartment door as her cell phone rings. A recorded message greets me. I hang up and dial again. My stomach churns as the sing-song message invites me to leave a message.

He's already there. That's why Kat can't answer her phone.

I jog toward my car as I call the police station. I yank open my car door, swinging my purse onto the passenger seat.

"Guntersville Police Department."

"Hi." I struggle to catch my breath as I situate myself onto my car seat and close the door. "This is April Snow. I need to report..."

What the heck? Leaning forward, I squint at the squiggle of lines imprinted on the multiple tones of gray before me.

"Ma'am? April?"

I reach out and touch my windshield with the tip of my forefinger. Dragging it across the glass, a bead of water etches a track below my finger. In combination, my finger and the released bead of liquid obliterate the letter *P* in the threatening message. I swallow so hard it feels like I downed a golf ball as several immutable facts cross my mind simultaneously.

First, the message, "Butt out, or you and your entire family die," accompanied by a crude drawing of a stick person with x's for eyes and a portion of its head detached, isn't what I would expect. The lettering, miraculously consistent considering that it was written on a fogged window, comprises sharp, minimalist slants to the point that the letter *T* has a minuscule crossbar. If the cross were any smaller, it would appear as a bump on the letter *l*. It in no way matches the earlier notes I received from Liam.

Second, my car door was locked, yet the writing is on the inside and not the outside of my windshield. Now that I am over my initial anger and my adrenaline has waned, the incident with my car makes me realize that my apartment door was definitely locked when I went to bed. It was even locked when I came outside this morning. This means Liam has some cat burglar skills that are impossible to deny, and he can reach out and hurt me any time he wishes.

"Ma'am, I need your address."

The police officer's voice draws me back to our phone call and what I believe is happening at Kat's trailer. "I don't have one just yet."

"Excuse me?"

It's true. I don't have an address because I need to know if something nefarious is happening. I look at the time and realize I must have fallen asleep before Liam entered my apartment because it is two in the morning. And it's not unreasonable to think that Kat would have turned her phone's ring tone down when she went to bed. "I'll call you back."

"Call us back?" Her voice cracks. "That's not how this works."

"Sorry."

"Don't hang up."

I do, however, and fish my keys out of my purse to start my car. My plan, if you can call it that, is to drive to Kat's, and if I find Liam's car there, I'll call the police back.

But I can't chance being incorrect and accidentally calling

in an erroneous report. I must collaborate with the police too often to let my imagination set me up as the crazy lady who calls in gut feelings.

Oh, how I miss Jacob right now. It would be nothing for me to call him and explain my uneasiness about Liam. He wouldn't think twice about meeting me there.

Captain Lau might extend the same professional courtesy if I develop a working relationship with him. The difference being if I were wrong, Jacob would be understanding and not hold it against me in the future. I get the feeling Captain Lau is more of a one-strike-and-you're-out sort of man.

I dial Kat's number and again hear her recorded message.

Jacob belongs in Guntersville as much as I do. I wish he had never left. And it's not like we couldn't still be friends after he declared his love for me.

Look at the situation with Shane and me. It's similar, and yet we're successfully navigating the awkwardness. Jacob chose to leave rather than figure out how to make it work.

I can't be upset with him for living his life and deciding what will be best for him. All the same, I believe he is wrong. His place is here, and if he remained patient, he would eventually be the police captain. I don't see Pete Lau, an outsider, holding the position long-term.

I call Kat's number again. I'm barely paying attention since I'm wondering where Jacob is currently and what he is doing.

"Captain Lau here."

Pete's voice startles me. "I'm sorry. I must have misdialed."

"Is this April Snow?"

"Yes, sir."

"Kat can't come to the phone at the moment. She is giving a statement to one of my officers."

I gasp. "Oh Lord, is she okay?"

Pete sighs. "She will be. I think she's in shock right now. It's tough the first time you are forced to kill someone. I can only imagine if it were someone you're close to."

"Liam... He is dead?"

"Unfortunately. He had already passed by the time the first officers arrived."

"Oh."

"It's a run-of-the-mill self-defense case, Counselor. You won't have to be going to trial now."

I have slowed my car well below the speed limit. Subconsciously, I already realize there is no longer a need to rush.

"Why are you calling anyway?"

"I wanted to review a couple of items about the case with Kat."

"At two in the morning?"

"I guess I'm dedicated."

"I see."

"Can I come by and speak with Kat? Given the gravity of the situation, I should."

Pete clicks his tongue. "It's a free country, Counselor. Just don't interrupt my detectives until they have her statement."

∞∞∞

I don't know what I expect to see when I drive up. Still, it gives me a jolt from my car.

Between the six emergency vehicles, I spot Liam's lifeless body sprawled in front of Kat's trailer, his left foot still on the bottom stair. Nervously, I bounce my left fist against the side of my head, trying to psych myself up for what is going to be an epically emotional interaction.

Meanwhile, I am still running different scenarios through my mind where I might have been able to cut this off at the pass. Liam may still be alive if I had simply given the police the report and risked being wrong.

With a huff, I get out and shut my car door. I lean against it and hesitate. It may not be my place to be here. I am Kat's lawyer, but this is the realm of emergency workers and police officers, not lawyers.

Still, Kat is my client, and in a small community, it's about more than just what is and isn't my job. We have a connection, however tenuous and new as it may be, and the least I can do is check in to see how she is doing and if I can help in any way.

At least, that's what I tell myself as my fanny remains plastered to the side of my car door.

One of the responders stands, and our eyes meet. It's Shane, and he makes a come-here gesture with the movement of his head.

I pull in a settling breath and accept his invitation. The swirl of the blue-and-red emergency lights and the much-too-loud crunch of gravel under my boots give the moment an unbelievably surreal feel.

Thankfully, Shane steps toward me, saving me from having to look directly at Liam. "It's good of you to come." His face twists into a rare frown. "Kat is tore up about this, understandably. It might do her some good if you talk to her."

My throat has gone dry and I can't speak, so I nod.

He tilts his head to the side in response. "Yeah, I know. What do you say at a time like this?"

I scoff and nod again.

His brow furrows as his expression turns stern. "When you're done, come back and talk to me."

"I will."

He angles his body to shield my view of Liam and still allow me a path to the stairs of Kat's trailer. I enter the open door, and more people are present inside than the fire marshal would allow if he weren't already here.

Kat is at her kitchen table with two officers filling out a report. Maude is in the kitchenette area, tapping her foot feverishly. She flicks her cigarette into the sink and strides toward me.

"I told you this was gonna happen," she says.

I shake my head and frown at her aggressive declaration.

"Liam was always dangerous. I knew he wasn't right for my baby girl."

"What happened, Maude?"

Her eyes open wide as she purses her lips. "What happened? What happened is he came here threatening to kill her, and she did the only thing she could. She chose to survive and put the dog down."

"When was this?"

Maude rocks back on her heels. "Maybe fifteen minutes ago."

Bless it. Maude confirmed my fears. If I had sent the police directly to Kat's trailer, Liam would be alive. Instead, I let my career aspirations get in the way of doing the right thing. I was so concerned about being wrong and what it would do to my career that I didn't place the report.

The sinking feeling in my soul that I could've prevented this, but didn't, causes my lungs to constrict as my stomach bubbles with the burn of acid. I could have thwarted this, and I wasn't brave enough.

What is it with me? Why can't I move forward?

Will it always be two steps forward and one step back with me? I helped Thelma, and I helped reunite Dionis and Randolph, yet I let a man do something stupid and get himself killed.

I just can't anymore.

Because of my shame, I look away from Maude in the one direction that doesn't have a human being who can convict me of being narcissistic and selfish. My line of sight goes to the tiny, now empty kitchenette, and my breath catches.

Kat has a chalkboard on her wall listing her week's menu. Next to "Monday," written at the top, is "Dinner at Mom's."

The small circle serving as the dot above the lowercase *i*, and the flair on the right side of the letter *n*, reminiscent of the curled toe of tiny elf boots, are identical to the writing on the threatening notes I've been pulling off of my car windshield this week.

The trailer spins and suddenly has too little oxygen for the number of people in it. I should exit now.

Maude grabs my arm, and a slick coat of oily aura slides up to my shoulder, making me shiver in disgust.

"Kat needs you. I'd appreciate it if you'd stay and talk to her."

"I'm just stepping outside for some air."

"You do that. But don't go far. The police chief's already said it was self-defense, but you know how that uppity DA likes to go after people like us."

Maude is spewing so many things at me at one time that do not align with my beliefs about my community that my professional façade dissolves. My face squinches into a frown so severely I nearly close my eyes.

She leans away from me. "I'm just saying."

I point toward the door. "I'll be outside."

I'm torn between standing on the first step and drawing in as much fresh air as possible or getting as far away from this place as quickly as possible. As I push back the queasiness building in me, I notice Shane watching me with a concerned expression.

I muster a smile and, for good measure, wink at him. His left cheek quirks upward in an adorable half-smile, and he crooks his finger toward me in a come-hither motion.

Have I mentioned that Shane can effortlessly convince me to do anything, regardless of my current condition? I dutifully step down the stairs and make a wide circle around the photographer, who is still ghoulishly taking hundreds of pictures of Liam.

"If you're going to invite me to get a bite, this is the one time I'll turn you down," I joke as I approach him.

He makes a comical expression that forces me to giggle. "You're hungry?"

I shake my head. "Uh, no."

"That would be a first."

"Whatever. Did you have something you want to tell me, or were you simply attempting to keep me from gawking at Liam's dead body?"

"I thought I should inform you that your job isn't done."

I am afraid to ask. It's best to let lying dogs lie. "Why do you say that?"

"I thought you would never ask."

Darn it. My curiosity got a hold of my humongous mouth again.

"The timeline doesn't check out."

I lift my hands in frustration over another one of Shane's maddening riddles.

He grins. "Maude said that Kat was in her trailer and Liam busted down the door. And that it was fifteen minutes ago."

"Yes."

"First, if I broke into your apartment and you had a gun, where would the bullets hit me?"

"I would never shoot you, Shane."

His smile is so all-consuming that it makes me grin. "Okay, so if the meanest man in the world broke through your door."

"Front, center mass."

"And how long will it take for this mean man to bleed out completely?"

I screw up my face in shock. "Lord, Shane. Morbid much?"

"It's important."

"I have no clue. That's more along your specialty."

He shrugs. "As a point of reference, because you may need this type of information in the future, the first responder was here in five minutes. According to him, Liam had already bled out—way too soon to be out of blood. Plus, Liam seems to have busted down the door with his shoulder. At least that's the only plausible explanation for the three rounds hitting him on the left side."

My mouth drops open as I consider what Shane is saying.

"Of course, it isn't inconceivable that he broke in using his shoulder. I would've thought it easier to kick in a trailer door, though."

"He didn't."

Shane peers toward the trailer. "Yeah, it's minimal damage,

but doors on trailers are pretty cheaply built. The locking mechanism may break long before the door gives way."

"Liam was right-handed."

"Yes."

"If you're right-handed, you won't lead with your left shoulder."

Shane squints as he lifts his left and right shoulder while evaluating my observation. "Good night. That's a good catch, Bama."

Biting my lower lip, I shake my head. "It still doesn't prove anything."

Shane favors me with a good-natured smile. "Nope. But understanding crazy will allow you to keep your sanity, even if the person doesn't do jail time for it."

"Very sage advice, my friend."

"Thank you, Bama."

I hike a thumb over my shoulder and sigh. "I think I've had enough crazy for today. I'm going home to catch a nap."

"You do that. Drive safe, and I'll call you tomorrow with any updates on the case."

"I'll hold you to it."

We share a lengthy smile, and I find myself leaning forward to pull him into a hug. It's best I don't touch Shane often, so I turn toward my car.

I'm unsure exactly how I feel as I walk toward my car. Even if it seems somewhat perverse, I am relieved that even if I had called in my suspicion to the police, it would've done nothing to help Liam.

Yet something is still off about the timeline. It didn't take me but a few minutes to decide to leave for Kat's trailer. He never said exactly, but Shane made it sound like it would've required an hour or more for Liam to bleed out.

That's why Shane makes the big bucks. His training and expertise allow the police to develop an exact timeline. It may be days before he is confident his hypothesis is correct.

What really irritates me is that I believed Kat. I did not

retain a healthy level of cynicism that Liam was stalking her and meant to do her bodily harm.

Kat's notes were successful in deceiving me as she intended. Both messages riled me to the point that I became obsessive about protecting her from the man who thought he owned her.

I lost my professional objectivity and found myself a firm supporter of Team Kat. The only person getting owned in this whole situation was me. I had bought her entire shtick hook, line, and sinker.

I'm too embarrassed to even be angry about my lapse in professionalism.

As my car comes into view, the unmistakable scent of a Winston cigarette fills my nostrils. The red, glowing dot draws my attention, and I make out the silhouette of a man leaning against the nose of my car.

"Did you get an eyeful, Goldilocks?"

My traitorous knees turn to Jell-O, and I struggle to keep my feet. Luckily, unlike my untrustworthy legs, my brain is still in full gear. "I am sorry it came to this, Liam."

"Shucks. Your warning about it not ending well for me came after the deed was done." He offers me a wry smile. "You know she left me to die like a dog hit by a car on the highway. No help..." He drops his eyes. "That's cold."

"Yes. It is, and I'm sorry you experienced that, Liam."

He scoffs. "Heck, two hardheaded people at odds over something they both want—you don't have to be a psychic to know how it will end."

His reflective tone is not what I predicted, and I step closer. As Liam comes into view, I wish I hadn't closed the distance.

In his right hand, he methodically taps the blade of a fifteen-inch Bowie knife on his thigh. My mouth gapes open, and I look up into his eyes.

Liam smiles and puts out his cigarette against the blade, flicks the stub toward the woods, and wipes the blade slowly across his jeans.

I swallow my fear and plead, "Liam, don't."

He pushes off the hood of my car. As he walks toward me, there is no crunch of gravel beneath his boots.

Liam rests his finger under my chin. The coolness and energy tingle, forcing my eyes up to meet his. He removes his finger from my chin and places it against his lip, warning me to keep the promise I made under duress in my apartment.

I watch the ghostly hunter's broad back as he walks up the gravel drive. He slides between a firefighter and a police officer, unseen as he walks up the stairs and disappears into Kat's trailer.

Oh, Kat. What have you done?

Chapter 63

Two months later...

"That went smoother than I ever could have imagined," Elizabeth Johnson gushes as she looks toward me.

I point forward to remind her we're crossing the bridge leading into Guntersville. I'd rather her keep us out of the lake than pay me so much attention.

"You were well prepared, Elizabeth."

She beams a smile and shimmies her shoulders from side to side. "Thank you. I appreciate that." Her attentive stare returns. "Still, your testimony sealed the deal with Judge Rossi."

I snort a laugh. "That's only because Judge Rossi knows I'm the Queen of Crazy. What's that old saying? 'It takes one to know one.'"

Elizabeth sighs. "Well, I like your crazy. Maude ... not so much."

Maude is not crazy. She is afflicted with an obsessive disorder regarding her daughter Kat. Her mama bear privileges allow her to write "Dinner at Mama's" on her daughter's chalkboard ... and murder the boyfriend she finds unsuitable for her baby girl.

And she is touched with a thin partition to the veil.

My belief is, in the minutes after his death, Liam realized

Maude was susceptible to seeing ghosts. He devised his revenge as he lay dying in the dust after being ambushed at Kat's trailer door.

Shane's autopsy of Liam revealed three rounds entered his left ribcage at a steep upward trajectory. DA Lane and Captain Lau agreed it was consistent with Liam busting in the door and Kat shooting him while seated on the sofa.

Shane disagreed. The angles were too steep. And miraculously, Kat was free of gunshot residue.

While Shane grumbled about his displeasure of not understanding what had happened that night, I was concerned for Kat's safety. Still, I never heard about a peep of weirdness coming from the Krasinski's trailer park.

No news is good news. Right?

Apparently not.

Last week, I received a voicemail from Maude. Her message would have been nonsensical to anyone other than me. When her voice rose an octave, and she said, "I need your help, please!" I had no choice but to go to her.

Those two words together—"help" and "please"—Mama always said they were magic, and she is correct. Despite my not caring for Maude and my heart being as hard as a stone toward her since I had felt her true nature crawl up my arm the day she grabbed me, my heart softened to her plea. I dropped everything, driving out right then to meet with her.

Maude's appearance shocked me as I entered the smoke-filled trailer. She had lost thirty pounds, her hair that hadn't fallen out was shock white, and her eyes had sunk deep into her face and become dull and lifeless.

She began our conversation by relaying that she is an obsessed fan of my brother's work—the television series, not his books. She continued by saying that only I could help her because she needed a demon cast out.

Liam sat beside her every night, tapping his knife blade against his thigh. *Whack, whack, whack.* He never spoke, only menacingly smiled at her for hours.

I would like to say that Maude's nature had transformed because people often change during stressful situations. She hadn't. She held to the lie that Kat had shot Liam in self-defense.

Despite knowing her evil would make me ill, I reached across the table and took her hands in mine as I promised I would do everything I could to help her.

Maude had focused solely on Liam's death since he appeared to her. The two-minute snippet came fierce and fast into my memory in such complete detail it was as if I was Maude.

Liam's voice booms over the rattle of the aluminum door as he beats it with his fists.

A neighbor pokes her head out of her trailer door, and Maude raises a pistol toward the woman threateningly. The woman's pink curlers swing wildly as she disappears into her trailer.

Maude steps around an old holly bush at the end of Kat's trailer. Her pistol reaches eye level as she approaches the stairs from the side.

Liam pounds the door again with his fists. He opens his mouth to yell more insults—the words never come. A puff of smoke lifts into the air. Liam flinches to the right. Two more puffs of smoke appear in quick succession.

Liam's eyes open wider as he clutches his left side. I read his lips. "You." His legs give way, and he falls head first down the stairs.

Maude stands over him. "I warned you, Liam."

I promised Maude I would return that evening and do my best to expel Liam. If I had been honest with Maude, I wasn't considering an expulsion. I was in for what I predicted to be a very contentious negotiation with Liam.

It turns out I was wrong. Liam had become quite bored with haunting Maude and was ready to draw the whole ordeal to a close and move on to the next plane. He was adamant about one fact, though: Maude must serve time for her crime.

If the testimony of ghosts and memories gleaned from suspects by a psychic were permissible in court, it would be easy to convict Maude of killing Liam. If frogs had wings, they wouldn't bump their butt when they leap too.

It took three long nights of negotiations. Liam was right about them being two very hardheaded people. The breakthrough came from Liam.

Maude, I feel, still felt she had pulled off a near-perfect murder and didn't want to pay for her crime, but finally agreed to the terms. She would admit to killing Liam because she continually dreamed about him killing Kat and felt the need to protect her daughter.

Given her physical condition and willingness to tell anyone who would listen how Liam watched over her continually every night, it wasn't hard to sell Lane on having Maude evaluated. In return for her testimony, and in conjunction with the psychiatrist's report, Elizabeth convinced Judge Rossi to remand Maude to a state mental institution rather than be tried for first-degree murder.

Because of my interaction as Kat's lawyer and because Maude contacted me about her ghost situation, I was a witness and was required to recuse myself. Thankfully, Elizabeth was willing to take the case and did an excellent job finishing the deal, as I knew she would.

Liam was satisfied and Maude will be able to sleep, but Kat is devastated. In short order, the two most significant people in Kat's life are gone. I understand she loved them both, whether they were healthy relationships for her or not.

I hope she finds her footing and grows in her new freedom. Time will tell.

The Liam oddity was wrapped up while the rest of my fast-paced-circus life continued. Whoever said Southern life has a slower pace hasn't walked a mile in my heels.

Under the category of a positive byproduct of working on my brother's paranormal team, when Mama finally got in touch with Joan Nott, the sole heir of the Berger sisters, Mama mentioned my name. Joan, too, is an avid fan of Dusty's show. Oddly, she told Mama that if I was the woman buying the property, per the trust, she could sell the lot to me.

I find it humorous that the Berger sisters would only allow Joan to sell the property to a woman who had been on television. Still, I won't overthink my good fortune since it kept the property available until I noticed it and was able to buy it.

Thank the Lord there is a small house already on the property. Joan didn't offer me any hometown deal. Mama says it was fair market value. My bank account begs to differ.

If it weren't for the cottage, which requires much work, I would have, in effect, bought April's private campground. Because as I restart my business, a tent is all I could afford to put on the property.

"I'm excited for you to meet this new instructor. He is so impressive," Elizabeth says.

"You already have me in your car. There's no need to continue to sell it."

She looks toward me and raises her eyebrows. "I know. I'm just excited."

She is. Elizabeth practically has a halo around her curly, slate-colored hair. It draws a huge smile from me.

I've done an excellent job building my core in the last six months. Rowing, biking, and yes, even the occasional jog—which I still haven't learned to enjoy—have all helped me regain my correct weight and, more importantly, feel good when I wake up in the morning.

Still, for my long-term physical health, cross-training will be essential for me. I become bored with things quickly. When Elizabeth suggested the karate class, my first reaction was to ask, "Why?"

But she is right. And it is an excellent opportunity to continue building the other core. The one that is more foreign to me, but I've been working on improving over the last month. My core of female friends.

No matter how much I enjoy being around my male friends, it tends to become ... awkward.

The more time I spend with them, the more we laugh and

share secrets, the more I want to kiss them. I'm an adult. I've learned how not to act on these urges. Still, having men for friends introduces many X factors that I sometimes don't care to deal with.

As much as I hate to admit it, my brothers were right. I need a group of girlfriends.

Rather than denying or doing nothing to correct the situation, the new-and-improved April immediately pulled together a group of women to form a circle of friends.

Elizabeth and I have already formed a bond. Her ability to go over the top about some things when talking about them tickles me because I do that, too.

Of course, I had to include my CPA friend Elsa because she's the coolest woman I know. I fully expected her to say, "Thanks, but no thanks." I was shocked when she agreed. She even thanked me for the invite. Who knew even former CIA agents need friends?

Because she is my oldest friend, I had to invite Jackie Raines, even if we took a long hiatus from our friendship. It's funny how reconnecting with her is like pulling on a favorite, well-worn coat. She makes me feel warm and secure.

Three weeks ago was the first time we got together for dinner, and it was a blast. We've yet to commit to any specific amount of time, but if this karate thing goes all right tonight, we'll have an activity two nights a week. Plus, we will learn some self-defense skills.

Elizabeth pulls into Marvin's Marvelous Consignment's parking lot. I smile as I catch sight of Jackie and Elsa talking next to Elsa's Hummer.

"Are we late?" I ask as I get out of the car.

Jackie waves her hand at me. "We're early."

"Everybody ready to learn how to kick butt?" I joke as we form a circle.

"This might be a bit below Elsa's skill set," Elizabeth says as if it just occurred to her that the CIA researchers are trained in martial arts.

Elsa raises her eyebrow. "I must need a refresher. Every time I bathe King, I swear he will kill me. I must be getting rusty."

"I keep telling you to bring him in. We bathe cats all the time," Jackie says.

Elsa scoffs. "I would feel guilty for the damage he would do to your crew."

We walk, clutching our arms across our chests to defend against the brisk December air. Decorations adorn every streetlight, and the store windows are decorated with colorful lights and wreaths.

There is a law office three blocks down with the most adorable wreath on its mahogany door, trimmed completely in fresh garland. The thought brings a warm feeling from the inside out, and I smile.

I have found my place, my position, and my people, all with persistence, good luck, and much help from family and friends. There is so much for me to be grateful for this Christmas.

"We're so fortunate to get slots for this class. The instructor is from the West Coast and does this part-time in the evening to keep his skills up and stay in shape."

"Goodness," Jackie says as we look through the plate-glass window at the scores of women inside the karate studio.

"You aren't kidding, Elizabeth."

She holds the door open, and I'm the first to enter the much-too-warm studio. A man, his back turned toward me, towers over the women.

I stop. One of my friends bumps into my back.

The mountain of a man turns toward the tinkle of the door's bell. His expression changes as if he has spotted a unicorn. "April?"

My face twists into an expression akin to finding poop on the bottom of a new pair of sandals. "Hi, Scott."

Bless it.

The end.

Have you read all of April's stories?

My psychic lawyer life series.
https://www.amazon.com/gp/product/B08G8BL2B4

My magical psychic life series
https://www.amazon.com/gp/product/B0BY5ZXGSS

Never miss an April May Snow release.
Join the reader's club!

www.mscottswanson.com

M. Scott lives outside of Nashville, Tennessee, with his wife and two guard chihuahuas. When he's not writing, he's cooking or taking long walks to smooth out plotlines for the next April May Snow adventure.

Dear Reader,

Thank you for reading April's story. You make her adventures possible. Without you, there would be no point in creating her story.

You are the magic that breathes life into these characters.

M. Scott Swanson

The best way to stay in touch is to join the reader's club!

www.mscottswanson.com

Other ways to stay in touch are:

Like on Amazon

Like on Facebook

Like on Goodreads

I hope your life is filled with
magic and LOVE!